A Perfect Divorce

A Perfect Divorce

Francesca Clementis

PIATKUS

Visit the Piatkus website!

Piatkus publishes a wide range of best-selling fiction and non-fiction, including books on health, mind, body & spirit, sex, self-help, cookery, biography and the paranormal.

If you want to:

- read descriptions of our popular titles
- buy our books over the Internet
- take advantage of our special offers
- enter our monthly competition
- learn more about your favourite Piatkus authors

VISIT OUR WEBSITE AT: www.piatkus.co.uk

Copyright © 2004 by Francesca Clementis

First published in Great Britain in 2004 by
Piatkus Books Ltd of
5 Windmill Street, London W1T 2JA
email: info@piatkus.co.uk

The moral right of the author has been asserted

A catalogue record for this book is available from the British Library

ISBN 0 7499 0700 2

Set in Times by
Phoenix Photosetting, Chatham, Kent
Printed and bound in Great Britain by
Clowes Ltd., Beccles, Suffolk

For Auntie Billie,
With thanks for introducing me to the good things in life
including daytime television, Babycham with cocktail cherries,
soap operas and Kunzle Cakes. And for all those summer
holidays of Barry Island, Peyton Place, sweets, chips and
Bunty Annuals.
Good times.

It took over twenty years, from the day we met, for Mark and I to decide to get married and less than ten months to decide we were getting a divorce.

I think this might be a record. Maybe Jerry Springer would be interested. Although perhaps there is some culture somewhere in which this is a sign of success, where short marriages are regarded as beautiful in the same way that in some African societies very fat women are seen as beautiful.

I'll look that up one day. Maybe when I'm a divorcee living alone with fifty-six cats and talking to myself and wearing tweed slippers and looking for ways to occupy the empty hours.

It's not the typical tale of a couple living together for years who become restless and interpret this feeling as a sign that it is time to get married. Then, months after the wedding, they discover that they'd made a mistake, that the feeling had actually been a sign that it was time for them to split up.

That wasn't us because we weren't living together in the most committed sense of the words. Although Mark had effectively moved in years earlier, he still kept his own flat and even slept there occasionally. Everyone found this strange but it made financial sense. For some time now, property had been such a fast-returning investment, that it would have been considered insane not to hang on to a decent London apartment if affordable. And if it bothered me occasionally . . . often . . . well, I was too reasonable to say anything.

We got married because I wanted to. To be precise, I wanted children and it seemed a natural progression to formalize our relationship first. Besides, that's what couples do. They get married and then they have kids. Statistics still bear that out.

1

OK, so maybe it was a tactical error not actually spelling this out to Mark. But after two decades together, you'd think that some things didn't need to be said. Or is that just me being defensive?

When I casually mentioned that I was ready to try for a baby last week, I was not prepared for his reaction.

'But we agreed we weren't going to have children. You've never wanted babies. Not ever.'

·'That was when I was younger. I changed my mind. Loads of women do. Even you've heard of the biological clock.'

'But you promised me that you didn't have one, that you were born with the battery missing.' He was becoming agitated, a state of mind that he'd been displaying quite frequently recently.

'Mark, I'm not being unreasonable. When we were eighteen we said that we'd never own property, that we wanted to live in a gypsy caravan and travel around the country, eking out a living selling my work at craft fairs, while you wrote a novel. Are you holding me to that too?'

'Now you're being ridiculous.'

I was becoming scared now. With most of our rows, I could always see the conclusion. I'd always win, of course, but I'd make him think that he'd obtained a partial victory then we'd take a bag of Revels to bed and make up.

But this time, I saw a big black wall ahead of us.

'Why are you so opposed to the idea?' I asked.

'Because kids will spoil everything. We won't be able to do any of the things that we like doing, that we've always liked doing. We won't be able to stay in bed until midday or watch violent videos on Sunday afternoons, or leave a Scrabble game on the floor for days on end. Look at this.' He pulled me over to our games cupboard. 'All of our games have warnings on them: Not suitable for children under thirty-six months because of small pieces. It's official: our lifestyle comes with health warnings.'

My voice was starting to shake. I was running out of arguments. 'But children could bring us new pleasures.'

Mark became exasperated. 'Jenny, I like our old pleasures. I don't need new ones. We've always agreed that most couples only have kids because they're bored with each other and don't know what to do next. Well, I'm not bored with you and I never could be. You're my best friend and I just want to be with you!'

2

I calmed myself down, or I tried to. 'Mark, I don't think you understand what I'm saying. I really, really want a baby.'

'And I don't think you understand what I'm saying. I really, really don't.'

We had this same argument, with a few variations over the next few days. It always ended the same way, without resolution. If there was a compromise to be found in this situation, then we couldn't find it. We couldn't settle on having half a baby or a cocker spaniel.

Do couples, happy couples who've been together forever, get divorced over the subject of children? Well, what else are they to do? You see, while I love Mark, I have a physical need for a baby. It crept up on me unawares. It is so real it hurts. And it's not exactly unusual. If I suddenly announced I wanted us to join the Hare Krishnas or move to Upper Volta and study locusts, he'd be entitled to feel that I was being unreasonable. But a baby? The most natural thing in the world for a woman of my age.

'Out of interest,' I asked him the other day, 'what would you have done if I'd become pregnant accidentally?'

He shrugged. 'I'd have supported you and gone through with it, of course, because we'd have been starting out from the same position of reluctant resignation.'

I felt sick that I could have avoided all this if only I'd been deliberately careless. But we'd always been honest with each other and this had never occurred to me. And I couldn't possibly now forget we'd had this conversation then go and get myself pregnant anyway. He'd never forgive me.

'So why can't you pretend that this is the situation we're in now?' I argued. 'You've admitted that it is theoretically possible to stay married to me, to continue loving me, even if I became unexpectedly pregnant. So surely that means that you can't feel as strongly against kids as you insist?'

This just made him angry. 'So what *you* are saying is that you *couldn't* stay married to me, continue loving me, without kids? That all of a sudden your love has become conditional? So now who's the unreasonable one?'

I couldn't make him understand that this was nothing to do with my love for him. This was all about a need that just happened to be stronger than anything else.

I knew that nobody was going to understand that I needed a

baby more than I loved Mark. But I've come to understand in the last week that this is not the real reason why I'm divorcing Mark. All these years when I thought we'd been moving together, we'd actually been on slightly warped tracks, gradually veering off on an imperceptible tangent.

And now, when I wanted – needed – us to embark upon our biggest journey together, when I'd packed my emotional sandwiches, paid for the overpriced ticket, spent hours on the Internet working out the route and finally declared myself ready to climb aboard, I learned that Mark had deceived me, that he was, in reality, nothing but a trainspotter.

Chapter One

At the moment, Mark and I still live together. By that I mean, he didn't storm out of the flat and I didn't rip his shirts up with my teeth and hurl them out of the window after him. Nor did we scrub the toilet with each other's toothbrush or bother with any of the other acts of revenge so beloved of TV dramas.

He simply moved into the spare room with his Ryder Cup 1982 T-shirt, his Terry Pratchett books and his one-armed teddy that he swears he only keeps as an investment, having watched *Bargain Hunt* once and seen an antique German teddy sold for £15,000.

Instead of snarling and trading accusations of decade-old transgressions, we drew up lists and evenly divided our possessions.

But every word had to be carefully filtered through a civilizing sieve and we both had to pretend that we no longer knew what the other was thinking.

Mark went first. 'Why don't you have the coffee set?' (Do you remember when we bought it in Crete? I got drunk and started juggling which is why we have six saucers and four cups.)

'OK. But I think you should have the hideous dishes shaped like cabbages.' (Do you remember when you won them in that tombola at the Christmas Fair? I tried to switch the ticket secretly with the one on a bottle of wine and we got thrown out – the first ever recording of an eviction from a church hall.)

'We'll split the photos down the middle. I'll have the ones where my head isn't shining.' (Even though you always liked my head and enjoyed playing assorted film themes on it with your fingernails).

'I'll keep the ones where I'm wearing a skirt, just to prove I occasionally wore one.' (Even though you preferred me in jeans and told me I looked like Calamity Jane, which led to that time when I pretended my umbrella was a rifle and accidentally chipped a silver of bone from your jaw. I said that it was romantic to be spending a Saturday night in Casualty together, better than watching it.)

Every single possession was a bond that glued us together and simply putting them into separate boxes didn't seem to break the bond. It just stirred up memories, film clips that reminded us why we'd been together for so long as well as why we were breaking up.

I found the hand-decorated photo frame that some friends' children gave us as a wedding present. I fingered it with affection.

'Do you remember when Jocasta and Ellery gave us this?'

'Yes, I do,' Mark replied tightly. 'It was shortly after they'd ruined our wedding reception by fighting throughout the meal and refusing to eat any of the food. We were then all forced to sit at the table and wait twenty minutes – until they'd eaten three mouthfuls – by their parents who appeared to have forgotten whose party it was. When they'd finally swallowed it, they were both sick. Then when it was time for us to have our first dance as a married couple, Ellery kept karate-chopping me and screaming "Pokemon!" while Jocasta wrapped her arms around your right leg.'

'I thought that was quite sweet,' I said faintly.

'She was wiping her nose on your dress! Jenny, they were a nightmare! Even the baby didn't stop crying for the whole day despite my suggestion to put a measure of gin in her bottle.'

'But it doesn't have to be like that! There are nice children, kids who don't destroy other peoples' houses, who read books and do cross-stitch and never remove their underwear in public places.'

Mark stared at me in disbelief. 'But we don't know any of them, do we? Think about all the happy times of our lives, thousands of them . . .' his voice broke abruptly and it took him a while to get control back. 'Do you see any kids in those memories? No. Now think of all the miserable afternoons and weekends we've spent, not able to finish conversations, not able to relax for a moment in case some child comes and drinks our wine, or sticks a steak knife into their eye, or throws up over our shoes. Sound familiar?'

It did. We'd always shared our loathing of these enforced family encounters in the past. Just now I felt – knew – that it would be different for us. But I couldn't think of another way to say this, having tried communicating it continuously for the past week.

Mark shrugged helplessly. 'I don't like kids or babies. Maybe it's something to do with being an only child. They seem so alien to me. I'm not even sure I was a child myself. I think I was born middle-aged – maybe that's why I lost my hair so young.'

'But I'm an only child too,' I argued.

He smiled suddenly and I ached. 'Maybe that's why you and I have always had such fun together, making up for a lost youth.'

I smiled too. We *were* like kids, the two of us. The trouble was, I wanted to grow up and Mark didn't. How do you build a bridge across that kind of gulf?

But nobody could accuse of being uncivilized. We smiled so politely, so incessantly, that yesterday I went to the dentist in pain thinking I had a jaw infection.

And Mark never once saw or heard me cry. I kept all my make-up in the bedroom so that I could repair the damage each night inflicted on my face. When this is all over I'm going to have to go to the optician because I think I might have cried so much that my prescription must have changed. My contact lenses sting like needles but I put them in anyway. I don't know if Mark cries. If he does, then he's better at applying under-eye concealer than I am.

We've never been big weepers. We're very English like that. If films get a bit teary, I chew my nails and Mark tugs his earlobes as if he can't believe what he's hearing. Since we both know the other is doing this to avoid crying, I don't know why we haven't just abandoned the pretence and let ourselves bawl.

But we don't do that. And we don't shout. So why would we be any different now this is happening? We're nice people, we were a nice couple – everyone said so. And we had a catchphrase, a slogan, for this divorce. 'Nothing will change, not really.' That's what we agreed.

We were determined that we would break the mould, prove the sceptics wrong. Ours would be an amicable divorce. How could it be anything else after spending all our adult lives together? We would stay friends, we agreed, meet up all the time, move in the same circles without any awkwardness.

No lawyers, we agreed. We wouldn't need them. Instead we bought a £9.99 Handle Your Own Divorce kit from the newsagent down the road. It even came with a free CD-ROM. Now you don't get one of them from a lawyer.

The CD-ROM was not presented by a reassuring American with a shiny suit, fluorescent teeth and big hair making us feel good about ourselves. In fact, it just seemed to have a whole load of forms to download but it was a focus away from ourselves, a non-judgemental recording facility, allowing us to note who was keeping what. Everything was shared out without any argument in this, the world's first completely blame-free divorce, although there was a bit of tension when we were dividing up the videos.

We bought nearly all of them together. They were our most valued possessions, a lifetime's collection of the most lowbrow films ever released, our shared passion. Some of them were so bad they'd become cult classics in the meantime and possibly quite valuable. Obviously not *Xanadu* with Olivia Newton-John, which is too marginal in its appeal even to be called ironic, but that was the first film we saw together at the cinema in 1980. Mark smiled sadly and told me he wanted me to keep it.

He's not making it easy for me to stop loving him.

We watched every single one of these hundreds of videos together. In the past. Ago. Once. All our terms of reference have changed. Since we were sixteen, we've always talked about the now and the future. But 'now' has been replaced with 'yesterday'. And I can't quite get a handle on the concept of a future without Mark.

All I have to do is make someone else understand all this. Maybe then they can explain it to me. And I can explain it to Mark.

'I can't talk to you while you're wearing your hair like Princess Leia in *Star Wars*.'

I can always rely on Maria to make me feel faintly ridiculous. It's a gift.

'If you'd ever seen *Star Wars*,' I pointed out, 'rather than just played *Star Wars* Monopoly with us once, then you'd know that she had her plaits wrapped around her ears like doughnuts. Mine are plain pigtails and I am wearing them like that because I haven't washed my hair.'

Maria leaned over and began undoing the plaits. 'I still can't let you do this. It's a crime against my eyes.' She pulled them loose into a long, heavy sheet of relentlessly straight black hair. 'There, that's more like you. You need to wear your hair down to minimize your long nose and high forehead.'

I've heard that there are some things your best friends won't tell you. Sadly there is nothing Maria won't tell me.

She took a deep breath. 'Now I need a drink.' With the merest rise of her hand, a waiter miraculously appeared to take the order.

'A bottle of house champagne, two glasses and six packets of cheese-and-onion crisps please.'

'I've already ordered champagne,' I interjected, holding the waiter's arm before he disappeared. Not because there was anything to celebrate but because that was all Maria drank.

She laughed. 'So we'll have two bottles. On the phone you sounded as if this was going to be a multi-bottle evening.' She then dismissed the waiter with a dramatic flourish of her hand. 'So, tell me, when are you due?'

I expected this. No I didn't actually. It was only when she said this that I realized this was the obvious assumption. 'I'm not pregnant.'

Maria looked perturbed. 'But I had it all planned. You would insist that you couldn't drink too much and then I would persuade you that this was a perfect opportunity to introduce my future godchild to the life I have planned for her. I even got all this stuff on the Internet.'

She pulled out sheaves of paper, all closely printed, all bearing titles such as: ALCOHOL IN PREGNANCY – THE GOOD NEWS. 'I had to find some pretty obscure sites to come up with this many reasons why drinking champagne in pregnancy is a good thing, most of them sponsored by the French wine industry, but if you can't trust a champagne producer, well then . . .'

I closed my eyes. 'It was a reasonable assumption. My life has been the same for me since I left university. It's been Mark, Mark's business, living with Mark, marrying Mark, what else would I have to talk about apart from a baby with Mark?' My voice was rising disturbingly.

Two waiters arrived at the same time with champagne. I wondered if now was an appropriate time to order a third.

Maria lifted her glass. 'So what are we drinking to?' she asked apprehensively.

'Well, you won't be surprised to hear it's about Mark.'

9

Maria couldn't help herself. She never could, self-control being one of many virtues she'd not bothered acquiring, along with legible handwriting, table manners and a way with animals. 'Don't tell me – he's finally giving up the gym game and getting a proper job?'

'No.' I realized that Maria would continue to make inappropriate suggestions until forcibly restrained, so I decided to get it over with. 'We're getting a divorce.'

'What do you mean, getting a divorce?' Maria put her glass down to give this mystery her full concentration.

'Getting a divorce. What no man is supposed to put asunder, we're putting asunder. Going our separate ways. Splitting up. What don't you understand?'

'You don't mean splitting up completely?' Maria wanted to clarify this baffling announcement. 'You're just getting a divorce, right? It's only the marriage thing that wasn't a great success? You're still staying together?'

I ought to point out that Maria and I have been friends for eighteen years and, in that time, I have always been half of Jennyandmark. I've never existed for her as anything else. The concept of me as a separate entity is a new one for her. For me too, if I can bear to admit it.

We met when I was working in a department store as a holiday job and Maria was already working her way up to becoming one of the high street's youngest fashion buyers. She even looked the part, with her swirly skirts and tailored blouses that, with her long corkscrew brown hair and pale skin made her look like a 1950s Hollywood siren, a style she never abandoned even while she became more sophisticated in her interpretation.

To me she would always be utterly exotic and a bit foreign, even though I eventually learned that she came from Walthamstow and all her influences were derived from the films she loved. I suppose this made her no different from me. In occasional moments of introspection, I often wondered how my life might have turned out if I'd met a boyfriend who exposed me to punk rock or Renaissance art rather than bad movies.

We'd got through the first bottle of champagne without noticing and moved onto the second.

'I presume he's got another woman, although I can't imagine who else, apart from you, could see anything in him.' Maria has never been a great admirer of Mark on any level. Mark's hair started thinning at the age of twenty-two, a gift from his father ('I'd rather have had a car') and decided he couldn't face the agonizing process of watching his youth decline so visibly. He had his hair cropped as short as he could without looking like Steven Berkoff and scaring small children and he's kept it at that length ever since.

Maria likes men with lots of hair. She hides a lot behind hers and feels that everybody needs a veil of some kind. 'If you can't play with a man's hair, there's nothing else to do except look into his eyes,' she would argue.

I've always liked to believe that, one day, Maria will meet a man and want to do nothing but look into his eyes. She's not convinced.

But the thing that Maria has always really disliked about Mark is his existence. He has robbed Maria of my company on all the single woman's adventures that she's enjoyed through the years. All the early cheap package trips to Magaluf, the later treks to the Himalayas, long weekends in Barcelona flirting with waiters, singles nights in tacky West End nightclubs, experiments with Lonely Hearts ads and expensive dating agencies. Maria would have loved me to go through all that with her but I was Part of a Couple.

She also blamed Mark for what she saw as my stunted personal growth. 'He's kept you sixteen,' she complained. I thought about this a lot and wondered if it was, in fact, the other way round.

'No, he hasn't got another woman and, before you ask, I haven't got another man.'

Maria raised her eyebrows. 'I wasn't going to ask.'

I knew what she was thinking, that I'm a prude. And maybe I am. I look away during sultry sex scenes in the cinema, I've never used the word 'womb' in a public place and I don't even own a thong. But I'm sure there's a trollop inside me too, fighting out of its low-heeled shoes, desperate to break out and wear a Wonderbra. I've just never had the courage. Breaking out always implies, well, breaking something. And Mark and I worked hard to keep our life intact.

Yes, we are nice people, who don't, didn't, cheat on each other. But we're not completely repressed. I mean, we once went to a Frankie Goes To Hollywood concert, still have the T-shirts.

11

'So why are you splitting up?' Maria asked. 'Mark's realized he's gay? A transvestite? He's becoming a Roman Catholic priest? He's dying and doesn't want to put you through the ordeal of nursing a terminally-ill man? He's become mentally unstable? Mid-life crisis?'

'You hit a raw nerve when you asked if I was pregnant. I want a baby and Mark doesn't.' I shrugged. 'Simple as that, really.'

Maria screwed up her eyes, trying to comprehend all this. 'But I thought that was why you got married?'

'So did I. But Mark didn't. Maybe he just believed it was a way of undoing the damage caused when he gave me that sandwich toaster for my birthday and I accused him of not loving me. I suppose, to him, marriage was the ultimate good present.'

'But surely you talked about it?' Maria was completely baffled. And she was right. It sounds silly now, but I never actually got round to mentioning to Mark why I wanted to get married. I thought he would realize.

'We did,' I said. 'I remember vividly us having a conversation where we agreed that if we ever decided to have children, we would get married.'

'When was that?' Maria asked.

I thought about it. 'I think we were in my bedroom revising for our A-Levels.'

Maria slapped her forehead in despair. She hit herself quite a lot in my presence. I have that effect on people. 'But how could you have been together all this time without at least catching up on where you both stood on kids? You must have made comments of some kind when your friends had children or when your parents started dropping hints about grandchildren. What did you talk about all that time?'

'If you'd ever lowered your standards in men to the faintly reasonable and taken a chance on a long-term relationship, you'd know that after the first couple of years, you've covered all the big topics. After that, you discuss congestion charges, easyJet fares and, in Mark's case, whether male film stars are losing their hair.'

'So what does the Rottweiler have to say about this?' Maria had wisely changed the subject.

I sighed. It's not easy when your two best friends don't get on. Maria doesn't like any of my university friends, mainly due to a

12

real complex about not having a degree, but she particularly dislikes Lisa. 'I haven't spoken to her about this, yet.'

Maria smiled wryly. 'I'm not surprised. This will play havoc with her lists. I presume she still has her lists?'

Ludicrous question. At my last lunch with Lisa, two weeks ago, she even had a new list.

I already knew that Mark and I were in trouble and I wanted to talk to Lisa about it but, as often happened, my real problems got swept aside to make way for her perceived ones.

She pulled out her leather list folder and turned immediately to the Christmas schedule. 'The problem is, Jen, the last posting dates. Nobody ever lets me know until the last minute if we're going to be seeing them over the holiday. So I never know whether to get something light for the post or whether I can buy whatever I want. And all the best turkeys will be gone if I don't order quickly. Well, how am I supposed to know what size to get if people refuse to get their acts together and let me know if they're coming over on The Day?'

'It *is* only August,' I pointed out reasonably, fully aware that reason was the enemy of the neurotic.

'Yes, but anything could happen between now and December. I want everything sorted, just in case.'

When Lisa writes her autobiography, it will be entitled *Just In Case*. Even her fiercely short blonde bob and unmoveable make-up are designed Just In Case she should be rushed to hospital after an accident which robs her of the facilities to take care of her appearance for more than twenty-four hours. OK, that's not why she does it. She just believes that once she has spray-gunned her hairspray and super-glued her make-up on, she can face the world knowing that there is one part of her life that will not require attention.

'What could happen?' I asked her, forgetting that this wasn't the point.

'I could get pregnant,' she said quickly.

Oh yes. How could I forget? She and her husband Kieran had been trying for a baby since Mark and I got married. Not that we'd planned to have babies at the same time.

Our wedding was a turning point for Lisa in a different way. Mark and Kieran had set up a business together straight after graduation. But it never made the sort of money they'd envisaged. Then when Mark sold his flat to move in with me last year, he put the whole £100,000 profit into the company. With this investment, they were expecting big returns. This eliminated Kieran's arguments that they couldn't afford to start a family.

Lisa was flicking through her folder again. I felt queasy. 'Lisa, tell me that you don't have a Making A Baby list.' I had this awful feeling she was going to show me graphs with temperatures and positions. I've never been comfortable talking gynaecologically, not even with my own doctor. I always wish they'd bring out those dolls that they use for children so I could just point and mumble.

'Not a list as such. Obviously I've done research and drawn up notes and a plan. You have to be methodical when you're thirty-eight. No, this is my maternity leave plan. I've prepared a sliding schedule of handing over my duties to all my sub-editors and assistant editors. I'm going to try it out on them, have a dummy run.'

I groaned inwardly. Having met her colleagues on *Uptown Woman*, I didn't think they'd respond well to trying out another of her sliding schedules, however excited they might be that they were potentially getting rid of Lisa in the imminent future. At a drunken office party to which I'd been invited, they'd all confessed their loathing of Lisa, assuming that I must feel the same way since I looked so sensible.

'So how does Kieran feel about all this baby-planning?' I asked her, already aware that Mark and I had a big, big problem with this very subject.

Lisa suddenly became over-animated. 'Well, he says he's not sure about it. But he'll come round.'

'You mean, he doesn't want a baby?' I was suddenly interested.

Lisa raised a finger to object. 'He *thinks* he doesn't want a baby. He'll be fine when it comes along. I'll organize everything.' She waved her hand vaguely.

'So you're just carrying on trying even though Kieran isn't keen?'

'Of course!'

And for the rest of the lunch I wondered if it might be that easy for me and Mark.

The last thing I remember saying to Lisa was, 'Of course we'll be coming over on Christmas Day as usual.' That enabled her to make a big tick on her list and made her very happy.

I can only hope she hasn't ordered the turkey.

Now I had a list of my own to consider: People Who Need To Be Informed That There Is No Jennyandmark Any More. Mark and I looked at the list. There was only the one list because our lives are so closely intertwined. Apart from Maria, all of our friends are shared friends. Even our families have grown closer together over the decades since Mark and I started going out together in the sixth form.

Romeo and Juliet didn't know how lucky they were. They could have eloped, lived in isolation, cut off by their respective families, spent twenty years watching the mediaeval equivalent of back-to-back Burt Reynolds films, then split up without any who-are-we-going-to-invite-for-Christmas recriminations from disgruntled relatives and friends.

The phone rang. For the past week, we'd been letting the answering machine screen callers. It wasn't intended, neither of us being very good at intentions. But I picked up without thinking.

'Hi, Jen, it's Auntie Lynn, we were wondering what you and Mark were doing on Sunday . . .'

'Auntie Lynn!' Mark pulled a cushion over his ears. 'Oh, er, Sunday, well, that's a bit tricky . . . it's Mark, you know . . . no, nothing serious . . . I'll tell you what, can I call you back in a couple of minutes, I've just got to . . . fetch a . . . pot. Bye.'

Mark removed the cushion. 'Fetch a pot? What's that supposed to mean? Now she'll know something's up.'

'Why did you bother covering your ears if you could still hear?'

'Then I can pretend this is nothing to do with me. Since you've promised to call her back, perhaps now's the best time to tell her.'

'I can't do it over the phone. That would be cruel. I think we should tell them together.'

He didn't argue and he didn't hide behind any more soft furnishings so I took this as a sign of assent. I called Auntie Lynn back. 'I've just been talking to Mark and we were wondering if you and Harry could come round to dinner tonight.'

At the mention of 'tonight', Mark bypassed the cushion and left the room completely. I found him in the kitchen rummaging maniacally through the cupboards.

15

'Are we going to cook with your half of the kitchen equipment or mine?' he asked tightly. 'Because if you're planning to use the George Foreman Lean Mean Fat-Reducing Grilling Machine or the Microwave Rice Steamer or the Electric Chicken Rotisserie or any of the other useless unused wedding presents that you kindly placed on my pile, we'll have to unpack some boxes.'

He was tense, I could tell.

'Mark, I'm not looking forward to this any more than you are,' I said shakily.

He began to move towards me then stopped, wanting to comfort me and not knowing how. Normally, he'd stroke my little finger which would mean: 'Sorry, I love you, but I can't help being a pillock.' I would run my hand over his head which would mean: 'But you're *my* pillock and I love you.' But we didn't do touching any more. We had to find words and it was hard.

'Who's going to make the announcement?' Mark asked. This was a good question. Because while Lynn was my aunt, Harry, her husband, was Mark's dad.

'What about Dad's heart?' Mark asked, suddenly worried.

'We'll break it to them gently.' Now it was my turn to want to comfort him. His father had only recently recovered from a third heart attack and I loved him as if he were my own dad.

Mark became serious. 'They'll know something's up as soon as they see the flat. It looks as if we've been burgled now my stuff is packed away.'

I looked around. I love this flat. I loved it when it was mine and I loved it even more when it became ours. I bought it when it was a shell and when Battersea was considered the poor man's Chelsea. Even in its run-down state it was expensive and I wouldn't have been able to afford it without the money Dad left me. It took me almost ten years to make it into a home. I put in new windows to let light into the dank basement area, knocked the two small sitting rooms together to make one large open space, and turned the tiny patio garden into an extension of the living area. All the furniture was second-hand but I'd reupholstered, repainted, covered and dressed everything to make it an extension of me.

It had been a wrench to get rid of some of my things to make room for Mark's larger pieces but I felt it was worth the sacrifice for him to bring his commitment into my home.

16

But Mark's furniture was now in a storage company and the rest of his possessions were in twenty-four boxes alongside the bed he was currently using in the spare room. The walls were looking very bare and the floor was littered with little craters like gravestones marking where tables and chairs had once lived. I half expected tumbleweed to come rolling through the door to the sound of *The Good, the Bad and the Ugly*.

I found some boxes of candles, spread them around and lit them, trying to disguise the voids. When the doorbell rang, neither of us knew who should answer it.

For two people who'd vowed that nothing would change, everything was different.

want children. Maybe I love being

Chapter Two

'Lisa! What are you doing here?'

'I thought you must be dead! You haven't been returning my calls. Good God, what's happened in here? It looks as if you've been burgled. I assume that you've lit all the candles to hold a séance to try and find the burglar? I would stick to the police if I were you.'

She'd walked straight past me before I could come up with a plausible or plain rude excuse for why she couldn't come in. Mark stared at me in panic. He didn't like surprises any more than I did. It had taken him all day to summon up the courage to confront his dad and my aunt with our news. Now Lisa was here and he wanted me to make her go away. His eyes told me that.

Funny how I've always been able to read his mind yet I had no idea that he didn't ever want children. Maybe I have selective telepathy. If I end up having to join a dating agency to find a man to father my child, I'll have to mention that. Can't be many women with selective telepathy. Perhaps it will compensate for my long nose and high forehead.

Lisa took her coat off and looked for somewhere to put it. Before she could march into the spare room, I snatched the coat from her, opened my bedroom door a few inches, flung it in and shut the door quickly. Lisa glared.

'That coat is cashmere and I doubt you've hoovered in there for a year so I hope it landed on the bed.' She was scrutinizing the room and was about to make an uncomfortably astute observation when the doorbell rang again.

Mark waited for me to answer it. Clearly I was to be squadron leader in this venture. As I walked to the door, I thought I could hear *The Dam Busters*. I was beginning to wish Mark and I had developed a passion for silent movies. Or macramé.

'Auntie Lynn! Harry!' We all did lots of kissing including Lisa who knew Lynn and Harry well. It made me feel uncomfortable to realize that this was yet another connection that was going to become knotty after the divorce.

'Very Bohemian, dear,' Harry observed after acclimatizing to the dim candlelight.

Auntie Lynn was less impressed. 'It's a fire hazard,' she declared. 'And where are Mark's nice Ikea units?' As a blood relative, she doesn't have to be polite. She was about to comment on the bareness of the rest of the flat when I exclaimed, 'Let me get you drinks!'

They both jumped at my unnecessarily loud voice.

Mark and I shuffled from the kitchen to the living room trying not to touch each other. It wasn't as easy as it sounds, not with Lynn and Harry hovering in the middle of the living room, Lisa popping up unexpectedly and candles threatening to topple over at every turn. All that was missing from the obstacle course was the additional handicap of an egg-and-spoon. It must have been exhausting to watch us bobbing back and forth like shadow-boxers and, frankly, I think Harry's heart would have been less stressed by seeing Mark hold my head under a guillotine than have to endure this performance.

Lisa was following us around, preventing us from formulating a strategy. It meant we had to improvise and we were strictly script-readers.

'So why haven't you called me back? I know something's wrong. I even asked Kieran to ask Mark what he was up to and apparently he became all mysterious.'

'I've never been mysterious in my life.' Mark was becoming defensive.

'He's right about that,' I agreed. 'And to be fair, I'm not sure Kieran would have noticed if he had.'

Lisa was forced to concede the point. In all the years we'd been friends, the men's conversations had generally consisted of such oblique comments as: 'Funny old world,' to which the other would reply something along the lines of: 'Mad, isn't it?' Somehow this served as communication and we could only hope that, in business dealings, they at least used complete sentences.

'I still know that something's up. If you're pregnant, there's no need to hide it from me even though I want a baby more than you do. I won't resent you. Well, I will a bit, but you can wear that silk blouse I bought you that you've never worn and that will appease me.'

Mark was stirring the soup a little too energetically.

'I'm not pregnant.' I wish I didn't have to keep saying this. I can't find a tone that makes it sound anything other than unhappy.

'Then what is it?' Now I know why Maria calls her the Rottweiler. I was saved by Lynn coming in to see if she could help.

'Is Lisa staying for dinner, dear?'

'No!' Mark and I answered in one voice.

'That would be lovely!' Damn. All by herself, Lisa was louder than the two of us.

'Why don't you go and sit at the table, Auntie Lynn. We'll bring everything through.' I had to use physical force to move Lisa out of the kitchen.

Mark was struggling to get past me to carry the starters to the table. I inhaled, pulling my stomach in until it practically touched my spine. Mark thrust his pelvis backwards like Mick Jagger to avoid any contact. We'd become so skilled at this over the last week, that we could contort our bodies as nimbly as any Chinese gymnast while dividing our lives into two perfectly equal halves.

Lynn and Harry sat down. Lisa was looking from Mark to me. She'd obviously noticed our little dance and was going to comment on it.

'Sit down, Lisa!'

She obeyed but without once taking her eyes off me. Before she could say anything, Lynn spoke. 'Oh Jenny, I can't wait another minute. We know something's up, we're not silly. Please just come right out and tell us. We don't know whether to be worried or happy. I mean, are you pregnant?'

Lisa took it upon herself to answer that for me. At least it saved me having to summon up a cheerful tone from my back catalogue of 'Brave Voices For Difficult Scenes.' 'No she's not. That's as far as I got. I've been worried all week. She hasn't returned any of my calls and that's not like her. I thought she must have a brain tumour or something terrible like that to be avoiding me.'

Thank you, Lisa. That helped.

Lynn went pale. They were all waiting for me to say something, including Mark. For the first time, I couldn't think of a film situation that I could draw upon. Perhaps there isn't one. There are lots of tear-jerking scenes where parents tell their cute children they are getting a divorce. I know all those lines. I could even tell a whale that we were to be parted, that it wasn't him, it was me. But I can't think of a single film where grown-ups break the news of a marriage split to their friends and relatives. How's a person supposed to know what to say if Meryl Streep hasn't said it first?

'We're getting a divorce.' I just said it. It was slightly easier after my maiden run with Maria. At least that's what I thought until I saw Lisa's face. And Lynn's face. And Harry's face.

Nobody spoke.

'Shall I serve the soup?' Mark's hand was trembling.

'I don't think anyone's very hungry,' I said, flatly.

Mark stood up and started edging the long way round the table to avoid me. Now that everyone knew why he was doing this, the action seemed pathetic.

'I'll go and make coffee.' The old diversionary tactic.

He had no idea that he could hitch-hike to Guatemala and pick the beans in person and Lisa, Lynn and Harry would still be waiting for him when he got back. But I'd forgotten that, as a man, his presence was not compulsory at such inquisitions. Within seconds they turned on me. Lisa went first.

'What do you mean, getting a divorce? That's stupid. You've only just got married.'

Lynn took a different approach. 'I told you this would happen! I had one of my feelings on your wedding day, do you remember, Harry? I said, if it ain't broke, don't fix it, didn't I? You were so happy, Jennifer, why did you have to spoil everything? I know I used to say that it was potty the two of you keeping two flats when you were practically living together, but at least there was none of this nonsense.'

The ranting went on for a while but I tuned it out. I didn't need to hear it, having anticipated every reaction over the past week. I absorbed every tenth word or so, waiting for cues that they'd become rational: '... crazy ...' '... selfish ...' '... insane ...' '... just thinking of yourself ...' Nope, still irrational.

Harry joined me in silence. I expect he felt that wild speculation

22

and accusation were women's territory. Perhaps he's right. I've always been better at it than Mark.

By the time Mark came back with the coffee, Lisa and Lynn had run out of recriminations. If they'd seen as many courtroom movies as I had, they could have kept going much longer.

Mark made a major production of bringing cups, milk, milk frother, sugar, biscuits and after-dinner mints through, one item at a time. At one point, I wondered if he was going to fetch his George Foreman Grill just to prolong the whole episode.

Finally he had no choice but to sit down. Go on then, I thought. Everyone have a go at him now. But of course they didn't. They were still looking at me.

'Give me one good reason, Jenny.' Oh dear. Lisa has become rational. This is a rare occurrence and very worrying. When she diverts all her neurotic energies into lucid thought, she is a formidable adversary. I hoped that Lynn would start ranting again to buy me some thinking time. But no, she clearly approved of this question and was waiting for an answer. They all were, including Mark. As well he might.

'I think you might be having a breakdown,' Lisa concluded. Coming from a woman who probably had personality disorders that hadn't been named yet, this was quite a judgement. 'You don't just end a lifelong relationship over one issue.'

I tried to make her understand. 'But what if it's the most important issue and it's totally irresolvable?'

Lynn had left in tears and Harry had apologetically gone after her. Mark had retreated to the spare room with his Game Boy and portable CD player. He would have his headphones on so that he wouldn't be able to hear us talking. It was more effective than a cushion.

Lisa was opening a bottle of wine. 'Surely after all these years, you know how to make Mark agree with you.'

I shrugged. 'I've never needed to. We've always agreed on most things, Steven Spielberg over Ingmar Bergman, dolly mixtures over smoked salmon, Elvis over Bach, musicals over opera. We even like the same clothes.'

Lisa closed her eyes briefly as she pictured the lifetime of randomly co-ordinated jeans-and-shirt combos that Mark and I had subjected her to. 'Don't change the subject. If you think I'm

23

going to start on your clothes and forget what we were talking about, you're wrong.'

It was worth a try. 'I'm just saying that we've never had really serious arguments before, so I've never needed to acquire any of those skills.'

Lisa didn't look convinced. 'The two of you possess more board games than any adults outside of an institution should possess. You should be a master at manipulation.'

'Beating him at Stratego is slightly different from persuading him to want a baby.' Lisa doesn't understand our love of games. She never does anything that doesn't have a guaranteed outcome.

After three large glasses of wine, Lisa finally said what was really on her mind. 'And what about us? The four of us. And the business? And what about Tally and Phil? What'll happen about skiing? And Easter? And which of you are we going to have for Christmas? For dinner parties? What . . .?'

I reached for her hand to stop her from expiring. 'We'll still be friends. You'll still give me cashmere jumpers, I'll still give you articles on Obsessive Compulsive Disorder. The others will get used to it too. We'll sort something out with the holidays and . . . and everything else.'

But the six of us had been close since university. We'd grown up together, moulded into a single amorphous mass, each of us forming a fixed element in the structure. We were joined together with the ties of a shared past and none of us could know what would happen when one of the bonds broke. I continued trying to persuade Lisa that everything would be all right. Maybe I'd believe it too if I said it enough.

'Couples divorce all the time,' I emphasized, 'friendships survive. And the business will be fine. It's really Mark and Kieran's after all. I just help out occasionally.'

But we both knew that I do a lot more than that. As well as designing their logo and writing the text for every promotional leaflet and piece of paperwork they generated, I decorated their offices, acted as receptionist, secretary and cleaner when necessary, produced their adverts, often modelling in them as well.

And let's not forget that I was cheap, i.e. free, and had neglected developing a proper career of my own so that I would always be available for Mark. Not that I begrudged it, not really, when everything we did was for our future. There had never been a line where Mark ended and I began. It was how we are. Were.

I even supported him financially as well as I could. I made a decent living doing occasional freelance work as an origami artist. And, yes, you can make money doing origami. Pretty much any advert you see on the television that uses a giant artichoke or mobile telephone made out of paper, I will have made. I've done children's parties and even entertained at the occasional team-building conference. It's not brilliant money but it's kept us in popcorn and replacement Scrabble tiles for many years.

'So you're just going to go out and find a replacement for Mark?' Lisa was having difficulty controlling her emotions so I'll forgive her if she sounded harsh.

'Lisa, I'd love to spend a few years getting over Mark, finding myself, reading self-help books, joining an ashram, that sort of thing. But I'm thirty-eight and I want children. What am I supposed to do? Go to a sperm bank? Buy a baby on the Internet? Would that be any better or worse than looking for a man whose values and goals coincide with my own?'

Lisa softened and put her arms around me.

'I don't know, Jen. But I would like to know how you are planning to find a new man and have a baby with him at thirty-eight, when no other women of that age seem to be able to manage it right now?'

I met Auntie Lynn at the garden centre she owned and managed with Harry. We'd arranged this in whispers just before she left yesterday.

They didn't spend so much time here since turning sixty, but Lynn still liked to pop in to stamp her personality on the place. 'Come through to the café,' she said, after kissing me with a little more anxiety than usual.

The café was full as usual. If you wanted a pot palm and a home-baked cake, then this was the only place in Fulham to visit. Lynn went out the back and dragged a small table and two chairs out. There are advantages to being related to the owner. Without asking me what I wanted, she jumped the queue at the counter and took two date slices and a pot of tea.

She brought it back and served us. It transported me back to the day after my mum's funeral. I was twelve and Auntie Lynn was trying to tell me that, before she died, Mum had asked her to help Dad look after me. I resented the offer and punished Dad and Lynn by imposing a nightmare adolescence on them. Not by crashing other people's cars or buying drugs from men in stained raincoats. Even then, I was too conventional for that.

I simply stopped talking to them so that they wouldn't know that I wasn't pregnant or stealing car stereos. In fact, when I was out late, I was usually at a friend's house working on geography projects, but I always mussed my hair up and put on make-up before I came home to worry Dad.

All that changed when I started going out with Mark. No wonder they'd loved him so much.

'Now, what are we going to do about all this silliness?' Lynn asked brusquely.

I sighed. I'm thinking of making a tape-recording which I can bring out and play on such occasions. It will be on a loop, continually repeating: 'I want a baby, Mark doesn't. It cannot be resolved. And, by the way, yes I did think about this before I did it.' I'm coming to understand that it'll need to be heard a hundred or so times before it sinks in.

'Auntie Lynn, there's nothing to do. But at least we've managed to agree to this split without any nastiness. That's an achievement these days, isn't it?'

Lynn shook her head. 'Listen to you! I reckon you must be having some kind of breakdown.' I'm going to have to get used to this diagnosis. 'Of course it will get nasty. Personally I think it's all down to the two of you insisting on keeping separate flats for all these years.'

I screwed up my face in bewilderment. 'How do you work that out?'

'Normal couples would have moved in together after a few years, once they realized they were committed to a joint future. They talk things through, get a lot of things clear about what they want. But you were both so stubborn and I'm sure it prevented you from really getting to know each other properly. Harry and I never understood it.'

'If Harry hadn't lent him the money for the deposit, he wouldn't have bought that flat in the first place,' I argued. 'So we both had flats we loved and neither of us wanted to be the one to give it up entirely.'

26

In rare moments of honesty, I acknowledged that I'd always resented Mark for holding onto his flat. He'd effectively moved in with me when we were twenty-five and merely paid lip-service to home-ownership by furnishing his flat with a bare scattering of functional accessories. He rarely slept there, perhaps on the odd night when I was away and he'd been working very late at the office which was close to his apartment block. But Lynn was right. The flat's existence was a wall between us, a constant reminder of the absence of firm and final commitment between us. Once Mark sold it, I expected us to meld together miraculously. Bit of a miscalculation.

Occasionally during our years together, I wanted to ask him the sort of questions I felt should be asked, where we were going, did we have a future, that sort of thing, but there were always films to watch, other people's lives to occupy us, to fill in our blanks.

'As I said, you're both stubborn,' Lynn mumbled. 'And now, because you're both too stubborn to compromise or back down, you're breaking up over one little thing with someone who's loved you all your life.'

'But it's not little, it's the biggest thing there is to me.'

Lynn was close to tears. I felt sick at upsetting her like this. 'Oh sweetie, were you thinking that I didn't understand? I understand only too well. You know I do.'

I did. Lynn had never hidden from me the fact that she had badly wanted children. But her first husband had died when Lynn was only twenty-eight and she had remained alone until she married Mark's dad twenty years later. By then she had accepted that I would be the closest thing to a child she would be able to experience.

'So you'll support me?' I asked nervously.

'Oh, Jenny, how could you even ask me that?'

We ate our date slices, both feeling that all this outpouring was too painful. In our family, as in many others, food offered a great refuge from emotion.

'How is Harry feeling about all this?'

Lynn looked behind her to make sure he wasn't nearby. 'Jenny, it was terrible. We had an awful row about it. In fact . . . sorry, I wasn't going to tell you this, I don't want you to feel guilty, but it was our first row.'

Guilty? If a giant divine finger had come down from the sky and pointed at me, with four shifty horseback riders hovering behind, I couldn't have felt less wicked.

'Sorry, Auntie,' I said feebly.

Lynn rushed to reassure me. I would have felt better if she'd smacked me with a slipper. 'Don't worry about us. It was just a shock, that's all. We'll sort it all out.'

'What did you argue about?' I wasn't sure I wanted the answer but I felt obliged to ask.

'Nothing. That's the problem. He refused to talk about it. Said we mustn't get involved or start taking sides.'

'But that's good, surely?'

Lynn shook her head. 'I hadn't even thought about taking sides until he said it. So we rowed about that. Then we took sides.'

When I hear about other couples' rows, I'm always relieved that Mark and I spent twenty-two years playing Uno instead.

'Mark and I talked about you and Harry. We're going to do everything we can to avoid making things awkward for you.'

Lynn smiled sadly. 'I know you'll try hard. But it's already awkward. I didn't even tell Harry we were meeting today and I don't know why. Everything's changed since you told us.'

I knew why. I'd had a week to work it out. It wasn't hard. Not only were Mark and I the reason Lynn and Harry met, we were also part of the glue that held them together. We were, individually and as a couple, the most important people in their lives, individually and as a couple. There was no division of real parent and in-law, they were both parents to us both. How could I have thought that this wouldn't damage them?

'Will you be angry with me if I ask you something that sounds a bit harsh?' Lynn asked finally.

Yes I will, but at least it can't possibly be as bad as Lisa's last question. 'No, of course not.'

'How do you intend to stay friends, or even stay friendly, with Mark, when you've just wiped out each other's lives?'

'You can always rely on family to make you feel suicidal when you only felt clinically depressed to begin with.' I knew that Maria would understand, with a childhood straight out of *Kramer versus Kramer*.

We were walking around Battersea Park. Mark was moving his things out and I couldn't bear to be there when he left. Maria had

28

immediately left work to meet me when she heard how desperate I sounded, even though it was only mid-morning.

Maria was unusually quiet. I became aware of a disturbing noise behind us and looked around in panic, thinking we were about to be attacked by a heavy-breathing sex fiend.

Maria was the heavy-breathing sex fiend, staggering along on unfeasibly high heels and hyperventilating. 'Is there any chance you could slow down before I have an asthmatic crisis or pull a ligament?' she gasped.

I'd forgotten that Maria was an adult who wore grown-up shoes rather than a girl who found a style of moccasins that were comfy in 1983 and had stuck with them ever since. My excuse is that I've always worn flat shoes because I don't drive and so I've become a fast walker.

Maria, on the other hand, is a fast driver and therefore only needs her shoes to make a statement. Today's statement was: 'I am in touch with my sexuality but please don't make me walk more than twenty yards or my lower spine will pack up.'

I waited for Maria to catch up with me. 'Are you OK?' I asked.

'No. I don't care if you need to commune with the elements to sort your head out, I need a sit-down and a cigarette.'

I held her arm and managed to get her to the café. We sat outside because Maria was determined to smoke. I went and got coffees for us. When I returned, she'd lit up and was looking human again. We spent a few companionable moments soaking up the sunshine and trying to ignore the children running around, screaming for ice creams and poking their siblings with stolen forks. I'd forgotten that these were the last days of the summer holidays. At moments like these, the idyll of babies seemed oddly distant.

'Do you feel better now?' I asked.

Maria exhaled smoke dramatically, looking like Lauren Bacall. I'm sure if I smoked, I'd look like Columbo. 'So where is Mark moving to?'

'He didn't say, he's going to give me his new address later. I think he's being deliberately secretive to punish me.'

Maria cleared her throat knowingly. 'A few days ago, you were going to be civilized, do lunch every third Tuesday and wear hats to each other's next weddings. Surely you're not at the subtle punishment stage already.'

29

She was supposed to be tender and supportive. Instead she was on the attack. I wondered how long it would be before she asked if I was having a breakdown.

'Do you think you might be having some kind of a breakdown?'

I must have full-on telepathy with Maria, rather than the selective type I have with Mark.

She hadn't finished with her medical theories and I cursed myself for buying her that encyclopaedia of women's health for Christmas. 'I was wondering if it might be some premature menopause type of thing. Some women can become clinically psychotic, you know. It's important that you start taking HRT as soon as possible.'

'I'm not having a breakdown, I'm not psychotic and I'm not having an early menopause.' At least I don't think so. She's got me worried now. 'I just want a family and found I was with someone who didn't. And yes, I realize I should have discovered this earlier, but I didn't want kids myself until last year.'

Maria leaned forward. 'You see, that sounds like your hormones talking. Perhaps you have Polycystic Ovarian Syndrome. That can make your hormones go crazy. Have you noticed the beginnings of a moustache recently?'

'Maria, have you been reading that medical book from cover to cover?'

She looked quite proud of herself. 'Yes, I have. It's fantastic. I want some of those syndromes myself. Especially the ones that give you big chests and rounded backsides. And I can't wait for the menopause. Apparently HRT gives you the ability to climb mountains and seduce young men. If I'd known, I would have started taking it when I was twenty-eight.'

I groaned. 'Much as I appreciate you researching my "condition", there is nothing physically or mentally wrong with me and I wish everyone would stop saying it. I just want you to accept my decision and help me move on.'

Maria put her cigarette out. That's how bad I'd made her feel. I'll remember that for the next time I'm trying to get her to give up.

'I'm sorry, Jen. You'll never convince me that this isn't a temporary aberration, but I'll be there for you however I can.'

'Well, that's good because I was relying on you.'

'Here I am! What do you want me to do?'

I took a deep breath. 'Well, you know how you've always said you wished I was single because then I could join in all the single-girl things that you had to do without me?'

Maria became tense for some reason. 'Yes.'

'Well, using your own words, here I am!'

She looked at me blankly. 'What do you mean?'

She was mysteriously dense without a cigarette. It must be a syndrome. I'll look it up. 'I can now go out with you to all those places, Singles Nights and those Date-a-thon dinner parties and cruises with like-minded men. We can relive my youth. But we have to speed up the process because, according to you, I could hit the menopause any day now and I haven't got long to have a baby.'

Maria was looking worried. 'Ah.'

'Don't say "ah". It always means you're going to give me bad news, usually about my appearance.'

Maria's expression became pinched. 'The thing is, Jen, there's something I've been meaning to tell you.'

'Tell me what?'

'Somebody's moving in with me.'

I didn't understand what she was saying. Maria hadn't had a flatmate in her entire life. She always said she was impossible to live with. Three hours in her company generally persuaded me. 'Have you got money problems? Is that why you need a lodger?'

'It's not a lodger, it's a man, a . . . a boyfriend.'

'But you haven't got a boyfriend.'

'I only met him three weeks ago. Things developed a little more quickly than I'd anticipated so I didn't get round to mentioning him.'

I had so many thoughts crashing into each other, I was finding it impossible to say anything. 'But . . . I don't understand . . . who . . .'

Maria exhaled slowly. 'His name is Danny. He's one of my new suppliers. He took me out to lunch and we got on really well so we went out that evening. And we've been out every night since – apart from when you phoned me in a state on Thursday and dragged me to that terrible bar. Anyway, we seem to like the same things and want the same things. And yesterday I asked him to move in with me and he said yes.'

I was stunned. 'And you were accusing me of being deranged! Three weeks and you're moving in together. That's lunacy!'

Maria raised her eyebrows. 'After fifteen years of maintaining two flats in London, you finally decided you knew Mark well enough to take the plunge and look how that ended. I think time is overrated as a factor in the relationship stakes.'

'Yes, but three weeks!'

'I love him and I think he's the one. And don't forget I've had more practice than you at knowing when a man *isn't* the one.'

I concentrated on my coffee, trying to work out how I felt. When I did, I was horrified. If this had happened six months, six years ago, I would have been cautiously thrilled for Maria. I'd longed for her to find somebody, knowing how badly she wanted to settle down. But now?

Her life was coming together at precisely the moment mine was falling apart. We were swapping roles in our friendship and I didn't know how we would be able to adapt to that. I summoned up my cheeriest voice.

'So you're finally going to live with a man after all this time! I can't believe you'll be going through all the same experiences that the rest of us went through years ago.'

'I could say the same about you,' Maria retorted. 'You've effectively been an old married woman since you were sixteen. You haven't got a clue about what life is like as a single girl.'

'I was relying on you taking me out and showing me,' I said gloomily, 'two single girls together on a great adventure. You were supposed to show me what to do, demonstrate how I sit on barstools without showing my pants, that sort of thing.'

Maria tutted. 'You've listened to me witter on about it all for years, you know as much as I do now. And if only Danny were a hairless grump with no dress sense and terrible taste in home entertainment like Mark, then I could have learned about man-management from you.'

I'd been banking on my friends to guide me through the difficult times ahead – maybe I should just have bought a labrador.

Chapter Three

It was the worst evening and night of my life. Even worse than the night when Mark and I agreed that we would be splitting up. That was bad enough but Mark's presence in the spare room was a residue of continuity from my rock-solid past to the uncertain future. Even in the last week, when things were so awkward, we were still together in a way that was meaningful to us.

We still watched videos, although we chose them very carefully, avoiding any that evoked too many memories. That restricted us to *Mad Max IV* and *Waterworld* although, when we saw them, we remembered how bad they were and that made us feel nostalgic all over again. I kept my hands clenched tightly together, so that there was no chance he might accidentally touch my little finger and melt my resolve.

We even played Rummikub while we were eating, rather than risk talking about anything.

But last night he was gone. Really, really gone. Even when he officially had his own flat, most of his things were at mine. As well as his clothes, he kept his favourite albums and computer games here. All of our joint possessions were in the bedroom that we called our bedroom.

For the first time in my life, I had nothing of Mark and I didn't know what to do. I couldn't watch a video. Not without Mark. Even if it were a film that Mark didn't like, it wouldn't have felt right. So I switched on the television. But all that did was make me feel more out of kilter with the rest of the world. I didn't recognize any of the characters in the soap operas. I didn't understand the stories. And when I did find a programme I could follow, it was always about a broken relationship and it was always portrayed as a tragedy. I knew that it was vital that I continue in the delusion that my divorce was not a tragedy but an unavoidable misfortune, one from which Mark and I would definitely recover. Definitely. So I switched the television off and built a replica of Stonehenge from dominoes. Me, having a breakdown? As if.

When the phone went, I let the machine pick the message up.

'Jenny, it's Tally. I can't believe it! Lisa has just told us the news. She thinks you might be . . . unwell. If you're interested, I can recommend someone, he does all the celebrities. Oh, and, I know this might be tricky but, erm, what will be happening about Phil's birthday next Wednesday? Only, we've booked the table for six people . . . well, anyway, perhaps you'd let me know what . . . well, you know. Bye.'

Was I imagining an absence of sympathy in her voice? She sounded more concerned about Phil's birthday than my tragedy – I mean misfortune – although maybe it was unreasonable to blame her for this. She'd had her kids, after all, how could she understand?

I managed to get to sleep after finishing off a bottle of wine and the last flagon of scrumpy from our last hiking holiday in Devon. To guarantee my stupor, I also ate a past-the-sell-by-date box of chocolate liqueurs that Mark had inexplicably left behind.

I was woken by someone banging on the door and ringing in my ears. Then I remembered that I have a doorbell. That was the ringing. Sitting up slowly, I identified the source of the banging as every nerve end around my forehead. I lay straight back down again, in dire need of water, painkillers, toast and, possibly, a bucket.

The bell rang again. I crawled to the door repeating slowly to myself: I will not be sick, I will not be sick. Pulling myself to a standing position gave me new respect for that first ape who dragged his knuckles off the floor and lurched up. It's not as easy as you think.

The postman took a step back, no doubt experienced in spotting projectile vomit potential at a doorstep's distance. He thrust a card at me to sign, dropped the post in my hand and retreated fast.

I collapsed gratefully to the floor and opened the Special Delivery letter. It was from Auntie Lynn and it was brief.

Dear Jenny,

Sorry if I seemed harsh with you on Friday. You know that you will always have my support. You mentioned that you would be concentrating on your career. Enclosed is a little something to tide you over while you get yourself started.

Lots of love
Auntie Lynn.

The little something was a cheque for £10,000.

It took a couple of hours, three cups of coffee, two slices of dry toast, two ibuprofen capsules and some fizzy tablets that made me belch all morning, but I eventually regained the full use of my limbs and partial use of my brain. £10,000 is quite effective as a hangover facilitator and I shall recommend that Lisa adds it to her traditional pre-Christmas party feature on How To Deal With The Morning After. It's not often I can contribute anything to her magazine for the Modern Woman and her Lifestyle, being neither a modern woman, nor ever having had a lifestyle. I think she'll be grateful.

Everything was clear in that blinding sense of clarity that only comes from an onslaught of artificial stimulants on top of an underlying state of hysteria. I switched on the computer.

For the last five years, since Mark had taught me to use the machine for something other than playing solitaire, I had toyed with the Internet. I had looked for markets for my origami skills and even placed my details on a few of those free websites that promise you access to thousands of blue chip companies. I eventually found out that not even oven chip companies used such facilities.

But now I had £10,000 and an urgent need to build a career. I spent three hours and £2,000 registering my website with search engines, paying premiums for good listings with the reputable directories and generally making myself known and available to the global creative community. Anyone in the world wanting a professional paper folder would find me. Now all I had to do was wait.

I was exhausted after my exertions and I was still irrationally angry with Maria for abandoning me to my search for a suitable man. That's my excuse for what I did next. Also, it was like a sign, an omen, when I was just staring at the screen and it appeared: PROFESSIONAL? 25–45? LOOKING FOR THAT SOMEONE SPECIAL? CLICK HERE.

So I clicked. Who wouldn't? By which, of course, I mean who in the tightly defined target group of deranged, recently separated, tired, unevolved women who have no idea how to move their lives on.

Five minutes later, I'd paid a reassuringly large registration fee on my credit card and typed in the following ad: LATE THIRTIES LONDON WOMAN, LOOKING FOR MAN WHO LOVES FILMS AND GAMES, ORIGAMI AND TRANSPORT CAFES, JEANS AND FLAT SHOES, WALKING AND COMICS, MUST HATE PARSNIPS AND KENNETH BRANAGH. DOESN'T NEED HAIR, I HAVE PLENTY.

Even I knew that the mention of children was not a smart thing to place on an Internet ad, so I hoped that if I found a man who liked all the same things as me, there might be a good chance he would share my views on families as well, even if the theory fell down miserably with Mark. I resolved to ascertain this fact before getting involved with anyone again.

Maybe if I'd taken Maria's advice and started taking HRT, I wouldn't have done something so impetuous, but I pressed 'SEND'.

So that's my life sorted then.

I got to Mark's office at about three o'clock. Some post had arrived for him, including a recorded letter from Harry. I assumed he would be getting a cheque too, although I didn't think he needed it having made such a killing from the sale of his flat before our wedding. But I decided I mustn't think ungracious thoughts. I must always bear in mind that this situation is of my own making. Frankly I think I prefer the idea that I'm having a breakdown. A month in a clinic being indulged and patronized sounded glorious to me. And I've heard that everybody dresses badly there so I'd be conforming for the first time in my life.

Mark wasn't at the office and Kieran appeared alarmed to see me.

'Don't worry, Kieran, I haven't come to smash my wedding

ring through the computer screens. I've just come to drop off some post for Mark.'

His relief was evident but he then immediately looked guilty at showing his relief. 'That's OK. He won't be long. So how are you?'

'Fine, fine. Why shouldn't I be? The worst is over and we've survived. Nothing has changed. Not really.'

He applauded slowly. 'That was good, I almost believed you. Now try again, this time remembering who you're talking to.'

I'd known Kieran since he was a particularly young eighteen-year-old student. While Lisa had, in recent years, dealt with his clothes and had his fair straw-dry hair shaped into a smart layered style and even persuaded him into contact lenses, only electro-convulsive therapy would teach his long, gangly arms and legs to move with any kind of dignity. He was Mr Bean in Paul Smith casuals and he was Mark's best friend.

Setting up the business together after university had been their single expression of intimacy, the equivalent of Lisa and I going to a health spa, lying naked on massage tables next to each other and having our facial pores vacuumed, which Lisa forced me to do last year as a horrendous birthday 'treat'. While we bared our bodies and souls, Mark and Kieran signed binding contracts and shook hands over a pint and a steak-and-kidney pie, committing all their time and money for the foreseeable future to each other.

But we were connected by more than Mark. He was also my secret friend. We'd liked each other since we met and if we hadn't both been attached, I often wondered if we might have got together. That was half of the secret. The other half was that we often had long phone calls without Lisa and Mark knowing.

It had started with casual chats when Lisa wasn't available until, gradually, we found ourselves telling each all those awkward truths that couldn't be confided elsewhere. He knew how much I hated Mark hanging on to his flat for all those years and I knew how much he hated Lisa's lists. I sympathized when he found his jeans had all been replaced with chinos and he sympa-thized when I found my first grey hair.

We never met up alone. That would have been . . . wrong. And when we were in a foursome, we never referred to our conversa-tions. It afforded us all the thrills of an affair but without having to book cheap hotel rooms and develop furtive expressions.

37

The disadvantage was that he knew when I was lying. 'OK, I'm not fine and everything has changed. And if you accuse me of having a breakdown, I'll tell Lisa that you actually threw away that pink tie you said was stolen from your car last year.'

'And I'll tell Mark how you cheat at backgammon.'

But neither of us would say anything. That would be crossing boundaries, redefining relationships that had been sealed for all time between the four of us with cheap beer in a college bar.

I patted his arm affectionately, innocently. 'I'm glad I can still rely on you to point out my faults.'

'Any time. So what are your plans now?' he asked.

I explained about my morning's work on the Internet. 'I'm hoping to pick up some jobs, make some more contacts.'

Kieran looked alarmed. 'Does that mean you won't be helping us out any more?'

'Well, I'll always help if Mark wants me to but . . .' I held my hands up, hoping he'd understand that it might not be as straightforward as it used to be. I noticed Kieran was adjusting his expression, not very successfully. 'Why? Is there a problem? I thought that, with all the money Mark put into the business, you'd be laughing. You can even probably afford to get some professional help. If you're cranking up your profile, you ought to produce some more upmarket-looking promotional material than my amateur efforts.'

Up until last year, Mark and Kieran subleased and supplied fitness equipment to companies who wanted to set up in-house gyms for their employees. They were both fitness freaks and had toyed with the idea of running their own gym before deciding that there were better prospects in the corporate market.

They always knew that they would never make serious money until they bought their own gym equipment to rent out, keeping all the rental fees for themselves. When Mark sold his flat, he immediately decided that he would use the whole lot to buy state-of-the-art machines and lease warehouse space to store them until they got new contracts or some of the old contracts' leases expired.

Kieran turned away from me. 'So Mark hasn't said anything to you about . . . anything.'

'We've been somewhat preoccupied with other stuff,' I reminded him. 'Why? Is there something you're not telling me?'

Mark arrived before Kieran could reply, looking pleased to see me for, ooh, two seconds. Then he stopped smiling, then he remembered we were still supposed to be best friends and he smiled again.

He stood by the door unsure how to greet me. I understood his discomfort. Do I peck him on the cheek? Give him a cheery wave? Shake hands? Maybe he wanted to slap me. I wouldn't blame him. 'Is everything all right?' he asked immediately.

'You're wearing new clothes.' I couldn't help myself. 'You hate new clothes. We both do. Did. Do. I mean, we both still probably do, but we're not a "both" any more.'

Mark touched his shirt without thinking, ignoring my discomfort or more likely not noticing it. 'It just seemed an appropriate time to buy new stuff.'

'Even though it's exactly like the old stuff.' I pointed out.

'Just because I'm a man doesn't mean I can't be irrational. I read that in men's magazines so it must be true.'

Now it was my turn to smile. 'They also say that any man can get a six-pack stomach on just ten minutes a day and that turned out not to be true.'

Mark raised a finger to object. 'That all depends on how you define the six-pack. I think you'll agree that I have the perfect abdominal muscles on which to rest a six-pack.'

It took a massive effort not to throw my arms around him and shout: 'I'm sorry, let's forget all this and go back to how we were. Let's go and buy a packet of eccles cakes and hire a rowing boat in Battersea Park then go home and play Monopoly until I get Mayfair and Park Lane and you pretend to sulk, and then we'll have fish and chips and . . .'

'She's just brought you your post,' Kieran said, finding the silence agonizing.

Mark picked up the envelopes from the desk, fingering them absently. 'Our Video Club membership has expired.'

'How appropriate,' I whispered.

We stood there for a while like the villains at the end of *Reservoir Dogs* with guns at each other's heads. Neither of us wanted to shoot first. It was Kieran who broke the silence, probably because he hadn't seen the film.

'Jenny was telling me about building up her origami career,' he mentioned. I could have hugged him for his attempts to alleviate the tension.

I waited for Mark to smile that smile he always displayed when he heard the word 'origami', an inherently funny word, in his opinion.

'Perhaps she could fold herself a new life,' he said, 'with little paper children.'

Kieran smiled nervously, unsure if this was supposed to be a joke. I knew that it wasn't. It was a cruel, cruel comment and it took my breath away. We all stood like that for a few seconds more before I realized that there was nothing more to say.

'Right, then, I'll be on my way,' I ventured finally. There was no argument.

Kieran made a move to kiss me then pulled back, unsure if this was now appropriate. I mumbled my goodbyes and made a quick exit. I was glad to be out of there and vowed not to do it again. Before I had a chance to enjoy my solitude, I felt my arm grabbed from behind. All ready to apply the Heimlich manoeuvre to my attacker, it being the only manoeuvre I know, I saw that it was Lisa.

'What the hell are you doing?' I hissed.

'I'm watching the office to see what Kieran is up to. Come back here.'

I followed her to a taxi parked along the road. The driver was reading the *Sun* and seemed oblivious to my arrival, no doubt encouraged in his silence by the ticking meter.

'What the hell are you doing?' I repeated, unable to top this question.

'I'll show you.' Lisa took her mobile phone out and dialled the office. From our vantage point, we could both see right into the office window. Mark answered the phone.

'MarkieFit, Mark Stafford speaking, how can I help you?' He'd been on one business course in his life and they'd taught him to answer the phone like that. Sad.

'Hi Mark, it's Lisa. Can I have a word with Kieran?' She then held the phone up to my ear to hear the reply.

Without hesitation, Mark lied. 'Sorry, Lisa, Kieran's out seeing a client. Can I give him a message?'

'That's OK, Mark, I'll see him at home later. Bye.'

I was horrified at how smoothly he'd lied. I turned to Lisa. 'How long has this been going on?'

'About a week.' Lisa's voice was shaky. 'I thought there might be another woman so I've followed him a few times. But I haven't seen anything yet.'

I didn't like to argue that following her husband was the act of a slightly unhinged woman. My credibility in the sanity stakes was not particularly high right now so I decided to try and reassure her instead.

'I'm fairly certain that this is nothing to do with another woman. I think the boys might have some problems with the business. Kieran more or less admitted it.'

Lisa looked confused but relieved. 'But how can they have problems after Mark put all that money in?'

I raised my arms in ignorance but before I could say anything, Lisa tapped my arm. 'Jenny, what is Tally doing here?'

I looked back out of the taxi window. Tally was walking into the office. Although she didn't walk so much as shimmy.

Even when she was a student, Tally was different to the rest of us. She was so obviously a woman while the rest of us were girls and boys. And while we all secretly liked the idea of the rampant promiscuity that university was supposed to offer our working-class repressed souls, none of us ever got around to embracing it. But Tally did. She'd appeared to be on a mission to sleep with as many men as possible in the shortest time. Now that I'm grown-up (by which I mean I've seen a lot of films about women like Tally and read some of Lisa's articles) I recognize that she had low self-esteem and was just seeking male approval.

At least I hope so. If she was just doing it for fun and it didn't damage her in the slightest, then the rest of us had inhibited ourselves for nothing.

She didn't really join our crowd until late into the third year when she started going out with Phil, who played football with Mark and Kieran. We'd not welcomed her warmly, knowing her reputation and fearing for our boyfriends. She also made us feel shabby with her logic-defying jeans and clinging tops. But then she completely reinvented herself, becoming a devoted and faithful girlfriend to Phil and a pretty good friend to Lisa and me.

Yet she still made us nervous. Her curves were so much more visible than ours, her smiles more knowing. She married Phil straight after university, quite unusual at the time and, twenty years on, she's a stay-at-home mum to three kids and one of the more stable members of our group. But still she shimmies.

Watching her push the peeling door to MarkieFit's tiny office, above the Kashmir Kurry Kanteen, I couldn't help but notice that she was back in those tight jeans, that her long, highlighted blonde hair was loosened from its customary ponytail and the smile was in evidence. She was even wearing a skimpy halter-neck top and even I know that you're not supposed to wear those over the age of thirty-five, unless you're Lulu. I felt instantly shabby and vowed to make a ruthless cull of my faded T-shirts in the near future.

Even the taxi driver was fascinated by Tally. I wanted to swipe him with his newspaper. Excuse me, I felt like saying, I could walk like that if my jeans were a size smaller. I just choose not to give myself a sweat rash.

'You don't think . . .' Lisa couldn't complete the sentence.

I patted her knee. 'Don't even think it. There will be a perfectly innocent explanation for this.'

But I couldn't think of a single one. Every person we know has his or her place. That's how it is with friends. We women go out together. The men sometimes watch a football match in a pub. That's the way of things. Maria would never go on a bender with Mark, and Tally would never meet Kieran in the daytime. That would mean something significantly different and we do neither significant nor different things in our crowd. (Of course, my telephone friendship with Kieran breaks the rules but that's OK, because they're my rules.)

So now I have to work out the significance of Tally leaving the office, two minutes later, laughing happily with Mark.

'So which one's that, then?' the taxi driver asked. 'Is that the husband who won't answer the phone or the one whose wife left him just because she wants a baby even though she didn't tell him that before?'

I glared at Lisa, who had the decency to blush. 'I see you've updated our chauffeur on the status of my private life.'

'Sorry. I had to explain what I was doing to convince the cabbie that I wasn't doing anything illegal.'

'Lisa, you didn't need to explain anything. He's a taxi driver, he dreams that one day a woman will get into his cab and say

42

"Follow that car!" or "Park over there and turn the lights off!" If you must talk to strangers, then tell them about your life, not mine.'

We both knew that I was only overreacting because I was shaken by seeing Mark with Tally. Lisa understood this and didn't argue with me. 'It's like you said, Jen, there's probably a perfectly innocent explanation for this.'

'Yeah, right. Perhaps she's helping him choose a divorce present for me. After all, Tally and I are so similar, she'd be the perfect person to ask. She could recommend a push-up bra or slutty shoes.'

'That's it!'

'What's it?'

'He must be helping her choose a present for Phil's birthday.' Lisa was looking cheerfully smug after making this logical deduction.

I was uncertain. 'But she's never asked him before. We don't ask each other's husbands to do things like that.'

But that was the point. He wasn't my husband any more, not really. The rules had shifted. And now I had to wonder how far Tally intended to shift them.

It was all changing too quickly. I wanted everything around me to stay the same, to act as a safety net for me while I flailed about, reliving my life, correcting my mistakes. The only change I wanted was a baby. I didn't want to lose Mark and I especially didn't want to lose him to a married friend. I kept seeing her hair and Mark's smile.

I switched on the computer because there were no other appliances I could trust. The TV would be showing love films, the radio would be playing our song and even the microwave would smell of the last batch of popcorn Mark and I had made. I felt suddenly hot and sweaty. Opening the windows made no difference, all I did was let in those rancid smells that seem to stick to the air on a hot day.

Lights were flashing and alerts were beeping on the monitor. Not only did I have messages, I had 187 of them.

After opening the first dozen or so messages, I began to understand the shorthand and was able to filter them out more effectively. I was surprised that most of the emails had digital photos attached. This was useful. Having compared the photographs with the descriptions, I came to understand that 'good sense of humour' meant that the man generally resembled the photofit of a hired killer, 'intelligent' meant that he wore bad glasses and 'good-looking' meant that the picture was of somebody else, in one instance of Val Kilmer in *Batman Forever*. In full costume.

But there were some interesting replies that had clearly taken some time to compose. I had no idea that there were so many men in London who were interested in origami. I eventually ended up with nine men whose eyebrows didn't meet in the middle and who had kept their clothes on in their photos.

While I thought about what to do next, I logged onto my professional account. I was astonished to find forty-nine replies there. I discounted the reps with names like Darren and Geoff who were trying to sell me photocopiers, water coolers and pornographic calendars.

But there were a dozen others that were promising. The requests were varied but, coincidentally, they were also mainly from men.

'I'm looking for someone to make a full-size paper boat that can be sailed down the Thames. Can you help?'

'URGENT! Can you turn crisp packets into pandas?'

'I'm a fashion designer and I want to do a catwalk show with designs made entirely from paper to match the actual clothes. Is this possible?'

I could do all these things and I even recognized some of the names. This could involve serious fees. I was about to respond to them all when I stopped and thought. Whoops, here come Mark and Tally again, shimmying through my head, dancing to our song, watching our videos . . . Strike them out quickly.

It must have been the jumble of these unfamiliar anxieties – I hadn't even considered the notion of Mark with another woman, not ever – mushed with the excitement of all my new possibilities, both personal and professional. I had nobody to bounce my ideas off. Mark had been my springboard, always. I could have asked Lisa or Maria but I wanted to make this decision alone, to prove I could.

And I was angry. *And* irrationally jealous of Mark who seemed to have moved on with such ease. *And* the only thing that could possibly make me forget the pain I was now experiencing at the loss of Mark was a child. *And* at thirty-eight the chances of me having a baby would be diminishing every day. These were mitigating circumstances, I would argue later. All I could think of was that I had two choices: I could sit in my flat and imagine fifty ways to subject Mark and Tally to violent deaths. Or I could move on myself. Very, very quickly. The rational part of me (and yes, I was aware of just how small an area this part occupied) warned that things were happening too fast, that I needed to take stock, settle down a little before taking any radical action.

But if Mark could do it?

Now I'm not stupid, well, OK, I'm a bit stupid or I wouldn't be in this position in the first place, but I knew I couldn't just go off and meet all these strange men by myself. I also knew that the professional contacts, respectable people from respected companies, could open lots of doors for me.

So why not meet them all together? The lot of them. The men from the personal ads and the business ones too. How much safer could that be? I'd invite them all to a . . . a . . . party for origami-minded folk. An origami party. I could even delude myself, if I lost my nerve, that I was just making new chums and forging new business connections, not looking for a new partner at all. I mean, if my future was moving in that direction, it was a fast, effective way of getting myself known. And it would be an unpressured way of meeting the men. I really couldn't face going on dates, never having been on a date in my life, unless you count the first few times I went out with Mark. Except they were during a Duke of Edinburgh's Award field trip when we sneaked off to eat buns in a teashop, so, technically, possibly not dates.

I was impressed with myself. I went through all the possible arguments before deciding that this was a great idea. After a quick phone call to the pub down the road to book the upstairs room, I emailed the nine personals men and twelve professional men/women (was Ashley male or female?) and invited them to an origami party in two days time.

Proud to have taken decisive action to stop myself from being dragged down into a depressive pit, I emailed Lisa and Maria to let them know what I'd done. Their responses were rewardingly fast. Strangely, they both used capital letters. I think they wanted to make a point.

45

Maria was first. But then she always has been a talk-first-think-later sort of friend.

NOW I KNOW YOU'VE LOST IT! ARE YOU COMPLETELY INSANE? YOU CAN'T JUST INVITE TWENTY-ONE MEN AND ASHLEYS THAT YOU'VE NEVER MET BEFORE TO A PARTY. AND WHAT THE HELL IS AN ORIGAMI PARTY? THEY WILL ALL BE PERVERTS AND YOU'LL BE FOUND MURDERED IN A WHEELIE BIN DAYS LATER. I AM GOING TO BE THERE TO MAKE SURE YOU DON'T DO ANYTHING TOO STUPID (ALTHOUGH IT WILL TAKE SOME DOING TO TOP THIS FOR MADNESS). DON'T DO ANYTHING ELSE BEFORE CONSULTING ME FIRST. UNLESS IT'S GOING TO SEE A DOCTOR WHICH I STRONGLY ADVISE.
MARIA
XXXXXXXXXX

Apparently, Lisa shared her concerns.

YOU COMPLETE IDIOT! I SAID YOU WERE HAVING A BREAKDOWN AND YOU WOULDN'T LISTEN. WHAT MORE PROOF DO YOU NEED? YOU ARE IN NO FIT STATE TO BE MEETING NEW PEOPLE AND YOU SHOULDN'T BE ALLOWED ACCESS TO THE INTERNET WHILE YOU ARE UNHINGED. DO NOT, UNDER ANY CIRCUMSTANCES, TALK TO ANY OTHER STRANGERS WITHOUT ME BEING THERE. I WILL BE COMING TO THIS 'ORIGAMI PARTY' AND WILL PERSONALLY THROW OUT ANYONE WHO LOOKS ODD OR CREEPY OR WHO SAYS ANYTHING NOT DIRECTLY RELATED TO ORIGAMI. PERHAPS YOU SHOULD HAVE A CONDITION OF ENTRY THAT THEY ALL HAVE TO BE ABLE TO FOLD SOMETHING BEFORE THEY'RE ALLOWED IN, LIKE A DUCK OR SOMETHING, SO WE AT LEAST KNOW THAT THEY'RE NOT PSYCHOPATH STALKERS, PRETENDING TO LIKE PAPER-FOLDING AS AN EXCUSE TO GET CLOSE TO A DISTURBED, VULNERABLE WOMAN.
I KNOW YOU FEEL YOU NEED TO GET MOVING ON THE MAN FRONT AND I WANT TO HELP. I HAVE AN IDEA

THAT MIGHT MAKE YOU FEEL BETTER ('AND IS SAFER
THAN YOUR OPEN HOUSE TO THE LONDON UNDER-
WORLD). COME TO MY OFFICE TOMORROW MORNING
AT 9.30.
LOVE
LISA

Well, frankly, I think they're both making a lot of fuss about
nothing.

Chapter Four

I woke up without a hangover. A result indeed. I was knackered, of course, from having spent most of the night inventing and playing out every possible scene involving Tally and Mark. I don't know why I never considered writing film scripts myself. I'm very good at it.

In one, Mark only married me because Tally's husband, Phil, and I were getting close to discovering their secret affair and they needed to distract us.

There was a surreal version where Mark was the father of all Tally's children which was why he didn't want kids with me. OK, so the plot makes no sense, but the *Highlander* films with Sean Connery are proof that cohesive plots are not essential for a film to be commercially successful.

In another, Mark rushed into her arms *after* I broke his heart, although it couldn't have been that broken if it only took a couple of days to make it available to another woman. OK, I reasoned, maybe it might look as if I'm doing the same thing but then my actions are rational and heart-free. Oh yes they are. Perhaps I'll have a badge made that makes this clear, just in case anyone might be tempted to accuse me of hypocrisy.

I couldn't switch the images off. I felt physically sick and wondered if this was just the normal response to the end of a very long relationship. I made a note to myself to ask Lisa for some appropriate articles when I saw her this morning.

It hadn't helped that Tally had phoned me during a particularly lurid imaginary scene that would never have made it past the censor. Unless the film was released in France, of course.

'Hi Jenny, it's Tally. Hello? Are you there?'

I pulled myself together, reminding myself that life was not a film and that, quite possibly, she was not the marriage-breaking harlot I was imagining her to be. Quite possibly she really did just need Mark's help to choose new golf shoes. 'Hi Tally. Sorry about that. I, er, had something in my mouth.' Some filthy words of abuse, actually.

'How *are* you, Jen? I don't know what to say. I just can't believe this is happening to you and Mark.'

I think you can. 'I'm fine, Tally. And before you ask, no, I'm not having a breakdown.'

Tally laughed nervously. 'I wasn't going to ask. That's not why I called. Well, the reason is . . . oh, this is all a bit awkward.'

Here we go. 'What is it, Tally?' I asked coldly.

'It's about Phil's birthday next week. The thing is, we all feel really bad about you and Mark and we want to help in any way we can. But we're presuming you're not both intending to come to the restaurant.'

'Well, Mark and I didn't discuss it specifically. We had bigger matters to discuss.' That's a lie. We discussed the bigger matters as little as possible. But I'm keen to at least give the impression that this was a mature separation. 'But we were agreed that we didn't want this to change everything. So I don't see why we can't both be there next Wednesday.'

The silence told me that Tally disagreed. 'The thing is, Jen, that this is Phil's fortieth. He's the first of us to get to forty and I wanted to make it as special as possible.'

'And you're worried that, if Mark and I both come, we'll throw lobster claws across the table or bore you all rigid with incessant "he saids" and "she saids"?'

'Well, it would be a bit uncomfortable, you have to admit.'

'So you're saying that we can't both come? You want one of us to bow out?'

No, she wasn't saying that or she would have agreed with me. What she was saying, in her painful silence, was that she felt Mark ought to be there rather than me.

'I feel terrible about this, Jen, but Mark is really Phil's friend. What we thought we could do, is have you round to dinner on the Friday, get another cake and do the whole thing again.'

Lovely. I could go to the B-List celebration. But I didn't have time to dwell on the new two-tier system that had been put in place within days of our separation and without any consultation. I had just been confronted with a truth that had never previously mattered in the past but that was now all-important. All of our joint friends had been Mark's friends before they were mine.

They went to his university in Bristol. I had friends of my own in Exeter, but Mark never once came to visit me there so he didn't meet them. I don't know why we'd done things this way, but it had evolved that I went to Bristol most weekends. Gradually, Mark's friends became my own and I never resented it. I've learned that this state of affairs is unusual in a couple. In general, the women make and maintain the friendships and the men get dragged along for the ride.

The friendships I made in Exeter were less intense, probably because so much socializing was done at weekends when I wasn't there. When I graduated, I didn't keep in touch with anyone, already enmeshed with 'my' Bristol crowd. A few girls phoned and wrote when they moved to London, anxious to touch base with a familiar face in a new town. To my shame now, I didn't reply to any of them.

Well, I'm paying the price now, aren't I?

'Fine, Tally, whatever.'

'Now you're angry with me. But what am I supposed to do, Jen?'

You're supposed to act as if nothing has changed or be on my side, those were the only two options I'd considered, you shimmying old hag. Well, that's mature of me. I'm one step away from her beautiful detached home, boiling the family guinea pig in her Nigella Lawson spaghetti pan. And she probably hasn't even done anything. But I'll never know now and I don't have the right to ask. Great. I'll just have to brood on it obsessively, instead.

'Sorry, Tally. This isn't your fault.'

'I know that,' she replied, a little harshly, I thought. 'But I am trying to make the best of a difficult situation.'

Well, you're failing miserably.

Lisa was in a bad mood when I arrived at her office. 'Kieran and I had a foul argument last night.' She'd come down to the lobby of the huge building to collect me.

'I can't imagine you and Kieran fighting. I thought you told him what to do and think and wear. Surely if he doesn't, you just send him to his room with a glass of milk and a biscuit to think very carefully about his behaviour?'

Lisa ignored my sarcasm. 'Not this time. I presume Tally's called you?' I nodded. 'Well, I was furious when she told me what she was planning, especially after what we saw yesterday. I said that Kieran and I wouldn't be going if you weren't going. Then when she told me about the second dinner for your benefit, I said, fine, we'll come to that one.'

'That wasn't necessary,' I said weakly. 'The last thing I wanted was to cause trouble for everyone else.'

Lisa ignored my objection. 'Then Kieran asked what I had been talking to Tally about and announced that he fully intended to go on Wednesday. That he owed it to Phil *and* to Mark to be there on the birthday itself.'

'Didn't you use your special tricks to make him agree with you?' I asked, desperately trying to lighten her mood.

'He wouldn't budge. So that's that. He's going on Wednesday and I'm coming on the Friday.'

This was terrible. It didn't matter how sincerely Mark and I intended to spare our friends from too many repercussions from our split, they were rushing into a freefall decline of their own accord.

The lift arrived at the twentieth floor before I could argue with her. I hadn't had a chance to find out exactly what I was doing here so I was naturally apprehensive. 'Can I just say, Lisa, that if there are men in white coats with a stretcher and a straitjacket, you didn't need to go to all that trouble. I will definitely go quietly. I quite fancy a year of sedation and isolation.'

Lisa strode out of the lift and I followed, noticing with wonder how quickly she could walk in high heels. It reminded me painfully how different I was from other women, that even the way I walked betrayed me as a separate breed, not quite a woman as such. She opened some double doors with a dramatic flourish to reveal a large table, a whiteboard and a dozen or so enthusiastic minions staring at me.

I stood still, reluctant to enter what looked like a gladiatorial arena, where I was either going to be Russell Crowe or the lion. Either way, I didn't fancy my chances.

Lisa guided me in confidently, like a mother dragging a small child into school for the first time.

'Everybody, this is Jenny. Now you all know that she is a very good friend of mine, so I want you all to use your skills and sensitivity when you are working with her.'

Perhaps they are a team of surgeons and boffins, who are going to rebuild me like the Six Million Dollar Man. They will turn me into a socially-presentable woman who wears suede skirts, maybe with a chip implanted in my brain that will make me like *The Archers* and Pimms.

I wasn't as wrong as I would have liked to be.

'As I've explained to everybody here, Jenny, the fact that you've recently found yourself unexpectedly single coincides with our planning a whole issue dedicated to the problems of women just like you, in your late thirties, desperate for children, but out of the dating scene for so long that you don't know how to get back in and also facing a declining pool of available men.'

She spoke with such well-meaning sincerity, that it was possible, very slightly possible, to ignore her staggering thoughtlessness at exposing me to this humiliation.

'Is there a "good news" bit to this bad news, Lisa, because I'm getting depressed and I felt fine before I got here.'

'The good news, Jen, is that you don't have to do anything at all, we're going to do it all for you. We have style consultants who will prepare you for the singles marketplace, psychologists who will advise you on how best to handle the men you meet, relationships counsellors who will show you where you've gone wrong in the past so you don't repeat your mistakes and –'

'Maybe the manager of Arsenal to ensure that my Keepy-Uppy skills don't let me down on the field?'

'Sorry?' She finally noticed that I had raised my hand. I wanted to hit her with a chair but this was her workplace and I had to respect her position in front of her team. I knew that most of her colleagues disliked her but I felt I needed to show that she did have at least one friend, just to give her a hint of a human side that might redeem her in their sight.

'Sorry to interrupt, Lisa, but what hallucinogenic drugs did you take before concluding that I would go along with any of this?'

Lisa turned to the room. 'Just excuse us a moment.' She grabbed my elbow and yanked me outside. 'Now I know this is a bit of a shock. But I had good reason not to tell you about it in advance.'

53

'Because I would have laughed in your face? Found a thousand good reasons not to turn up including root canal work and a time-share presentation?'

'I knew you wouldn't come, yes. And I want you to hear what these people can offer before you say no.'

'I don't need to. I'm saying no already. No and goodbye.'

But Lisa was still holding on to my elbow. 'I know what you're thinking.'

Bet you don't.

'You're thinking this is too much too soon, but the magazine won't come out for a few months by which time you'll have run out of crazy paper-folders, become sane again and will be grateful for some lovely normal men.'

I quickly applied my Lisa-filter to her words. She couldn't avoid appearing insensitive, it was her special gift. I knew that this was her way of trying to 'help', of showing me that she cared but I would rather she'd offered me silent support. Or a kidney. Anything but this.

'I'm only asking one thing. That you listen to each of these people before you make up your mind. I have briefed each of them personally and comprehensively and insisted that they don't do or say anything without my written approval.' I'll bet that helps her popularity standing. Then she delivered her winning salvo. 'You'll make me look bad if you walk out now.'

I had no choice. But I did have a question. 'Even if you perform all your hocus pocus on me, I thought you said there was a shortage of eligible men out there for women like me. How are you intending to find someone?'

Lisa beamed. 'That's the best part. We have a partner publication called *Upscale Man*, it's a lifestyle magazine that –'

'I know all about it. Mark and Kieran advertise in it.'

'Well anyway, it has a circulation of 225,000 and they've agreed to run a feature asking men to write in, saying why they think they would be a good match for you.'

No, this made no sense. 'I don't get it. It sounds as if you're going to advertise me, inviting offers. Like an unwanted kitten. You can't mean that.'

Lisa became animated. 'Not advertising, promoting, Jen! Think about it. Can you come up with a more efficient way of achieving your aim? You've got twenty-one mad people coming to your origami party; I'm offering you over two hundred thousand men who we will have screened first. What have you got to lose?'

My dignity. My pride. The will to live. Pick a number.

After my traumatic six-hour ordeal at Lisa's offices, I had to work hard to organize my origami party. I did what Lisa had asked, listened to everything her colleagues had to say, didn't slap any of them, and promised that I would make a measured decision over the next forty-eight hours. Only joking.

I now had just the one day to get everything ready. As Maria and Lisa were insisting on coming, it was important to me that this wasn't the disaster that reason dictated it must be. I bought twenty boxes of filo pastry and began using it to fold some intricate models which I then baked.

Some of the models looked rather obscene when they came out of the oven and I had to snap off some unwelcome pastry appendages. I hoped I was doing the right thing. I was trying to create a civilized ambience for my origami party and there are not many articles on that. Maybe there's a book opportunity in this for me.

I spent a long time deciding what to wear. I don't know why because my wardrobe limits my choices drastically. I decided to appease Lisa and Maria by wearing the one pair of jeans that fit me properly and my least offensive shirt, the one not made of checked brushed cotton and not worn down at the cuffs. I would have preferred to wear a T-shirt on such a warm evening but the memory of Tally in her glamorous top had dented my confidence in clothes that had once made me feel comfortable.

I got to the pub at 5 pm, which gave me two hours to set things up. Maria arrived ten minutes later.

I greeted her warmly, knowing that she'd left work early twice this week for me. 'Let me guess, you've got an armoured van outside with a metal detector and a very big, tattooed man called Frankie.'

'I know you think this is very amusing but, if you ever watched made-for-TV movies, you'd know this is the classic woman-in-peril situation that ends in spooky music and a bloodbath. You think that everyone is as sweet and nice as you. But while you and Mark have sleepwalked in your little cocoon through two decades, the rest of the world has become mean. They even have serial killers in *Coronation Street*.'

'Yes but the origami world has been uniquely free of murder in modern times, as far as I know.'

Maria took off her coat. 'You're so naïve if you believe that all these people will be interested in is paper.'

'Maria, you look amazing! I can't believe you've dressed up for this.' She was wearing a white wraparound top over a magnificent red satin skirt with a dramatic black pattern swirled around the hem. It was more pinched at the waist than Maria normally wore and gave her the hourglass figure of a young Rita Hayworth.

'It's nothing,' she said, appearing to be embarrassed that I'd noticed. 'Right, now here's what we're going to do. You must never be out of earshot of me or the Rottweiler so that one of us can intervene if you are doing something stupid like giving out your home address.'

I sighed. 'I'm hardly going to do that. I do have some common sense. Why did you think I hired the pub in the first place?' Because my flat was too small. But she doesn't know that.

'Because your flat is too small,' Maria replied sweetly.

As of now, Lisa is officially my first best friend.

Lisa arrived at that point. I looked at my watch. She never left work this early. I was really touched by this display of concern from the two of them. And she'd also made an effort with her appearance. Not that she didn't always look great, but she was more glittery than usual and she'd had her hair cut even though this wasn't haircut time on her Personal Care List (I know her lists intimately, since I appear on most of them).

I watched Maria and Lisa eyeing each other appraisingly and suddenly understood why they'd both gone to so much trouble with their clothes – it was to impress each other. I stifled a laugh as I imagined each of them this morning, determined not to be outshone by their arch rival in the glamour stakes. They'd met several times and now, when I reflected on those meetings, I suppose they always did this.

I wondered what they got out of it. I didn't care who dressed the most stylishly (as if I would have even noticed) and it had no impact on my friendship for them. I filed this away for future contemplation. For now, I had origami on my mind.

'So what do you want us to do?' Maria said finally, her

confident tone indicating that, in her eyes, she'd won the fashion competition.

Go home? Leave me to handle this myself so that, when it all goes horribly wrong, nobody need know about it? Be kind, I told myself. In just over a week I've lost a husband and alienated one friend, Tally, already. If I'm not careful, they'll all be sick of me and I'll end up having to travel round London buying the *Big Issue* every week from all the sellers, just for the human contact.

'Can you help me lay the food out, Lisa? And then there are these decorations to put up and the sculptures to display.'

I unpacked the boxes, pulling out some of my demonstration pieces. Lisa and Maria stared at them. I waited for the jokes.

But Lisa was shaking her head in astonishment 'Jen, these are amazing! You've done a whole Noah's Ark. I can see what every animal is and they're even accurately proportioned.'

'They're supposed to be,' I observed dryly.

Maria had picked up a vase that I'd filled with a mixed bouquet of paper flowers, all arranged according to traditional Japanese Ikebana principles. 'Roses, lilies, freesia . . . and look at all the leaves, I had no idea you could do this. These are pieces of art!'

I was not used to so much praise from them. 'What did you think I did then?'

Lisa shrugged. 'I assumed you made flapping birds and those open-shut finger things that tell your fortunes that we all made in school.'

'How did you think I made any money if that was all I did?'

'To be fair, Jenny, you never showed us any of this stuff.' Maria had unconsciously moved a step closer to Lisa. I was amused by this new affinity they were finding for each other as they closed ranks against me. 'The only thing I ever saw you make was that little frog you folded from my business card that you flicked onto the next table in that bar.'

'Well, you wanted to attract that guy's attention, didn't you?'

'He complained to the manager about us and we had to leave. An inviting smile would have been less confrontational.'

I always did think that Maria's unadventurous attitude to men was part of the reason she hadn't been able to get one to stay with her in the past.

Lisa was admiring a tiny jack-in-the-box that I'd constructed from a chocolate wrapper and a selection of assorted hats, each of which was folded from the front page of a different newspaper with the title prominently displayed. 'Do you know how much I pay stylists to create things like this for my magazine?' she asked. 'And all the time you had this amazing talent and were sitting at home, wasting your time writing pamphlets and slogans for our husbands.'

'So now we're all agreed that I'm an undiscovered genius, can we see if I can kick-start my neglected career tonight without any more jibes about psychopathic perverts?'

Maria had to get one last dig in. 'At least when you're lying in a gutter stabbed by a paper knife, nobody will be able to accuse you of having aggravated the attack by wearing provocative clothes.'

Thank you, Maria.

By five past seven, eleven guests had arrived, including Ashley, who had turned out to be male. I'd made stickers for each of them with miniature folded animals on them. They were colour-coded at Maria's request, so they could distinguish between the professional contacts, to be treated with respect, and the men from the personal ad, who were to be treated with contempt to see if they could be goaded into a homicidal frenzy that each had hoped to hide from me.

I hadn't argued with this since it had occupied my friends for thirty minutes, leaving me to get on with the decorations. They'd looked quite companionable as they worked on the stickers and I was surprised at the twinge of jealousy I experienced as I watched them.

I don't know what's happening to my emotions at the moment, I thought. Perhaps Lisa was right and it was my hormones all along. I don't have any HRT at home but I could always light that aromatherapy candle that Auntie Lynn gave me for my birthday. Mad women light candles a lot in films, I've noticed. Perhaps it helps.

'Hi, this is a great idea!' A man was thrusting his hand at me. His label said that his name was Ed but I didn't know what the blue dot indicated. I should have asked for the colour key from my brilliant friends. Still, he didn't have any tics and he looked quite clean. He was also well dressed, by my standards at least. That was all I could go on, really.

'Hi, Ed, I'm Jenny. Thanks for coming.'

I waited for him to identify himself as either 'creative director seeking someone who can turn five pound notes into penguins' or 'single eccentric with a collection of lifesize paper *Star Wars* figures'.

I liked his face. He had lots of laughter lines, no frown ones, eyes with life and curly brown hair that he'd made no effort to tame into shape. For the first time, I got Maria's point about hair. He was wearing a smart jacket and trousers that had creases in the proper places. I had no idea if they were fashionable or expensive, but I felt a little shabby next to him.

'I'm glad you organized this so quickly. The timing couldn't have been better. As I mentioned in the email, we've got a shoot on next week and I need to construct a white landscape with origami mountains and trees emerging from the flat surface. We'd film the folding and then speed up the footage to make it look as if it were happening spontaneously.'

I couldn't help being relieved that he was one of my professional contacts. I could relax and not worry about saying the wrong thing. Out of the corner of my eye, I saw Maria and Lisa giving me a thumbs-up. First admiration, then approval. Will our friendship ever be the same again?

'That would be no problem. In fact, I've got some country scenes on the table over there, some pine trees and a three-hill group. Why don't you take a look and see what you think?'

'Thanks.' He seemed gratifyingly reluctant to leave and I felt an instant thrill that was just as instantly replaced with the certainty that this was absolutely wrong and that I ought to be at home with Mark, eating wine gums, stroking his head and watching Neil Diamond in *The Jazz Singer*. I was shaking inside as if I were going down with flu.

'What's wrong? He was great!'

Maria came over to me, leaving Lisa talking about lists with a man in a quilted waistcoat who'd taken his Topics Of Conversation list out of his pocket as soon as he arrived. If Lisa hadn't already been married, it would have been a perfect match.

'I don't know what I'm doing here,' I whispered. 'You should have talked me out of this.'

'I tried, if you recall,' Maria hissed indignantly.

'You were right. I'm having a breakdown. I should never have left Mark. I should have gone to the doctors and asked for pills that would stop me wanting babies and make me content with my lot.'

Maria touched my face with a gentleness that made me want to cry. 'Sweetie, if you want, I'll chuck them all out and you can call Mark, tell him this was a big mistake and you want him back.'

'Of course I want him back!' I exclaimed. 'I'll always want him back. But I want children more. And besides, he's already off shimmying with someone else.' I knew how pathetic I sounded.

'Then maybe you just need some time to adjust before you start rushing into this new life thing,' Maria suggested.

I shook my head. 'The reality is that all the time in the world isn't going to help. It will be years before I get over Mark, if ever, he's been so much a part of me for so long. But if I wait until I feel better, it will be too late for me to have kids and then I will have put us both through this for nothing. No, I've just got to get on with it.'

I dodged past Maria before she could say any more wise words and make me do something rash like come to my senses. I went and poured myself a glass of wine from a bottle around which I'd sculpted a swan.

'This would be perfect for the banquets I cater for!' I stopped to talk business with a man who had emailed to ask if I could produce elaborate paper flower displays.

I worked out that the men with red dots were the ones who'd answered my personal ad. They were all disappointing, although none appeared certifiable, violent or even particularly odd. (But bear in mind that my own friends consider me the oddest person they know.) I'm sure that another woman would have been perfectly happy to meet any one of them. But I couldn't rid myself of the strong sense that I was being unfaithful to Mark simply by talking to them.

One man had brought along a paper box as a gift for me. When I opened it, there was a wad of cotton wool on top of which were some gems, beautifully crafted from coloured cellophane. 'I didn't know what to bring to an origami party so I thought this would be different.'

His name was Cesar. He had strange eyes.

'Cesar, these are fantastic. Do you make these for a living?'

'No, I'm an IT consultant.'

'But I've never seen anything like this!'

'Most women I meet find it childish,' he said. 'And I think they prefer real jewels.'

I was about to defend my sex when I thought of Lisa and Tally with their truckloads of discreet, but expensive, real jewellery. Would they be moved by this hand-made gift? Probably not. 'Then you need to find someone who appreciates your talent for what it is.'

'It's just a hobby.'

His shyness was evident in his stilted conversation. Perhaps I should have introduced him to the man with the Conversation List, he could have given him some tips.

'I will treasure these. Thank you. It's good to meet other people who share my interest. I thought I was the only person over the age of ten who enjoyed paper-folding.'

Cesar became animated. 'That's why I was so excited when I saw your message on the website. I've never seen an ad from a woman that mentioned origami, not in fifteen years.'

His face lit up and then I realized what had been strange about his eyes. They'd been the saddest I had ever seen. When he smiled, the strangeness disappeared and was replaced with hope. I felt a complete bitch for raising this sweet man's expectations. But I needed to quash them fast.

'There are some people here who will pay a lot for someone with your skills. Let me introduce you.'

But he tensed, recognizing the rejection, probably an expert after fifteen years of it. 'That's OK. I'll be on my way. Thank you for inviting me.'

Then he was gone.

I hoped I wasn't going to decimate the origami community of London by sending them all into suicidal despondency with my inept brush-offs. But most of them appeared to be enjoying themselves. Two men, who apparently knew each other, were standing on chairs, dropping paper helicopters that they'd made from napkins. They shouted with pleasure as they twirled slowly to the floor.

Maria and Lisa watched in horror, wondering if they should call the police before the men pulled chainsaws from their belts and went berserk. But they eventually climbed down and sat calmly, eating plate after plate of pastries.

Some of them stood quietly to the side, accustomed to being alone. Lisa and Maria talked to them all, acting like perfect hostesses and, I hoped, skilfully hiding the motives behind their intense interrogation.

I made sure I spent at least five minutes with each of them. There was no doubt that there was something a little unusual about them, that rendered them out of synch with the contemporary world. But I felt a kinship with them that left me to wonder about the way other people perceived me.

I enjoyed myself, learning some new models that I would look forward to demonstrating to M . . . Whoops, almost forgot. But Mark had always enjoyed my origami. He never joined in but he humoured me. Must stop thinking about him. Must stop thinking about him.

It was the sort of party I wish somebody would invite me to. None of these people seemed to care about my clothes or their own. They were impressed by my creations. We made spiders and pagodas and got down on the floor to have jumping competitions with our paper fleas. These were my kind of people. But I didn't want to have babies with any of them.

'So what's the significance of the red dot/blue dot?' I turned round quickly. Ed was watching the room with interest and amusement.

I reddened. It went well with my red shirt. I hoped Lisa was observing my first success at colour co-ordination since my wedding, when I'd allowed her to choose my outfit. 'Oh, it's just an idea my friends had.'

Ed waited for clarification. Mark wouldn't have needed clarification. I missed him.

'So you're not going to tell me what the dots mean?' Now he was amused. 'I've been conducting an experiment to see if I could work it out for myself.'

'And your conclusion?'

Ed considered his reply. 'The blue dots are people who want to employ you and the red dots are from a subversive Rent-A-Paper-Folder organization that you've hired for the ambience.'

'Wow, so I achieved an ambience, after all! That's a first.'

Ed laughed. 'Am I right?'

I relaxed again. It was quite easy being in his company, maybe because he had hair and didn't remind me of Mark. 'More or less,' I agreed.

'Listen, is there any chance we can meet up before the shoot? I want to go over the project so that you can make any suggestions, tell me if we need to supply you with anything in particular.'

'Sure. When did you have in mind?'

'How about next Wednesday?' He hesitated before adding tentatively, 'We could have dinner.'

I would have said 'no' immediately, having, this second, been on the down section of my emotional rollercoaster which dictated that this was all a terrible idea. But Wednesday was Phil's official birthday dinner, the one I was no longer invited to and that Lisa was boycotting. I knew that I would spend the whole evening drinking alone and imagining them all having a wonderful time, talking about me. Perhaps Tally would stroke Mark's head and he'd stroke her little finger and disprove the innocent birthday present theory, but I wouldn't know because I wouldn't be there.

'That would be great, Ed,' I replied, mainly to stop the image escalating.

'I'll call you to arrange,' he said, picking up one of the business cards I'd had printed that morning. For a scary moment, it looked as if he was going to kiss me, but instead he shook hands warmly and left.

I felt . . . How did I feel? I don't know. Still bad, but better than before.

By 9 pm, all the guests had left. Lisa and Maria were a little drunk. I'd had much more to drink than both of them but I was utterly sober.

'So?' Lisa was waiting for a verdict on the evening. Her job was done, no blood had been shed and she'd been there to ensure I didn't throw off my clothes in a hormonal frenzy and scream 'someone give me a baby *now*!'

'I'm having dinner with him next Wednesday.'

She and Maria exchanged glances. I must have missed a signal between them because they turned to me simultaneously and announced, 'Then we're coming too.'

'Sorry, Jen,' Lisa said, 'but you don't know anything about this man, you are mentally unstable and we don't trust you.'

'But he was wearing a blue dot. That makes him respectable according to your rules.' I was determined to talk them out of this suggestion.

'I'm with Maria,' Lisa argued. 'Under normal circumstances,

the blue dot would be sufficient. But you are behaving bizarrely at the moment and he could turn into a red dot at the slightest provocation.'

Maria was encouraged by Lisa's support. 'Don't worry, though, we're not going to sit at the same table, we don't want to scupper the deal, we'll be a few tables away.'

Well, that's OK then.

Chapter Five

When some more post arrived for Mark the next day, it occurred to me that he hadn't given me his new address. I phoned the office and Kieran answered.

'Hello?' He hadn't been on a phone-answering course.

'Hi Kieran, it's me.'

'Sorry, I'm unavailable to give you a baby this morning, can I interest you in an abdominal cruncher or some knowing ironic banter?'

'My conversational skills were used up last night so repartee of any kind is out of the question,' I apologized. 'Can I just speak to Mark?'

Kieran hesitated. 'Sorry, Jenny, he's out with a client.'

'I don't believe you,' I barked. 'So where is he?' It wasn't only that I recalled Mark saying the same thing to Lisa when she'd asked for Kieran the other day. Mark had always told me that he didn't see the point in meeting clients before 11 o'clock because they weren't fully awake until then and never made decisions. He also liked to be able to extend the meeting over lunch to close the deal.

'This isn't fair, Jen. Mark is my friend.'

'You're supposed to be my friend too,' I snapped, before slamming the phone down.

I had a lot to do, calls to make to discuss work offers from the night before, some design preparation on the winter scene that Ed had commissioned me to fold for next week, more enquiries on my website to sift through, both personal and professional.

But I didn't do any of them. I grabbed my coat, rushed outside and hailed a cab, thanking my late father that he'd enabled me to buy a flat on a main taxi route.

'Where to, love?'

'If you can get me to Warwick Way in Pimlico, I'll direct you from there. And I'm in a bit of a hurry.'

These were the words all London cab drivers dream of hearing. He performed a U-turn that sent me hurtling to the floor and then bombed over Albert Bridge, as if we had life-saving organs to deliver to a dying child.

As we approached Pimlico, I briefed him further. 'When we get near St Cecilia's School, can you slow down?'

He did so, oblivious to the horns and screams of abuse from the traffic behind him. 'Can you stop now!' I called out.

His emergency stop was awesome. So were those of the cars behind. That's why I don't drive, because of taxi drivers like him with passengers like me. But we'd got there in time.

I had no idea where Mark might be otherwise I would have been following him, but I knew where Tally always was at this time, so I decided to follow her instead. What did I hope to achieve? I'm having a breakdown, I don't need to have logical aims.

She emerged from the school grounds in her Range Rover at exactly 10 o'clock after dropping her children off at their holiday club. I immediately judged her a terrible mother for offloading them so readily when I would have been playing educational games and making *Blue Peter* models with them if they'd been my children. And, yes, I know that I'm only saying that because I haven't got kids and don't know what it's like. I'm irrational. I've got a syndrome.

'OK,' I announced to the taxi driver. 'I want you to follow the woman in the over-tight top in that green car.'

'And you don't want her to know that she's being followed?' he asked, eagerly.

I tried not to laugh. 'You could sit on her tail and flash your lights at her all the way from here to Glasgow and she'd ignore you. You're a taxi driver, she's a woman driver, it's what she expects.'

He showed his displeasure by slamming the dividing window shut. Doing his best to inflict a whiplash upon me, he sped away. I was grateful for the silence that gave me time to think about what I was doing. But instead, I found myself fixated on the driver, wondering if he was ninety years old, as he certainly looked, wondering where he'd bought his flat cap that I thought had only existed in *Steptoe and Son*, wondering if he had discussed the question of children with his wife before getting married.

My instincts were rewarded when she turned left over Battersea Bridge, the opposite direction to her house in Fulham. She stopped and parked outside a patisserie off Wandsworth High Street. The taxi driver pulled up a couple of cars down, opened the window and waited for me to insult him again.

But I was distracted by somebody getting off a bus and running over to join her inside.

It was Mark again. He was wearing another new T-shirt. Had he done anything apart from shopping since he moved out?

'Quickly,' I shouted at the cabbie. 'You have to go in there and listen to those two people over there and tell me everything they say.'

'No problem, madam. I'll use the recording device I have hidden in this button here and then I'll transmit the tape to you via the antenna I have had surgically built into my left ear.'

I preferred him when he was sulking. But I needed his help.

'OK, I'm sorry I was rude earlier. But that man is my husband. Well, he was my husband. And that woman, is, was, my friend. And I just need to know . . .'

He'd got out of the car before I needed to finish the sentence. Why wouldn't he? He would have enough material from this fare to bore his future passengers for weeks to come.

They seemed to be in there for ages. Mark and Tally left first and I slid down in my seat so that they wouldn't see me. There was nothing untoward in their parting kiss but that didn't mean anything. My taxi driver came out a minute later, looking smug.

'Well?' I didn't bother masking my impatience, I was paying by the minute after all.

'I couldn't hear much, they were talking quietly.'

'Well then, how did they behave. Did she stroke his head?'

He looked at me as if I was mad. Well, I am mad, that's the general consensus.

'No, she didn't stroke his head and that would be a very weird thing to do if you don't mind my saying. No, the only touching they did, which I'd hardly call touching, was when he touched her little finger.'

*

The cabbie kept the dividing window open as he drove me home, giving me a running commentary of every incident of adultery he'd encountered in his taxi.

'None of them are worth it, that's what I always say.' He'd become quite concerned when I burst into tears and tried to back-track. 'Maybe it wasn't her little finger,' he said, 'maybe it was her middle finger.' He watched me carefully to see if this made a difference, aware that I was a disturbed individual in whom any minor detail could push me over the edge. I wondered if he would work his way through every finger until he found the one that calmed me down.

'Maybe,' I mumbled, to shut him up.

'And didn't you say that you'd left him?'

Why do people tell taxi drivers these things? 'Only a few days ago. I didn't think he'd run after my best friend hours later.' Oh no, I'm now turning into a taxi driver myself, adding pointless, false embellishments to my story for dramatic appeal.

'But didn't you also say that you had started looking for a man the same day and that you have a date with someone with a blue dot next week?'

'Do you have some kind of truth gas pumped in your cab?' I complained. I had no recollection of telling him all this. I was becoming more convinced that I was suffering from a something-oma or -itis, something physiological at the very least.

He ignored my question. 'I think you just sensed I was someone you could trust.' Now I know I've entered the Twilight Zone. 'You're about the same age as my Katie. She's married to a swine as well. They emigrated to Australia and every time I get the opportunity to help out a lass in trouble, I do it, in the hope that someone might do the same for my Katie when she needs help.'

Great. To punish me for all the abuse I've hurled at cabbies during my life in London, I've got myself saddled with one as a guardian angel. As we pulled up outside my flat, he gave me a card. 'On that are all my numbers. Now any time you need a taxi for anything, you give me a call and I'll be there. I'm coming up to my retirement so I only go out for a few hours a day. Most of the time, you'll be able to catch me. I won't even start the meter running until you get in the cab.'

This last offer was unprecedented in taxi history. Even if Nelson Mandela were a cabbie, he would always start the meter running before picking his fare up. It was a comforting absolute in an unpredictable world. 'Thank you . . .' I looked at the card, 'Alfie.'

He jumped out to open the door for me. For one cinematic moment, I thought he was going to waive the fare with a flourish. But not even in a surreal Latin-American film about tangoing armadillos would that plausibly happen. 'That'll be forty-one pounds and fifty pence, but we'll call it forty quid.' Surreal enough.

I walked down the stairs to my front door. Just as I put my key in the lock, I heard someone inside. Only one person had the key to the flat. Mark was home.

'Only me, Jenny!'

I stand corrected. Two people have the key. 'Auntie Lynn! What are you doing here? What's happened? Is it Harry? Is it his heart? Is it Mark?'

Lynn was cleaning my kitchen. This was a major exercise since neither Mark nor I had been very good at cleaning. Well, we might have been good at it, we just never got round to testing our abilities because we weren't interested. As long as the TV screen was shiny and there were no visible mouse droppings, we were content with our environment.

'It's nothing like that. Well, it is to do with Harry, but it's not his heart. In fact, I'm beginning to doubt if he even has one. Maybe when he had his last heart attack, something was destroyed, if there was something there to begin with.'

'Have you had a row?' I asked, impressed by my own heightened sense of perception.

'It was more than a row. It takes two people to have a row and he wasn't talking.'

She was scrubbing the surfaces with bleach and a Brillo pad. I wondered if I ought to be offended that she had judged the level of squalor worthy of such drastic action. No, I couldn't be offended, I don't care enough.

'What happened, Auntie Lynn? Please don't say that this is about me and Mark again!'

'Not exactly. Well, sort of, I suppose.' I felt that now familiar sickness seep through me. 'I wasn't very happy about Mark moving in –'

'Wait a minute! Mark has moved in with you?'

'Yes. Surely he told you?'

'No.' I mentally added that to my new list of Things Mark Hasn't Told Me. It was a surprisingly satisfying exercise and I'm beginning to see the appeal of lists to Lisa.

Lynn was too preoccupied to notice my own plummeting mood. 'Well anyway, I didn't say anything because I thought it was just a temporary measure until he found somewhere of his own. But then all the whispering began.'

'What sort of whispering?'

'Maybe it wasn't whispering as such. But every time I went into a room, Harry and Mark would be standing close to each other talking. Then they'd stop as soon as they saw me.'

I understood her concern. For Mark to be standing close to his dad and talking at all was a totally unreal happening. Unless they were in front of a barbecue turning chops and massacring sausages, they would never willingly put themselves in a position where personal conversation might be encouraged. They both favoured the English approach to father/son relationships whereby they talked about sport and politics a lot and occasionally patted each other on the arm in acknowledgement of the blood tie.

'Did you ask Harry what was going on?'

'Of course I did,' Lynn snapped. 'Obviously I tried eavesdropping at the door first.' Obviously. That's exactly what I would have done. 'But I couldn't hear a thing. So I asked him what they were talking about and he said that he'd promised Mark that he wouldn't tell me.'

'But that's outrageous!' I confess I was more outraged that I was not going to hear the subject of all the whispering than the betrayal of trust in Lynn and Harry's marriage.

'Exactly! So I started shouting about how he shouldn't take sides with Mark in all this because otherwise I'd have to take your side. And do you know what he said? That it was nothing to do with you, that it was something completely separate.'

I took a deep breath. 'I think I know exactly what it was about.' I told her about my discovery today. She didn't lecture me on the advisability of following people when already in a state of mental upset, for which I was grateful. Nor did she try and find innocent explanations for the little-finger-touching incident. She knew exactly what that meant.

'Oh, love, I'm so sorry. That must have been horrible for you.'
Now I was beginning to wish she'd tried to jolly me out of my
misery, because I had the terrible feeling that I was going to cry.
'That makes sense. Harry would know how much I'd disapprove
of any shenanigans like that.'

'Even though I'm about to embark on some shenanigans of my
own?' I asked in amusement.

'That's different.' But neither of us was sure why.

'So you decided to cool down by coming over and murdering
the germs in my kitchen?'

Lynn stopped cleaning and looked at me. 'Didn't I say? I've left
Harry. I told him that he and his precious son could whisper to
their hearts' content. I'm moving in with you.'

I survived the day – just. Fortunately my flat was filthy enough to
both occupy and exhaust Lynn. By 7 o'clock, she was asleep in
front of the telly, the remains of a pizza on her lap. She'd
studiously picked off every speck of anything unrecognizable
from the pizza, including a few pieces that she refused to accept
were tomato. At least this was good practice for when I finally
become a mother. I couldn't imagine that any toddler could be
fussier than my Auntie Lynn, who thought that jacket potatoes
were unrelentingly foreign.

The spare room was all ready for her to fall into after Mark's
departure. It was also bearing the hallmarks of her hyperactive
cleaning onslaught, so I was confident that I could leave her for a
few hours. I just had to get out.

It was a lovely evening so I decided to walk over to Lisa's
house in Stockwell. Walking always had a positive effect on me so
I was unhappy to discover that it now aggravated my obsessions.
I found myself mentally beating Mark with a bicycle chain in
rhythm with my footsteps. I kept seeing Tally dressed in white
throwing herself across his body to defend him from my attack. I
arrived at Lisa's just before I murdered them both but was found
not guilty on grounds of diminished responsibility.

I'm not sure if the concept of 'diminished responsibility' exists
outside of films. I hope so, because all of my future plans are
currently founded on this Get Out Of Jail Free card.

Lisa answered the door in a state. I knew that she was in a state
because she still had her jacket on and Lisa never wore her jacket

in the house. It was one of the rules on one of her many mental lists, the ones that don't need writing down because they are referred to continually.

'Jenny! What's the matter? Is it Mark? Your Auntie Lynn? Harry's heart?'

I followed her into the house, taking care to remove my shoes first and only walk on the plastic covering along the centre of the hall carpet. Kieran was in the living room pouring himself a large glass of wine.

'I didn't know you were coming round, Jenny.' If he'd placed a bell around my neck and handed me a placard labelled UNCLEAN, he couldn't have made me feel less welcome. I hoped he was just mad at me for putting the phone down on him earlier.

'I popped round for a chat with Lisa.'

'You've never done that before. Not ever.'

I hadn't realized that until he mentioned it. Just days into my new life and I was already acting out of character.

Lisa had her hands on her hips in classic confrontational mode. 'Are you going to pour Jenny and me some wine or shall we just watch you enjoying it?'

Kieran grabbed the bottle and poured two small glasses, spilling some drops on the carpet. 'Have you lost the ability to pick up a bottle yourself or have you got used to your slaves at work performing every non-executive function for you?'

I suspected I might have called at a bad time. Lisa dashed to the kitchen, returning seconds later with a spectacular array of specialist cleaning products. Kieran and I could only watch with helpless fascination as she removed the rogue stain with extreme prejudice.

'Shall I come back another time?' I suggested, wishing I'd stayed at home with Auntie Lynn and amused myself by throwing bits of uneaten pizza into her open, snoring mouth.

'No! In fact, you can help us out. Kieran and I were having a little disagreement. Perhaps you'd like to tell us what you think.'

No, no, no. Anything but somebody else's argument.

'I hardly think this is appropriate,' Kieran objected.

'But I thought we'd agreed that I don't care what you think,' Lisa said, sweetly. 'So this is totally appropriate behaviour.'

I was having a very bad day indeed.

Kieran slammed his glass down on the table, spilling more

drops, this time onto the tablecloth. 'OK. If you insist. Here are the facts, Jenny. I have reluctantly, *extremely* reluctantly, agreed to go along with Lisa's determination to try for a baby, even though I would rather have waited for another couple of years –'

'By which time, I would be forty,' Lisa interrupted.

'But that's not enough for Lisa. Oh no. Despite all the books saying that you have to try for eighteen months before you start investigating for any problems, Lisa wants us to spend a thousand pounds seeing some expert in Harley Street who will tell us to come back in eighteen months.'

'I'm just talking about planning. What's wrong with planning?'

'In anybody else, nothing at all. In you, it's one plan closer to being certifiably barking mad!'

I was drinking as fast as I could. 'Oh well, I'm sure you'll work it all out,' I said feebly.

Lisa glared at me. 'But you know what I'm talking about. You were prepared to leave your husband over this. All I'm asking is that Kieran agrees to speed things up now that he's agreed to it. I mean, it's not as if we can't afford it, is it?

Kieran didn't reply. Something must be seriously wrong with the business and he hadn't confided in Lisa. Or in me. I was irrationally hurt, knowing I had no right to expect him to tell me everything he kept from his wife, my friend.

She was still waiting for me to say something loyal or sarcastic. Here goes. 'The last thing I want is for you to break up over this. It happened to me and Mark because we couldn't resolve our differences. But, Lisa, Kieran has agreed that you can have a baby, so I don't think it's unreasonable that you agree to his suggestion that you just let things happen naturally.'

Kieran was unnerved by my defence. Lisa looked devastated. I fingered my empty glass nervously and cursed myself for wearing lace-up shoes – it would make a swift exit more complicated.

'Well, that will teach me for asking a friend who chooses her clothes for comfort,' Lisa snapped.

'Don't blame Jenny for being honest.' Kieran felt obliged to defend me in return.

'I must be off,' I shrieked brightly. 'Thanks for the wine. Goodbye.'

My abrupt announcement shook Lisa from her fog of resentment

73

at me. 'But you've just got here and you haven't even told us why you came.'

I waved my hand vaguely. 'It was nothing. Really. Bye.'

Lisa stood in front of the door to block my exit. 'Sorry, Jen. We shouldn't have dragged you into our argument. Something must be up for you to come round like this.'

I'd wanted to talk to Lisa alone. This came under the category of subjects I shared with her, not Kieran. I was hoping that he would tactfully leave. Like most of my recent hopes, this one was thwarted too.

The awkwardness of the preceding moments robbed me of my discretion. Everything just spewed out. 'Oh it's nothing much. Auntie Lynn has left Harry because Mark has moved in and now they're keeping secrets even though I explained to Lynn that it's hardly a secret now that I've actually caught Mark in the act. More or less.'

'Am I alone in not understanding a word you just said?' Kieran asked me.

'I sort of followed it,' Lisa said, meaning she didn't but was being loyal.

I explained the whole story slowly, right down to my new best friend, Alfie, who could personally testify to the act of adultery in the coffee shop.

'You followed Tally?' Kieran had paled at this detail. I didn't justify this by pointing out that I got the idea from his wife, who had indulged in this on a regular basis recently. My first loyalty still had to be to her. That was the rule.

'Only because I had to.'

Kieran was looking at me curiously. 'So just because a taxi driver tells you that Mark touched –'

'Stroked,' I corrected.

'Stroked Tally's finger –'

'Her *little* finger,' Lisa interjected, understanding the distinction perfectly.

Kieran nodded patiently. 'Whatever. Because of this, you have concluded that he must be having an affair with Tally.'

'Exactly. We both always hated couples who kissed and touched each other a lot in front of other people. Even when we were at school, we didn't hold hands. So he started this thing of stroking my little finger when no one was looking. It's the most

74

intimate public thing he ever does. If he's now doing that to Tally, then it means that he must be intimate with her in other ways.'

Kieran considered this. 'Maybe, but not necessarily recently.'

It was as if we all experienced a freeze-frame. I was trying to decipher Kieran's oblique comment, while Lisa's eyes were darting back and forth maniacally, looking for a distraction.

'What do you mean by that, Kieran?' I amazed myself with my serenity.

Lisa jumped in front of him, I suppose to prevent me using any lip-reading skills. 'He doesn't mean anything. He's just being a moron.'

Kieran stepped aside. 'Thank you, Lisa, That really helps our current situation. All I was saying, Jenny, was that Mark was probably touching Tally's finger completely innocently because he was out of sorts, with all this divorce stuff going on, and because he remembered that they had a fling once.'

'They had a fling once,' I repeated.

Lisa turned to Kieran. I didn't see her expression, but I saw Kieran's, which told me that she'd conveyed her displeasure at this revelation.

'I mean, you did know this, didn't you?'

'Of course she didn't, you idiot!' Lisa snapped.

'But evidently, you did, Lisa,' I said.

'Surely it doesn't matter, it all happened a long time ago.' This was Kieran, the voice of reason, the voice of sense who was very close to ending his life either at my hand or his wife's.

'How long ago would that be?' I asked. My face must have been very scary because both Kieran and Lisa had taken a step backwards.

'First term at university. It was nothing, everyone was doing it, we'd just left home, you remember what it was like?' Kieran didn't know when to turn and run for his life. He just kept ploughing on, compounding his blunder in the hope he might unexpectedly say the right thing.

'Yes, I do remember. I was at university too. I had offers too. The difference being that I said no. Because Mark and I had promised, *promised*, to be faithful to each other.'

'Yes, but –'

'Kieran, *shut up!*' Lisa was red and flustered. 'Look, Jen, I'm really sorry about this. Kieran's got a big mouth.'

75

'You obviously haven't. You've managed to keep this secret for twenty years.' I didn't bother trying to conceal my hatred for her at that moment.

'But that's it,' Lisa pleaded. 'It was twenty years ago and I hardly even knew you until the second term. We weren't proper friends for a year or so after that. When was I supposed to drop it into the conversation?'

'Any time would have been fine. But you didn't. And now I will never be able to trust you again.'

Before I could make a fool of myself by crying, I pushed past her, grabbed my shoes and left, running down the street barefoot, wishing I'd worn my moccasins.

'Wait for me!'

I sped up, grateful that I was so much fitter than Lisa. She caught up with me in a stunning high-heel sprint that would probably shorten the lifespan of her calf muscles by a number of years. Her close-fitting linen dress was riding up and she was losing her balance as she attempted to pull it back down. She lurched towards me and clutched my arm for support. I shook her off and kept walking. Childish, I know, but it made me feel better.

'Jenny! I'm sorry, I'm sorry, I'm sorry. There's no excuse. I should have told you. I'm just a hopeless coward and I know you must hate me, but see it from my point of view.'

'I don't want to.' I was now enjoying my childish standpoint and fully intended to maintain it for the foreseeable future. 'You should have told me before I married him.'

Lisa couldn't stifle a laugh. 'Yeah, you'd have been really grateful to me for that. On your hen night, I could have said, "Oh by the way, Jenny, Mark had a juvenile little fling with Tally when she was the college slapper. I think you should ignore the fact that you've shared your whole adult life with the man you love and you should leave him immediately, punishing him and yourself for all eternity for this one error." Would you really have thanked me?'

'You still should have told me. I would have told you.'

'I doubt it,' Lisa mumbled. 'Where are we going?' She was becoming out of breath. Good.

'I'm going to see the one person I can trust, the one friend who wouldn't hide anything from me.'

'Maria? Oh great, she'll love this. I thought she lived in Clapham? Aren't you going on the tube?'

'No, I'm walking. I need to clear my head. Why don't you rush home to your imbecile husband and argue about having children? I could give you some good lines if you're a bit short. They're guaranteed to kill a marriage in a week.'

'I'm not leaving until you've said you forgive me. I know you're hurt but once you see this in perspective, especially in the light of everything else that is happening now, you'll see that this is not worth destroying a friendship over.'

'Then you've got a long walk.'

How she did it, neither of us will ever know. She talked the whole way there, reminding me incessantly of all the life-changing events we'd gone through together, all of the lists that included me at the top. She developed a pronounced limp which I worked hard to ignore. Finally we reached the massive terraced house in which Maria owned a tiny two-bedroomed flat.

I'd planned some cutting words to use as my dismissal of the treacherous Lisa, but when I turned to deliver them, she was crying.

'I've broken a heel and I've got blisters on both feet and I came out without my handbag and I don't have any money to get a taxi home and there are no black cabs round here anyway so I'd have to get a minicab and be murdered in an alley in Brixton and it's all been for nothing because you're never going to forgive me.'

I forgave her at that instant. So call me weak. 'I've got money. Better than that, I have access to the world's first trustworthy taxi driver.'

We sat on the steps outside the house and I dialled Alfie's number.

'Hello, Alfie, it's Jenny Palmer, I mean, Stafford, I mean . . . Oh anyway it's not me this time, it's a friend of mine. She could do with a knight in shining armour.'

I gave him the address and he promised to be there in ten minutes.

'Come on, let's go and wait inside. This isn't the nicest street to be hanging around on. I'm sure Maria won't mind.'

But when she answered the door in a hastily pulled-on dressing gown, I wished we'd taken our chances with the kerb-crawlers.

*

77

'What's happened? Is it your Auntie Lynn? Harry? Mark?' Then she noticed Lisa's broken shoes, torn tights and bleeding feet. 'You've been mugged! Come in, come in!'

'We haven't been mugged. Lisa just wore the wrong shoes for a long walk.'

Maria exchanged a glance of utter empathy with her erstwhile rival for my friendship. 'I made the same mistake the other day,' she commented, companionably.

She offered an arm to help Lisa up the stairs and I followed behind, feeling irrationally betrayed at Maria's acceptance of my new enemy. Maria rested her hand on the door handle before opening it.

'Are you decent?' she called through, awkwardly.

'No, but I'm dressed!' a cheerful voice called back.

Maria opened the door to reveal that her flat was full of candles that a man was hastily blowing out. He was wearing nothing but boxer shorts and his arms were full of the detritus of the sort of romantic session that only happens in the early weeks of an affair.

'Danny, this is my friend Jenny. You've heard me talk about her. And this is *her* friend, Lisa.'

'The Rottweiler?'

I laughed. Lisa didn't. Maria blinked her eyes in dismay but she was still too infatuated with this man to be cross with him. That'll pass, I thought, cynically.

'It's actually a compliment,' she said hastily to Lisa. 'The Rottweiler is the most loyal dog, I mean, pet.'

Lisa relaxed. 'Don't worry about it, Maria. Being married to Mouth of the Year, I'm in no position to give lectures on tact.'

I leaped to Maria's defence. 'Lisa is just waiting for a taxi. It shouldn't be more than ten minutes.' I filled the minutes with a severely edited version of how I met Alfie, omitting the part about me following Tally and the finger-stroking episode. It wasn't much of a story without those details, if I'm honest.

The bell rang at exactly the right moment and I bustled Lisa downstairs to give Maria and Danny a few minutes to compose themselves.

'I wish I could come with you,' I whispered to Lisa. 'It looks like we interrupted them, well, you know . . .'

Lisa smiled. 'You should have lived in the 1940s. I find it

amazing that you're almost forty and you still can't talk about anything remotely –'

'Yes, quite! Well, anyway.' Lisa was laughing out loud by the time I got her into Alfie's cab.

'Is this anything to do with the finger business and your rotten husband?' Alfie asked after ascertaining that Lisa was not badly injured.

'I'm sure Lisa will fill you in on the journey home. She talks to taxi drivers.'

Lisa touched my hand gently. 'I'm really sorry about all this. And I'm going to make it up to you.'

I shuddered at the prospect of Lisa taking a more proactive role in my life. 'That's not necessary. I'm sorry too. I shouldn't have blamed you, I would probably have done the same in your position.'

'And I would have hated you when I found out. I want you to promise that you'll always tell me if you find anything like this out about Kieran.'

'I promise,' I intoned, solemnly, chuckling inwardly at the idea of Kieran doing anything worse than wearing a red tie with a green shirt.

'Back to the lion's den,' Lisa said, hugging me affectionately. 'I'm going to kill Kieran when I get home.'

'No, don't. I'm relying on you to be the stable one while I fall apart so if you could try and hold on to your marriage for a while longer, I'd be grateful!'

Alfie prepared to pull away. 'You leave her to me. I'll explain what's what!' Lisa closed her eyes in horror. I decided that, after this, I could consider her punishment complete.

When I got back upstairs, both Maria and Danny were fully dressed and bustling about, looking for clean glasses and drinkable wine. I had my first opportunity to take a good look at this, the first man to make an impact on Maria's life. Except he wasn't a man. He was a boy.

'How old are you?' I blurted out, without thinking. I suddenly sympathized with Kieran's blurting and vowed to forgive him the next time we spoke. Maria froze.

'Twenty-six,' he replied unselfconsciously. 'Didn't Maz tell you?'

Maz? He calls her Maz? Even when she was five, I couldn't imagine anyone calling Maria Maz.

I cleared my throat. 'No, she must have missed that part out.'

'To be fair, Jen. We have had other things to talk about, like everything going wrong in your life.' Maria sounded defensive.

I winced. 'Sorry. I was just surprised.'

Danny didn't appear bothered. 'We're used to it. All our colleagues think we're crazy. And my mother cried. But they'll get used to it.' As he walked past Maria, he kissed her nose. The transparent affection made me want to cry. Everything makes me want to cry right now. I'd probably cry if I saw *Terms of Endearment* now, a film that Mark and I always considered a comedy of the first degree.

'You didn't say why you were here,' Maria said. 'You've never turned up here unexpectedly. Not once.'

'Of course I have,' I argued.

'Not once,' Maria repeated. 'We have always met up after a week or two of planning when you have a night when Mark is otherwise occupied.'

Could this be true? Was I such a terrible friend that I expected Maria and Lisa to be available when I was at a loose end but was never willing to sidestep Mark and put them first occasionally?

'Sorry.' Apologizing is becoming as frequent as almost, but not quite, crying.

'Forget it,' Danny said, unexpectedly. 'She's just grumpy because you interrupted her when she was introducing me to the pleasures of Supertramp. I'm not complaining, I thought it was incredibly pretentious.'

But that was the whole point of Supertramp, I wanted to explain.

And they think the age difference doesn't matter. Actually, Danny looked even younger than twenty-six. His blonde hair was longer than (I believe) is acceptable or fashionable and he smiled more broadly than (I believe) is officially cool. I wanted to buy him sweets to thank him for being so kind.

'So?' Maria was still waiting for an explanation of my appearance. I felt uncomfortable going through the whole story in front of Danny, so I edited it right down. Apart from the bit about the finger-stroking which is key to the whole story and is the one fact that stops me looking like a crazed stalker. I had the additional

80

piece of information about Mark's university infidelity to explain why Lisa had followed me there.

To Danny's credit, he listened to the whole story and asked intelligent questions that showed he was paying attention.

'You must have been gutted,' he said.

'Thank you, I was!' At last, someone taking me seriously. 'Do you, by any chance, like origami?'

'Jenny!' Maria was glaring at me.

'I was just asking, that's all. You'd be amazed at how the most unexpected people turn out to be closet folders.'

'How could I be amazed? I was at your origami party.'

'I wish I'd been invited, it sounds great!' Danny was so enthusiastic, I thought he might explode.

I vowed to find myself a younger man if nothing came of my dinner with Ed. And that was the next day.

'Look, I feel awful for just bursting in like this. I'll catch up with Maria another time.'

'I'll be seeing you tomorrow at the restaurant, don't forget.'

'Thank you for reminding me, Maria.'

'I had no idea you women chaperoned each other. Were you hiding behind a pillar the first time I went out with Maria?' Danny asked me.

'No,' I answered. 'Apparently, she's allowed to embark upon relationships without any interference from her friends.'

'That's because Danny wasn't some psycho from an Internet ad.'

'But I could still have been a psycho,' Danny interjected reasonably.

I liked him. He was on my side. But Maria's patience was dwindling and I thought they might be on their way to their first row. It would be my fault as every row in Greater London appears to be at this time.

I jumped up. 'I'm off.'

Danny stood in front of me. 'No you're not. Don't be silly. I want to get to know all Maria's friends. Now I hear you love games.'

Maria wailed in the kitchen. 'Don't encourage her!' she cried.

'There's nothing wrong with games!' Danny called to her. 'I mean, I haven't played any since I was eleven, but I can see the appeal.'

'Then it's a shame I haven't got any otherwise we could all have a lovely game together, the three of us!' Maria's relief was audible.

'But I saw Perudo in your cleaning cupboard. I've heard that's a great game!' Danny would last another week, tops, that was my theory.

I couldn't help myself. 'I bought that for Maria years ago. I even taught her how to play it.'

Maria rushed in to defuse this enthusiasm. 'But I hated it. Just as you hated the low-cut clinging jumper I bought you.'

'I wore it, didn't I?'

'Yes, with a fleece over it that you refused to take off even in that sweltering restaurant.'

While we bickered over unsuitable presents, Danny was rummaging around, searching out the game. He emerged bearing it triumphantly like the flag of an enemy regiment.

'Why don't I leave you two alone?' I suggested before Maria suggested something less diplomatic.

But Danny was determined. 'No, let's just have one game. Come on, you can teach me. It'll be great! And I *did* listen to Supertramp.'

Maria grimaced. 'Fine.'

I could tell that she was already planning her revenge on me.

Chapter Six

I was woken by the smell of bacon frying. And I didn't have a hangover. My quality of life was improving with each passing day.

I walked into the immaculately clean kitchen to find Auntie Lynn cooking breakfast, looking the part of Bed & Breakfast land-lady in an apron that she must have brought with her.

'What time did you get in, dear?' she asked.

Great. I've regressed to the age of fourteen. Was it worth it for a fry-up? I decided that, yes, it was.

'About midnight. I went round to Lisa's then to Maria's. I ended up playing Perudo with Maria and her new boyfriend all evening.'

Auntie Lynn started whisking the eggs, satisfied with my response. I wondered what she would have said or done if I'd announced that I'd spent the evening buying Kalashnikovs from a Russian arms dealer for the terrorist cabal I had just joined. I'd probably have had to settle for Coco Pops.

'Auntie Lynn, how long are you planning to stay? Not because I don't love having you here, but I think you know that you belong with Harry.'

Lynn sniffed. 'When he apologizes and tells me what all this secrecy is about.'

That's what I thought she'd say. I had no alternative. I was going to have to talk to Mark and get them to sort this out. I took the cordless phone into my bedroom and dialled Harry's number.

'Jenny! Is it Lynn? Has something happened to her? Has she had a fall?'

'Harry, Harry! Nothing's wrong with Auntie Lynn. Nothing that can't be put right by you coming to your senses and talking to her. You shouldn't have secrets in a marriage.' I was speaking in the light of my newly acquired knowledge.

'Sometimes they seem easier and less destructive than the truth.'

I could see why Lynn was so angry with him. But I didn't want to alienate him. 'Can I have a quick word with Mark?'

Harry hesitated. 'He's not here right now.'

I looked at my watch. It was 7.45. Mark was not a morning person. That was another reason he didn't like early meetings.

'Where is he?' I asked.

'I'm not absolutely sure. Why don't you try him on his mobile?'

'Thanks Harry.' I cut him off abruptly before I screamed at him for protecting his worthless son.

I called Mark's mobile but it was switched off. I left a curt message asking him to call me when he had a minute. And then I had to do it. I was restrained enough not to call my private cabbie up to drive me round London searching for the philandering pig. But I could do something. I called Tally.

'Hello?' Phil sounded very stressed. There were screams and crashes in the background.

'Hi Phil, it's Jenny. Can I have a quick word with Tally?'

'No you can't. She's gone to a spa for a twenty-four hour detox before my party, I think she calls it. And of course, the au pair has gone down with the flu and the kids were throwing up all night because I gave them prawn curry, which apparently doesn't agree with them.'

'Sorry, Phil. You get back to the kids.'

'Thanks!' Phil put the phone down before I could.

So that's the end of my short-lived belief that maybe Tally was no more than an extinguished old flame. The escalation was unbelievable. Just over a week ago, we were a married couple, now he's taking the wife of a close friend away for the night and stroking her little finger in cafés.

I was having difficulty breathing.

'Breakfast is ready!'

I'd lost my appetite.

I called Lisa to apologize for the night before and to update her on the Tally/Mark affair.

'God, Jen. I'm really sorry. Kieran had me convinced that you were imagining this.'

'Anyway, the reason I'm phoning is to say that I'll do your magazine feature.'

'You're joking?'

'I lost my sense of humour a week ago. So no, I'm not joking.'

'Then what changed your mind?'

'I've finally accepted that my whole marriage was a sham. I'm not going to waste one more day on Mark. I'm going to do anything and everything to get my new life up and running and if that means subjecting myself to some kind of *Blind Date* humiliation, then I'll do it.' I could hear my voice increasing in pitch and volume. I was either genuinely excited about my prospects or on the verge of imploding into a black hole.

Lisa was doubtful. 'You sound a little . . . edgy just now. Maybe you shouldn't be rushing into things.'

'So it's all right for Mark to rush into a new relationship days after he claimed that he was devastated by my leaving him?'

'He could be saying the same about you, if he knew you were going out with a man tonight.' Lisa made this suggestion nervously, not wanting to offend me when she'd just won me back.

'The difference is that . . .' But the difference suddenly seemed spurious to me. I wanted a baby. Mark wanted another woman. Who was I to say that one was more noble, less base and selfish than the other?

Whoops, here come the ever-threatening tears again. I rallied gamely. 'Anyway, I suppose you haven't changed your mind about shadowing me tonight?'

'Absolutely not! Besides, I've already arranged things with Maria. We're meeting for lunch to discuss strategy.'

'Lunch? You and Maria?' What's going wrong with the world? Everything is topsy-turvy, all the friendships are swapping round, our situations are transposing. How am I supposed to keep a hold on myself when all the rules are changing?

'We arranged it after your origami party. We shared a cab and decided it then. She's mellowed, in my opinion. Must be the new toyboy.'

I was curious. 'Do you think a big age difference can be a problem?' Not only had I lost all my reservations about Danny after nine games of Perudo, I was even a little jealous of Maria, not that I would confess that to anyone.

'Personally, no. Not any more. Although I think I'd miss all the points of reference that make communication easy. I can't imagine living with someone who doesn't see tartan and immediately think of the Bay City Rollers.'

I could imagine it and I quite liked the image. Which was more than I could say for the image of my two best friends having lunch without me. I didn't like that at all.

I became increasingly apprehensive during the day as I anticipated my dinner with Ed. I refused to call it a date. Auntie Lynn leaped into action, taking me in hand and preparing me for the evening. I had to remind her that this was the twenty-first century and that going to the hairdresser for a shampoo and set fell into the category of Trying Too Hard. Lynn didn't believe that a nice shampoo and set was ever unsuitable, but I compromised and agreed to wash my hair and even use conditioner.

That's a big compromise for me. I'm not big on preening and pampering. Not because I'm lacking in personal vanity – I've just never got the hang of it. If I ever have made an effort to improve myself, it always alarmed Mark and reduced Lisa and Maria to hysterical laughter.

I observe minimum standards. I shave my legs in the summer when I wear shorts. I'm meticulous about talc and deodorant and I spend a fortune on gadgets that clean my teeth – mainly because I have a phobia about dentists.

I also thought I'd please Lynn and iron my clothes. Normally, I spray them with water and stick them in the tumble dryer. That's good enough for me and Mark. I mean, was.

By 5 o'clock, I was ready – ready for my 'date' and ready to kill Auntie Lynn. When she sprayed lavender water in my shoes, I knew that these living arrangements could not continue indefinitely. Before I could think how we were going to fill the next two hours before I was due to leave (I might have miscalculated the timing of my preparations), the doorbell rang.

'Surprise!'

Maria and Lisa marched into my flat like Trinny and Susannah, ready to dismantle me and reassemble me into a clone of themselves.

86

Maria glared at me. 'And I don't want to talk about last night. Nine games. *Nine.* I don't ever want to do that again.'

I sensed that she wasn't joking.

Lisa clapped her hands like Hattie Jacques in *Carry On Matron.* 'No time for any of that. Right, Jen, we've decided that we couldn't let you do this by yourself.'

'But I wasn't by myself. Auntie Lynn helped me get ready.'

They both closed their eyes in despair. 'So what were you planning to wear?' Lisa asked.

Hello? Couldn't they see that I'd ironed my clothes? That I was wearing my best jeans and top (i.e. the same things I'd worn to the origami party that hadn't deterred Ed and had even, dare I say it, attracted him)?

'You are kidding!' Lisa looked at Maria as if to say, it's worse than we thought.

'The thing is, Jen, from what we can recall, this Ed was very smartly dressed. Now while he wasn't repulsed by your appearance, he was primarily looking at you as a weird, paper-folding character. It was only at the end that he saw your potential and asked you for dinner. So now you have to show him you're not just –'

'A weird, paper-folding character. Yes, I get the picture. But I've only got this and my black dress and I can't wear that. He'll get completely the wrong impression.'

'I agree,' Lisa said.

'Me too.' Maria was nodding.

Now I was very suspicious. And rightly so. They produced two holdalls that they'd been concealing behind them.

'What's in the bags?' I asked, knowing what was in them and, at the same time, praying that I was wrong.

'We've brought a few of our clothes for you to try on. Between us, we must have something that you're prepared to wear.'

I recoiled from this horror. Anything but this. Even the image of Mark stroking little fingers all over London didn't appal me as much as this. But resistance was useless. Especially when Lynn took up a position alongside them.

'Will somebody pour me a drink, please?' I asked resignedly.

'Wow!' They all said wow a lot, possibly shell-shocked at the results of their endeavours.

Maria had brought her most exotic printed skirts, some of which only needed an accompaniment of tropical fruit piled on top of my head to make me start dancing and screaming 'Ay-ay-ay-ee!' The gypsy blouses were hopeless because I am fundamentally clumsy and would have trailed the frilly cuffs in all my food.

Lisa had brought pencil skirts that prevented me from moving my legs and some tops that were clingier on me than on her. I think she might have experienced her first ever pang of envy of me at that realization.

In my role as peace negotiator I had settled on one garment from each, pacifying them both (slightly) and resigning myself to looking ridiculous.

I looked in the mirror with curiosity. I mean, it was recognizably me: same hair, same face, but wearing one of Maria's swirly skirts that gave me a waist that I didn't know I possessed, and one of Lisa's tailored blouses that emphasized the chest I knew I possessed but had spent my adult life trying to camouflage. I looked different.

We could only find one pair of Maria's shoes that I could actually stand up in. They were brown and gold and six inches high. OK, that's not true. But they were definitely over an inch high which made me feel insecure and a bit giddy.

Maybe the giddiness was a symptom of Post Traumatic Stress Disorder. I definitely felt that I had been trawled through a battlefield. Although no blood was shed, it was painful being caught in the crossfire between Lisa and Maria, each determined to stamp her own personal style on my blank canvas.

I was very miserable in this get-up and yet it seemed right that I should look so different. If I'd gone out in my Jennyandmark clothes, I would never have been able to forget my ties to the past. I was curiously liberated and was even on the verge of thanking Maria and Lisa.

But they hadn't finished with me. Lisa had a list and Maria had contributed to it. Like a superbug, Lisa was spreading her madness and I could only hope that I was strong enough to resist it.

They took turns. 'OK. First. You need to make sure he's not married. Don't assume he'll tell you.'

'Second, ask him loads of questions. Men like that and you'll find out lots about him. Maria and I can then interpret the data and let you know if he's hiding something.'

This went on. I don't know for how long because the skirt was cutting into my waist, the shoes were pinching and I was fixated on the pain.

'Are you listening, Jen? Because this is important.'

I jumped when Maria prodded me. 'Of course I am.'

She was holding my mobile phone. 'OK, now I know you're not very good on technical things –' that's because Mark always took care of technical things. '– so I've put your phone on Silent/Vibrate. Your skirt has a pocket where you can keep the phone. Lisa and I will be two tables away, near enough to hear what you're saying. We actually went to the restaurant today and persuaded the manager to show us where you'll be seated. Then we asked the people at the table to talk quietly to see if we could hear them. And it was a complete success.'

'Just remind me which one of us is having the breakdown,' I muttered.

Lisa ignored my interruption. 'We won't be able to talk to you, so we'll just text you. That way, you can discreetly look at the message without Ed being any the wiser.'

Lynn felt obliged to add her piece of advice. 'Now you're not to worry about a thing. If he so much as touches you, just give him a good kick.'

I felt like practising on the three witches before me. They were saved by the doorbell. Alfie was half an hour early. Hah! And he claimed to be Mr Reliable.

Lisa, Maria and Lynn all kissed me and then stroked me as if I were a chimney sweep who might bring them unearned luck. I took a deep breath and opened the door ready to leave.

It was Mark.

'Mark! What's happened? Is it Harry?'

Lynn rushed to the door. 'What's the matter with Harry? Is it his heart?'

'Harry's fine. Erm, can I come in?'

'Oh, of course.'

It was gratifying to see how intimidated he was to find Maria and Lisa glaring at him. Maria had never liked him but he probably couldn't work out what he'd done to offend Lisa. I wondered if Kieran would enlighten him.

'You look different,' he said, noticing my new appearance for the first time.

'So do you. Going somewhere special?' I couldn't help myself.

'It's Phil's fortieth.'

Of course it was. 'I'd forgotten. What are you taking him?'

'Don't you remember we had a set of Pathé newsreels from 1965 made up for him?'

'You mean, *I* had them made up. I was planning on giving them to him myself on Friday.' I was furious with him.

'Sorry, but I didn't have time to sort anything else out.'

But you had time to cavort with Tally. In the time you spent with her, you could probably have knitted him a golf club cover or written him a short novel in Latin blank verse.

I didn't say any of this. Not in front of the others. 'So what do you want?' I asked coldly.

He winced. 'You left a message on my mobile for me to call you, so I thought I'd just pop in. I didn't have a problem when you dropped into the office. I even thought . . .'

Yes, I thought so too. But that was when I thought you'd bought new clothes because the old ones evoked too many painful memories. Now I know they were to wear for your shimmying tramp. I buried my accusations for now. We'd never fought in public before, or much in private either, and I wasn't going to start now.

'This isn't a great time, as you can see.' I couldn't talk about Lynn and Harry when Lynn was hovering over us. Also Maria and Lisa had both sat down on the sofa, ready to enjoy any show we might be about to put on.

Mark shuffled uncomfortably from foot to foot. 'I need to speak to you privately as well.'

We waited for the others to retreat diplomatically. We could have waited until Christmas. 'Why don't we go onto the patio?' I said finally.

I tried not to look at the shrubs we'd planted together or the miniature apple trees we'd bought together.

I decided to say my piece first. My new clothes must have made me unexpectedly assertive. 'I called you because I'm worried about Lynn and your father.'

'So am I. My dad's in a terrible state. He doesn't need this so soon after his last heart attack.'

'But this is all your fault! You told your dad not to let Lynn know what was going on between you. You've caused this gulf and you can un-cause it.'

'We're both just trying to protect her.'

From seeing you for what you really are. 'Well, don't bother because it's not working.'

He didn't respond. 'I'll think about it,' he finally conceded.

That was the best I was going to get tonight. 'So what did you want to talk to me about?'

'This is very difficult for me and I don't want to make things any more strained between us.' He couldn't even look me in the eye.

'You want a quickie divorce so you can marry again?'

'What? Don't be so ridiculous. You're the one pushing for a divorce, not me.'

My mistake. 'Then what is it?'

'I wondered if we could go to the bank as soon as possible and sort out the division of all the money in our various joint accounts. It's just I've got a lot of expenses, finding somewhere to live, that sort of thing.'

I was stunned. 'You want half my money?'

Mark was still avoiding eye contact. 'It's our money, if you think about it.'

'When you made a hundred thousand pounds from the sale of your flat, that was *your* money, that went into *your* business. So everything that I've earned plus the insignificant amounts you've put in since we got married, all of that is *our* money? I can't believe what I'm hearing.'

Mark was now squirming. Good. 'I don't expect half, but I thought we were always a partnership, even before we got married.'

'Then, in that case, where is my share of the profits from the business?'

Mark turned away from me. 'When there are any, you'll get some, I promise.'

I looked at him carefully. He was acting completely out of character, even by the lowered standards I'd come to expect from him in the past few days. Neither of us had ever been overly interested in money. We shared cheap tastes in our lifestyle and not once had we argued about our finances. Now all of a sudden he'd become

91

Michael Douglas in *Wall Street*, mercenary and grasping (but without the bouffant hairstyle, of course).

Even worse, he was being unreasonable. And Mark was a man who was usually so reasonable that other people wanted to punch him.

Once more, I was struck by the strong suspicion that he was hiding something serious from me. 'Mark, what has happened to the company?'

'If you're going to interrogate me, then just forget it!'

He walked straight out, almost knocking over Lynn, Maria and Lisa, who were standing by the patio door eavesdropping.

'Well, I don't know what all that was about,' I commented.

Lisa had become completely pale. 'Something is going on with the business and I'm going to make Kieran tell me when he gets back from this wretched party. Then I'll tell you, Jen.'

In a way, I hoped she wouldn't tell me. I just knew it was going to make everything even worse.

Since I couldn't walk in the shoes, I was glad I'd arranged for Alfie to drive me to the restaurant. He didn't do anything until he'd taken instructions from his new protegée, Lisa. 'Take her straight to the restaurant. Don't let her make you pull over so that she can change into jeans. Wait until she's in the restaurant and you see us before you pull away.'

'I thought I'd hang around and take her home afterwards. On Wednesdays I'd normally stay at home and listen to a concert on the radio. I might just as well do that in my cab.'

Lisa had told me that Alfie had been widowed for ten years. I'd felt bad that I hadn't taken the trouble to find that out about him myself. I'm obviously as selfish as everyone thinks I am.

'That would be so kind, Alfie,' Lisa accepted on my behalf. I didn't bother arguing. Maybe I'd lost the ability since having my jeans forcibly removed, like a superhero without his magic pants.

He double-parked outside the restaurant, causing a tailback along Battersea Bridge Road, but now that I was best friends with a taxi driver I regarded this as a marvellous initiative rather than an intense irritation.

San Ferdiano had been my choice, mainly because it was one of the few places Mark and I had never been to. No memories. When I saw the tables, I knew why we'd avoided them. We'd had a theory that the quality of food was inversely proportional to the size of the pepper mills. The round-shouldered waiters here were staggering under the weight of the menacing towers and could well have grounds to sue for the damage caused by being forced to carry them without the benefit of cantilevering or a neck brace.

'You look smashing, love,' Alfie told me continually. 'The young man will be knocked out when he sees you.'

But I was the one knocked out when Ed stood up to greet me, dressed in well-worn jeans and a very casual shirt. I blushed furiously.

We sat down and he held up a hand to stop me from speaking. 'Don't tell me, you've dressed up because you thought I was a smartly dressed man who despises over-casual clothes?'

'And you've dressed down so that I won't feel out of place like the poor relation just come up to t'Big Smoke from t'country?'

'Sorry to disillusion you, but I actually came to your origami party straight from a meeting with a client and was wearing clothes that I'd bought purely for the occasion. I'm strictly a jeans man.'

'Whereas I actually always dress like the girl from *The Dukes of Hazzard* – without the chest. I had to borrow these clothes from my friends to look the way a normal woman is supposed to look.'

I stood up abruptly when I felt my phone start vibrating against my leg. Ed stood up too in alarm. 'Is something wrong?' he asked.

'No, nothing. It's just my phone. I'm not used to it.'

Out of the corner of my eye. I spotted Maria and Lisa gesticulating wildly at me. I stared at my phone. The message was simple: SHUT UP. ASK HIM ABOUT HIMSELF. THIS IS A DATE NOT A THERAPY SESSION.

Thank you. In retrospect, I knew I should have mentioned to my friends that I'd never texted before. Unsure of how to delete the message, I pressed buttons randomly until the screen cleared. That worked.

'Problem?' Ed asked, fascinated and amused by my fiddling about under the table.

'None at all. I know this is probably a rude question, Ed, but are you married?'

Maria's audible groan saved the need to text me. Ed laughed. 'No I'm not. But I am divorced. I'm forty-two and I've got some new hairs growing in my ears. Are there any other personal questions you want to get out of the way while you're on a roll?'

'Sorry. I've been told what to say. I'm not very good at this. Maybe if I had a drink or two, we could start all over again.'

Ed ordered some wine and I drank the first glass quickly. This reminded me that I'd already had a couple of glasses at home while I was getting ready. I made a mental note to slow down. I'm not good when I'm drunk. I talk too much, say the wrong things. Then again, after my performance so far, how much worse could I be?

The answer: much, much worse.

'Watch this!' I'd made my ever-popular barking dog from a menu that I'd torn into a square and was pulling its tail to make its head bob. I made a loud barking noise to add to the full effect. Ed seemed to find this entertaining. The diners at the adjoining tables were glaring at me.

My phone vibrated. This time I was a little clumsier in reading the message without drawing attention to myself. I dropped the phone and felt inexplicably dizzy when I sat back up.

STOP ORIGAMI NOW. STOP TALKING NOW. STOP DRINKING NOW.

I pressed the same buttons that had worked before to delete the message. I don't think Ed noticed anything.

'I suppose I should ask you if you're married,' Ed asked while I composed myself, 'since you're wearing a wedding ring.'

Oh. I'd forgotten about that. I could sense Maria and Lisa fighting over their phone, jabbing the keys desperately before I could step into this minefield. It wasn't necessary. I was in command of myself. 'I'm separated,' I said, calmly.

I already had my hand on the phone, ready for the inevitable message.

DON'T MENTION BABIES. CHANGE THE SUBJECT NOW.

I got rid of it efficiently.

'How long were you married?' Ed continued.

'Only ten months,' I replied.

Ed raised his eyebrows. 'A whirlwind romance?'

'We'd been together over twenty-one years since we were at school, so I'm not sure it could be called a whirlwind, more like a dull unceasing breeze.'

94

Ed became subdued. 'Twenty-one years. That's a whole life-time. How do you get over something like that?'

I began creating alpine landscapes on the tablecloth with sea salt. I was nervous and needed to do something to occupy my hands. In the absence of an instructional text from Lisa and Maria, I thought this would seem less off-putting to my date than moulding an effigy of Mark from the candle and poking it in the eye with a lighted match. 'It's easy, when you learn something about the man every day that makes you realize you didn't know him at all and that your entire relationship was a sham.'

My voice had become louder and shriller, not an attractive quality outside a woman's football match.

Ed looked alarmed at my outburst. 'Are you OK?'

'Perfectly OK. I just haven't had anything to eat all day.'

Ed called a waiter over and I quickly ordered food. 'I'd like the tortellini to start, then the lamb cutlets with fried potatoes, zucchini and those peas with the onions and a side salad. And some garlic bread, please. And some breadsticks.'

'Are you expecting company or are you ordering for us both,' Ed asked in amusement.

'I'm a big eater,' I explained simply. I hadn't expected this to be anything that needed explanation. The world of dating was more complicated than I'd anticipated. 'So tell me about the job,' I suggested, to buy me time to demolish a basket of ciabatta and a litre of water.

Unfortunately it only took him a few minutes because he'd gone over most of the details over the phone the day before. I had to start concentrating again.

'You're very talented,' he said. 'I'm surprised I hadn't come across you before. I know most of the creatives working in London.'

'I've only dabbled up until now; this is the first time I've consciously marketed myself. Mark, my soon-to-be-ex-husband, felt it was a rather silly thing for an adult to do, so I didn't take it seriously.'

Ed picked up my paper dog, which had lost the power to nod since I'd spilled some wine over it. 'How many job offers have you had since your party?'

I thought about this. 'Five, so far. Mark would say they just felt sorry for me.'

'But the work you had on display was incredible! It sold itself.'

'Mark thought they had about as much value as balloon models.'

The phone again.

STOP TALKING ABOUT MARK. MEN DON'T LIKE HEARING ABOUT EXES.

After pressing buttons deftly for the last time, I switched the phone off.

'Are you finally giving up on them?' Ed asked.

I looked up to see that he was having difficulty stifling laughter. 'Did you know what I was doing?'

'It was fairly obvious,' he said. 'Also, I recognized the harpies from your party. They interrogated me before allocating me my dot. I was surprised they didn't shine a bright light in my eyes and speak in a funny German accent. So what was their plan?'

I glanced sideways. My friends were studying their menus with an intensity worthy of a surgeon approaching a life-saving operation.

'They have no faith in my ability to get through a meal with a stranger without either scaring him off, enrolling in a cult or getting myself lured away to a ritual death. So they are giving me instructions and I'm supposed to do as I'm told.'

'Would these be the same friends who dressed you up like a Barbie doll?'

I nodded. 'I'm thinking of swapping them for a nice hobby, like calligraphy or line dancing.'

Lisa and Maria scowled at me, Ed waved back cheerfully. I liked this man. He was on my side. I had enough confidence to slow my drinking right down and enjoy the rest of the evening. I could even ignore the appalling food, although that might have been due to the drink as well as my huge appetite that has always led me to value quantity over quality.

'I know I'll be seeing you tomorrow but it will be pretty hectic, and we won't get much of a chance to talk. Perhaps we could do something at the weekend?' Ed asked, tentatively.

'I'd like that.'

'What do you like doing?'

That was easy. 'I love Chessington World of Adventures.'

Lisa and Maria were holding their heads in their hands. What had I done wrong now? Who wouldn't like a day at Chessington

World of Adventures? A second later, my brain caught up with my mouth and told me exactly why I shouldn't have suggested Chessington World of Adventures. *Because you're not fourteen years old*, it yelled.

Ed seemed to be waiting for something but I couldn't think of anything more grown-up. Finally he held his hands up in stoic acceptance. 'I was thinking more along the lines of a film or play, but I suppose Chessington would be . . . fine.' After making arrangements to meet at the commercial shoot the next day, we left the restaurant at 11.30. Alfie drove me home, after making it clear to Ed that he could make his own transport arrangements. We parted with one of those kisses where we both proffered our cheek and turned our lips at the last minute. It was awkward and a bit thrilling at the same time. I was Meg Ryan for an instant.

'Shall we wait for your two friends?' Alfie asked as I sank back into the cab, smiling secretly.

'They can walk,' I replied. 'They love walking.'

When I got home, Lynn had gone to bed and I could enjoy some glorious peace and solitude. I went online to check my emails. There were dozens, both professional and personal and I lost track of the time reading them, although I found myself uninterested in the personals after my successful evening with Ed. I was restless and ended up entering the bizarre world of late-night TV, game shows that made no sense, films too awful even to have been released on video, repeats of *Prisoner Cell Block H*.

I must have dozed off because when the doorbell rang, I jumped up and looked at my watch. It was 2 am.

I ran to the door, not wanting the intruder to ring again and wake Lynn up. She'd insist on making tea all night and asking me about my pension plan. At this late hour, it had to be Mark and it had to be bad news.

Well, I was 50 per cent right. It was bad news, but it was Lisa bringing it.

Chapter Seven

Lisa's presence alone in the middle of the night was bad news without her needing to open her mouth. But once she was through the door, I couldn't shut her up.

'Oh, Jen. I'm so sorry to land on you so late, but I didn't know where else to go. I could have gone to Tally and Phil's but, well, you know . . .' I knew. 'I had the most terrible row with Kieran and stormed out of the house. And I can't go back because I said I refused to stay in the house with him and –'

'Lisa, calm down! It's 2 o'clock in the morning. I'm exhausted and you're worrying me. Just tell me what happened. Really, really quickly,' I added, wanting to go to bed really, really soon.

Lisa took a deep breath. 'You know that Mark put all that money into the business last year?' I knew. 'They lost it all.'

I shook my head. 'They can't have. They bought all that equipment. From Clive Whatsisname.'

'Wrong. They *ordered* all that equipment, from Clive, Clive Rushforth. I don't know if you remember him that well from Bristol. He was one of their football buddies who ended up living in France. The problem is, the guy took all the money knowing he was about to go bust and couldn't deliver the goods. He's now run off with their cash.'

'But surely they didn't pay all the money upfront? Nobody does that, not even if it's for a so-called friend.'

Lisa shrugged. 'Our dear husbands trusted him because the crook said it would help his cashflow. And because he was a so-called friend.'

'I bet he did.'

'The only reason Kieran told me was that he got drunk at Phil's party, so when I laid into him, he crumbled straightaway.'

I would have felt sorry for Kieran but I was too tired and muddled. It was a lot to take in. I was furious with Mark for being so stupid, but also for not trusting me enough to tell me the truth. But more than this – much, much more – was the terrible possibility that our whole split might have been caused by this. Maybe the only reason he was so adamant he didn't want kids was because of this financial disaster. After all, it had given Kieran second thoughts and he and Lisa had been struggling under some unspecified pressure.

I could barely breathe for the growing realization that my appalling timing had forced him into a corner. But at the same time, I felt the stirrings of an upturn, a hint of hope that this might all be resolved.

I would speak to him the next day, make him talk to me, let him know I understood and would support him. With all the well-paid work I was getting, I'd even be able to put some more money into the business to help them get started again. Then when he started to feel more positive about the future, we could talk about children once more.

In twenty-four hours, we could be back together again. Everything would be perfect once more. The same.

'I can't possibly wear any of those.' Lisa was flapping around the bedroom fingering my best clothes disparagingly. 'I have an editorial meeting in forty-five minutes and my team have certain expectations.'

I refrained from pointing out that I knew exactly what their expectations would be: that Lisa would make unreasonable demands of them, then, when they miraculously met them, she would take the credit for herself. One day, I fully intended to sit down and explain to her that her management techniques could do with some drastic revision if she were to have any friends left at work before she hit forty. Maybe when I knew her better, in another twenty years, say.

'Lisa, you have three choices, you go to work in your dirty clothes, you go home and change and face Kieran or you borrow something from me.'

She couldn't squeeze into my one dress, a fact that gave me a momentary pleasure. After a lot of sighing and bustling, she found a pair of brown cords which had been in the cupboard for so long that they had developed a central crease. 'This is as close to tailoring as I can expect to get here,' she grumbled. 'Where are all the clothes I've bought you in the past?'

'The charity shop,' I replied, sheepishly. 'Sorry.'

Lisa was too tired to lecture me on the insanity of giving away silk and cashmere when Milletts could close at any time, leaving me bereft of my last supplier of fashionwear. 'This will have to do,' she said, settling on a cream brushed cotton blouse that looked like suede if you scrunched up your eyes and stood ten yards away. She'd boil in it today when a mid-September heatwave of 30 degrees was forecast but, after a cursory flick through my faded, stretched T-shirts, she abandoned all hope of comfort.

'You'll have to talk to Kieran later anyway, unless you're planning to come back here later.' I hoped that my tone accurately conveyed the less-than-open-armed welcome I was offering her. Three women in a smallish flat was two too many. Lisa had spent twenty-five minutes in the (only) bathroom doing who-knows-what. I mean it must surely only take four strokes of a comb to restore that ruthless bob to order. And the make-up? It takes me twenty-five seconds to do my face: ten seconds to spread some tinted moisturiser, five seconds to dab some powder on and stop me getting shiny (not sure why this is supposed to be a problem, but it's a way of making Lisa happy without having to wear a tight blouse) and a further ten seconds to smear on some pinky vaseline-type gunk that Maria bought me as a compromise when I refused to wear lipstick.

Twenty-five seconds and I'm a 38-year-old woman who has a new man willing to take me to Chessington World of Adventures at the weekend. In twenty-five minutes, Lisa had turned herself into RoboEditor. You'd need crampons and an ice-pick to scale that face and crack through the rock-hard covering. I don't think Ed would want to take her to a theme park, currently my sole criterion for judging the success of a beauty regime.

Remarkably, when Lisa put on my clothes, she looked glamorous and I wondered if I had more style than anyone (including myself) thought.

'You'll have to borrow a pair of my shoes,' I said. 'Those

stilettoes make the cords look too short and even I know that's not an acceptable look outside an Ibiza nightclub.'

Resigned to a day of fashion suicide, she ran her eyes over an impressive selection (in my opinion) of high-quality practical footwear, before sighing dramatically and gingerly placing her feet (wearing my best *Lord of the Rings* socks – the only ones that were clean) into a pair of dark-brown moccasins with attractive little tassles.

'You look great!' I said, admiring the final picture. 'Hey, do you know that this is the first time you've ever had to dress in my style, whereas I've had to put on all sorts of monstrosities to shut you up over the years.'

Lisa scowled at me. 'Now I have grasped the hard consequences of walking out on my husband, I fully intend to become the model wife. I can handle the separation, the grief, but your clothes? Never again. And I will take my revenge. Don't forget you're coming to the office on Friday to have the photos done for the feature. Wait till you see what my team have in mind to do with you.'

I shuddered at the prospect. Still, it might all be unnecessary. If I patched things up with Mark today, I could legitimately pull out of the dating exercise.

The buses were packed at that time of the morning, but I was too tired to walk all the way to Hammersmith. I'd dressed carefully (by my standards), choosing clothes loaded with memories. I'd gone for the embroidered khaki combats and green vest that I'd bought for our walking honeymoon in the Lake District. This was an important meeting and I wasn't taking any chances.

The bus stop was right outside Lynn and Harry's home, an imposing five-storey building with ivy and climbing roses covering the lower wall.

I prepared myself, not wanting a single wrong word to slip out. I had told Lisa that I wasn't going to mention Tally, that if I had any hope of pulling my marriage back together, there had to be no recriminations. I rang the doorbell and tried to slow my heart rate down. I experienced a terrible panic that Mark wouldn't be here, that he'd found an excuse to spend another night with Tally, but I reminded myself that Phil's party the previous night would surely have prevented the treacherous couple from disappearing for any length of time.

I'd expected Harry to answer the door, groomed and dressed as he and Lynn always were before 7 o'clock each day. But instead the door sprang open and I was faced with Mark, bleary-eyed and clutching one of his dad's cardigans over a pair of boxer shorts. New boxer shorts, I noted. I smiled nervously, aware that Mark was never at his happiest when he was woken up prematurely from a deep sleep.

I watched his expression change slowly from irritable to venomous. Maybe he had a hangover, I told myself, be patient. He'll be fine once he's had a cup of tea and I've told him the good news. He didn't invite me in, a lapse that I put down to his weakened state and I gently pushed the door and walked past him, still careful not to touch him.

He slammed the door behind me. A very, very bad hangover apparently. This was not going well. I went straight into the kitchen and put the kettle on, sliding efficiently back into wife-mode.

'Where's your dad?' I asked, cheerily, ignoring the increasingly hostile set of his face.

'The garden centre,' he replied abruptly. 'What are you doing here?'

Boil, kettle, damn you, boil! If Mark didn't have tea quickly, it was going to take a tranquilliser dart to mellow his mood. 'I thought we were supposed to be staying best friends, as you reminded me yesterday when you dropped in on me.'

'That was yesterday and, incidentally, you weren't very welcoming. A lot has happened since then.'

He was obviously thinking of Phil's party. Surely nothing else could have happened in one evening. The kettle boiled and I busied myself making tea, praying that each second would dissolve Mark's resentment but, for some strange reason, he seemed to be bubbling with rage. Then I remembered why he'd come round the day before. He was probably still mad at me for hedging over the division of our finances. At least I now understood why money was such a sensitive issue.

I couldn't wait any longer for the tea to have its soothing effect. I rushed forward and grabbed both of his hands. 'Listen, Mark. It's OK. I know everything! Kieran told Lisa and Lisa told me so I understand why you got so anxious about having kids, although I wish you'd trusted me enough to tell me about the money but, anyway, we can get through this. You won't believe how much I can make from my origami and we'll put all of it into your business and then, in a year or two, we'll think about the baby thing again and –' He interrupted before I'd even taken a breath.

'What were you doing last night?'

'Sorry?' I didn't understand what he was talking about.

'What were you doing last night?'

It didn't sound any less confrontational the second time around. 'I went out with . . . one of my new business contacts. We were . . . discussing a job he's hired me for today, creating some origami for a TV ad. It's paying nine hundred pounds for three hours work and I'll get more every time the commercial is aired.'

'Over dinner?'

'Pardon?'

'It's just that I have my business meetings over lunch or coffee or simply in an office. I don't take women out to dinner for business. Not ever.' His voice was unfamiliar and accusing.

I was beginning to feel sick. Somehow he'd found out where I'd been, probably from Kieran, who knew about the dinner. I needed to drag this conversation back before even more damage was done. 'I presume you know exactly where I was last night, so you must also know it was completely innocent.'

'I don't know anything of the sort. What I do know is that you were trying to impress this man, in fact you were so keen to impress him that you employed your two friends to coach you. Learning chatting-up techniques by text over a business dinner? I don't remember any of that when I was doing my MBA. Funny.' He wasn't laughing and neither was I.

I poured the tea out automatically. I didn't know what else to do. 'It wasn't like that. They talked me into it and it was really more a joke than anything else.' Then something occurred to me. 'How did you know about the texts?' Lisa had told me that she'd kept this from Kieran, not wanting him to accuse her of being overly manipulative. I managed to keep a straight face when she told me this.

'You sent me the texts,' Mark said coldly.

'I sent you the texts?' I repeated stupidly.

'All of the texts you received from your buddies ended up on my phone. One of the highlights of the evening was guessing what you'd been saying to inspire such dramatic responses. Tally was

104

reading them over my shoulder. Out loud. So it might please you to know that my humiliation was total. And of course we were all fascinated to know how you did it when you have always been such a determined Luddite with your phone in the past.'

I knew exactly how I'd done it. I could even show him the combination of keys that one needs to press to achieve this end. Since I'd never even sent a text before, let alone forwarded one, I was almost proud that I'd stumbled upon a function that Mark had never discovered himself. I opened my mouth without thinking. Maybe it was frustration at my own stupidity that made me abandon all my good intentions.

'So I went out to dinner with a man. That's all I did. Unlike you.'

'What's that supposed to mean?' Mark had gone from a rolling simmer to a volcanic eruption. 'I was out to dinner with *our* friends.'

'You weren't the day before. Or last week. I saw you alone with Tally. Twice.'

I wanted to take the words back, rewind the film. But Mark had sped ahead to the next frame, the big battle scene. 'So? She was trying to track down Clive Rushforth, see if she could get any of our money back. She was close to him at university. We had to meet privately. Phil didn't know she had a thing with Clive when they were together.'

'Well, this is becoming a familiar tale, isn't it? Because I didn't know that *you* had a thing with Tally when *we* were supposed to be together.'

This worked far more efficiently than the tea at deflating his anger. I'd have to ask Lisa if there were any other hideous secrets that I could hold as weapons in reserve for such occasions.

'It was nothing, absolutely nothing. It was just a first-term thing when we were all drinking too much and getting used to the novelty of living away from home.'

'It's not nothing to me,' I whispered, suddenly experiencing the pain of betrayal as if it had happened an hour ago. 'I didn't go out and drink too much in Exeter. I studied like a maniac all week so that I would be free to enjoy the weekends with you and I thought you'd be doing the same.'

Now Mark was holding my hands. 'But it was twenty years ago! I can barely even remember it.'

105

'You remembered it last week when you were stroking Tally's finger in that café.'

Mark let go of my hands. 'Were you following me?' He was looking at me as if I had morphed into an enemy alien from the planet Zarg.

'No. Not exactly. A . . . friend of mine just happened to see you, that's all.'

Mark took a step back and leaned against the kitchen units. 'Shall I tell you something amusing? That morning in the café, Tally did make it clear that she was available for me, but I turned her down. Maybe I did stroke her finger. I didn't do it consciously, I was just letting her down gently. I told her I would feel that I was being unfaithful to you after such a short time of being apart. But now that I know how easy it's been for you to move on, I'm wondering if I should take her up on her offer. Maybe I should even thank you for helping me to come to this decision.'

This was too much. We hadn't even talked about the money situation and now I couldn't. We'd each landed some killer punches and I felt too winded to think clearly. I pushed past him, not caring about the physical contact this time, and walked towards the door.

'Out of interest,' Mark called from the kitchen, 'who told you about Tally and me at Bristol?'

'Kieran accidentally let it slip,' I replied without thinking.

Mark laughed unpleasantly. Before slamming the door, he delivered his winning ace. 'Did he? I bet he didn't "accidentally let it slip" that he'd done exactly the same when he was going out with Lisa.'

That went well, I thought glumly at the bus stop.

An hour ago, I thought I was going to be reconciled with Mark and that we would now be planning our new future. Instead, I had somehow managed to talk him into an affair that he'd previously resisted and shot the final bullet into our lingering marriage. Oh yes, and now I knew something about Kieran that threatened Lisa's marriage too.

As I said, that went well.

The bus journey seemed interminable and, by the time I got home, I had to rush around the house to grab everything I needed to take

106

to the film shoot. Auntie Lynn followed me like an annoying toddler, asking me difficult questions when I wanted her to go and watch *Teletubbies* and eat Farley's Rusks like a good child.

'How did it go? What did he say about the money? Have you sorted everything out? Is he moving back in? What did Harry say?'

'Auntie Lynn!' She recoiled and I spoke more gently. 'Sorry, I didn't mean to shout. I'm in a bit of a hurry. No, we didn't sort everything out. In fact, everything's ten times worse. But that's for me to worry about. The important thing is that there's nothing for Harry to hide from you any more. It was obviously all this business about the lost money that was the big secret. So you can go home now.'

Lynn looked doubtful. 'You make it sound easy.'

'Auntie Lynn! Just go back to him. Please. Talk to him.' Then I remembered what had happened when I talked to Mark. 'On the other hand, don't talk to him. Just go back, say you love him and forgive him. Please.'

I kissed her and left in a hurry. At least there was one person whose life would be sorted out today. Two, if you included Harry.

Alfie was waiting for me outside. I didn't like calling on him so often but I was short of time and I didn't want to be late for the first paid job of my new professional life.

'After you've dropped me off, could you come back and pick up my Auntie Lynn and help move her back to Hammersmith?' I asked him.

'Of course I can. Now what's the story with her husband or is she the only woman in your circle who has a normal marriage?'

I realized that everyone in my circle had normal marriages until mine broke down. So much for nothing changing.

The shoot was a success. Ed had seemed particularly pleased to see me although I was grateful he didn't kiss me. I was still fragile from my face-off with Mark.

'You look fantastic,' Ed said warmly.

I looked at my clothes. I'd forgotten that I'd dressed up for Mark and blushed that Ed might think I'd made this effort for him. 'It's nothing,' I replied feebly.

There was no time to elaborate. The work had to be completed in three hours to keep on budget and I ended up folding my models over twenty times before the director was satisfied with the results.

By the time we were finished, I was starving. I'd rushed over to Mark's without breakfast and it was almost 3 o'clock when my stomach reminded me that I hadn't eaten.

'Do you fancy a late lunch?' Ed asked.

I hesitated, reassessing my status following the appalling scene in Hammersmith. It was official. I was single. 'I'd love a late lunch,' I answered firmly.

Ed looked pleased. 'I know I'll be sorry I asked, but where would you like to go? McDonald's? The popcorn booth at London Zoo? The ice-cream van outside the playground down the road?'

I knew he was teasing me and I liked it. It was familiar and comfortable, the way Mark teases me, used to tease me. Before. 'TGI Friday's,' I suggested, choosing somewhere that served alcohol, that was open all day and didn't sound too unsophisticated to my hopelessly unsophisticated ears.

It didn't help when I was offered a balloon at the entrance. And accepted it without thinking. I shoved it behind my seat and ordered the most expensive cocktail on the board, ignoring the kids' menu to try and correct the (accurate) impression that I had the tastes of a twelve-year-old.

I finished the drink in three nervous swallows. The impact was fast on an empty stomach and I ordered a lot of pasta to absorb the alcohol. And a side order of chips. I also asked Ed if I could try one of his Fajitas.

'You eat a lot, don't you?' Ed asked, amused by the speed at which I demolished both plates before starting on his.

I sat back, happy now that I was full. 'Is that a good thing or a bad thing?'

Ed didn't need to think about this. 'It's a good thing, definitely a good thing.'

I'm not sure at what stage he took my hand but, when he did, I didn't pull it away. And after we left (without the balloon, I'm impressed to say), we automatically held hands. So that's that then, I supposed. We must be, I don't know, boyfriend and girl-friend. Except that sounds so teenage. There must be a grown-up phrase. I'll ask Lisa, she's probably written an article about the terminology; it sounds a fatuous enough subject for her magazine.

I walked him back to his office where he was going to go over the footage we'd just shot. He kissed me affectionately, more meaningfully than the evening before, but not passionately. I think. I mean, I'm no expert. Mark and I went out for weeks before we even kissed properly but then we were sixteen and hopelessly shy.

How does it all work from now on, I wondered. I mean, what's the exact timing of such things? I wish I'd paid more attention to Maria when she recounted all her disastrous dating sagas from kiss to kiss-off. Will Ed be turning up at my flat tonight with a Barry White CD and some flavoured condoms? Should I be wearing my best pants, just in case? I decided to make sure I was out this evening to avoid having to face all this.

But I couldn't put off the next stage indefinitely. I was going to be seeing Ed on Saturday when we went to Chessington and I needed to be prepared.

Perhaps he'd be expecting a gradual build-up of seduction as we went from one white-knuckle ride to the next. We'd start off pressing thighs on The Vampire, then be flung closer together on the Runaway Train, arms tightly around each other on Rattlesnake, then throwing up together after a stomach-churning spin on Rameses Revenge. After all that enforced intimacy, surely the day could only end one way.

But I wasn't sure I was ready for that.

'Tell me again why we have to do this,' Maria sighed as she showed me out.

'I just think Saturday night is going to be awkward and it will be easier if you're there. Please.'

Maria was still angry with me over the Perudo session Danny and I had inflicted on her the last time I'd visited. And she wasn't very pleased at me popping in uninvited for a second time. Once more I'd clearly interrupted them in the middle of a romantic evening on the carpet without a board game in sight.

'Great to see you again, Jenny!' Danny had said enthusiastically. He was beginning to become fixed in my imagination as an untrained puppy. I resisted the urge to pat him on the head and tickle him under the chin. Maria barely resisted the urge to smack him.

'Is this another emergency that couldn't be shared over the phone?' she asked me sarcastically.

'But you and Lisa both accused me of never just dropping in so I thought I'd do it more often. Anyway I won't stop. I just wanted to invite you both over on Saturday night for dinner with me . . . and Ed.'

'Red dot or blue?' Danny asked.

'Blue,' I replied, wishing my friends were more discreet.

'Great! We'd love to come, wouldn't we, Maz?'

I scrutinized Maria's face, to see if she had reached the point when she threw things at him for calling her Maz. No. Not yet, but I was sure the hour was close.

'I thought we were going to the cinema,' she objected.

'We can go in the afternoon,' Danny suggested.

'I suppose so,' Maria conceded, but the absence of the offer of a drink or even a welcoming smile communicated perfectly that she might well withdraw her agreement if I didn't leave promptly.

'Right then, thanks. I'll be off now. See you Saturday, Danny.'

'Don't rush off,' he said. 'Why don't you stay and eat with us? We could have a repeat of our Perudo tournament.'

I didn't need to see Maria's face behind me to know what her reaction to this was. 'I've got to get back, Danny. Another job tomorrow I need to prepare for.'

'So what's the job?' Maria asked as she walked me out.

'It's not exactly a job. I'm supposed to be doing this photographic shoot for Lisa's big dating feature.'

Maria nodded. 'She told me about that. It's a fantastic opportunity, speaking as someone who has tried and failed at every other method of meeting a man, even though it's about as lacking in dignity as a grown woman could imagine.'

'Since I've never had any dignity, I'm not going to miss it,' I commented. 'But I've decided not to do it anyway, because things with Ed are looking so promising. It seems as if I've managed to find someone all by myself. Maybe I could write about that for Lisa's magazine instead of having myself put up for auction in branches of WH Smith all across the UK.'

'Lisa won't be happy.'

'That's not all she has to be unhappy about.' I explained what Mark had told me about Kieran. 'So do you think I should tell her?'

Maria didn't hesitate. 'It's a tricky one, but do you remember how badly you took it when you found out that she'd kept the secret from you? And then how bad she felt for you? She made you promise that you would tell her if you found out anything like that about her husband.'

I pressed further, not wanting to make such a huge decision on my own. 'But would *you* want to know?'

Maria considered this. 'Definitely. Absolutely. I'd tell you and you must promise that you would do the same.'

It was an easy promise.

'What's happened now?' Lisa was about as pleased as Maria had been to see me on the doorstep.

'Now you know why I never did this before,' I grumbled, when she reluctantly invited me in. 'You and Maria haven't exactly been killing the fatted calf when I've turned up. I haven't even been offered a ham sandwich.'

Lisa apologized. 'It's just a bad time. Kieran's still angry about me going with you to Phil's alternative party tomorrow night.'

'God, I'd completely forgotten about that! I can't go now. Mark's admitted that Tally has been throwing herself at him for the past week even though I believe him when he says he hasn't taken her up on the offer. Yet.'

I told her about Mark's veiled threat, leaving out his parting shot about Kieran. I still hadn't worked out how I was going to break this news to Lisa.

'You have to come! If you don't, then Kieran and I will have gone through all this for nothing. And what will we tell Phil if you don't come? It's not fair on him, is it?'

Kieran walked in, looking mortified to see me. 'Oh, er, hello, Jen. Listen. I'm really sorry about . . . you know, my indiscretion. Mark mentioned that you had something of a set-to.'

What a fabulous understatement for the violent death of a marriage. I wondered if Mark had also mentioned his own indiscretion about Kieran and Tally. That would explain why Kieran was so alarmed to see me.

'Well, that's in the past now,' I announced cheerily, inanely, unconvincingly.

Kieran nodded understandingly. 'Oh, of course. I suppose you're here to talk about Lisa's big idea to sell you like an unwanted lawnmower. That'll shift a few hundred thousand copies, won't it? Will you be posing topless, showing exactly what you have to offer? Or just staring desperately into the camera with a speech bubble emerging from your mouth asking for potential suitors to supply details of sperm count and genetic desirability?'

'Kieran!' Lisa shouted at him. 'Just because you're angry with me, there's no need to take it out on Jenny!'

He was silent for a few seconds. 'Sorry. Really I am. But none of this is easy for any of us.'

'I think I'd already figured that out,' I observed dryly.

Kieran smiled weakly and left, avoiding eye contact with Lisa. That wasn't looking good. 'OK,' I said, finally. 'I'll come tomorrow, but it will be the last time. I don't know if Tally and Mark will start something or not but I don't want to see it or even know about it.'

'Sure,' Lisa agreed, eager to accept any conditions that would get her through the next difficult evening. 'So I'll see you tomorrow for the shoot?' She was not very subtly moving me towards the door in a gesture that I was learning to expect from my friends.

'That's really why I came round,' I began. 'You see, now that I've been out with Ed a couple of times, and it's going so well –'

Lisa clutched my arm firmly. 'I know what you're going to say.' She always did, that's the downside of close friendships. I would never have had this problem if I'd been a mad cat woman, confiding all my deepest secrets and desires in feral creatures that only loved me for my tuna. 'You think you don't need any help, that you've met Mark's replacement and that everything will be perfect from now on.'

That was exactly what I was thinking. 'I wasn't thinking that at all,' I said feebly.

Lisa wisely ignored me. 'But the magazine won't appear for three months. By then, this thing with Ed could well have fizzled out. I don't want to sound cruel but you are vulnerable at the moment, on the rebound. The chances of this turning into something serious, only days after leaving a twenty-year-plus relationship, are negligible. I should know, I write about this for a living.'

I wanted to cry or hit her. Instead I nodded pathetically. 'You're probably right.'

'And if, by some astonishing miracle, you and Ed are still

together when the issue is published, then ...' She waved her hands about vaguely.

'Then what? What will we do?'

Lisa smiled brightly, insanely, dismissively before saying goodbye. 'Something. We'll do something.'

That's OK then.

The door had closed before I remembered that I hadn't told her about Kieran and Tally. Tomorrow. I'd tell her tomorrow. After I'd spoken to Kieran.

He had dirty marks on the ... his trousers. I sat with a kilt

Chapter Eight

'Why are we meeting here?'

Kieran sat on the swing next to me. We automatically began competing to see who'd go the highest.

'Because there's no chance of anyone seeing us.'

He looked around him. 'Granted, none of our acquaintances are likely to be passing a playground in the middle of a council estate in Wimbledon. By the way, well done for sending the text.'

'Thanks.' I brushed the compliment away modestly. With the help of the instructions, it had only taken me three hours to send the two-line message. Nobody else had received the text and I hadn't alerted the emergency services to a nuclear incident. In my opinion, this was an achievement.

Kieran jumped off the swing, showing off like a ten year old. He had dirty marks on the back of his trousers. Lisa would kill him. 'So what's the problem?'

I told him. 'And now I'm in a really difficult position after all the fuss I made about Lisa keeping the same information from me.'

He became very subdued, sinking onto a chicken that began to wobble randomly on its coiled base. 'You can't tell her! It wouldn't be fair on either of us.'

I gasped at his hypocrisy. 'But you're the one who told me about Mark and Tally.'

'That was because I thought you knew. You and Mark were always so close, I just assumed he'd told you years ago.'

I wandered towards the rusty roundabout and perched on the splintered seat. 'Well, the damage is done now. And I have to decide what will cause the least damage to Lisa since she's the victim in all this.'

Kieran sat alongside me, moving us slowly around with his feet. 'We're trying for a baby. If you tell her it will destroy her and you know how fragile she is.'

He was right. Purely because of that I reluctantly promised him that I would keep his secret. But as we left, I had the sense that, while my friendship with Lisa was diminished by this decision, my relationship with Kieran had just entered a new phase.

I don't know what I expected. Maybe a girl with a big make-up brush and a man with a big comb. Definitely lots of camera trickery which would make me look like someone different while actually leaving me the same. I'd seen all those celebrity magazines where they catch film stars unawares and you realize that they don't look anything like their publicity photos.

I certainly didn't expect scissors and tweezers and racks of clothes and computers and machines with nozzles. Everything looked permanent and undoable.

'Right, Jen. The photographer will be here in one hour, by which time we need your hair and make-up almost finished.' She stood in the middle of the throng and began to shout. 'Everybody! Do you all have your lists?' Pieces of white paper were waved by unsmiling assistants. 'Then why are you just sitting about wasting time?'

I found myself yanked by invisible hands into a chair where countless faces appeared staring at my head from different angles. My hair was pulled up and scrunched tightly to the scalp.

'No!' I exclaimed. 'I will not have my hair cut short. Not under any circumstances.' I have had long hair all my life. There's no deep emotional significance to this – I just happen to think it suits me and it's my only vanity. Besides, Mark always loved it. I gulped at this recollection. I wondered when, if ever, I would be able to think five consecutive thoughts without Mark intruding like essential punctuation.

Lisa crouched down in front of me. 'Jenny, here's the deal. We won't do anything you really hate, like turn you into me.' I grimaced at her perception. She smiled at my discomfort. 'But let the experts do their stuff. Your hair will grow back and you can wipe all the make-up off. OK everybody, I want this done properly, you all have your schedules, so let's stick to them!' And with that, she went off to have coffee.

The hostility that greeted this announcement intimidated me into acceptance. It all happened fast and without the aid of mirrors. That was Lisa's idea too, so I wouldn't be able to object. But I could see big chunks of hair on the floor and bright colours on brushes and sponges approaching my face like instruments of torture.

I was no happier with the clothes. Lisa had culled the racks of anything resembling my existing wardrobe: no jeans, no T-shirts, nothing made in brushed cotton or overstretched lycra. But, like Samson, I had lost all my strength when my hair was cut and I was unable to protest when they squeezed me into skirts and dresses and trousers in totally unfamiliar fabrics.

I left the final decision to the stylists and they settled on a purple bias-cut silk dress that floated just above my knees with a white short-sleeved cashmere cardigan. My stubborn self was spurred back into existence when the shoes came out. Nothing could induce me to wear heels and, in desperation, they had to lend me a pair of flat jewelled Indian sandals that belonged to the girl who ironed my thighs. They were so beautiful that I gave her £20 for them.

Finally the photographer arrived. Like an invalid I was guided to a white screen where I allowed myself to be posed in various catalogue poses with assorted cheesy grins and moody expressions.

Four hours after my arrival, I was shown the first polaroid. I thought they'd accidentally shown me the picture of someone else. But when I stared carefully, I could see that it was me. And that it wasn't me. I wished I'd studied German literature because there was probably some long German philosophical term with lots of Zs in it that literally meant 'simultaneously me and not me'. This was way beyond Lisa and Maria's amateur attempts to dress me for my first dinner with Ed two nights earlier. I was transformed.

I would never admit this to anyone but I looked . . . good. My hair was now slightly above shoulder length which made me feel naked but liberated. Layers had been slashed in with a razor blade that made the hair flicky and natural. I tossed my head back and forth dramatically like a model trying to make it as an actress with no talent.

Somehow, the make-up artist had given me cheekbones and

117

enlarged my eyes. Despite my fears, I didn't look like a Soho stripper with my bright red lipstick. I just looked grown-up. Now all I had to do was start thinking and acting like a grown-up and the transformation would be complete.

Yeah, right.

'Jenny, you look fantastic!' Phil kissed me affectionately. Tally smiled tightly, or was that just my imagination?

She was dressed more sedately than she had done for Mark recently, I observed cattily. Her hair was clipped back in a loose ponytail and her treacherous, shimmying hips were camouflaged by some satin palazzo pants. I'd never heard of palazzo pants until I tried some on this morning and learned that they were not pants at all, but baggy trousers. Tally looked like Audrey Hepburn in hers; I'd looked like Omar Sharif in mine.

As a surprise, Lisa had announced that I could keep all the clothes I'd worn in my photograph. I cursed myself for handing over the £20 for the slippers. She and I had arrived together in Alfie's cab and even Alfie had been impressed when he saw me. 'You look gorgeous, love. Your young man will be bowled over!'

'My young man won't be here tonight,' I explained patiently, not having yet asked Lisa what women call their young men outside of 1950s sitcoms. 'This is the repeat performance of the fortieth birthday dinner that I couldn't go to on Wednesday because my ex-husband went and we're no longer allowed to attend things together. My young man doesn't know these people.'

'I'm here to support her,' Lisa added.

Alfie nodded wisely in the driving seat. 'I really want to understand, but I'm still having trouble remembering the difference between the red and the blue dots. The rest makes no sense at all, I'm afraid.'

'To me, neither,' I commented, mournfully.

Tally was at the front door when we arrived, putting some bottles in the recycling bag.

Alfie leaned forward to peer at her. 'Isn't that the woman with the finger?'

'See! You are getting the hang of this,' Lisa said, admiringly.

Alfie shook his head. 'I think you should all just stay at home with your husbands. The human brain wasn't made to cope with all this complication.'

I was beginning to agree with him.

Phil was genuinely pleased to see me and hugged me affectionately. I wanted to cry again but restrained myself. I'd managed to keep my make-up intact all day and knew that I would never be able to reproduce it if tears smudged it.

Phil appeared different to me now that I knew how often he'd been deceived. My whole opinion of him was softened by my pity. Everything was appearing different to me but this was worse because I was indirectly responsible for the damage about to be inflicted on his future.

I'd never felt that I knew him very well. He was the most successful of our group, as a senior corporate lawyer for a massive City firm. But he had little time for anything else apart from the occasional game of golf with existing or prospective clients. I always found it a strain knowing what to say to him. He didn't like bad films and felt that origami belonged in the playroom with his beautifully dressed, privately educated children.

I suppose he just seemed so much older than the rest of us. While Mark and Kieran were still boring us with their endless repetitions of the *Monty Python* Dead Parrot sketch that they'd been enjoying since they were eighteen, Phil recounted golfing anecdotes and recommended cheeky little Sauvignons.

And the strains of his gruelling working life had led to him ageing physically as well. His hair was thin and greying and his face was prematurely drawn. He was even displaying the early bulge of a paunch.

'Thanks for the great present,' he said warmly. 'Mark told me that it was you who chose the Pathé newsreels.'

'That was good of him,' I admitted. No wonder he'd been so furious about the texts on Wednesday night when he'd just made a generous gesture on my behalf.

Phil linked his arm through mine. 'Come and have some champagne.'

Lisa and I followed him into the dining room where the table was lavishly set for four.

'Is it just the four of us?' Lisa asked anxiously, echoing my own worries. I didn't know who else we'd been expecting but the reality of this intimate dinner was grim.

'It was just the four of us on Wednesday too.' Tally was not sounding very friendly as she carried the warm plates through.

119

Shimmy, shimmy. 'It's hardly our fault that it all appears a bit flat.'

Reading between the lines was the direct accusation that this was my fault. Well, if she wanted to get on to the subject of accusation . . .

The conversation dried up by the time we'd finished our smoked salmon. My fingers were twitching. Unless somebody spoke soon, I'd have no choice but to fold the napkins into the white cliffs of Dover.

Tally broke the silence. 'Mark tells us that you're getting a lot of work.'

'When did he tell you that?' I couldn't resist asking.

Tally reddened. 'He told us all over dinner on Wednesday. He sounded quite proud of you. Of course that was before all the texts started arriving.'

Phil leaped to my rescue. 'I'm sure Jen doesn't want to go into that.'

I smiled coolly. 'That's OK, I'm happy to have everything out in the open.'

Tally stared at me. 'Don't you think that some things are best left unsaid?'

Then I knew that Mark had told her of my accusations. That meant they had met or spoken since yesterday. That meant that she now knew that I knew that . . . oh, Alfie was never going to be able to follow this. Not unless he had a lot to drink first.

'Could you go and check on the kids?' Tally asked Phil abruptly. 'I think I heard something.'

Phil raised his eyebrows but complied, kissing his wife affectionately as he walked past. He had never stopped being grateful to Tally for marrying him and his loyalty now struck me as unbearably poignant.

Once we heard him reach the second floor, Tally turned on me. 'Just because you're willing to throw your own marriage away, it doesn't give you the right to destroy mine!'

'You're doing that all by yourself,' I hissed back. 'I don't believe you. I thought you were supposed to be my friend.'

'You can't complain,' Tally whispered, glancing nervously towards the stairs. 'Not only do you not want Mark any more, but you've found someone else, so what he does should be of no interest to you.'

I folded my arms defensively. 'I'm not talking about now. I'm

120

talking about twenty years ago when you slept with my boyfriend.'

Tally closed her eyes wearily. 'I didn't even know you then. And I didn't know he had a girlfriend. Blame Mark, if you must, but not me. And I don't see the point in telling Phil about it. It happened before I even knew him but it might spoil his friendship with Mark if he found out. I don't think he deserves that.'

Lisa touched my arm gently. 'Jen, let's not go all over this again. This is Phil's night and he hasn't done anything to hurt you. Afterwards, you don't have to see Tally again, if you'd rather not.'

Tally looked relieved at this prospect. But all I could see was an eighteen-year-old Tally seducing my eighteen-year-old Mark and everybody knowing about it, laughing about it, lying about it. The problem was that this was dead news to them but fresh and raw to me. And I wanted to lash out.

I turned on Lisa because she seemed to be defending Tally against me. 'It's OK for you, you've had years to enjoy the nasty little secret that you've all been keeping from me. I'm still getting used to it.'

Lisa became impatient. 'Don't you remember what it was like to be eighteen, Jen? We were kids, really, so of course we did stupid things. If we can't forgive mistakes from twenty years ago, what chance do we have with all the mistakes we're going to make in the next twenty?'

I was completely thrown off balance by her being so rational. That was my role in our friendship; her role was to make me feel smug about my calm, ordered existence. Those were the rules and I hated the way all the rules were being eroded on a daily basis. 'You wouldn't be so calm and understanding if you were in my position,' I snapped.

Lisa smiled at me patronizingly. 'Frankly, Jen, with all the real problems Kieran and I have at the moment, I don't think I could afford to get too excited about things that happened twenty years ago.'

I was furious with her. 'Then you won't be "too excited" when I tell you that it wasn't just Mark who had a fling with Tally in Bristol. Kieran did as well, while you were going out with him. I only found out yesterday so at least you don't have to worry about me knowing about it and lying to you for years.'

As soon as I'd spoken, I regretted it.

121

The first thing I noticed was that Lisa's hands were shaking. The second thing was Tally's white-faced stare. The third was the object of Tally's stare, Phil standing in the doorway, holding a bottle of champagne that chose this precise moment to pop its cork.

'Lisa, wait, wait for me!'

She'd grabbed her coat and rushed out of the house leaving Phil slumped in an armchair and Tally crouching by his side frantically trying to console him. Alfie jumped out of the cab to open the door but Lisa ran across the road and began jogging clumsily towards the river.

'What's going on?' he asked me, as I dashed past.

'I've got to catch up with her!' I cried. 'No time to explain.' I hadn't anticipated any difficulty in catching up with Lisa, except she had kicked off her high-heeled shoes and I was tripping over my own feet in my ludicrous Indian mules. I finally followed her example and removed the sandals. Eventually, I caught up with her.

'Can you slow down, Lisa? It's a long walk to Stockwell.'

She stopped and turned to me. I couldn't help but notice how her hair and make-up hadn't budged. Apart from the streak of wildness that had inflamed her eyes, her face was a perfect mask. 'Why did you have to do that to me?' she asked. Then she started marching. This time, I kept up.

'But you told me to! After last week, you insisted that you'd want me to tell you rather than keep a secret.'

Lisa threw her arms up. 'Obviously I didn't mean it! I only said it because I didn't believe it would ever happen. You should have known that I wouldn't want to know even though I said I did. Look how miserable it made you!'

Once Mark and I had accidentally gone to see *The Battleship Potemkin* at the Student Union. Through a series of miscommunications, we'd thought we were actually seeing *Battlestar Galactica*. The film was being shown without subtitles and we were in the middle of a row of intense Russian Studies undergraduates before we realized our mistake. By then it was too late to escape.

That experience was very similar to this. Even though Lisa was at least speaking English, her words made as little sense as if they were Russian. But the gist was that I should have ignored her when she told me to be honest with her. Maybe if I'd read her magazine more carefully, I would have appreciated the subtle distinction.

While I was absorbing these indigestible truths, she was walking ahead. I ran to catch up.

'Lisa, I can't pretend I understand, but I'm really sorry. Would it help if I said all those things that you said to me last week about it being a long time ago, not meaning anything and so on?'

Lisa considered this. 'Did it help?'

I considered this. 'Not in the slightest.'

She allowed herself a half-smile. 'Then please don't.'

I linked my arm through hers but she gently removed it. I felt sick at this rejection of my friendship.

'Are you ever going to forgive me?' I asked, trying to sound jokey.

'Course,' she replied shortly. The smile followed a fraction of a second too late to be convincing.

We walked on in an uncomfortable silence. I wondered how sore her feet were. Mine were killing me and I was used to walking these sorts of distance, but not barefoot. Unfortunately I was the guilty one this time so I had to endure the suffering and wait for her to release us from this ordeal.

Now London is not a quiet city at any time, even on a chilly late evening like this. But we both began to be bothered by the rising volume of car horns around us.

'What's that noise?' she asked.

We looked around to discover a long, slow-moving line of traffic hooting Alfie, who was following us at 5 mph, unbothered by the commotion behind him.

'What are you doing?' I shouted above the noise.

'I'm not leaving you alone in this state,' he answered smoothly. 'If you don't kill each other, the muggers will do it for you.' He fixed his attention back on the wheel, not interested in our pleas for him to go home.

Lisa and I increased our pace to avoid a major road rage incident. She appeared to have been distracted by the unfolding drama behind us and I took a chance on speaking to her again. 'What are you going to say to Kieran?' I asked, apprehensively.

I could be mistaken, but I think I detected a crack in her make-up. 'It's more a question of when rather than what,' she said sadly. 'The thing is, Jenny, do I confront him with this before or after I tell him I'm pregnant?'

Oh no, not again. Auntie Lynn was sitting on the doorstep with her bags. Except there were more of them this time.

Alfie had pulled up outside my flat after we'd dropped Lisa off. It had taken ages to persuade her to get into the cab and I'd been forced to resort to a cheap underhand trick. I'd jumped out in front of the taxi and rather enjoyed watching all the other cars screech to a halt around the Wandsworth one-way system.

Frankly I don't know why taxi drivers are given such a bad press – having one of my own has been the single shining light in my recent pit of darkness.

'Alfie, Lisa is pregnant and I can tell she is tired. Will you make her see sense and get her in the cab so we can take her home?'

Alfie jumped straight out without bothering to pull over. Lisa was so overwhelmed by the wave of hostility that emerged from all the other drivers that she quickly climbed into the cab without any argument. As I said, our cabbies are wonderful.

When she got out at her house, I rushed ahead and stood right in front of her.

'Can we go out next week, just you and me?' I asked. 'I promise not to turn up unexpectedly.'

'Sure,' she replied. 'I'll call you.'

'When?' I asked desperately. 'When will you call me?'

'Soon,' she promised before leaving and I spent the cab ride home wondering if she meant it.

'Auntie Lynn! What are you doing here?'

'I left my spare key here when I left.'

Alfie automatically picked up two of her cases and carried them downstairs. I picked up the last bags and followed him.

'I don't mean, what are you doing outside, I mean here, at all. I thought you and Harry had sorted everything out.'

Lynn's voice was shaking. 'We have now. Everything is well and truly sorted out. I can never trust him again. That's sorted that out.'

'I'll be off, love,' Alfie whispered. 'I took the liberty of putting the kettle on. You look after your aunt, now.'

'But I haven't paid you for tonight.' I fumbled around in my bag.

Alfie dismissed the offer. 'Leave it till next time.' He patted my head affectionately before leaving.

Before I could face Lynn, I had to call Kieran and warn him. His mobile was switched off so I texted him. I had to hope he'd understand when I explained how it had slipped out. The message was brief: SORRY. I BROKE YOUR PROMISE. LISA KNOWS ABOUT TALLY. TALK SOON. Jxx

'So what's happened now?' I asked Lynn. I resented her being here when all I wanted to do was go to bed and think about the lives falling apart around me and my day at Chessington with Ed tomorrow.

'What's happened is that I went back to Harry and told him that I knew everything so we didn't need to have any more secrets. He was relieved of course. But after a few hours, I suspected that we were talking about different things. Then when he started talking about remortgages, I knew that this was yet another secret and, probably, one that you were ignorant of as well.'

In my new life, it seemed that every time a kettle was boiling, I was to be given bad news. I intended to switch to Diet Coke from the very next day.

'So tell me,' I said resignedly.

'Harry's remortgaged our house without telling me. *Our* house. He's lending Mark seventy-five thousand pounds to get the company out of debt and see them through the next six months.'

'Seventy-five thousand pounds?' I repeated dumbly.

Lynn nodded. 'Mark's had to buy some more equipment to meet the contracts they already have and pay the next six months rent on the warehouse.'

'Seventy-five thousand pounds?' I repeated again, still stunned by the amount.

Lynn was making tea, having watched me ignore the boiling kettle. Maybe the curse of the kettle will now pass to her. 'It's not the money, it's the deceit.'

'Oh Auntie Lynn, all this is my fault!'

'How do you make that out?' she asked.

'If I hadn't insisted on Mark getting married, he wouldn't have sold his flat and he wouldn't have had all that money to play with in the first place. Then if I hadn't been so determined to have a baby, he might have told me about his problems and we might have been able to get through this without involving you and Harry.'

Lynn shook her head. 'You watch too many films, Jenny. Actions and consequences aren't as straightforward as that, everyone else plays their own part. Besides, you and Mark couldn't have gone on the way you were indefinitely.'

'We'd managed for twenty years,' I pointed out gloomily.

Lynn patted my arm. 'You just concentrate on your own problems, love. Don't worry about me and Harry, or about the money. Besides, Mark seems confident that he'll eventually get the money back from Clive.'

'Really,' I said, sceptically.

Lynn handed me a cup in which I'd spotted her surreptitiously stirring a couple of sugars. It seems I'm now in shock. 'In fact,' she went on, 'he told Harry that a mutual friend is working on it and he's going over to France with this friend at the weekend to see what they can find out. He seemed quite upbeat about it.'

I'll bet he's upbeat, I murmured to the mirror the next morning as I struggled to chisel off the remainder of yesterday's make-up. I'd been shocked by my own appearance. I resembled a corpse who'd risen from the grave with ominous coloured flecks peeling from my face. I'd never worn enough make-up to justify removing it at night and was grateful to have this mistake pointed out to me before I embarked on my very first affair.

As I scrubbed the debris from my skin, I tried to imagine I was ridding myself of the last vestiges of Mark. Why should I care where he was going this weekend and with whom? I was off to Chessington World of Adventures with a new man. In my best underwear.

I'd forgotten my haircut and, after my shower, I didn't know what I was supposed to do with the style. After five seconds of contemplation, I accepted that I had neither the equipment nor the ability to do anything with my hair apart from blast it into a Don King Afro. So I just let it dry and sent up a quick prayer that I hadn't done my long nose and high forehead a disservice.

Wearing the green trousers and top that Ed had seemed to like in the week, I grabbed my bag and walked into the living room, where Lynn was cleaning again.

'Auntie Lynn, what are you doing? The flat is still spotless from your last visit.'

Lynn tutted. 'But you said you're having guests for dinner tonight. So I thought I'd just put the duster around.'

I sat down in despair. 'I'd completely forgotten about dinner. I haven't even done any shopping, I'll have to order a takeway.'

Lynn put her duster down. 'Don't give it a moment's thought. I'm pleased to be able to help. I'll pop out this morning then have it all ready for you when you get home. And don't worry, I'll get out of your way. You won't want an old fogey like me hanging around.'

Not only had I forgotten about my dinner party, but now I had to think about Auntie Lynn. 'Don't be silly,' I protested unconvincingly. 'I can't have you doing all the cooking then send you out to walk the streets.' Unless I really had to.

'I'll go and visit friends. Don't you worry about a thing!'

'What about Harry?' I suggested hopefully. 'With Mark away, you could talk without any interruption. Surely it's worth another try?'

The doorbell rang. Ed had arrived on time. I looked to Lynn for her answer. She was concentrating on rubbing an invisible stain from the coffee table. 'Oh love, it's all gone too far for talking to help. I thought I'd made that clear last night. I've made up my mind. I'm going to ask him for a divorce.'

'You hair looks amazing.' Ed stroked it admiringly.

'You're supposed to say how grown-up it looks.'

Ed tilted his head to one side. 'Well, put it this way, you did look about eighteen. You've now aged to, oh, about twenty-four.'

This pleased me. 'Since I feel as if I went straight from sixteen to thirty-eight, I'm quite happy to revisit my twenties.'

'Can I say something that will probably be taken as an insult?' Ed asked cautiously.

'Please do. It will make me feel better if I do the same thing to you later.'

'I hadn't noticed the tiny lines around your eyes and mouth before. I mean, you really did look eighteen. But the new hairstyle has opened up your face –'

'And now highlights my wrinkles perfectly. How lovely! I am in possession of the first ever hairstyle that accentuates crow's feet.'

'I've insulted you.' Ed looked miserable.

I stroked his hand. 'No you haven't.' But I wasn't sure I meant it. I've always assumed I looked young because people tell me so. Maybe that's why I've resolutely refused to change my style of dressing throughout my adult life. Just putting on high-heeled shoes would be screaming to the world that I have finally grown up. My delusion allowed me to perpetuate the myth that I have my whole life still before me, the big goals still to reach, the important decisions still to take. I had chosen to believe that time stood still for me when I met Mark and decided that he was the one. Now that I acknowledged this to be a mistake, I didn't like the idea that this was a mistake that had robbed me of all my young years. Lines, even tiny attractive ones, were permanent stains on a canvas that I'd always imagined still to be blank, loaded with potential.

Ed turned my face to his. 'You do know that you're beautiful, don't you?'

Actually I didn't. So I changed the subject instead and told him about my Auntie Lynn's news.

'Would you rather not go to Chessington?' he asked, when he saw how upset I was.

'Don't be silly!' I said. 'If I cancelled something every time I received bad news, I'd have to get used to spending most of my days skulking in a dark room.'

'But we could go somewhere more low key. I really don't mind.'

I shook my head. 'I've been looking forward to this for two days. Those big rides are the one thing guaranteed to take my mind off all this.'

It took an hour to get there and I watched with interest as Ed drove into a private car park right next to the entrance.

'Do you know someone?' I asked.

'Our company did some filming here a while back.' We got out of the car and walked over to a side gate marked PRIVATE.

'Are you sure this is OK?' For me, the normal experience involved a thirty-minute queue then an argument with a belligerent sales clerk who didn't know how to work the credit card machine. Ed took my hand and led me to the gate where a uniformed attendant admitted us without hesitation.

'How does he know you?' I asked.

'All right, I'll come clean. I came here yesterday to introduce myself and organize tickets. They think I'm planning a major film session here and they're giving us VIP tickets that allow us to jump the queues and go behind the scenes.'

'That's fantastic,' I exclaimed. 'You know what that means? We can go on *all* of the big rides. Normally you just have to pick a few favourites because of the queues.'

Ed seemed less enthusiastic. 'We'll see how the day goes, shall we?'

I assumed he was just a Chessington novice and vowed to convert him, especially now we could pack so much in.

I started him off gently on the Vampire. As I'd expected, he held my hand tightly. I must confess he was cutting off the circulation in my fingers by the end and I was glad to get off. I took him straight from there to the Runaway Train. On that, Ed didn't make any attempt to hold my hand, he seemed to prefer holding onto the safety rail. Very firmly. I suppose it's a shock to the system the first time, but personally I can't remember. Mark and I had been coming here since we were teenagers. It was more a glorified zoo in those days as far as I could recall.

'Why don't we go and see the animals?' Ed asked shakily. 'I've heard there's a monorail that takes you around.'

I laughed. 'That's a kiddies ride! There aren't even any queues for it, which means it's not worth going on.'

'Still, it might be nice,' he persisted. 'And I'd like to get a feel for the whole place.'

I shrugged. 'OK. Come on then.' He was right. It was nice. We held hands and he didn't dig his nails into my palms. I quite enjoyed the absence of pain.

'Perhaps we could go to the zoo, next time?' he suggested.

I smiled at him. 'I also like the theatre, the cinema, hillwalking and just drinking wine and talking. You don't need to hire a children's entertainer for me. Don't forget I've got the haircut of a twenty-four year old now.'

Ed kissed my hand. Then he kissed me as if I really were twenty-four, or even thirty-eight. I decided that we would stick to the sedate kiddies' rides if they had this effect on him. So we sauntered round on carousels and roundabouts and water rides, becoming closer in each section of the park.

But Rameses Revenge beckoned to me straight after lunch.

Ed was very reluctant. 'I don't think we should go on a big ride so soon after eating.'

'That's the best time to go,' I told him from experience.

This was where Ed learned the disadvantage to his VIP passes. If we had been there on normal tickets, we would have joined the end of a ninety-minute line, Ed would have seen close-up exactly what happened on the ride, seen people staggering off and known, without any doubt, that he should not go on this. But instead, we walked straight to the front while the ride was stationary, before he even had the chance to see what he was being buckled into.

Then it began. And so did Ed. 'What's happening? Where are we going? Oh no, we're turning upside down! Everything will fall out of my pocket! Oh God, no . . . I'm going to be sick. I want to get off. Stop the machine . . .'

The centrifugal force seemed to shut him up at this juncture, either that or he was hyperventilating or, quite possibly, dying. When we got off, he leaned on me for support. 'That was horrible. Horrible. I'm never going on anything like that, ever again. I need a drink.'

I managed to dissuade him from having a drink until his stomach had completely settled down and he'd stopped shaking. I bought him a bottle of water and we sat watching a stunt show on seats that didn't move. It took over half an hour for the colour to return to his face.

'Why didn't you tell me you hated these sorts of places?' I asked him amusedly.

'You were really keen to come so I didn't want to let you down.'

Now it was my turn to stroke his hair. 'In future, I'd prefer you to be honest.'

'OK, then, I'll be honest. Right now I'd like you to come back to my flat and make love all afternoon.'

So we did.

Chapter Nine

When I looked at Ed's bedside clock, it was displaying 17.50. It took my brain a while to work out that this was ten to six, and a while longer to remind me that Maria and Danny would be arriving at my flat for dinner in just over an hour, and that Auntie Lynn would be there now cooking.

I shook Ed ferociously. 'Wake up! Wake up!'

He sat upright, his eyes flashing maniacally. 'What's happened? Are you hurt? Is there something wrong?'

I leaped out of bed and started pulling on my clothes that were distributed around the flat like a cartoon parody of a seduction scene. I was relieved I'd worn my best undies and was grateful for all the films I'd watched that had given me this specific hint.

'You have to get up quickly. My friends are coming over to have dinner and play Trivial Pursuit.'

Ed rubbed his eyes. 'Why did you invite them over when you knew we'd be spending the day together? Didn't it occur to you that we might end up spending the evening together as well? And possibly the night?'

'Of course it did!' I was struggling to get dressed in a hurry without losing my mystique. 'That's why I invited them. I was nervous and thought that, if they were there, it might help defuse the tension. I was really worried. Don't forget I haven't been out with anyone since I was a schoolgirl. I don't know the rules, or anything.'

Ed was watching me with amusement. Obviously my mystique was gone already. At least that meant I didn't have to worry about my pants being inside out. 'You didn't seem to me to be worried earlier.'

I dropped my left sandal in embarrassment. 'Please get dressed!' A terrible thought occurred to me. 'Unless you're not coming with me.'

He grabbed my wrist and pulled me back onto the bed. Seemed like my mystique was back after all. 'Of course I am. Although I still don't know why you're going ahead with this dinner party. I don't understand anything you do and I haven't since you made that ridiculous dog in the restaurant. But I . . . like you a lot and will go along with your crazy schemes if they make you happy.'

I let him kiss me but nothing else. The thought of Auntie Lynn slaving over a chicken brick killed my newly awakened libido very quickly. 'If you want to make me happy, then please, *get dressed.*'

He was totally unselfconscious as he climbed out of bed and began rummaging around in his wardrobe for a clean shirt. 'Do you want to borrow something?' he asked me. 'I think your own clothes look a little the worse for wear.'

I looked at myself in the mirror. It would be obvious to anyone that these clothes had been pulled off, trampled on and generally mistreated in ways not associated with theme parks. I blushed furiously. Ed threw over a pair of jeans and a clean T-shirt.

Now if this were a film, they'd fit me perfectly and it would be a sign. But just because I'd been able to wear Mark's clothes didn't mean that I would share the same size as any other man. I mean, what were the chances of that?

The jeans fitted perfectly and I felt like Cinderella. Will I never grow up?

'You've got changed,' Auntie Lynn said as soon as we walked through the door.

'I, er, spilt something on my clothes so we popped back to Ed's and he lent me something of his to wear.'

'And where do you live, Ed?' she asked, basting the chicken innocently.

Oh, no, I know where this is going.

'Highgate.'

Lynn looked up. 'But surely if you were coming back from Chessington on the M25 or even the M3 or the A3, it would have been easier to come back here than to go to Highgate?'

It occurred to me that, if Lynn was really going to divorce

132

Harry, I could pair her off with Alfie. With her knowledge of London's arterial roads, she would be the perfect foil for a cabbie. They could test each other on the quickest route from The Angel, Islington to the Theatre Royal, Drury Lane.

'Oh well, we didn't think it through,' I mumbled.

'Something smells great.' Ed rubbed his hands together appreciatively.

Lynn looked from him to me suspicously. 'Well, it's all ready to serve whenever you want. I'll be on my way now. Don't wait up.'

Suddenly Ed spoke. 'Why don't you stay?'

Lynn looked surprised. 'Why?'

I couldn't think of a good reason myself so I, too, was interested to know why.

Ed counted the reasons on his fingers. 'Because you're living here, you've done all the cooking and because I think you'll be useful on our Trivial Pursuit team. I hear you're a walking encyclopaedia of science and nature. And also, you're Jenny's aunt and I want to get to know you.'

I'm not sure who was the most astonished, Lynn or I, but I think that she too fell a little in love with him after that.

'I'd better go and get changed then,' she said, flustered, undoing her apron with excited hands.

I walked over to Ed and kissed him. 'That was a lovely thing to do. But you know this isn't going to be the most romantic evening and –'

'I won't be able to stay the night, yes I know. But that's OK. Because I'm playing the long game here.'

And if I was a little disturbed by the concept of this relationship being any sort of game, I didn't dwell on it. Not then.

Maria and Danny arrived late. I wanted to drag Maria into the kitchen and tell her that I understood, that I'd spent a wonderful afternoon with a new man as well and that I hadn't wanted to get up for this either.

They both stood in the doorway, just staring, I had no idea at what.

'Jen, Your hair! You've had it cut.' Maria walked around me as if I were a surreal sculpture on a plinth.

My hands shot reflexively to my head. I'd completely forgotten about it. I'd forgotten about everything since this afternoon. Even

Mark. Damn, there's Mark again, creeping into my thoughts. I thought I'd finally banished him.

'Do you like it?' I asked casually, no longer needing her approval, not now I felt so totally validated by Ed.

'I think it's terrific. But I've been telling you to get it cut ever since I've known you. What made you take the plunge now?'

'It was Lisa,' I replied without thinking. Then I stopped. I didn't want to go into the story of the dating feature in front of Ed. It made me sound so desperate. Anyway, he didn't need to find out about it now. Lisa would have to pull me out of the magazine once she knew how things had developed with Ed.

I felt a stab when I remembered that my friendship with Lisa was currently on a very wobbly footing. I had been looking forward to sharing my good news with her, but decided it would be sensible to wait a few days before calling her.

Maria was smart enough to know that this was a subject I'd want closed. 'Good for Lisa,' she said simply.

Thank you, I mouthed silently to her.

Danny was still gazing at me. 'I think you look absolutely incredible! Much older!'

Maria slapped his arm. 'Wrong thing to say!'

Danny ignored the slap. 'How can you say that? You know I love older women.' He continued to stare at me with open admiration.

I felt uncomfortable at all this attention, particularly from someone I barely knew. 'Thanks anyway. I think. Danny, let me introduce you. This is Ed and this is my Auntie Lynn.'

He greeted everyone warmly and then Auntie Lynn slid into her adopted role as hostess, pouring drinks and dashing in and out of the kitchen.

Danny sank into an armchair, pulling Maria down onto his lap. It was good to see her so happy, so loved. I longed to do the same with Ed but Auntie Lynn's presence made that a no-no. I needed to talk to her before confessing that my relationship with Ed had moved onto a more serious footing.

'So do we eat first or do we play first?' Ed asked.

Maria looked at me quizzically. 'Play what?'

Whoops. 'Oh didn't I say? I thought we'd all play Trivial Pursuit.'

'No, you didn't say that,' Maria said tightly. 'You invited us to dinner. You know I hate games.'

'How can anyone hate Trivial Pursuit?' Danny protested. 'It's just questions and answers.'

'That's not why Jenny enjoys games,' Maria argued. 'She and Mark always played them together to avoid talking to each other and they played them with other people to stop any serious conversation from enveloping them.'

I was taken aback by her perception. I had no idea she'd known me so well.

'Dinner's ready,' Lynn announced hastily. I thanked Ed inwardly for his foresight in inviting Lynn to stay. Maybe he could make all my decisions in future. I started drawing up a mental list.

'So come on, tell me everything!' Maria had followed me into the immaculately clean kitchen where I was wondering how Lynn had prepared a full meal without unleashing my usual armageddon of smears, splashes and stains.

I pulled her away from the door so that we couldn't be heard.

'There's nothing to tell. No, that's a lie. We went to Chessington World of Adventures . . .'

Maria closed her eyes in despair. 'Jenny, unlike you, I am a grown-up, I have no interest in all the roundabouts you went on and the ice creams you ate. I want to know what put that smile on your face and that flush in your cheeks.'

My hand reached up immediately, wondering if my actions really had left visible traces. 'Well, Chessington was a bit of a disaster, actually; it wasn't Ed's sort of place.'

Maria nodded approvingly. 'He's my sort of man.'

'So we went back to his flat,' I continued, not needing Maria to tell me that my face was growing very red.

'I knew it!' she exclaimed. 'You're incredible! I thought you were the most repressed woman I'd ever known but within a couple of weeks of ditching one husband, you're already well on your way to number two. How do you do it? No, don't answer that, it would only depress me to find out that all I had to do was learn origami and wear terrible clothes. Just tell me, how was it?'

I swallowed, trying to find the words. 'Well, you know, it was . . . nice but a bit . . . awkward.'

Maria raised her eyebrows. 'Don't you think it's a little too late to become all coy? After all, you are now a fully-fledged adulteress, since you're still legally married.'

135

'Remind me why I consider you a friend?' I asked her miserably. 'Anyway, I was too nervous and self-conscious to pay much attention to what was happening. I didn't know any of the rules, what I was supposed to say or do.'

'You mean you didn't know at which point you needed to break it to him that you wanted a baby and you wanted it *now*?'

'That was not . . . presented to me as an option,' I pointed out uncomfortably.

I watched Maria deciphering my oblique references, wishing I'd just once watched *Sex and the City*, which I'd heard from Lisa portrayed this kind of conversation all the time. I simply didn't have the vocabulary to talk like this. It was a bit too real, too earthy for me.

I was saved from Maria's protracted interrogation by Lynn bustling in to ask why it was taking two people so long to find one serving spoon. As Maria obediently returned to the living room, I asked myself all the questions that my friend had not had the time to pose.

OK, if I was honest, my overwhelming emotion during the afternoon was one of embarrassment and self-consciousness. I'd felt inexperienced and naïve, painfully aware that I'd only had one partner before Ed. Even worse, I'd kept thinking of Mark but I surprised myself by intuiting that this was probably not a good thing to mention to Ed. So I didn't.

But if I'm continuing the honest theme, I also felt more distanced from Mark afterwards and that was surely my aim. Wasn't it?

It was a great meal. I'd forgotten what a good cook Lynn was and what a bad cook I was. She'd done something with chicken breasts and almonds and cream that didn't require any jars or packets labelled 'instant', an essential requirement of Mark's and my cuisine. For pudding, she'd created a fantastic chocolate roulade – and it wasn't even a shop-bought swiss roll that she'd unravelled and filled with squirty cream from a can. I hoped I wasn't the only person who did that.

The quality of the food had an uplifting effect on us all. And after the truncated dinner at Tally's the night before, this was a haven of goodwill and easy company.

When Lynn was out of the room, Ed would touch my hand or face affectionately.

'When are you going to tell your aunt about us?'

'Probably tomorrow,' I said, clinging to his hand for a few seconds, not wanting to be separated from him.

'I see our company wasn't necessary after all,' Maria was watching us with interest. 'We were supposed to be helping the conversation along, sitting in between you to stop any unwelcome contact. But now we can't keep you apart. Danny and I could have been doing something else, instead of being bored rigid playing board games with two people who would also probably rather be doing something else. Oh, and an aunt who is here for who-knows-what reason.'

'Home-made chocolate truffles!' Lynn bore her plate proudly aloft like a newborn child. 'If you like, we can have coffee in the living room and start playing. That way, we might have time for two or even three games.'

Maria closed her eyes in misery. I was going to owe her a lot of favours after tonight.

By eleven o'clock, I'd made a mental note never to let couples play on the same team in the future. Maria and Danny argued continually throughout the game.

'Who won the Best Actor Oscar in nineteen seventy-two?' Lynn read out.

'I wasn't even born then,' Danny replied cheerfully. 'How old were you then, Maz?'

Maria ignored him. When a Glenn Miller question came up, Danny patted her hand encouragingly. 'I'll leave this one to you, Babes.'

'I think I'm going to kill him,' she mumbled, as he left the room. When he came back, the question was about a Britpop band. The rest of us weren't absolutely sure what this term meant exactly but we presumed that 'The Beatles' would not be a sensible answer.

Danny sat forward confidently. 'Trust me, Maz. This is my era. I was there. I remember it.'

Irritatingly, the set seemed to have been created in the mid to late 1990s and most of the cultural references were placed firmly in Danny's era rather than ours. There were no less than three questions about rappers and none of the answers were Snoop Doggy Dog, the only rapper the rest of us could name. While Mark and I had played with the set in the past, this anomaly hadn't bothered us because all of our friends were from the same era as us. We could laugh at our shared exclusion. But tonight we just felt old.

'Why aren't there any questions about Gilbert O'Sullivan?' Maria asked irritably.

'Or Gilbert *and* Sullivan?' Lynn added. But she was having a marvellous time on our team. Ed turned out to have a bottomless pool of useless knowledge that was so vital for this particular game and, in the areas where he was lacking, Lynn was frequently able to fill in.

'You see, Maz,' Danny observed on one occasion. 'Ed is the same age as you but he knows the names of Blur albums and the childrens' TV presenters from the days of colour TV. The trouble with so many people is that they stop expanding culturally at the age of twenty-one when they finish their education.' I cringed inwardly, wondering if he knew that Maria had not been to university and had a complex about it. He ploughed on. 'They stop listening to new bands. The only new music they expose themselves to is anything used in TV commercials and the occasional album plugged on Radio Two.'

'Can't we just admit defeat and go home?' Maria asked in desperation. 'I'm very tired.'

'Actually I'm tired too,' Ed added, innocently. 'I've had a busy day. I could do with an early night.'

'As long as we can have you all back to us for a rematch,' Danny demanded.

'That would be lovely,' Lynn exclaimed.

Maria didn't hide her dismay at this suggestion. 'We'll see. I just need to use the bathroom before I go.'

I piled up some plates and carried them through to the kitchen, while Lynn and Ed read some more of the questions, arguing merrily about the answers. Danny followed right behind me with some coffee cups.

I took them from him and began loading the dishwasher. 'Thank you.'

Danny helped me with the loading. 'No. Thank you. It was a great night. I could really get into all these games. All Maria seems to want to do is sit around talking. I feel we're running out of conversation after just one full week of living together and we're now getting to the stage where we find out how little we have in common.'

138

'There's a lot more to Maria than you could discover in one week,' I told him. 'Make an effort.'

'Maybe I don't want to.' His strange tone made me look up at him. At the exact moment our eyes made contact, he kissed me. I pulled away immediately, but not before noting that it was a grown-up kiss. I was becoming an expert at spotting the difference after my first day as a bona fide adult, wrinkles and all.

'What do you think you're doing?' I whispered at him snatching a glance at the door.

'I know you feel the same way.' Danny was trying to remove a dirty cup from my hand. 'After the other evening, we both felt it. Then you turned up again on Thursday. And when you invited us round tonight, I was certain. Maria said that you hardly ever invited her round when you were married, I mean, married and still actually living with your husband, so it had to be me you wanted to see. And I know why. We have so much more in common than I do with Maria.'

Did we? All I knew was that I felt nothing for Danny except a horror that he was going to break Maria's heart when it had taken her a lifetime to entrust it to anyone.

'Maria is my best friend and you've just spent an evening being friendly to my new boyfriend. For those reasons alone, this is never going to happen again.'

'What's never going to happen again?' Maria asked, coming into the kitchen.

'This disastrous excuse for a sociable evening,' I lied fluently. 'It won't happen again, I promise. Back to you and me out alone from now on. No more games.'

Maria rolled her eyes up. 'Thank God!' She hugged me warmly. 'We'll talk next week,' she whispered, gesturing back at Ed. 'Thanks for a truly dreadful evening.'

'Actually it was a great evening, Jenny,' Danny interjected. 'I can't wait to do it again.' He kissed me on the cheek, letting his lips linger there for so long I couldn't believe Maria didn't notice.

After they left, I stayed in the kitchen, replaying the kiss. It was like a recurring nightmare. For the second time in two days, I'd discovered something that would hurt one of my closest friends.

Both of them had maintained that they would want to be told but look what had happened when I told Lisa. That friendship was now hanging by a thread.

I wished I wasn't such a nice girl. Then I would have stayed in bed with Ed all evening, cancelled the dinner and none of this would have happened. Maybe I won't be so nice from now on. Look where it gets you.

I helped Lynn with the clearing up. I understood why she enjoyed cleaning and bustling so much. As soon as two people sit down in a room without a video on or a board game on the go, they have no option but to talk. And frankly, since Mark and I split up and I've been talking to people, Mark included, everything has gone badly wrong. I'm already worried about what will happen to Ed and me when we stop making love and start talking.

But eventually there was nothing else left to move, wash or put away. We sat down and talked.

'So is this Ed someone special?' Lynn asked.

'I think so,' I agreed, shyly.

'I can't pretend I approve,' Lynn said. 'You're still married to Mark and I haven't given up hope that you might get back together. I thought you'd decided that this separation was just down to Mark's money problems.'

God, I really wanted to switch the TV on. 'It's more than that, Auntie.'

'Maybe,' Lynn sniffed. 'But what chance have you got of a reconciliation if you're seeing a new man?'

'I'm not the only one seeing someone,' I objected. I told her about Mark's threat to take Tally up on her ongoing offer. 'And I'm fairly certain that they're in France together this weekend.'

'But you said that she's been trying to help him get his money back, and that nothing's happened so far.'

'But it has in the past.'

She wasn't moved by my tragic tale of undergraduate betrayal. 'That was twenty years ago. Grow up!'

I sank into a juvenile sulk. I wanted to be with Ed. He had never betrayed me. He loved me even though I have lines and don't know how to behave in restaurants and don't have much mystique. He was on my side. There's nothing childish about that.

'So it's all decided, then?' Lynn asked.

'What do you mean?'

'You're going to divorce Mark quickly, marry Ed quickly and have babies quickly?'

I was shocked at her blunt assessment of the situation. 'Well, I don't know, I mean, it's early days . . .'

Lynn looked at me coldly. 'I thought you left Mark because you wanted a baby, not because you wanted an affair with someone else. Has that changed as well? Last week, you seemed absolutely certain of what you were going to do. So what's happened to the plan now? I presume Ed knows that you are desperate for children?'

'Obviously I haven't mentioned that. Not yet.' My stomach was churning. I didn't like where this was heading. I hadn't thought all this through, it was true. But it all felt right, so surely that was a good sign. How could Ed not want children?

And what had he said about playing the long game? Before I had a chance to decide what this meant, the phone rang.

It was the hospital. Harry had suffered a heart attack.

It was late Saturday night and there were no taxis to be found. I called Alfie. 'I'm really sorry to phone so late.' I explained what had happened.

'Don't you worry about it. It's an emergency and, anyway, I was still up. I don't need much sleep at my age.'

He was here in twenty minutes and drove like a cabbie on the way to the Chelsea and Westminster Hospital, almost causing four accidents and irritating the hell out of every driver he passed and cut up.

I left Lynn on the ward where Harry was being treated. After getting the full story from the doctor, I went outside, trying to reach Mark on his mobile.

'Do you know what time it is?'

I'd woken him up and I doubt if he was pleased to see my name appear on his handset.

'I'm really sorry, Mark, but it's your dad.'

'What's happened?' He was fully awake now and his voice was shaking.

'He's had a heart attack. Don't panic, he's comfortable, but it was a serious one this time.' I gave him the details as I knew them. 'Lynn's with him now.'

'I'll come right back,' Mark said. 'If I drive to the airport now, I can get a cancellation on the first flight out.'

'Make sure your mobile is on and I'll keep you posted on his progress. I'm going to stay at the hospital with Lynn.'

'Thanks, Jen. Listen, I'm going to make a move now. See you as soon as I can. Bye. Love you.'

Now I know that last bit was just an automatic response that spilled out while he was in shock. But it took my breath away. With one phone call, with two words, it was as if everything had gone back to how it was.

His voice had lost all its hostility. I had been able to talk to him without having to consider all my words first. There were no accusations implicit in the simple phrases. He was no longer the man who was depriving me of a child or a teenager cheating on me. He was the man with whom I'd spent all my adult life, the only man I'd ever really known and loved. He was suffering and I wanted to comfort him.

Even more, Harry was as much of a father to me as he was to Mark and I felt sick with worry. I wanted Mark here, now, so we could get through this together.

It was a long night. I encouraged Lynn to stretch out on a couch so that she could get some sleep. I had to make do with a plastic upright chair that stuck to my arms. I didn't think I slept at all but there were moments in the dark silence when I seemed to be drifting back from somewhere, not quite from a dream, but from a hazy, peaceful place.

The morning routine began early with breakfasts and drugs and needles coming and going from dawn onwards. Harry had woken up a few times in the night but hadn't made much sense before dropping off again. It was about eleven o'clock when he finally showed signs of lucidity.

'Lynn,' he whispered.

Lynn was sitting by the side of the bed holding his hand. 'I'm here, love.'

'I'm sorry about all the . . . well, you know.' He was finding it a struggle to speak. Lynn placed a finger tenderly on his lips. 'That's enough of that nonsense. None of it matters any more. We're going to get you better and I'm not going to leave you alone again.'

I closed my eyes in relief that they'd been reunited, that they'd had the chance to be reunited. If Harry had died while Lynn was living with me, because of my selfishness . . .

'Jen?' Mark stood nervously at the entrance to the cubicle, looking from his dad to me, but mainly looking at me.

142

Harry had drifted back off to sleep and Lynn had nodded off with her head on his hand. I tiptoed out and took Mark down to the café on the first floor. He ordered coffee and cakes for us both and I luxuriated in the easy pleasure of someone knowing what I wanted without my having to say a word.

We sat down opposite each other and wasted a few seconds unwrapping buns and sugar sachets.

'I didn't expect you back so quickly,' I said.

'We were at the airport by four o'clock and there was a six am flight we managed to get on.'

We? He said 'we' twice. I drank the coffee even though it was too hot and burned my mouth. At least it stopped me from saying something I'd regret.

'The news is quite positive. Your dad will have to think about retiring completely and taking things easy. The doctor made it clear that this was a final warning.'

'This is all my fault,' Mark said, stirring his cup furiously to stop himself from crying.

I instinctively took his hand. 'It's not anybody's fault.' I wasn't sure if I believed this. 'Or maybe it's my fault for trying to change things.'

'It was my fault you had to change things.' Mark looked at my hands as if he'd never seen them before. He stroked my little finger and the last few weeks disappeared. Ed disappeared.

'The most important thing is that Lynn and your dad have made up.' I hesitated. 'Did you make any progress in France?'

Mark stretched his arms out tiredly. 'We found out where Clive is living. I wanted to confront him but Tally stopped me.' So she was there. 'She said that he would do a runner if he knew we'd tracked him down.'

'So what are you going to do now?' And what did you do once you'd found his address, you and Tally with her shimmying hips in beautiful Bordeaux in sultry September? I don't think I asked that out loud.

'I could go to the police. But Tally is staying there for another day or two. She's going to try and "accidentally" bump into him, pretend that she doesn't know about his rip-off and see if she can find out what he's doing with all his money. Then she's planning to appeal to his better nature.'

'I'm sure Tally can get anything she wants from a man,' I muttered coldly.

Mark looked at me sharply. 'Her marriage is falling apart and she had to make up a ridiculous story to get away this weekend. She feels responsible for us losing all this money.'

'She's a saint.'

Mark wisely changed the subject. 'You've had your hair cut.'

I laughed. 'You've noticed!'

'It looks . . . different.'

'Do you like it?' I asked, suddenly caring about his response.

'I think so. It's just . . . different. Jenny, nothing happened with Tally and it's not going to. I thought about it when I heard you had dinner with that guy, but I still feel married to you. I know I over-reacted about all those texts but I've got over it. I was just being stupidly jealous. It was just a dinner after all; I realize that now. I don't want anyone else and I'm hoping you feel the same way.'

Could he see my heart pounding through Ed's T-shirt? Oh God, I was still wearing Ed's clothes!

I gently extricated my hand from his. 'I'm so tired I can't think. I need to go home and get changed. I've been up all night in these.'

'Let me come home with you,' Mark begged. 'I mean, really come home. We can talk now that there are no more secrets. About money, children, everything.'

'We should have talked three weeks ago,' I said weakly. 'I wish we'd talked then.'

'Well, now I've come to my senses. It's been a terrible time for us both but now we have the chance to turn the clocks back. I mean, no real harm has been done, has it? Nothing has really changed.'

Now didn't seem a good time to tell him just how much had changed.

'Alfie, this is Mark, my husband.'

Mark seemed surprised that we now counted a taxi driver in our list of close personal friends. Since our circle of friends had been, and continued to be, decimated by the fall-out from our recent separation, I felt he should be grateful that anyone was still pleased to see us.

'We'll be needing a good taxi service. I don't think I mentioned it but I sold the MG.'

'But you loved that car!' I exclaimed.

144

Mark rubbed his hands together casually. 'It was just a car.' But I knew that it must have been a wrench for him.

Alfie didn't show any reaction to the unexpected appearance of my husband. He said nothing about red and blue dots or mysterious finger-stroking incidents in cafés. He was the king of inscrutability and I was beginning to love him.

'Pleased to meet you,' he said, blandly.

He drove us back to my flat, I mean, our flat, I mean, my flat, keeping up a safe, steady conversation, asking about Harry and Lynn. I don't even remember agreeing for Mark to come in with me but, when we got to Battersea, he automatically got out and reached into his pocket for his front-door key. It was still on his keyring alongside other keys from his other life.

Mark took out his wallet to pay the amount shown on the taxi's meter. I rushed to intervene before Alfie could register his disapproval. 'I'll sort it out with Alfie later,' I said hastily.

Mark was mystified at this odd state of affairs. 'Do you have an account or something?'

'It's the or something,' I replied, exchanging a knowing smile with Alfie. Over the past few days, I'd taken to slipping him an envelope with the amount I'd worked out I owed. He accepted it without acknowledgement. It hadn't been planned that way, it just seemed right for the evolution of our particular unique relationship.

Alfie touched his cap, reinforcing, for Mark's benefit, the belief that he was simply my chauffeur, rather than a friend. 'I'll go back and pick up your aunt later,' he said. 'And will she be needing her bags going back to the other house?'

'She certainly will,' I said with relief.

Alfie nodded. 'I'll do that later as well. Bye for now.'

Then he was gone. Mark had already let himself into the flat. When I followed him in, I found everything as Lynn and I had left it after the dinner party. I wondered whether Mark would be suspicious at the five settings of cutlery and plates in the dishwasher. But why would he?

Mark turned to me. 'So what do we do now?'

He looked at me for an answer. So it was up to me then. OK, so maybe I was tired, maybe just confused. I'd spent a sleepless night confronting images of death. Mark had turned up and, within minutes, had been stroking my finger, insisting he'd done nothing wrong, practically promising me a baby, vowing that everything could return to the way it always was.

I was exhausted trying to erase images of Ed and origami parties and my friends' fragile marriages. I wanted to be by myself, to think about all this. But, in the absence of blissful solitude, the next best thing must surely be familiarity, where I wouldn't have to think, I could just be and do, the way I'd always been and done.

So I took Mark's, my husband's, hand and led him into my bedroom, I mean, our bedroom, I mean, well, I don't know what I mean any more.

Chapter Ten

It was only when I got up a couple of hours later that I noticed the answering machine flashing. I'd completely forgotten that I'd promised to call Ed as soon as I got up. The messages were bound to be from him. I listened to them on a low volume before deleting them. Checking that Mark was still asleep. I carried the phone into the spare room and closed the door before dialling Ed's number.

'Hi, it's me,' I said quietly.

'Where have you been? I've been really worried that I'd said or done something to offend you and that you were never going to have anything to do with me again!'

'I'm sorry I didn't call.' I told him about Harry and being at the hospital all night. I left out the part about my reconciliation with Mark. I hadn't found the words that could explain this, not to him or even to me.

'Shall I come over?' he asked. 'You must be exhausted. We could have an afternoon nap together.'

'No!' I heard myself shouting. I quickly calmed down. 'Sorry, I didn't mean it to sound like that. It's just that I'm going to have to go straight back to the hospital to try and persuade Auntie Lynn to come and get some sleep here. Look, today's going to be a write-off and I can't use my mobile at the hospital, so can we leave it that we'll talk tomorrow?'

'Sure.' Ed couldn't conceal his disappointment. Before I had a chance to reassure him, the door opened and Mark was standing in front of me, probably awoken by my raised voice.

'I have to go now. Bye.' I cut the connection before lying smoothly. 'That was Lisa. Just seeing how your dad was.' Now I was going to have to phone her secretly and let her know what was happening.

'Did you tell her about us?' he asked.

Did I? 'Well, no. I think we should keep this to ourselves while your dad is ill.' And while Lisa decides whether to forgive me for tainting her marriage. And Kieran forgives me for breaking a promise. And while Tally tries to retrieve £100,000 before returning to rebuild her marriage. And while I decide whether the love I felt for Ed yesterday was real.

Mark sat next to me on the spare bed. 'We are going to be OK, aren't we?'

I patted his hand absently. 'Course we are.'

The phone rang. 'Hi, it's Lisa.'

'Hi again,' I said emphasizing the 'again'.

I clenched the handset tightly against my ear so that Mark wouldn't be able to hear my conversation. Fortunately he chose to wander off and make tea, remembering that relentless phone calls were a permanent feature of life with me.

'What's with the "again"?' she said.

I lowered my voice and spoke quickly. 'It's complicated. Mark's here. Harry's had a heart attack, a bad one but he's stable, but Mark thinks I've already told you. He thinks you just called me.'

'I can't take all that in. Why is Mark there? Did you just say that Harry had a heart attack?'

I became impatient. 'Yes, yes. Look I'll fill you in later.'

'Aren't you going to ask me why I called?' Lisa asked, sounding offended.

I didn't think I wanted to know. 'Oh, I'm sorry, Lisa. Things are really, really difficult. So have you told Kieran about the baby?'

'Yes and he was thrilled.'

'Really?'

'Well, not exactly thrilled. Stunned is probably a more accurate word. But I was stunned myself at first and now I'm thrilled so that will probably be the next stage for Kieran.'

I made a mental note to inform Kieran that he would be entering the 'thrilled' stage imminently when I spoke to him next. That was one of the functions I performed in my friendship with him. I reminded him to notice when Lisa had a haircut, policed the presents he bought her and told him of the expected emotional

148

responses to situations he couldn't possibly grasp by himself. 'Did he tell you that Tally and Mark went to France this weekend to try and get the money back from Clive?'

Lisa was amazed by my equanimity. 'Well, yes, but I didn't think you'd be very happy about it.'

I was too tired to explain what had happened. 'I'll tell you all about it when I see you.'

'We need to go out and celebrate my good news so that you can tell me yours. It *is* good news, I presume?'

'I honestly don't know. I think so.' I took a deep breath before asking her the question I dreaded. 'So, did you confront Kieran about him and Tally?'

Lisa sounded surprisingly calm. 'No. And I'm not going to. I'm taking the advice I gave you, letting it go. It was a long time ago and has nothing to do with who we are now. We're having a baby and I can't afford to let anything spoil that. I'm learning from your mistakes.'

I was too relieved to be insulted. Obviously my warning text to Kieran hadn't been necessary. I hoped he hadn't been in too much of a panic when he received it. 'I'm really pleased. You are definitely doing the right thing.'

'Can I just say something, Jen? If you ever find out anything about Kieran, *anything* – that he's a serial killer, or dresses in my clothes when I'm out or has five illegitimate children from a bigamous marriage, I don't want to know. I really, really don't want to know. It would cause more pain than anything.'

And that was why I knew I wouldn't tell Maria about Danny.

Sunday, Monday, Tuesday, they passed so quickly. It was a blur of hospital visits punctuated by Mark popping into the office and me fulfilling the contracts that were still trickling in. Occasionally Mark asked me how we went about retrieving the divorce papers that we'd previously sent into the court. I kept promising to find out what we were supposed to do, but I never did. There were other, more important things to do. Like maintaining elaborate deceits.

I called Ed a few times, usually leaving messages on his home machine when I knew he wouldn't be home. Cowardly? That's me. During the day, he was as busy as I was so calls were brief, but on Tuesday he did pin me down and make me agree to spend the coming Saturday with him.

I said 'yes' knowing that I'd cancel on the day. Ed was already fiction to me, a vague memory, something intangible from a dream. The reality was Mark, Harry and Lynn, just as it always had been.

Wednesday brought good news, bad news and a nasty rash. The rash was nothing sordid, just some spots on the back of my neck. Mark had them too. They were annoying enough that I planned to ask a pharmacist for advice.

The good news was fabulous news. Tally had managed to persuade Clive to give Mark back £65,000 of the £100,000. We don't know how she did it, or perhaps Mark just didn't want to tell me. But Clive had a pool of cash and a list of creditors that he'd arranged in order of severity of threats placed against his life. We'd moved closer to the top of this list. He was never going to be able to pay them all off so we were relieved that we were going to get anything back at all.

You see, I was already back to thinking in terms of 'we'. Mark had agreed to let me put some of my earnings into the company. I think he was astonished to find out how much I was being offered for my origami.

And we'd even agreed that we'd start talking about trying for a family. Just talking, but, wow. It was even Mark's idea. The money was no longer an issue, he pointed out, because I could carry on doing my particular work even with a baby. The mortgage on the flat was still in my name and was tiny. Of course, neither of us mentioned the fact that Mark's objections were never merely financial. I was quite sure that he was still not keen but he was desperate to make our marriage work and knew that this issue wasn't going to disappear. I didn't dare ask myself whether I would be as willing to make a compromise. There were a lot of questions I wasn't prepared to ask myself.

If it hadn't been for the unfinished business with Ed and the nagging sense that I was back with Mark purely because it was the easy option, I would have felt a little smug. Until the first phone call. It was Lisa.

'I hope you're happy,' she snapped. 'Just because you've subjected your marriage to torment and torture, we all have to do the same.'

'What have I done?' I implored.

'I think you know what you've done.'

She's not going to make me guess, is she? 'Please, Lisa, just tell me.'

'Mark decided to inform Kieran that the secret about Tally was out. He thought he was doing my husband a favour by warning him.'

I groaned. I'd told Mark about the awful events at Phil's birthday dinner the previous Friday, but I thought I'd told him not to mention it to Kieran. Maybe I hadn't – I was finding it difficult to keep up with all the deceptions. On the plus side, at least this didn't appear to be connected with my text. I was puzzled as to why Mark's warning should spur him to action when mine didn't. But I wasn't going to lose sleep over it. This was one thing that was definitely Mark's fault and I could kiss him for that. 'What happened?'

'What happened?' Lisa parroted. 'He insisted on coming straight home and talking about it, of course. I was perfectly happy in my state of self-induced denial, but he wouldn't shut up. He kept apologizing over and over again for Tally.'

'But you'd already decided that you were going to be calm and forgiving,' I reasoned. 'So surely it wasn't that bad.'

Lisa snorted. 'You would have thought so. But because he was so amazed at how calm and forgiving I was about it, he decided to apologize for the other fling.'

'What other fling?' I asked in shock. I was still having difficulty imagining Kieran with Tally. The emerging picture of him as a quiet Lothario was ludicrous. Maybe it was his old glasses that got in the way of the image. Or maybe it was because I'd flattered myself that I knew him well.

'Do you remember when Mark and Kieran went on that golfing weekend in Portugal about five years ago?'

'Of course I do.' That was when Lisa dragged me to that sadistic health farm to have my colon irrigated of the 350 calories a day I was allowed per day.

Lisa was becoming tearful. 'He met someone. Mark was having some extra lessons with the pro and Kieran joined an organized walk and –'

'God, Lisa, I'm so sorry. I didn't know.'

'Didn't you?' she spat. 'How can I be sure of that?'

'Because you're the one who kept a secret from me for all those years! As soon as I knew anything about Kieran, I told you.'

'Well, I wish you hadn't bothered.'

This was awful. We were bickering and we'd never bickered.

'Lisa, I'm really sorry about everything.' I was about to say that I didn't think that this could be my fault but I was coming to accept that everything was my fault: the declining standard of acts on *Pop Idol*, the rise in Council Taxes, the questions in Trivial Pursuit, Third World poverty – all my fault for asking Mark for a baby three weeks earlier.

'It's not your fault,' Lisa conceded. I was relieved I'd said nothing so that she could come to this conclusion all by herself. It restored my confidence that this might all be sorted out. For five seconds.

'So are you going to make him suffer for a while, then forgive him when he presents you with a big piece of jewellery?' I asked playfully.

'Hardly,' Lisa replied. 'It was one thing to forgive something that happened two decades ago when we'd only been going out for a few months. This other thing happened when we were married. And how am I to know if there weren't lots of others? He might have been about to confess to affairs all over Western Europe until he discovered my reaction to the first one. Obviously he's not about to admit to any more now.'

'I'm sure it was a one-off,' I pressed.

'Are you?' Lisa asked wryly. 'Well I'm not. I can't trust him any more.'

'You're not going to be on my doorstep with your luggage in a couple of hours, are you?' I hoped my levity was audible.

'No, why should I move out? I pay most of the mortgage. I've thrown Kieran out and told him not to come back.'

This is not my fault. This is not my fault. I paced around the flat, cursing Mark for talking to Kieran about something personal for what must be the first time in their friendship. Why couldn't he have stuck to replaying Memorable Golf Shots of My Life with a pencil and a Malteser?

I cleaned the flat, having learned from Lynn how therapeutic it could be, before getting down to some preparatory work for a meeting the next morning. Later that afternoon, the phone went again.

'Thank you. Thank you very much.'

'Maria? What have I done?' I hadn't spoken to her since

Saturday, not even to tell her about Harry. It wasn't deliberate, at least I don't think it was. I'd already decided that I wasn't going to tell her about Danny, but I was dreading having to maintain the deception, so maybe I was putting off the first contact.

'I think you know what you've done.'

Was everybody passing the same script around? I looked around me for a hidden camera. Surely a toothsome presenter would soon leap through a door with a comic award for me. 'I really don't.' I hoped I really didn't.

'Danny told me about Saturday night,' Maria intoned.

In that case, I really did. 'I don't know what he told you, Maria. But it was nothing. He was drunk, he declared his undying love for me, I brushed him off –'

'He said he kissed you.'

Oh, that. 'He tried and I pushed him away. It was nothing.'

'If it was nothing, why didn't you tell me? Or if it was some-thing, why didn't you tell me? We'd discussed this and you promised you would tell me. So why didn't you tell me?'

I was developing a stress headache. 'I told Lisa about Kieran, because she made me promise to tell her and it caused her nothing but pain. She begged me never to tell her anything again. I thought I was doing the right thing.'

'Well, you weren't. He's left me.'

'Oh, Maria, I'm sorry!'

Maria exhaled loudly. 'Why did you have to change every-thing? I mean, we've been friends for eighteen years and, in all those years, we've done things the same way. We go out alone, just the two of us. I don't bring boyfriends, you don't bring Mark. Apart from the occasional compulsory birthday parties where I've stoically tolerated him as well as your boring university chums, that's how it's always been. We only share the parts of our lives we're comfortable sharing and no more. And I imagine you share completely different parts of yourself with the Rottweiler. But what I've always loved about our friendship is that we don't . . . encroach on each other's lives.'

So now I'm an adulteress, a deceiver and an encroacher. I wondered if any of these were Deadly Sins or whether they were just minor transgressions. When you've spent a lifetime consid-ering yourself a nice person, you don't give much thought to sin. Now I seem to be notching them up with ease.

Maria's voice became gloomy. 'Look, Danny and I had nothing in common really and it was never going to last; I was beginning to see this. But it could have gone on for some time. I was hoping I would at least be able to spend Christmas with a lover. I've never done that before. Besides, I liked having somebody there in the evenings and in the mornings. I liked eating casseroles with a knife and fork at a table every evening instead of dry Cheerios with my fingers in front of *EastEnders*. I liked holding my stomach in when I walked across the room. I was even looking forward to socks on the radiator so that I could learn to nag.'

'Sorry,' I said, pathetically. I must have sounded close to tears because she relented – not that I deserved it.

'Please don't make me feel sorry for you,' Maria protested. 'It takes away my pleasure at having shouted at you. Now I suppose I have to put you out of your misery.'

'A bullet would be very welcome at this present time,' I agreed.

Maria didn't argue. 'I did realize this afternoon that we're both finally single and available at the same time now.' This would be a good moment to tell her that I was back with Mark.

She continued. 'It's the only reason I'm forgiving you so easily.' Maybe it wasn't such a good moment.

Maria was encouraged by my silence. 'And now I know how irresistibly attractive you are to the younger man, we should do brilliantly. Next Tuesday there's a 1980s disco in Kingston. I've already got us tickets.'

'Sounds great,' I said, trying to sound enthusiastic. Something else I'd have to get out of nearer the day. I hoped my lying skills would be up to the job.

I forgot all about going to the chemist about the spots on my neck until Mark came home itching badly. 'I'll pick up some cream for us tomorrow,' I promised. 'I'm sorry I didn't get round to it, but I had a bad day today. How about you?'

Mark was on the floor unpacking his boxes of videos and replacing them in our joint cabinet in alphabetical order.

'I phoned the bank and they said that Clive had transferred the money across. It should be cleared by tomorrow. I'm going to give it to my dad and Lynn the minute it arrives. And then pay the rest back when I can.'

'How is your dad?'

He stopped what he was doing. 'The heart attack is all down to me. The consultant more or less said so. If he hadn't been subjected to any excessive stress, then there was no reason why Dad shouldn't have gone on for another twenty or thirty years without any trouble. When the doctor asked me if I could think of anything that might have caused him any undue pressure, I didn't know where to begin.'

I decided to join him in self-recrimination. 'I had Lisa on the phone today. She's thrown Kieran out. He took it upon himself to confess about some woman he met in the Algarve on that golfing holiday.'

Mark looked amused. 'It was a quick kiss on a sand dune!'

'Lisa gave me the impression it was a full-blown affair!'

'You know what Kieran is like. He probably felt as guilty as if he'd had a full-blown affair.'

Poor man, I thought, thinking he could get everything off his chest while his wife was proving uncharacteristically tolerant. 'It's probably the fact that he hid it from her, rather than the nature of the betrayal, that hurt the most,' I concluded, before recalling that I, too, was now a hider of facts.

'I shouldn't have said anything in the first place,' Mark admitted. 'That's what sparked this all off. I'm really sorry. Has it spoiled things between you and Lisa?'

I twisted my mouth. 'We'll survive it. Just.'

'I feel worse about Phil.'

'Is he not speaking to you and Kieran?' I asked, accepting my share of the responsibility for Phil's misery after my outburst at his so-called birthday dinner.

'It's even worse. He's taken our side against Tally and describes us all, him included, as her victims. And he's grateful to you for bringing all this to a head. It turns out that she's been having affairs all through their marriage, which I suppose isn't a great surprise, but he was always able to pretend that it wasn't happening.'

So his marriage was just like mine. Two people pretending that everything is fine and not having the courage to face the problems and fix them. Whereas Mark and I papered over our cracks with ceaseless activity and minimal talking, Phil buried himself in work and Tally occupied her empty days with other men. Until I opened my mouth on Friday and forced him to confront the truth.

'I've had a really bad thought, Mark.'

155

He came over and put his arms around me. I let myself sink back, close my eyes and let myself mould into him, enjoying the effortlessness with which we fitted together. Was this love? God knows. But it was easy and I was grateful for that.

'What's up?' he asked gently.

'Lisa and Kieran, Tally and Phil, Harry and Lynn, even Maria, they've all been badly affected by our decision to get a divorce.'

'We've worked things out. Maybe they will too.'

'But maybe they won't.'

Mark sat back. 'But what can we do about it?'

'It's what we *can't* do. Do you think that our friends are going to throw a party when they hear we've got back together? That they'll weep tears of joy that the childhood sweethearts have rekindled their love? They are all still reeling from the aftershocks that we've caused them. Right now, we're the only happy ones among the lot of them.'

'So what are you saying?'

'I'm saying that we can't tell them that we're back together, that they'd never forgive us for putting them through all that only to announce a few weeks later that everything is fine now. Because it's not fine for them.'

This was undeniable. While they were all wrapped up in problems that we'd unwittingly caused, they would be unlikely to share our happiness. But there was another reason for keeping quiet, one I didn't want to mention. Of course I was pleased that Mark and I had put all the unpleasantness behind us but we hadn't resolved the major problem that had caused our initial split. Until the baby issue was settled one way or another, I couldn't be confident that we were truly reconciled.

Mark didn't appear to have any such reservations and was trying to understand the situation. 'So we have to pretend that we're still separated?'

I nodded.

Mark shook his head. 'That's crazy.'

Finally, he understands.

On Thursday, the doctors agreed to discharge Harry from hospital. Alfie was going to pick him and Lynn up, bring him back to our flat to pick up the last of Lynn's things, then drive them both home.

156

I left Mark at the flat getting things ready while I went off to my meeting.

'Did you sort out getting the divorce papers back?' he called as I was about to leave.

Damn! 'No, but I absolutely promise I'll do it this afternoon.' And suddenly, I meant it.

The meeting was with an American bank that wanted me to turn dollar bills into origami representations of the presidents on Mount Rushmore. I'd spent three evenings preparing my models and they were very impressed. We agreed that I would attend a photographic session the following week and prepare some fresh folds for a forthcoming poster campaign. They were going to pay me £2,000 and I amazed myself by managing not to react to this generous offer.

When I came out of the bank, the itch on my neck reminded me that I was supposed to be picking up some cream for me and Mark. I went to the nearest chemist and looked for a man with a badge. Once I'd located Andrew Your Neighbourhood Pharmacist, I showed him the rash on my neck. 'My husband has the same rash. And, before you ask, we haven't changed our shampoo or our detergent.'

Andrew My Neighbourhood Pharmacist smiled. 'I wasn't going to ask. I know exactly what this is.' He lifted my hair from the back of my neck and parted it carefully. 'You have nits.'

I looked at him blankly. 'Nits?'

'Head lice to be precise. But you have the eggs, the nits as well. The spots are bites. Lice love the back of the neck. It's warm and . . .'

I felt suddenly queasy. 'Please don't say any more. I thought only children got nits.' I had a vague recollection of the nit nurse going through our hair with a metal comb at school.

The pharmacist smiled sympathetically. 'They're most common in children. But adults catch them too. Do you have children?'

'No,' I replied, 'not yet anyway.' I liked saying that. 'But I went to Chessington World of Adventures on Saturday. Could I have caught it from one of the rides?'

The pharmacist looked sceptical. 'Unlikely but possible. It's more likely that you caught it from someone who has contact with children. Now I presume you're going to want to get rid of the little creatures?'

'Creatures?' I repeated, trying to grasp the implications of the word. 'I have creatures, bugs, alive and running through my hair?' I thought I might faint.

'Actually they scurry more than run,' Andrew clarified. Our Neighbourhood Pharmacists are sticklers for terminology. I have bugs scurrying through my hair and they could have been there for days.

'I want them out NOW.' I had to concentrate on my breathing to stop myself from becoming hysterical.

Andrew was assembling an array of products. He started with a lovely green bottle decorated in leaves. 'Now this is the natural approach. It contains Tea Tree Oil –'

I seized his arm to stop him mid-flow. 'Tea Tree Oil? I don't want to give them an aromatherapy massage, I want to *kill them*, every last one of them.'

Andrew tentatively removed my hand from his arm. 'The natural approach is useful if you're concerned about side-effects or the environment.'

I would have seized his arm again but I couldn't risk being thrown out before getting my chemical weapons. 'Andrew,' I said, with awesome self-control. 'I have no concerns about side-effects or the environment, in fact, the longer the list of side-effects, the more confidence I will have in the product's killing ability. Something DDT- or napalm-based would be great and if it causes catastrophic environmental damage, even better.'

Andrew was assembling his face into his best Concerned Neighbourhood Pharmacist frown. 'Madam, I think you might be overreacting. Head lice are nothing to be ashamed of – most people get them at least once in their lives.'

One look at my face was sufficient for him to stop patronizing me. I was a woman with scurrying creatures in her hair, a woman not to be argued with. He selected the treatment with not a hint of green on the packaging and lots of small print, guessing correctly that I'd be pleased with that. I was.

He emphasized that I would need to treat my husband too and repeat the shampoo in a week's time, so I bought two bottles along with an electronic comb that zapped the lice when it touched them. I could electrocute the little buggers too. I wondered idly if you could also buy mini nooses to hang them or microscopic rock quarries to inflict hard labour on them.

Mark and I were going to have a fun evening tonight, delousing each other like chimpanzees, applying weapons of mass destruction to our hair and forgetting all our other problems. It might even become a new hobby.

I walked all the way home from the City which took an hour and a half but it was such a lovely day. The kids had all gone back to school and the grown-ups had reclaimed the streets. It was late September – hot but without the August humidity. I was wearing my purple dress and Indian shoes from Lisa's magazine shoot. I was different and the same again but, after the events of the past few days, I was the same in different ways and different in . . . oh, whatever.

Well, it made sense to me until I tried to articulate it. That's the problem with being with one person forever. You never need to acquire the skills of interpreting yourself to others. Mark would immediately know what I meant. He was there while I was being moulded into the person I am. He knows and understands all of my influences. The first time I got drunk, my first job, when my dad died, when I got my first cheque for producing some origami artwork for a small local business, when I made love for the first time, when I got married, when my marriage broke down, when it was fixed. He was always there, which saved me the necessity of having to explain it all.

When I got home, I expected him to say, 'Hi, Jen, did you enjoy the walk?' because he knew I'd walk home on a day like this. But when I opened the door, I found him sitting on my sofa, I mean, our sofa, staring at his hands.

'Is your dad OK?' I asked, anxiously.

'Fine.' He didn't look at me. 'Been and gone.'

Perhaps he was tired. Neither of us had been sleeping well. 'I got that job,' I told him, sitting down next to him. 'Oh and I went to the chemist. You'll never guess what we've got.'

'Nits,' he replied curtly.

I looked at him in surprise. 'How did you know that? Have you found a Neighbourhood Pharmacist of your own?'

Then he looked at me. 'I didn't need to. There was a message on the answering machine when I was seeing Dad and Lynn off. Your friend Ed rang. It seems you caught them from him.'

Mark was waiting for me to respond. I chose my words carefully. 'The pharmacist was telling me how easy they were to catch. Practically everyone gets them at some point.'

159

Mark tapped his chin intently. 'That's interesting because I've just been on the Internet. Did you know that lice can't fly or even jump. They just "clamber" from head to head. So your head has to be in contact with another head to catch them. I mean, I caught them from you because we've been sleeping together for the past few days. So I have to ask myself how you caught them from a man you merely had dinner with in a restaurant.'

'I'm not going to argue with you,' I said. 'This is what happened last week when I came to see you and look how that ended. I'm going to go and put this stuff on my hair.'

I walked towards the bathroom. Mark waited until I was about to close the door before calling out. 'By the way, if you'd rather wait until Saturday when you are apparently spending the day with Ed, he says you can treat each other's hair in the shower together. In fact, he's looking forward to it.'

And that was how my marriage ended for the second time.

At least the divorce was still in progress. We didn't have to go and spend a further £9.99 on another kit.

I couldn't deny anything. I listened to Ed's call myself and the evidence was damning. I'd told him that Lynn was moving back home which was why he'd been so explicit, thinking that I was the only person who would hear the message. He didn't need to go into any graphic detail to convey that we'd slept together.

'But technically I didn't do anything wrong,' I pointed out hesitantly to Mark. 'I mean, we'd split up, filed for divorce.'

Mark glared at me coldly. '*Technically*, of course, you're right. *Technically*, I could have taken Tally up on one of her offers, either here or in France and not been in the wrong, *technically*. But I didn't because it still would have been wrong and we both know it. At least, I thought we both did. I know you want a baby desperately but I thought you might at least go through some sort of grieving process for our relationship before you moved on.'

'But I thought *you'd* moved on,' I pleaded. 'You didn't look as if you were grieving to me.'

This infuriated Mark. 'I apologize for shaving and going to work and talking to *our* friends. Had I known that you would use this unreasonable behaviour to justify sleeping with the first man you met, I would have walked the streets in my pyjamas with a bottle of cider under my arm, shouting at strangers, *grieving* properly.'

'I didn't mean it like that.' Of course I did.

'Well congratulations,' Mark said finally. 'You've destroyed us.'

Who would have thought it? I was the one who cheated, really cheated, committed adultery, or whatever it is popularly called nowadays, while Mark had resisted Tally, even when they were alone under a warm French sky. Because *technically*, we were still married, even though we were separated. And could I honestly say that I did it because I wanted a child? I certainly hadn't been thinking about that on Saturday afternoon and Ed and I hadn't even discussed his thoughts on the subject.

I did it because I'd wanted to and had been punished by a headful of lice and the loss of Mark just when I'd got used to having him back. I wondered if Andrew My Neighbourhood Pharmacist had anything for a shattered marriage.

Chapter Eleven

Mark and I had never really enjoyed *Groundhog Day* as a film. The concept of a day being repeated over and over again until the hero gets the day right is clever but we didn't find it funny. I think its ceaseless repetition of daily routine was a bit too close to home for us to laugh at·it.

But surely Mark must have appreciated that there was a farcical irony to this. He was back sleeping in the spare room. The videos were being divided again. Fortunately the George Foreman Lean Mean Fat-Reducing Grilling Machine was still in Mark's Unused Wedding Present box so I was spared another sarcastic diatribe about that. We were even keeping our friends in the dark about what was happening once more. Since none of them knew that we'd got back together, it would have been tricky to tell them that we'd split up again.

We'd decided to stay in the flat while Harry was so fragile. He and Lynn had both been so happy when they heard that Mark had moved back in, that we couldn't tell them the bad news. Eventually Mark would move out again, but not until he could afford to pay for somewhere of his own. It was unthinkable for him to move in with Lynn and Harry after the last time. We agreed that we'd wait at least until Mark had paid them back the rest of the money before landing them with the bombshell of us separating once more.

So here we were, pretending to be living together, properly together, for the sake of Harry and Lynn, and pretending to be living apart, in separate places, for the sake of our friends.

Once, when I was a schoolgirl, Dad and Auntie Lynn had taken me to see a Brian Rix farce in the West End. I'd loved it, of course, with the endless scenes of doors opening and closing with split-second timing, men with trousers falling down to reveal funny socks held up by suspenders, women with enormous blonde perms in baby doll nighties.

But it wasn't plausible, it wasn't supposed to be, and that spoiled the effect a little for me. I could never have guessed that, years later, I would be living in my very own farce. If we were expecting Lynn and Harry, we'd move Mark's stuff back into the master bedroom (that's what I call it to get around the my room/our room dilemma) just in case they peeked round the door. If friends were coming round, we had an efficient system for moving all Mark's stuff out of the bathroom and into a box under the spare room bed.

The message on the answering machine now consisted of me speaking in a professional voice for the benefit of callers offering me work. Lynn and Harry seemed to accept that this was sensible.

Fortunately everyone else's lives were going so badly that nobody had the time to scrutinize our living arrangements more closely.

But I put up with it. And it wasn't difficult because I was seeing Ed again. Well, what else was I supposed to do?

'Did you get the message about the nits?' he asked cheerfully when I called him on Friday from a café in Brixton. 'Hope it wasn't too much of a shock to hear it like that but we kept missing each other on the phone and I needed to let you know as soon as possible.'

I closed my eyes at the memory. 'No problem. I've already treated myself.'

'Great! So we're free to do what we like on Saturday. What did you have in mind?'

'After my less-than-successful choice last week, I think that it's only fair if you choose this time.'

'In that case, I know exactly what we can do. But I'm not going to tell you. It can be a surprise.'

I cringed at the prospect of further surprises. I wanted advance scripts, guarantees and get-out clauses. 'Can you at least give me a clue so I know what to wear?'

'Jeans and T-shirt will be perfect. And sturdy shoes. I'll pick you up at 8 am.'

That meant I had to be outside on the doorstep at 7.30 to avoid him discovering that Mark was living here. Of course I was going to tell Ed all about Mark. When I had to.

'So what are you going to do now?' Alfie asked.

He'd invited me to his favourite café for a fry-up. He said I was looking thin but I think he was just missing our chats. He'd picked me up the evening before to take me to Hammersmith to drop off some tea towels that Auntie Lynn had left behind. It had really just been an excuse to escape the unpleasant atmosphere in the house.

I'd told him everything that had happened. Well, I hadn't been able to confide in Lisa or Maria or Lynn or even Kieran. I watched his eyes widening and narrowing as he did his best to follow all the implications.

He didn't comment, mainly, I expect, because he needed to write everything down in a flowchart, something he did with the plots of *Neighbours*, one of his great passions. 'It makes me feel close to my Katie in Australia,' he'd confessed during one of our earlier jaunts.

Just before the waitress brought us our Jumbo All-Day Specials (with extra fried bread and unlimited cracked mugs of tea) he gave me his painstakingly-considered advice. 'I think the best thing will be to tell everybody the truth.'

'I think that's a very bad idea.'

'What's the worst that can happen?'

I counted on my fingers. 'I can lose all my friends, Harry could die of shock, Lynn will never forgive me, Mark will ask me why I didn't talk to him years ago and Ed will leave me. But apart from that, it's a very good idea.'

The table was suddenly filled with two plates about the size of the Isle of Wight. At least I think they were plates, although there was not an inch of china showing underneath the mass of eggs, bacon, sausage, black pudding, beans, mushrooms, tinned tomatoes and a fortune cookie. A fortune cookie? I picked it up.

'The owner has a brother-in-law,' Alfie explained enigmatically.

I didn't bother asking him to elaborate. He may be my friend but he is still a taxi driver and doesn't know the meaning of a short pithy anecdote. To distract him from beginning his epic tale, I cracked open the cookie and took my fortune out.

BE TELL TRUTHING TO HIMSELF.

165

OK, I know it's a cliché as well as a really bad translation. But it was a strange coincidence leading on from Alfie's pronouncement on truth and I was unusually susceptible this morning. Maybe it was a side-effect from the nit treatment. I'd avoided succumbing to an asthma attack and my hair hadn't caught fire when I stood near an electrical socket but I was seeing meaning in fortune cookies.

Alfie watched me curiously as I fingered the wafer-thin paper. 'What did it say?' he asked.

'Nothing,' I replied. But it wasn't nothing to me.

Mark stayed at work until late. I don't know what he did afterwards but he didn't come home until after midnight when I must have dropped off. I'd tried not to watch the clock – all part of my resolution to stop encroaching.

I thought I'd be awake all night so, when the alarm went off at 6.30, I jumped out of bed in a panic, unsure why I needed to be up so early, unable to remember if Mark and I were separated or back together. My brain appeared to be missing the connections necessary to adapt to the unpredictable. Maybe Andrew My Neighbourhood Pharmacist had a shampoo for that.

Gradually, I remembered that Ed would be picking me up in an hour for a ramble or something. I showered and then spent thirty minutes combing my hair with the electronic nit comb. It was oddly compulsive and calming and my hair had never been so smooth and silky.

It was the first Saturday in October and the first time I'd felt chilly since the summer began. I had to jig about to keep warm outside the flat and I was grateful when Ed arrived ten minutes early.

He jumped out and kissed me affectionately but our noses bumped and my left elbow got in the way of his right arm. I wondered if it would take a further twenty years before this man and I could become as physically attuned as I'd been with Mark.

I'd expected a long journey to get out to the country but it was only three quarters of an hour before we pulled into a narrow opening near Box Hill. Ed parked near a portakabin, appearing very pleased with himself. I got out of the car and looked around. There was a strong smell of horses but that didn't necessarily mean anything.

Ed took my hand and led me along a path to a stable. A woman in an ancient anorak and worn brown cords strode to greet us.

'Edward! Lovely to see you. And this must be Jenny. We've heard a lot about you.' She hugged me warmly.

Ed beamed to see me enjoying the hug. 'Jenny, this is Brenda. She's my very own Auntie Lynn. When my mum died, she helped my dad look after me and my sisters.'

Brenda blushed with pleasure. 'All I did was make huge shepherd's pies, patch up school trousers and play a lot of table tennis. Come on then, Edward has a long day's trekking planned for you.'

'Trekking?'

'Have you ridden before?' she asked as she measured me up for a hat.

'Once, a long time ago.'

Ed was pleased with my answer. 'That's perfect! It'll come right back to you.'

I tried to recollect how I felt about horses and my single riding experience. It was at Exeter when I was still bothering to get involved in my own university life. But I was soon so bound up in the euphoria of my weekends in Bristol and my new circle of friends there that I lost interest.

Ed went back to the car and unpacked his own riding clothes. 'I can't wait to see your face when we get to the top. Last week you took me on your favourite rides, today I'm taking you on mine.' He turned to Brenda. 'Who are you going to give Jenny?'

'I think Toffee would be best. This way, Jenny.'

Toffee. I once had a stuffed panda called Toffee. That had to be a good sign. I followed her across the yard and watched with horror as a boy led a massive brown animal towards us.

'Samson!' Before I could run away screaming, Ed greeted the horse excitedly. Like John Wayne, he pulled himself up into the saddle. I closed my eyes gratefully and allowed my heart to start pumping again, giving Brenda time to bring my little pony through. When I opened my eyes, the sun had been eclipsed by a massive black bulk. When it shook its head, I fully expected trees to be uprooted.

'There . . . there must be some mistake,' I stammered. 'That horse can't be Toffee. With a name like Toffee, he is supposed to be sweet and small, at the very least he should be brown.'

'Toffee is short for Treacle Toffee,' Brenda explained.

167

Well, that was plain deception and I considered prosecuting Brenda under the Trade Description Act. A horse like this ought to be called Satan, just to warn the unsuspecting rider.

'This isn't even a horse,' I pointed out shakily. 'It's some kind of hybrid giant dragon beast that you see in nightmares. He probably breathes fire and eats babies.'

As I babbled on, Brenda was calmly steering me over to some steps. 'Toffee's the best horse for you if you're not very experienced and a bit on the nervous side. Don't be put off by his size, he's a softie.'

As if I was climbing to my execution, I felt my feet moving up the stairs. Then I froze.

'I've just remembered why I only went riding once,' I whispered to Brenda so that Ed wouldn't hear. 'I'm absolutely petrified of horses.'

Brenda placidly put her hands around my foot and guided it into a stirrup. 'You'll be fine, lovey. Now after three, I want you to reach up and put your leg over. One . . .'

'You don't understand. I really, really am petrified. I cannot get on this horse –'

'Two . . .'

'I will probably hyperventilate or have a panic attack. Maybe I'm allergic, that would explain why I feel nauseous now –'

'Three.'

The stable boy had come up behind me and helped Brenda shove my other foot and then my backside over and up onto the monster. I was on a horse. Then the nightmare really began.

'Isn't this great!'

Ed reached out a hand to me but I left mine where they were, hanging on to the reins as if they were my last hold on a cliff edge. 'Great. It's great.' It must have been me who said that but I thought I'd lost the use of all my bodily functions, speech included. I definitely couldn't move my head or my eyes because, if I did, I knew that I would fall off the horse and die. That was a scientific certainty.

'Are you OK, Jen?' Ed asked.

'Great. It's great,' I repeated tightly. Breathe, breathe, breathe.

'Shall we go then?'

'Great. It's great. Um, Brenda? You are coming, too, aren't you?'

'I'll get you started, then I'll leave you to it once you're happy.'

'I will never be happy on this horse. *Never!*' I whispered. 'Do not leave me under any circumstances.' I would have grabbed her hand or even her hair to emphasize my point but I couldn't let go of the reins because, if I did, the horse would shy up on its back legs and throw me across the Surrey landscape severing all four of my limbs in the process. This fact was beyond dispute.

'OK, lovey, whatever you say.'

It wasn't too bad for the next couple of minutes because we were on a flat, narrow track that we had to negotiate slowly. But then the track dipped. It didn't look like much of a descent until I lunged forward.

'Sit up tall, dear,' Brenda instructed evenly, not bothered by the low keening sound I was emitting from deep in my throat, 'or you'll fall off.'

That cheered me up. 'Are we going deep into the bowels of the earth or does it just feel that way?'

'You're doing brilliantly. You've gone down. Once you've gone up an incline and done a bit of trotting, you'll be just fine.'

Going up was like going down except the whiplash was reversed with my neck snapping backwards instead of forwards. 'Would you mind if we skipped the trotting?' I pleaded.

'Nothing to it. Just relax.'

Had this woman been in a parallel universe for the past few minutes? If I could relax, I wouldn't have had a problem. And unless she had some intravenous Valium in her pocket, I did not possess a single muscle that was going to unclench. I was even finding it painful to blink.

'Here we go,' she alerted me.

Trotting was very bad indeed. In fact I refused to believe that was trotting. I think that some all-powerful centrifugal force was being supernaturally applied to me, sending the molecules of my body hurtling outwards.

'How's it going back there?' Ed called five minutes later.

'Great. It's great.' Out of the side of my mouth I hissed at Brenda, 'How much further?'

'About another twenty-four miles,' she replied.

The path widened and Ed waited for me to arrive alongside him. 'You're not enjoying this, are you?' he asked, barely suppressing his laughter.

I was so glad he was having a good time. Maybe he could drip acid onto my naked body later. 'How did you guess?'

'I'm a new man, very perceptive and sensitive,' he answered with his most serious expression. 'Plus your lips are moving in some kind of prayer/chant thing and you have cut off the blood supply to your hands.' He let go of his reins in mock alarm. 'Careful, you nearly smiled! Horses can tell when a rider is smiling. They become possessed with evil equine spirits and start cantering malevolently.'

'You weren't laughing on Rameses Revenge,' I reminded him, wishing he would hold onto his reins.

'I think I'll leave you to it,' Brenda decided.

'No! Please don't!' I begged.

Ed trotted over to me. 'You'll be fine. Unlike on Rameses Revenge, you'll stay upright the whole time and never move at more than four miles per hour. Trust me.'

Brenda must have trusted him because when I dared to move my eyes sidewards, she had gone. Ed reached over to the guiding thingy and made a clicky noise that stirred Toffee back into action.

'Don't you find it amazing that you are sitting on a great, living creature like this?'

'After the experience with nits, I'm off living creatures at the moment.'

'Yes, I'm sorry about that. Hold on, this is a rocky bit.'

If I'd been jumping over Bechers Brook on Red Rum, I don't think I could have been more destabilized by the rocky bit. Using formidable willpower as well as clamping my thighs round Toffee as if I were a champion wrestler, I stayed on.

'I did it!' I had a great surge of satisfaction from my achievement.

'I never had any doubt. It's easy from here.'

'Easier' would be a more accurate term than 'easy'. Side by side we moved very slowly along the path. I found it impossible to relax because we were climbing and I was convinced that I would fall, but I enjoyed being with Ed in an environment that had no associations with any other part of my life. I'd never been riding with Mark or my friends, for good reason, I had to admit. But I was beginning to admit the slim possibility that I could build a new life with new memories and references.

170

I lost all concept of time but my reliable stomach clock was soon informing me that I hadn't eaten for a long time. 'I don't suppose there's a café at the top?' I asked hopefully.

'Not necessary,' Ed replied. 'We're nearly there and all will be revealed.'

The path gradually opened up into a clearing that was blissfully flat. Ed jumped down and tied his horse to a tree before tethering mine.

'Do you need a hand getting off?' he offered.

Stupid question. I needed a fork-lift truck. If I'd thought that sleeping with Ed was as intimate as I could ever get, I was about to be disillusioned. I took my feet out of the stirrups then my body packed up.

'I can't move,' I declared.

'Yes you can. There's a tree stump here – put your left foot on it, then simply bring the other foot over.'

'No, I mean I can't move at all. Even thinking about lifting my leg is agonizing.'

Once Ed grasped the severity of the situation, he went into action. He stood on the tree stump, took hold of my arm, then used all his strength to pull me off the horse, breaking my fall with his own body. We lay there for a few seconds before Ed released a tiny 'ow'.

'Are you hurt?' I asked.

He sat up carefully. 'I'll live. What about you?'

'If you give me food, I might survive.'

After checking that no bones were protruding, he pulled a bag from his horse's saddle. Out of this bag, as if it were bottomless, came a bottle of champagne, a flattened loaf of bread, a slab of cheddar, a packet of butter and a family-size bar of fruit and nut chocolate.

'Fantastic!' I exclaimed, happy for the first time that day. I painfully pulled myself into a sitting position. 'Have you got any glasses?'

Ed groaned. 'Sorry. We'll have to drink out of the bottle.'

Since the alcohol offered my only chance of pain relief up here, I wasn't bothered. I would cheerfully have slashed open an artery and poured the stuff straight in, if necessary. 'Not a problem. But I have to eat first before I faint. Do you have a knife?'

Ed rummaged about in the bag. 'No, but I have some dirty

tissues and a Reader's Digest from nineteen seventy-four. I'm not very good at this, am I?'

'You have food and drink. That's all I need. You'll have to bring it all over here. I really can't move.'

I tore off a chunk of bread, dragged it across the butter and broke off a corner of the cheese. Squashing it all together, I crammed it into my mouth without ceremony. It took some time to chew and swallow but I was revived and restored from the first mouthful. I hadn't been aware that my eyes were closed in ecstasy until I opened them to see Ed watching me with amusement.

'I suppose if you're still hungry after all that, we could kill one of the horses and barbecue it.'

'That's not such a terrible idea. I have to confess I'm not bonding with this particular animal.'

Ed sat next to me and I prepared one of my squashed cheese sandwiches for him. 'You were doing well by the end. I think you're a natural.'

Please God, don't let this man think I am ever going to do this again. We ate until there was not a crumb of bread or cheese left. And even I know that the sight of a woman eating globs of butter from her finger is not going to be appealing so I folded the paper over it and replaced it in Ed's satchel. My hand touched something at the bottom of the bag. I pulled out a toy horse, a pink toy horse.

'Ah.' Ed seemed resigned by my discovery. I just held it up, waiting for an explanation. 'I'd forgotten that was still there.'

'Is it yours?' I asked fatuously. 'Or did you buy it for me after our adventure at Chessington?'

'It belongs to my stepdaughter.'

I made a conscious effort not to react to this. 'Your stepdaughter? I could be mistaken, but I don't think you mentioned a stepdaughter? Or is there more than one?'

'I have one stepdaughter and one stepson.'

'Oh.' Something occurred to me. 'That's where the nits came from?' I felt idiotic. I hadn't even asked myself how Ed might have caught them. The horror of finding scurrying creatures in my hair had precluded any rational investigation. But now it was so obvious.

'I was going to tell you,' Ed explained. 'It was just not that straightforward.'

172

'How could it not be straightforward? Two children – they either exist or they don't.'

'But they're stepchildren. Obviously, if they'd been my own, I would have told you about them immediately.'

Obviously. I wanted to leap up and storm off in a sulk to think this new information through. But I was paralysed, therefore leaping and storming were not options. 'Are you close to them?' I asked miserably.

Ed didn't look at me. 'Yes. I was with Rachel, their mother, for eight years. They were two and three when I moved in so I was effectively their daddy. I miss them a lot.'

We hadn't talked about his divorce since this had been a topic I was keen to ignore whenever possible. 'Out of interest, why did you leave?'

'She left me for someone else, simple as that. So now they have a new stepfather and we haven't yet decided where that leaves me. I see them less and less frequently. I'm not even sure about the correct term for a man in my position. A father remains a father after a divorce but what happens to a stepfather? I have no rights.'

His distress was visible and I wanted to comfort him but I still couldn't move. 'You must miss them,' I said.

Ed nodded. 'You won't believe it but the pain is actually physical.'

I believed it. The pain I felt for a child I might never have was real enough for me. Perhaps this was the right moment to mention why my own marriage broke up. The first time, that is, not the second time which was because of Ed. I decided to take a roundabout approach. 'I can believe it. But one day you'll have kids of your own –'

He didn't let me finish my glowing depiction of family life. 'Not me. Never.'

'What do you mean?' I was shocked by his sudden harshness.

'I'm never going to go through this again. I couldn't. It would be a hundred times worse if they were my own children.'

'But you wouldn't lose them if you were their father?' I argued.

'Don't you read the papers?' he laughed unpleasantly. 'Fathers don't have rights either. A mother can just walk out on her husband when she's bored or fancies a change, take the kids with her, make visiting difficult, provide a new father, emigrate to Australia if she wants.'

173

I struggled to sit up straighter. It was hard to be forceful when I was slumped against a tree stump. 'But it doesn't have to be like that. Lots of families stay together. Lots of marriages work. Why shouldn't yours?'

'Look at the two of us. Neither of us could hold on to our marriage. Over half of my friends are divorced. Even your elderly aunt is threatening it! No, it's too risky. I'm not going to take a chance that I invest all of myself in a family that could be snatched away from me on a whim. I'll stick to being as good a stepfather as I'm allowed to be and, hopefully, an uncle someday.'

He stood up and started packing away the bag. The subject was closed, that was the unspoken message. I tried swivelling on my hips to raise myself to a crouch. I began to cry. From my pain, from Ed's, from the hopelessness of this situation.

'I can't do this,' I sobbed. Ed rushed over to help me to my feet.

'Why are you crying?' he asked. 'Life's not that bad. We've met each other, we're beginning to learn about all the things we don't have in common and it doesn't matter.' He looked worried. 'It *doesn't* matter, does it? That you don't like horses and I will never defy gravity in a theme park again.'

'No, that doesn't matter,' I reassured him. But other things mattered and I didn't know how to tell him.

He kissed me lovingly but he must have felt my body stiffen. 'Where does it hurt?'

'My neck, my back, the tops of my arms, my legs, all of me.' I was still crying, feeling utterly pathetic. 'I'm sorry! I can't get back on the horse, I just can't.'

So we walked all the way back to the stable, Ed leading both horses while I hobbled along, every step sending agonizing spasms right through me. The good thing about this torment was that it distracted me from the truth that Ed didn't want children. But already, my mind was starting to play a trick that I had only recently identified. At least he loved children, I reasoned – his feelings for his stepchildren were proof of that. If he felt confident enough with a woman, maybe she, I, could make him believe that she, I, wouldn't put him through this again. Maybe it wasn't completely desperate.

We didn't talk much on the way back, because I was keeping up a continual flow of guttural noises peppered with some occasional swearing. The good thing about this was that I now felt fully prepared for childbirth. There could be no contraction as strong as the band of suffering that was engulfing my nerve ends. I didn't share this observation with Ed.

By the time we got back, it was 4 o'clock. I was stunned. 'Where did the day go?' I asked.

Ed was grateful that I was now speaking normally. 'That's what happens when you ride – time passes at a different rate. It's the only time I ever feel that I've truly escaped from my reality.'

'Films have the same effect on me,' I agreed.

Ed wasn't convinced. 'But surely films just take you into somebody else's reality. You don't learn anything about yourself.'

'Maybe I don't want to learn anything about myself,' I replied playfully.

Ed stroked my face. 'I think you're worth getting to know. Why not have a go at it yourself?'

It was a major exercise to manoeuvre me into the car. There was a possibility that rigor mortis had set in because, after all the exertions to straighten my arms and legs, I could now no longer bend them. Ed pushed the passenger seat as far back as he could. I then lunged in backwards, banging my head on the gear stick, before Ed climbed in the other side and rotated me round to a semi-reclining position. He kissed my hand fondly. At least my fingernails didn't hurt.

'Can I take it that we are not going to be writhing around in passion on the carpet when we get back?' he asked lightly.

I laughed. 'Personally, I anticipate that I will be writhing around for quite a few days, but the only physical contact I want now is a hot water bottle pressed on my back. Sorry.'

Ed started the car. 'I can manage a hot water bottle and I'll even go to Blockbuster and get a video so that you don't have to make conversation, if you like.'

I glanced at him to make sure he was only teasing. Little dimples in his cheeks that I hadn't noticed before were the giveaway.

After twenty minutes, he pulled into a small pub. 'I presume you're hungry, since it's been a few hours since you ate most of a loaf of bread.'

Yes, I could definitely fall in love with this man, if I hadn't already. We found a table in front of a log fire and had an early

175

dinner of fish pie followed by jam roly-poly and custard. Tentatively, I stretched my arms above my head. They didn't extend fully but I now believed that a full recovery was possible.

'I've never seen the point in drugs,' I declared. 'I can't believe that Ecstasy or a joint could make me feel any better than a plate of good food.'

Ed helped me to my feet. 'I'm pleased I'm not going to have to track down some dreadlocked hippy in Brixton to feed "your habit". When you get desperate for a fix, I can just dash to Waitrose.'

It was easier to get back into the car and, as Ed drove off, I took his hand and placed it lightly on my knee. We listened to a Billy Joel CD and I wondered if it had any special significance for him.

It took me back to university days and the weekends when Mark and I used to stay awake most of the night, just enjoying the freedom of being in a tiny single bed together, talking endlessly. What did we talk about? I asked myself. Possibly Jean-Paul Sartre, a passion of mine, or the early developments of computer programming, Mark's subject. A vague memory suggested that we discussed everything, trivial and important, but I couldn't picture it. We didn't talk about marriage or children, or what we would be doing when we were thirty-eight. What else was there?

I felt myself being sucked back into the past, suddenly wanting to retrace my footsteps, look for the clues of where we went wrong, correct the mistakes. But, as the car crawled along a busy Fulham Road, an odd sight caught my eye.

'That's odd,' I mumbled.

'What?'

'I just saw Maria and Lisa in a restaurant back there.'

Ed looked bewildered. 'What's odd about that? They're both your friends.'

'Yes, but they're not supposed to be friends with each other.' He couldn't possibly understand that this was all wrong. It was one thing for them to go out together and check out a restaurant in preparation for my date with a potential psychopath. But what reason could they have for being out tonight?

Maria was the one who'd accused me of encroaching and now here she was encroaching on my other friendships.

'Why is this a problem?' Ed was trying hard to comprehend my objection.

'Because I tell them different things and they both know different things about me and that's the way I like it.' Even I could hear that I was sounding petulant. 'Look, would you mind if I go back to my flat tonight? I think I need to sleep in my own bed after today, just to give my back a chance to recover.'

'Sure,' Ed grinned. 'I can give you just as good a massage there as at my flat.'

'You can't stay!'

Ed flinched. 'Why not?'

Because my husband is living with me and not living with me at the same time. After Ed's revelation about his stepchildren that had drained us both emotionally, I didn't feel that now was the right time to explain about Mark. I hadn't prepared a plausible story either.

'I just can't face being sociable tonight. I want a long bath and to cover myself in foul-smelling cream to numb my muscles.'

He was going to argue with me but something in the set of my face must have made him see that there would be no point. I could tell he was angry with me and we spent the rest of the journey in silence.

When we pulled up outside the flat, I was relieved to see that none of the lights were on. During one of our curt exchanges of information that passed for communication nowadays, Mark had said that he was going to meet up with Kieran this evening. He was obviously still out.

'Can I at least come in to use your bathroom?' Ed asked.

I had no choice but to agree. I tried to look welcoming as I opened the front door. I had no idea what to expect but, hopefully, there would be no incriminating boxer shorts across the living room. We'd been careful to keep the flat looking immaculately bare and tidy in case we had unexpected visitors.

It didn't matter anyway, because Ed seemed uninterested in the accessories. He hurried to the bathroom, which gave me a few moments to ensure that there were no tell-tale signs of Mark's presence.

Once my check was complete, I lowered myself inch by inch onto the sofa. At once I was free from pain and resolved to sit here for a year, folding paper and enjoying my solitude. I was interrupted from the reverie by a worry about Ed. He'd been gone a long time.

177

I dragged myself out of the sofa and limped towards the bathroom. 'Are you OK in there?'

The door swung open and Ed almost knocked me over as he stomped out.

'At least I know why you weren't keen for me to come in.'

I glanced past him into the bathroom. I couldn't see any shaving things out. And even if there had been some debris, it would have been simple to explain away as having been left behind when Mark moved out.

'What is it?' I asked, following Ed as he strode angrily into the living room. When he turned round, he was holding one of the bottles of nit shampoo. On it was a post-it note that I'd completely forgotten writing. Ed held it up although, by now, I knew what it said. MARK, DON'T FORGET YOU NEED TO DO THIS ASAP. SORRY. J.

Since he hadn't been talking to me after our fight, I'd had to leave notes for him and this had seemed particularly important.

Ed reread it for himself even though he must now surely know the contents by heart. 'You see, what I don't understand is how you gave your husband nits when you'd separated.'

Before he stormed out, he returned to the bathroom, slamming the shampoo back on the shelf with such force that the glass broke.

So there we have it. My husband had left me because I caught nits from another man. And the other man left me because I passed them on to my husband.

It would make a terrible musical.

Chapter Twelve

It was Saturday night and everything was bad. I'd found some painkillers and some wine. That helped. If only I could find a good therapist in one of the cupboards, then all my troubles would be addressed. Mark and I always believed that shrinks were a waste of space, that they were only of any use to sad people who didn't have any friends. Well, guess what?

Of course, I had friends. Mark had been my best but I'd lost him despite all our intentions that nothing would change. Lisa was out with Maria and neither of them was answering their mobile phones. Kieran was out with Mark so that eliminated him. I couldn't possibly call Tally even though I'd lost most of my hostility towards her. Everything she had said was true. She had done nothing that I had any right to condemn. When she'd slept with Mark at university, she didn't even know I existed. And by the time she began approaching him again, I'd left him. What right did I have to complain?

And, when seen in the light of my own recent behaviour, she was looking relatively virtuous. Maybe I'd call her one day when this had blown over, and we could join a support group for slappers. I could set up an origami subdivision.

I suppose I could have called Phil – he had expressed gratitude for bringing his marital problems to a head. But I couldn't face him. I'd hurt him so carelessly, without any hesitation and I didn't want to be reminded of what I'd become.

Auntie Lynn was off-limits. She and Harry were to be left in peace, secure in their delusion that Mark and I were blissfully reconciled.

So how did this all happen? I thought I had lots of friends but, when I thought about it, I had Mark and a few friends. Maria seemed to have dozens.

'That's what happens when you grab the first man who comes along,' Maria always insisted. 'If it hadn't been for Mark, you'd have made lots of mates at Exeter, you'd have had lots of boyfriends who would have introduced you to other people, you'd have done lots of different jobs and formed a whole series of relationships everywhere you worked. You might even have met someone else, and be married with kids by now. Then you'd have hordes of scary PTA mums to coerce you into selling raffle tickets. But instead, you gave yourself entirely to one person and the small number of people around him. You've effectively not stepped out of your little circle since you were eighteen. Apart from me.'

'But I don't want an address book stuffed with the names of everyone I've ever stood at a photocopier with,' I would argue. 'I would hate a calendar like yours, having to go out every night, week after week just to maintain all these spurious friendships. I like staying in most of the time. What's wrong with that?'

Nothing's wrong with that. Until your marriage breaks down and your select band of friends switch off their phones.

Then you have no choice. You have to phone your taxi driver.

'Alfie, you look terrible.'

'It's just a touch of flu, that's all.'

'Well, I'm here now; let me come and heat you up some soup.' I heaved the three stuffed carrier bags onto his kitchen table.

'Blimey, love, where did you get all this stuff at this time of night?'

'I had to hail a cab and, before you ask, the driver was nowhere near as nosy as you. I got him to take me to an organic supermarket in Lavender Hill, then to a pharmacist at Clapham Junction that stays open late on a Saturday.'

'You didn't need to go to all this trouble.' But he didn't have the energy to put up a fight.

'Haven't you got anyone nearby who looks in on you?' I asked, horrified by the near-empty cupboards and fridge.

Alfie was offended. 'You make me sound as if I'm a hundred and need the local Women's Institute to come round and force-feed me cake. I'm a London cabbie. That makes me indestructible. I've just got a bug, that's all. I'll be fine in a day or so.'

180

But he sank back into his chair and let me flap around him. I got him some soup and found a tray for him to use. I could see it was an effort for him to eat. 'I've got you some Guinness, as well, to build you up.'

'That's more like it.' He drank it with enthusiasm and it even seemed to help him finish the soup. As he worked his way through the large bowl, I wandered round the tiny sitting room, fascinated by the hundreds of photos on the wall.

'Is this your wife and daughter?' I pointed at an enlarged portrait that, judging by the fashions, had been taken about twenty years ago. It could have been me and Auntie Lynn, or even me and my mum, if only she'd lived longer. They looked so alike, so close.

'That's my favourite picture,' Alfie said softly.

I found another one where Alfie had his arm draped protectively around his wife's shoulder. 'I like this one. She looks so safe and happy.'

'That one over there on the sideboard is the latest of my Katie and my grandchildren.'

I picked it up. It was a classic tourist pose in front of Ayer's Rock. The woman was pretty but very thin. I assumed that the man beside her was the husband that Alfie despised. He didn't have kind eyes. I'd never realized how important they were until I saw a face without them. Mark had kind eyes. So did Ed.

They had three children, all of whom looked remarkably like Katie and her mother. The glass of the frame was gleaming as if it had been polished every day.

'Have you ever seen the children?' I asked.

Alfie perked up. 'No, but I've been saving and I'm planning to fly out there this Christmas.'

I poured him another Guinness. 'All the more reason to get you better,' I urged.

He ate and drank compliantly. Some colour was returning to his face. 'So what's been happening to you this week? Now that I'm ill, I've got the time to concentrate on this, so there's a chance I may be able to understand it all.'

I told him everything, enjoying the liberation of not having to filter any of the details. This must be what it's like to be completely honest. Even with Mark, I'd held things back, not deliberately but automatically. I'd done it to protect him from confrontation, or me from an unwelcome truth.

181

'And I was the only one available on a Saturday night?' Alfie concluded.

I reddened. 'That's not why I came.'

Alfie patted my hand. 'I know it's not, love, and I'm glad you came, but you should be with someone else.'

I looked at him. 'Who?'

'Why don't you go home and work it out?'

I didn't want to be alone – I'd worked that much out. I was even looking forward to Mark coming home. My back and legs were feeling even worse after all the lifting and carrying. I took some more painkillers and drank some more wine, then sat up watching late-night television for hours with the sound down. Even German game shows were watchable without the volume. At some point I must have fallen asleep, because I was woken by the phone. Peering at the clock, I saw that it was 9 o'clock.

My muscles had seized up again overnight. I fell off the sofa onto the floor and employed a clumsy commando crawl to reach the phone before the machine picked up.

'Jenny, sweetheart, it's Auntie Lynn.'

Not more bad news. 'Is everything all right?'

'I wish you'd stop asking that all the time. Harry is going to be fine and so am I. That's why I'm calling. We want to talk to you and Mark over lunch today.'

I looked around me. Mark hadn't come home last night. 'I'm not sure if we can.'

'But you must! You said you weren't doing anything today.'

I must be getting old as well as having a breakdown if I was now forgetting entire conversations. 'When did I say that?'

'Maybe Mark told Harry, I don't know.'

I'd forgotten that she still believed we were still two halves of a single unit, each capable of speaking on behalf of the other.

'Oh. Then I'm sure it will be fine.' I wasn't sure of anything but I was becoming good at acting as if I was.

'Lovely. One o'clock then. Bye.'

The first thing I did was take some more painkillers and lie down on the floor until they kicked in. I had the phone next to me so the time wouldn't be wasted. I called Mark on his mobile. It was switched off so I left an urgent message asking him to call me as soon as he heard this.

182

Then I phoned Kieran. His mobile was switched off too. The pair had probably got drunk and crashed out in their office. It had happened a couple of times in the past when they were celebrating new contracts. I left a message for him as well. 'Hi Kieran. It's Jenny. It's Sunday morning and I'm trying to get hold of Mark. If he's with you or you know where he is, can you get him to contact me urgently. Thanks. By the way, you haven't called me for ages. I miss you. Bye.'

I didn't mean to sound so needy. I just ached all over and wanted someone to look after me or just talk to me until I stopped hurting. And I did miss him. I'd grown to look forward to our long calls. There was something about the phone, the distance, that permitted us to be more open than we would have dared to be face to face.

As I lay on the floor, I replayed our last chat some weeks earlier. Somehow or other he'd got onto the subject of marriage, even though it was months after my wedding.

'I can't think of one good reason why you married Mark or why you even stayed with him all these years,' he'd joked.

'It would be too complicated for us to spilt up – imagine the fights over the videos. So tell me why you married Lisa?' I asked him, teasingly. 'Was it because you needed your wardrobe organized by season, colour and collar shape and your spices placed in alphabetical order in the rack?'

'You mustn't ever tell her, but I have no memory of proposing to her. At some stage, folders appeared in my life, laminated with labels headed TABLE PLANS and PRESENTS. She was working for that fashion magazine at the time and somehow managed to borrow a £10,000 dress for herself and a full dress suit for me.'

I chuckled. 'She's always been good at persuading people to do things for her.'

'I think they're so amazed at her gall that they go along with her requests and it's only afterwards that they feel resentful. You know that everyone who works with her loathes her? I think that's why I married her.' He sounded surprised by his own deduction. 'That sounds all wrong. I loved her, of course I did. But I think I went along with the wedding so that I wouldn't hurt her feelings.'

I wasn't surprised by his admission. 'Don't feel bad, my motives were no more hearts-and-flowers than yours. Think about it. I wanted a baby. I married the nearest man.'

183

'If I'd known it was down to geography, I'd have moved next door,' Kieran said lightly.

I couldn't contain my sarcasm. 'Of course you'd have married me, Kieran. Because marriage to me would be so much easier than to Lisa. Apart from the fact that you hate tacky films and games and fast food and every other element of my lifestyle.'

'Ah, but maybe I would have decided that you were worth it!'

I played along. 'Ah, but would I have decided that *you* were worth it?'

Kieran sighed dramatically. 'Probably not. But maybe twenty years ago, if I'd asked you –'

I mimicked his sigh. 'A bit late to wonder about that . . .'

Funny. I can't remember where the conversation went after that. But shortly after that, I began pushing Mark on the subject of children, ultimately pushing him into divorce.

I must have fallen asleep again. The next time the phone rang it was deafeningly loud because it was next to my ear. I picked it up, finding it impossible to believe that it really was 11.55 as the clock was insisting.

'Hello?'

'It's me.'

'Mark!' I sat up carefully. The spasms were easing. 'Where are you? Oh, forget it. Did you know we're supposed to be having lunch at Harry and Lynn's at one o'clock?'

'No, we can't. I can't. I've just had a massive fry-up with Kieran and I've got a really bad hangover. I only just picked up your message.'

I was exasperated. 'Why didn't you switch your phone on sooner? Or Kieran?'

'I hadn't realized that the phone was switched off. And Kieran's lost his.'

Great. 'Well, there's no time to debate the matter. They've got something important to tell us, so you'll have to make an effort.'

'But –'

'We'll meet at the bus stop down the road from their house so we look as if we've arrived together.'

'But –'

'Think of your dad's heart.' I slammed the phone down.

Today had to be an improvement on yesterday. At least I could walk.

'My goodness, you both look terrible!'

'Thanks, Auntie Lynn, you look lovely too.'

Mark shook his father's hand. Harry poured a very large sherry and gave it to his son. That was the father/son bonding concluded.

Lynn wasn't going to let me off so easily. 'So tell me what you two have been up to that's made you look like that?'

'We went to a party.'

'We went to a show.'

It was nice to know that we were still perfectly synchronized. Now all we had to do was read from the same scripts and we might just pull this off.

'We went to a show and then on to a party,' I clarified.

Lynn and Harry looked puzzled. We were saved by a timer going off in the kitchen. 'That'll be lunch!' Lynn announced. 'It's roast beef and Yorkshire pudding, your favourite. Mark's too.'

Mark's eyes became misty. 'Come on,' I hissed. 'And you'd better eat everything or they'll know something is wrong.'

Lynn circled the table with platters. It seemed to us both as if she'd never stop. 'Three Yorkshires each, because I know how much you both love them. Plenty of roasties. Oh take another one Mark; I made them crispy the way you like them . . . parsnip purée with double cream as it's a special occasion . . . I sautéed the carrots with some cashews . . . and here's a whole boar stuffed with thirty-six quails.'

Maybe I imagined the last bit although, if there'd been any more room on the table, I'm sure Lynn would have continued to fill it.

'So what show did you see?' Harry asked.

'*Chicago.*'

'*Fame.*'

Brilliant. 'We wanted to see *Chicago* but it was sold out –'

'So we booked tickets to see that . . . next week . . . and we went to see *Fame* instead.' Mark was catching on.

I reached for the jug of water and cried out as my shoulder seized up.

'What have you done to your arm?' Lynn asked.

'I just overdid the decorating,' I blurted out without thinking.

Mark blinked several times and I realized how implausible the lie was. Well, maybe that's good. I'd never been a good liar and had been uncomfortable at the number of deceptions I'd been forced to maintain in recent weeks. My ongoing ineptitude was surely a sign that I was still, essentially, a decent person. But I'd have to give Mark a different story later. There was no point upsetting him about my day with Ed when it wasn't going to be repeated. We still lived in the same flat and I wanted to avoid as much unpleasantness as I could. There would be enough unpleasantness that I wouldn't be able to avoid.

'Finish that up, Mark. I've done you a bread-and-butter pudding for afters.' Lynn was too busy checking all the plates to spot Mark turning pale.

I couldn't let it continue. In my eternal cycle of blame and self-blame, I was currently deeply entrenched in the self-blame category. 'Lynn, Mark's being polite. He didn't want to hurt your feelings because you've gone to so much trouble, but he's got a stomach bug.'

'Oh Mark, you silly boy!' Lynn rushed round the table to hug him. He smiled at me in gratitude, one of our old smiles.

'Would you like to read the paper in the other room?' his dad offered, a veritable emotional outburst for him.

'I'll be fine if I could just stop eating for now.'

Lynn stroked his back, not a sensible action under the circumstances. 'The rest of us have finished, so why don't we go into the conservatory? I'll wrap up the pudding and you can freeze it for another day. Harry, you go and make coffee. I'll bring the plates through. Off you go, you two, and make yourselves comfortable.'

Mark and I made our way out of the dining room very slowly, each of us suffering in our own way.

'Thanks for that,' Mark whispered. 'Out of interest, what did you do to yourself?'

'I pulled a couple of muscles taking some shopping round to Alfie's.' I recounted the story, emphasizing the weight of the bags I carried and missing out the part about the Derby I ran during the day. I wished I'd had the foresight to use this excuse on Lynn – it was so plausible, I believed it myself.

Mark looked confused. 'So why didn't you tell Lynn that? She can't possibly have a problem with your friendship with an elderly taxi driver.'

Good point. Next time I embark upon a career as a serial deceiver, I will remember to plan credible stories for all contingencies. In fact, maybe that's a career in itself. First-time adulterers might pay handsomely for someone to write consistent, unshakeable narratives to cover their infidelities.

Mark was still waiting for a reply while I was considering this employment opportunity. I couldn't tell him that the first lie was clumsy and unrehearsed and that the second was the result of having a little more time to think. 'I didn't know what I was saying or why,' I admitted. It was an unusual display of honesty and Mark nodded, apparently understanding this total bemusement at a situation that made no sense at all.

If he wasn't convinced that I was telling him the whole story, he was too tired and hungover and nauseous to push further.

We picked up a Sunday paper each, the way we always did at Harry and Lynn's, intrigued by their combination of the *News of the World* and the *Sunday Times*. As was traditional, I showed him a picture of Jude Law that made him look as if his hair was receding. To return the favour, he showed me a picture of Jennifer Aniston looking fabulous with no make-up, flat shoes and tatty jeans.

I'd miss this. The pain I experienced on realizing it was far worse than the ache in my back. All the tablets and sherry in the world wouldn't make me miss Mark any less.

Lynn and Harry came in with even more apparatus than we'd imposed on them, that dreadful day when we told them we were getting a divorce. It was part of the ritual, one of the many rituals the two of them shared, their equivalent of me choosing the video while Mark loaded the popcorn maker.

Lynn arranged the cups and saucers; Harry poured. Lynn handed the coffee out; Harry offered the biscuits. Then Lynn sat on the winged cane chair and Harry perched on the arm of the ancient sagging couch alongside. Mark and I winked happily at each other. Everything here was as it always was and we were going to do nothing to spoil it.

Lynn placed a proprietary hand on her husband's arm. 'Shall I tell them or will you?'

'Since when have you allowed him to do any talking, Auntie Lynn?' I commented.

She glared at me affectionately. 'OK. Now Harry and I have

been doing a lot of talking since he was in hospital and we've decided that the time has come for him to retire, for both if us to retire.'

'About time too!' Mark raised his cup in a toast.

Lynn continued. 'So we're going to sell the garden centre and the house – everything – and move to Spain.'

We were both stunned. 'Isn't that a bit impulsive?' I asked. I didn't mean to sound rude but, after a lifetime spent avoiding extremes, I was finding the constant stream of surprises increasingly difficult to handle.

Harry cleared his throat. 'Not really. It was the consultant's idea. The climate will be good for us both. We can play golf, do some gardening, swim. And you can come out whenever you like.'

'Anyway, the decision's been made,' Lynn added, guessing that we would have our objections. 'But we've got more money than we need. Now obviously that would all come to the pair of you when we die, but we think it might be of more use to you now. So when all the formalities have been finished, we're giving you two hundred and fifty thousand pounds.'

While we were absorbing this news, Harry intervened. 'It turns out I didn't even need to remortgage the house to loan you that money, Mark. We both had all sorts of insurance plans and policies that had matured. Anyway, none of that's important. We should have released all the cash before we move after Christmas and we don't mind what you do with it.'

'Put it in the business, start a new one, buy a new house, have lots of babies. Whatever you want.'

So we can do whatever we want? Maybe now would be a good time to decide what that would be.

We sat on the sofa in my flat, our flat, still reeling from the shock.

'This solves all our problems,' I said, gloomily. 'Apart from all the money, after Christmas we can forget all this pretence of being together. I mean, I think I can keep it up until then; what about you?'

Mark took an age to answer. 'I think it's a sign or a gift or something. We're being given a second chance and I want to take it.'

I scratched my head. I wasn't sure if I'd ever stop after the nits horror. 'I don't understand. Are you saying you want us to get back together? Again?'

He moved his hand closer to mine but didn't quite touch it. 'I was already thinking about it last night. Kieran and I talked, really talked, for the first time since we've known each other, mainly about you. He thought I was crazy to let you go and said that if you were prepared to forgive me for Tally, even though that was years ago, I ought to do the same about . . . him.'

Thank you, Kieran, I whispered to myself. 'And?'

Mark took my hand. 'I wasn't interested but I couldn't get to sleep despite being smashed and, after lying awake for hours, I knew that he was right.'

I held my breath. 'Just like that?'

Mark smiled. 'Not quite just like that. But when Dad told us about moving and the money, I knew what we had to do. Once they are in Spain, it will be just you and me. I don't know about you, but I felt a little –' he became embarrassed '– scared about this.' He coughed loudly to separate himself from the emotion. 'I miss you, Jen. I don't know what to do with myself without you. Does that make any sense?' Oh yes. 'So why don't we see if we can really try and make things work between now and Christmas? We have to make some serious plans with the money anyway so let's use the time for ourselves as well.'

I was amused. 'You mean, instead of a trial separation, a trial reconciliation?'

'Exactly! So what do you think?'

Sitting on this sofa reminded me of the previous night spent lying here alone. That wasn't how I wanted to live. I'd blown it with Ed and, frankly, I couldn't face the prospect of more Eds, dinners spent not knowing what to say, days struggling to find anything at all you might have in common, the terror that it would all end.

'I think it's a wonderful idea,' I agreed softly, wanting to lock the door, draw the curtains and pretend that the past month had been a bad dream. My doubts must have been visible.

'But one thing will be different,' Mark insisted. 'We'll be completely honest, no more secrets or lies. And we'll talk, talk properly, I mean.'

'I'd like that,' I agreed. I wasn't sure I did agree but I felt that I ought to. What sort of person didn't believe in truth and honesty? The motto from the fortune cookie suddenly appeared in my memory, shining like a clumsy motif in a bad film. I blinked to dislodge it. 'Erm, if we're going to be open right from the start, I suppose we have to mention the baby issue.' I raised my hand to stop him impulsively suggesting something he'd regret. 'But before you say anything, I think we should put the topic on hold for the next few months, sort ourselves out first.'

I thought he was going to fall at my feet in gratitude but he showed awesome restraint and simply placed his hands on his head, an unconscious acknowledgement of being granted remission.

Then a more familiar objection sprang to mind. 'We do, however, still have the same problem we had before with our friends. Kieran might have felt obliged to encourage us to get back together but we both know that we would not be very popular if we're the only ones to emerge from this living happily ever after.'

Mark's eyes were shining. 'I've thought of that too! Look at us. Only weeks ago our marriage was over, completely beyond repair. But we've found a way to mend it.' He spotted my scepticism. 'OK. Maybe we haven't actually mended it, but we've started the healing process. So why shouldn't we do the same for our friends?'

I raised my eyebrows. 'Promise them a quarter of a million pounds and some nit shampoo?'

'Fix their marriages! Between us I know we can do it.'

He wasn't aware that I also had a problem with Maria, who was looking forward to the two of us becoming a heat-seeking, man-searching team. I decided to keep this poser to myself, shuddering at the prospect of the singles disco I was expected to enjoy in two days. The rest seemed easy to sort by comparison. 'And when we've "fixed their marriages"?'

'We can have Christmas the way we always have: Christmas Eve at Tally and Phil's, Christmas lunch at Lisa and Kieran's, then all of us will go over to Harry and Lynn for their final Christmas night party before they move to Spain. We'll announce that we're back together. Everyone will weep and sing *Auld Lang Syne* or something. It will be perfect, the same as ever and, afterwards, we can carry on as if none of this had ever happened.'

It sounded simple when he put it like that.

Chapter Thirteen

We slept separately that night, not because of any awkwardness but because I was still in agony and Mark had appalling indigestion that could only be eased by lying perfectly still on his back.

I woke up first, going through my new routine of determining where I was, where Mark was and the current status of our marriage. I peeked in the spare room, just to make sure he was really there, no longer trusting my own computations. I stopped myself from tiptoeing in, joining him under the duvet and dissolving into him.

I was putting the kettle on when my mobile phone beeped announcing that I had a text. I tensed at this, still convinced that I was going to dispatch air ambulances to Kilimanjaro with one careless press of a key. I didn't recognize the number on the display.

MEET ME AT THE RITZ FOR BREAKFAST 10 AM. IMPORTANT. K. XXX

Damn. It was already 9.20. He probably thought that Mark was on his way to work. I had to text him back to tell him I couldn't make it and that I'd explain later. I heard Mark stirring which probably made me careless, or maybe it was my general incompetence but I pressed something that erased Kieran's original message. Unfortunately that was my only record of his new mobile phone number and I had no other way of contacting him.

I felt Mark's arms slide around my waist, making me jump. I dropped the phone into my bag, feeling guilty and ridiculous at the same time. He turned me round and kissed me affectionately. I worked hard to ignore the memory it stirred of Ed's kisses.

'How are you feeling?' I asked.

'Better. And you?'

'Better. Are you going into the office?' I asked casually.

'I have to. Kieran is out looking at some new suppliers he found on the Internet. Otherwise I would have suggested we spend the morning together.'

Before he found a way to justify this, I came up with a hasty excuse. 'That would have been nice but I have a meeting this morning.'

'Wow, you're really making a success of your origami now. We'll have to think of a way we can use Dad and Lynn's money to help you get yourself established.' He stroked my hair sadly. 'I've held you back, haven't I? If you hadn't been spending all that time helping me out, you could have launched yourself years ago.'

'Please don't feel guilty,' I begged. Right now, I'm using up our joint quota of guilt for the morning. Less than twenty-four hours into our new life which was going be governed by the overriding principle of honesty, and I was lying. 'Right now my workload is growing as fast as I can manage it. You need to sort out the company. The money can be used better there.'

He kissed me again before disappearing for his shower. That would be the last lie I told him, I vowed.

I couldn't deny it was exciting to stroll into the Ritz in my purple dress and jewelled shoes. In honour of the location, I'd had a go at blow-drying my hair the way the stylist had showed me at the photographic shoot and even put on some make-up, more than usual, that is.

Kieran was sitting at a corner table reading the *Guardian*. He could have been eighteen and sitting in the university coffee shop with a plastic cup of coffee and a doughnut. He looked the same to me and I wished I could go back to rethink my choices more carefully. I didn't know if I'd make different ones, but I'd consider the long-term consequences more seriously.

He must have sensed my approach because he looked up and grinned to see me. He stood up, knocking the table and sending some of the cutlery flying. A waiter appeared as if from a puff of smoke to replace them.

'You don't need to do that,' I told the waiter cheerfully. 'This floor is cleaner than a hospital. I drop cutlery all the time at home and use it – and my floor is filthy!'

He looked mortified and, probably wisely, ignored me. Despite my protests, he arranged the new knives and forks with mathematical precision on the table.

Kieran kissed me warmly. I could tell that he wasn't back with Lisa. He was wearing a yellow shirt with blue cord trousers and the jokey Super Nerd tie we'd given him for Christmas a few years earlier.

'You got my text!' he exclaimed. 'I was worried you wouldn't see it in time but this was a last-minute idea.'

I sat down and picked up a menu, already starving. 'You nearly left it too late. If it hadn't been for me losing the message, I would have called you to cancel.'

'Then this was obviously meant to be.'

I glanced up sharply at the wistful tone. 'Why did you choose the Ritz?' I asked. 'If you were looking for somewhere that we wouldn't be seen, there are hundreds more playgrounds in London we could be working our way through.'

Kieran played with his tie nervously. 'I thought we might have something to celebrate.'

I needed food before I could deal with this. I signalled to the waiter, who seemed to have forgotten that I was a slattern and was bringing clean napkins even though I hadn't blown my nose on the first one.

'Can I have the English breakfast, please? With everything? Plus tea, orange juice and lots of toast.' The waiter beamed, my appetite clearly making up for my slovenliness.

Kieran ordered the same. I turned towards him. 'Right, now what's the good news that we're going to celebrate? Let me guess. You're going back to Lisa so that she can cull your ties and measure you up for your designer baby-papoose.'

He became pale. 'Actually, I haven't spoken to Lisa since she threw me out. I've been spending the last few days thinking.'

'About Lisa, I hope?' I picked up a croissant and began buttering it liberally.

'About you, actually. Us.'

I put the croissant down, my appetite diminishing rapidly. 'What about me? Us?'

'I wouldn't have said anything, honestly, but when Mark told me that you would definitely never get back together, I knew this would be my only chance.'

'Kieran . . .' I began.

He grabbed my hand clumsily. 'Please let me say this before I lose my nerve! Jenny, I've always loved you, ever since that first day you came to Bristol.'

My stomach lurched. 'Kieran –'

'Please. I'm ashamed to say that I was glad when I found out about him and Tally back then. To me it meant that he didn't care about you and I was sure you'd soon realize this. I even toyed with the idea of telling you myself. I planned to be there to pick up the pieces.'

'I wish you had,' I whispered.

'What would you have done?' he asked hopefully.

I looked down at my hand in his, trying to imagine what my life would have been like if it had always been there, instead of Mark's. I should have pulled it away but I didn't. 'That's a crazy question and absolutely pointless! It was twenty years ago and you didn't tell me. Now you're married to my best friend and about to become a father and I'm trying to repair my marriage to your best friend.'

He slowly withdrew his hand. 'Mark was adamant that he wouldn't be going back to you.'

I twisted my mouth wryly. 'Apparently, you managed to talk him into it.'

Kieran stared up at the lavish chandeliers dotted around the ornate ceiling. 'I can't believe I did that.'

It was my turn to take his hand now. 'You did it because you're my friend and it was the right thing to do.'

'But it wasn't what I wanted.'

'Since we're friends, I'll let you into a secret. I don't know if it was what I wanted either. But nothing can happen between us now. Not now that Lisa is pregnant.'

'So are you saying that, if things were different . . .?'

'Madame!' The waiter ceremoniously placed a large plate in front of me. He'd taken my request for 'everything' literally and was now offering me enough calories to sustain an entire SAS regiment on an Antarctic trek. Ten minutes earlier, I could have demolished it with ease. Now I felt queasy at the prospect of a boiled egg. Kieran looked as unhappy as I felt when he got his plate.

Since neither of us could think of anything that would make the other feel any better, we picked up our forks with resignation.

194

It was like the fairy tale of the Magic Porridge Pot that never became empty, no matter how much you ate.

Exhausted from the food and the emotion, we both gave up at the same time. But the experience had dissolved the tension between us, as if we'd just survived a plane crash together. We had somehow clawed our way back to the almost easy friendship we had been enjoying before his disastrous revelation.

'That waiter is going to be really disappointed in us, in you especially,' Kieran said.

I leaned forward conspiratorially. 'I know. I can't bear to let him down. Hold on a second.' I reached into my handbag, pulled out a wad of tissues and passed a couple to Kieran. I held mine out of sight under the table.

'What are these for?' he asked.

I scanned the area around me to make sure that nobody was looking, then swept the contents of my plate into the hankie. I smoothly transferred it into my bag. Kieran followed suit just as our waiter returned. In desperation, he thrust the package into his trouser pocket.

The waiter's expression was inscrutable as he took the empty plates away. We both began to giggle when he'd gone.

'Look at your trousers!' I exclaimed.

The yolk from a fried egg had seeped through the pocket. Kieran dabbed at it gingerly. 'Yeeuch. A perfect end to a perfect morning!'

The waiter returned with the bill and two boxes. 'For the left-overs,' he explained, coughing discreetly.

We were still chuckling on the tube back. 'What are you going to do now?' I asked.

'I'll go home and change out of these trousers, then go and drag Lisa out to lunch, and beg her to take me back.'

I hugged him amicably. 'I'm pleased.'

And I was 100 per cent certain that Lisa would be pleased too – 90 per cent anyway.

There was someone in the flat. I couldn't believe that Lynn had left Harry again so, by deduction, it had to be Mark.

It was Phil. Did everybody have keys to my flat, I mean, our flat? He was unpacking a box of legal books onto our dining-room table. A lot of books. 'Phil! What are you doing here?'

195

'Mark said it would be OK for me to stay here for a few days.'
'Did he?'

Phil's face dropped. 'Didn't you know? I'm so sorry. I'll go back to the hotel.' He started putting the books back into the box.

'No, no. I was just surprised, that's all. It'll be lovely to have you.'

'I thought it might actually help. Mark explained that he's only staying here to make his dad think you're back together. It must be uncomfortable for the two of you so, maybe, a third person will take some of the awkwardness away.'

Right. 'Look, I just have to pop out and get some milk. I'll be back in a minute.' Without waiting for him to discuss this, I dashed out and called Mark from my mobile.

'Why didn't you tell me that you'd invited Phil to stay?'

'It was an impulse. I was going to tell you later. I didn't think you'd be back so soon.'

'Yes, but why is he here? I thought we were supposed to be spending time together. And we can't even be nice to each other because he still thinks we're getting a divorce.'

Mark lowered his voice to maintain the air of secrecy although I knew that Kieran wasn't there yet. 'He was starting to enjoy living in that hotel and we didn't want him to develop a taste for the single life. I'm going to work on him, persuade him to go back to Tally. And you're going to work on Tally.'

I laughed out loud. 'We're such good friends now that she's bound to listen to me!'

'You have to try. You've known each other a long time; that counts for something.'

I was outside the corner shop where I had to buy milk even though I didn't need it. 'I'll see what I can do. But you haven't forgotten that I'm out tonight?'

'Of course not. That's why I asked Phil to move in today, so we can have a good old talk. I can't imagine it'll be easy, so stay out as late as you can. You're going for a quiet drink with Maria, aren't you?'

Not quite.

It was called Kittenz. The 'z' should have warned me. So should the pink neon hearts that adorned the façade. And all the exclamation marks on the big sign screaming:

196

WOMEN!
FREE ADMISSION!
FIRST DRINK FREE!
FREE T-SHIRTS!
FREE KARAOKE!

I thought the bouncer was going to lift us aloft and carry us through like trophies when he saw us. I felt unbearably depressed.

'It's not as bad as you think,' Maria reassured me. 'Every night is different. This is a 1980s session so they expect an older crowd and it's all a little more civilized.'

We walked straight into the set of *Saturday Night Fever*. The place was cavernous and dark apart from occasional strobe flashings, some mirror balls and garish coloured spotlights pointing at the dance floor. Abba was optimistically trying to convince me that I was that Dancing Queen, young and sweet, only seventeen.

'I need a drink,' I muttered.

Maria led the way to the bar and ordered me my first free drink which was a pink monstrosity topped with a paper umbrella and a piece of tinned pineapple called a Kittenz Kooler.

'Don't worry, I've ordered some champagne as well,' Maria explained.

We found a small table and sat down, giving me my first opportunity to look at the other victims, I mean, customers. I was, of course, wearing my purple dress but without the cardigan, which made me feel almost naked. Maria had warned me that it would be boiling hot and I was grateful I'd dressed accordingly. Most of the women were in small groups and were probably our age, although the kind light could be disguising a few optimistic grannies.

'It's not as tacky as I thought it would be,' I grudgingly admitted to Maria. 'I haven't seen anyone in white stilettos or PVC trousers, although I am possibly the only woman here wearing both flat shoes and a bra.'

There were more women than men when we arrived but the balance evened out after an hour or so. I reminded myself that it was my job to find a man for Maria, to return her to that state of bliss that she was enjoying with Danny before I encroached.

'We can't just sit here,' I shouted over the deafening tones of Earth, Wind and Fire. 'We have to go and talk to men!'

Maria looked amused. 'I assumed you'd want to have a lot to drink first. Although, going by your recent record, you could sit here with a paper bag over your head and men would collapse at your feet.'

I screwed up my eyes in puzzlement. 'What do you mean?'

'Think about it,' Maria explained, obviously exasperated at my incomprehension. 'In less than a month, you've turned into some kind of man-magnet. Without making any effort, you've had three men throwing themselves at you.'

'Three?'

Maria counted them. 'Ed, of course, then Danny, and let's not forget Kieran who's been carrying a torch for you all this time.' There was more than a hint of resentment in this exposition and I regretted telling her of Kieran's confession that morning.

'I don't understand it either,' I said weakly. And I didn't. I'd never considered myself pretty and had never attracted attention from any men apart from Mark.

'Maybe that's your secret,' Maria murmured wistfully. 'Not trying too hard, not caring about your appearance, not behaving like a normal woman. Perhaps these are devastatingly attractive qualities to men.'

'One day, do you think you might be able to say something positive about me without prefacing it with a sequence of insults?' I asked politely.

Maria considered this. 'I don't think so.'

I thought not. I turned my attention to the purpose of this evening. 'What about them?' I inclined my head towards two men standing by the bar. They were wearing smart clothes and they had hair. Good enough. I jumped up and walked over.

Maria tried, unsuccessfully, to stop me. 'Come back!'

'Hello!' I called, hoping I was coming across as a Meg Ryan kooky eccentric rather than a Glenn Close psychopath. The men appraised me expertly and I wished I'd worn my cardigan. 'I'm Jenny. Jen.' I pointed across at our table. 'That's my friend Maria. Er, Maz. She's lovely, isn't she? She's thirty-seven and a fashion buyer.'

They introduced themselves as Gary and Tony. I didn't pay attention to which was which. It didn't matter. I was auditioning them both for Maria.

'So what do you do?' I asked, pleased with the way I'd adjusted to my role in this unfamiliar environment. Before they could reply, I was yanked backwards as Maria dragged me back to the

198

table. See, I wanted to announce to the room, this is why I wear flat shoes.

Maria poured me a drink. 'Can I ask you a question? Have you ever been to a disco before?'

'Of course!' I replied. 'There were loads of football discos at university.'

'Did you ever go to any of them without Mark?'

'Of course not!'

Maria nodded. 'And have you ever made conversation with men without Mark being around?'

'My origami party!'

'It's as if some asteroid struck you when you were sixteen and froze you in time.' Maria had her head in her hands.

I became indignant. 'I'm not that naïve. You said this was a singles disco. And, in case you've forgotten, I've successfully placed a singles ad. So what's wrong with going up to a man and introducing yourself formally?'

'You weren't introducing yourself formally, you were selling me like a camel at an Arab bazaar. Why didn't you tell them anything about you?'

'Because you didn't tell me what to do.'

Maria narrowed her eyes suspiciously. 'What you are to do is say nothing and speak to nobody. Don't even smile because you look deranged. We are going to have a fun night, dancing and drinking, and forgetting all about men. Come on.'

Then she grabbed me again and soon we were on the dance floor. Wham were singing and I was instantly transported back to school discos. I thrust my arms up and flung my knees out, glad my dress was so fluid. I forgot all about Mark and our friends and all the objectives I'd taken on for our collective lives. Maria was right. I *was* still sixteen. I felt free and young and I didn't care about anybody or anything.

I whooped and clapped and jumped through Spandau Ballet and Duran Duran and Michael Jackson and George Benson. When the beat suddenly slowed down, I remained on the floor for a while, my head spinning from the noise and the dehydration.

'Would you like to dance?' I turned and saw either Gary or Tony standing in front of me, his arms out. I looked around in panic for Maria but she was already dancing with the other one. She stuck her thumb up. I'd done it. I'd pulled. My work on earth was done. I could die in peace. Without realizing it, I'd allowed Gary/Tony to guide me into a clumsy swaying embrace, the dreaded awkwardness of the slow dance. I couldn't pull away, not when his friend was dancing with mine. It was a rule – I remembered that from school.

We shared a few key facts about ourselves. I told him that I knew how to make a Formula One racing car from a five-pound note. He told me that he knew the mobile phone number of Eric Knowles, the BBC antiques expert. Yes, it was true, I was in Hell. Or I thought I was until, inexplicably, Lisa walked onto the dance floor. Before I could think of a single sensible reason why she might be here, she walked straight up to me and slapped me hard on the face.

She turned and ran out of the nightclub, followed by me, followed by Maria, followed by Gary and Tony. A few other stragglers also followed, either believing this to be a conga line or hoping there was going to be a fight.

'Lisa!' I called. 'What have I done?' Hadn't I been saying this recently on more than one other occasion?

She whipped round. 'I know about you and Kieran!'

I flinched in response. 'Lisa, we had breakfast at the Ritz but we were –'

'I didn't know about *that*!' she shrieked. 'When was that?'

Oh dear. Think first, speak later, I ordered myself. 'Well, we were only talking about you anyway. I was trying to help him persuade you to take him back. That was all.'

Lisa held up Kieran's missing mobile phone. 'I found this in his jacket pocket when I dropped off a pile of stuff at the dry-cleaners. Guess what I found on it when I switched it back on?'

Oh no. 'Lisa, I only asked him to meet me at the playground because I didn't want –'

'I didn't know about *that* either!' She was yelling now. I decided to shut up immediately. Lisa did not. 'Exactly how many times have you met my husband without telling me?'

Maria tentatively leaned over towards me. 'I would strongly advise that you wait and hear what Lisa has to say before you end up confessing to a weekly liaison in a Soho hotel and a love child.'

I gave her a forceful shove with my elbow. 'I know what this is about, Lisa,' I said apologetically. 'You're angry because I warned Kieran that you knew about his fling with Tally.'

Lisa was shaking her head wildly. 'That's not why I'm angry. I'm feeling betrayed because you'd *promised* him, my husband, that you'd keep a secret from me. What has been going on between you for all these years?'

I heard whispering behind me and spun around. There was now a small crowd gathering and the people in the front were explaining to the newcomers at the sides what was going on. Maria was listening intently. She'd heard everything and understood nothing.

Lisa became aware of the audience and marched off. I followed her. Maria followed me. At least this time the rest of the crowd held back. I wondered if there was time to order Maria to run back and get Gary/Tony's phone numbers to salvage something from this debacle.

I hurried to keep up with Lisa, who had worn her flattest shoes for the occasion. Planning must come naturally to her. It started to rain. Of course it started to rain.

We turned round the corner and saw the welcoming golden arches of a McDonalds. I gently touched Lisa's arm. 'Let's go in there and wait for the rain to stop. Get a cup of tea or something.'

'I can't drink tea!' she snapped. 'The smell makes me feel sick at the moment.' But she pushed the doors open violently and walked up to the counter. 'Milk please,' she barked.

I ordered coffee and went to join Lisa at a small table in front of the window. Maria sat a few tables away, determined not to let us out of her sight but tactful enough to respect that we needed to talk privately.

'How did you know where I would be?' I asked, hoping to defuse the situation.

'Maria mentioned it on the phone the other day,' Lisa replied.

So now they speak on the phone. I would have expressed a little resentment that the two of them were getting on so well without me had it not been for the fact that I was the villain not the victim in the current scenario. I was not entitled to resentment. Still, I filed it away. It was always useful to have something like this to draw upon when self-pity seemed an attractive option to pursue.

Lisa continued with her rant as if there had been no interruption. 'And that wasn't all. When we thought Kieran's mobile might have been stolen, we called the phone company and asked for an itemised statement so we could see where it had been used.

In an unusual display of competence, they sent us all the statements for the past year. Guess what I found?' I didn't need to guess this one. 'Kieran has been calling your mobile every couple of weeks or so, sometimes for an hour or more. She lifted her hands, palms upwards, in utter despair.

I'd never seen her cry before. Or with her hair mussed up and her make-up streaked and smeared. Even when we went to health farms and she had her face thoroughly cleansed, she still appeared composed. In this state, out of control, she wasn't Lisa, not the Lisa I'd always known.

'I promise you, *promise*, that nothing has *ever* happened with him,' I emphasized. 'We just talked.'

'For hours?' she cried. 'In secret? Why would you not tell me if it was innocent?'

I struggled to make her understand. 'Because you and I are the ones who are friends. I didn't think you'd like it if I was friends with Kieran as well.'

She glared at me. 'Because you wouldn't like it if Mark was friends with another woman?'

'I suppose not,' I said, miserably.

The milk appeared to be having a calming effect on her. 'It doesn't matter that you only talked. You both lied to me and betrayed me. Well, congratulations. You've destroyed our friendship as well as my marriage.'

She stood up and walked towards the door. Just before she left, she turned towards me. 'I suppose you'll be warning Kieran again, since you're such good friends. By the way, does Mark know about all this?' she asked levelly. I said nothing and Lisa gazed at me thoughtfully. 'I thought not.'

'What do you want to do now?' Maria asked.

'I just want to go home. I don't know if Lisa is planning to tell Mark. I didn't even get a chance to ask her if she'd confronted Kieran with this but I really ought to warn him as well.'

Maria laughed. 'Isn't this what got you into trouble in the first place? Confused loyalties?'

I shrugged wearily. 'Everything is confused in my life, so why should the loyalties be any different.'

I decided against calling Alfie. He'd sounded better when I'd spoken to him this morning but I'd persuaded him to stay in for a few days more. I couldn't ask him to come and pick me up simply because I'd made another mess that had landed me in need of a reliable chauffeur. Maria and I walked to the nearest main road and waited until we could flag down a passing cab. That took thirty minutes and I dropped Maria off at about 11.45. As she climbed the stairs to her front door, I called out from the cab window, 'I don't suppose you got his phone number?'

Without turning to look at me, her key already in the lock, she put her hand into her jacket pocket and pulled out a drinks mat, waving it triumphantly. I laughed raucously, amazed that I still could.

It was almost midnight before I got home. As I was searching for the keys in my bag, I heard music and laughter coming from the flat. I didn't know how two men could make so much noise.

That was because there were three men in there. Mark, Phil and Kieran were all slumped on the sofa, surrounded by beer cans, wine bottles and pizza boxes, singing along drunkenly to 'Swing Low, Sweet Chariot'. They all looked round when they heard me slam the door.

'Jenny!'

'The lady of the house is home!'

Mark dragged himself up with enormous difficulty. 'I didn't think you'd mind if Kieran stayed as well! Lisa's in a bit of a mood.'

'The more the merrier,' I replied, tightly.

'It's the old gang back together!' they all cried out. 'The Three Musketeers!'

I went straight into my bedroom and shut the door. Wonderful. Just as we were all supposed to be moving on, we were all regressing, some of us further back than others.

I wasn't the first one up the next morning at 7 am. Phil was already immaculately dressed in his suit, sipping tea and eating a bowl of cereal. He was reading our copy of the *Independent* as if it were in a foreign language. To a *Telegraph* reader, it probably was.

'How are you feeling this morning?' I asked.

'Never better! It was great to be with the lads again. I'd missed them. We never do this sort of thing any more.'

'That's because you've had homes of your own to sleep in,' I murmured.

He folded the paper up precisely and put it back. 'I must be off,' he said, pecked me on the cheek, as he'd always done, picked up his briefcase and left.

Kieran staggered out of the tiny junk room half an hour later. He collapsed onto an upright chair and begged for tea. When I brought it to him, his head was on the table.

Now was the time to warn him that Lisa knew all about our friendship.

'So what did Lisa say when you went home?' I asked casually.

'She was throwing up when I got home. She'd been so ill that she didn't go to work, which worked well for me because she was too weak to be sarcastic or to torment me with a chronological list of my wrongdoings.'

'Poor Lisa,' I sympathized. 'She must hate the lack of control over her body that pregnancy is going to impose on her.'

'Anyway, she was so mellow, she didn't argue when I offered to move back in. She didn't even ask how I'd managed to get a fried egg stain on the inside of my trousers.'

'I bet she took them straight to the dry-cleaners,' I murmured.

Kieran was too fixated on his hangover to find this an odd observation. 'Of course she did. The hormones may subdue her more extreme leanings but, where there is grime, Lisa will always manifest the need to launder.'

'Did you see her last night?'

'She flipped again, it's anybody's guess over what, and she threw me out. I called Mark and he told me to come over for the night. I'm glad I did. Phil convinced me that I have to expect this for at least the first three months; gave me a few tips for coping with the mood swings and general insanity.'

I could have told him then, warned him that this was slightly more than a mood swing. But I didn't although I seriously doubted whether Lisa would ever show any gratitude for this. 'You do know that Phil doesn't know that Mark and I are back together?'

Kieran rubbed his forehead. 'I know that but I don't understand it.'

'You don't need to,' I muttered. I left him squinting at the news-paper an inch away from his face because his eyes were too sore to put in his contact lenses.

Mark was the last to emerge, twenty minutes after Kieran. I had showered, dressed, had breakfast, picked up £800 worth of business and erased the details of thirty-four men who liked the sound of me. How ironic, I thought, that it's women who are warned about Internet dating, and told how perfectly normal-sounding men can turn out to be dangerous, manipulative confidence tricksters. In my case, the ad was giving the impression that I was a well-adjusted, nice woman with middle-class tastes and just the one offbeat interest. If any men were to be so unfortunate as to meet me, they would find that I was a destructive force, without a clue as to who I was or what I wanted.

Even worse, I came with an entire contingent of friends who spanned the full spectrum of destructive tendencies, most of which they had previously deployed on themselves but were now looking for external targets.

For the sake of world peace, I cancelled the ad.

'What are you doing?' I hadn't heard Mark approach. He placed a hand on my shoulder and I kissed it.

'Just checking emails.' It wasn't a lie.

'Sorry I didn't get a chance to warn you about Kieran.'

I brushed his apology off. 'What's happening with them?'

He looked sheepish. 'We all had such a great time last night, they thought it would be really cool if the three of us got a flat together.' I was doing rather well by comparison. 'What about you?' he asked. 'How was Maria?'

'Fine, fine.' He had no idea about the incident with Danny or my encroaching or the fact that I'd gone to a singles disco. Lucky him. I wish I could be blessed with more ignorance.

'So are you going to phone Tally today?'

'Ohh! Do I really have to? It's useless. She hates me. What good do you think it can possibly do?'

'Phil will go back if she begs him. At the moment, she's claiming that everything is his fault for neglecting her for all these years.'

'OK, OK.' I was tired of arguing. I picked up the phone and dialled her number before I could change my mind. I assumed she'd be on the school run so she wouldn't be able to swear at me. Wrong.

'Oh, hi Tally, it's me.'

'Jenny. What a delightful way to start the day. If you've found someone else I slept with twenty years ago, then feel free to send their wives over to me so that they can make me feel dirty.'

This was worse than swearing. 'I'm phoning to say that I'm sorry and to try and make amends.'

'That's great! Can you send my husband home and make us happy again?'

I couldn't help myself. 'From what I've heard, you weren't that happy.'

The line went dead. I redialled and Tally answered after ten rings.

'Go away.'

'I'm sorry, I'm sorry. I really am.'

Tally was silent. 'So you really want to help?' she asked coldly.

'Ye-es.' Now I was worried.

'OK. Come over.'

'When?'

'Now. I want you to come over now and spend the day with me.'

I'd been holding the phone away from my ear so that Mark could hear. He looked as bewildered as I felt. 'The whole day?'

'That's right. I want you to know what it's like to be me for a whole day, then you can judge me and tell me how to live my life. Otherwise, don't bother contacting me again.'

The line went dead again but, this time, I didn't redial.

'What are you going to do?' Mark asked.

I shrugged. 'I'm going to go and be Tally for a day.' After being me for the past month, I was keen for a change.

Chapter Fourteen

I didn't have any shimmying clothes and my purple dress was a crumpled mess after the night before. That meant I was back to my old familiar wardrobe of jeans. An autumn chill had set in so I brought my favourite check shirts out from their storage bag under the bed. When I say 'my', I mean 'our' because Mark and I shared these. Somehow, these had been forgotten in the big division of property a month earlier.

I chose the red one that Mark liked best, both on me and himself. I was dressed in under a minute. Before I left, I called Alfie at home and on his mobile but there was no answer. This was unusual. I would keep trying and go round to his house later if I had no luck reaching him.

I would have liked to walk to Tally's but that would take an hour and she'd seemed impatient on the phone so I grabbed a cab instead.

On the way there, I wondered what the day would be like. I imagined that, once the kids were at school, we'd go to an aerobics class, do some shopping, maybe have our nails done (Tally always had beautifully manicured nails), meet some other mums for coffee and lunch, boast about our children's SAT scores, bitch about other children's personal hygiene. Then we'd pick the kids up from school, sit them down and help them with their homework, make them supper, prepare dinner for Tally and Phil . . . we'd have to improvise that bit, since Phil wasn't coming home.

I arrived at Tally's house and was immediately struck by its outer coating of calm and respectability. I'd never been here during the day and the silence was daunting. There were no kids playing outside, not when they had playrooms and gardens of their own, no chatting over fences, not when social appointments were firmly fixed on school calendars attached to fridges with magnets made by artistically stunted toddlers. This was a street of fortresses and castles. There may not have been moats but each home was effectively isolated from the outside world.

Tally's was a four-storey Edwardian house, fronted by a beautiful garden. I couldn't imagine living in such a big place, having control over so many rooms and so many people. I always thought I'd forget a child or a room and would wake up one December and discover a bedraggled teenager in the converted loft, who hadn't been to school since the dawn of the millennium and had been living on pigeons.

I rang the doorbell and was horrified by the bedlam that broke out. I checked my watch. It was 9.25 – they were all supposed to be at school. The door opened, then slammed shut, as hands battled over the handle, then opened again. It struck Tally's six-year-old daughter, Jocasta, on the head and she kicked her ten-year-old brother, Ellery, in the knee. I cautiously entered the hall and accidentally trod on Martha. She was two. It served her right for crying all through my wedding and putting Mark off having children. The kids were wearing nothing but pants, scrapping on the floor, shouting hysterically, poking and punching each other while yelling for their mum.

Tally walked into the hallway and ignored my presence while she separated her monsters, checked for serious injury and then ordered them into the living room to watch unsuitable videos. She looked ill until I realized she just wasn't wearing any make-up. Her face was definitely older than mine, the lines more pronounced, no doubt because of all the time spent in the sun on Caribbean holidays. The advantage of holidaying in the UK was that my skin would never be sun-ravaged. And her hair was not its usual sheet of golden silk – it resembled a mass of dried tobacco hanging unevenly around her shoulders.

'Coffee?' she asked, without looking at me.

I followed her into the kitchen, which didn't look the way it usually did. When we came here for dinner, the whole house was always immaculate. Everything smelled of pot pourri or possibly pot pourri-scented Shake 'n' Vac. Candles twinkled on every surface and lights were only switched on if they contributed to the ambiance or highlighted an expensive painting or a rare flattering photo of the not-very-photogenic children.

The house was unrecognizable today. I'd had to use all my orienteering skills to navigate around the debris littering the floor. Toys, bits of toys, half-eaten crumpets, food remnants of indeterminate origin, library books, a white bra that had been washed with something blue and was now that tell-tale shade of grey. There were six piles of dirty clothes arranged by colour on the table. I hoped we wouldn't be eating lunch off it later. With great care, I perched myself on a stool by the breakfast bar.

I wondered if Mark had ever dropped in on Tally in the past and encountered this bloodbath. It would certainly explain his violent antipathy towards children and I would have understood perfectly if he'd demanded a vasectomy immediately afterwards.

'Where's the au pair?' I asked.

'In bed,' she replied curtly. 'She gets depressed and cries for days on end. When it happens she loses her English and I have to listen to her wailing in Polish and hope that she's not threatening to jump off a church tower and take the children with her.'

Tally put the kettle on and made instant coffee in grubby mugs that she'd swilled out under a tap. As if she had four hands, she put washing in, took washing out, loaded the dryer, unloaded the dishwasher, loaded it with breakfast things, sorted clean clothes, not shimmying at all.

A piercing scream reminded me that we weren't alone. 'Why aren't the kids at school?'

'Inset day,' Tally replied. Spotting my blank look, she continued, 'The staff go to the pub all day and think up ways to make lives more difficult for parents, projects on Ancient Egypt requiring three-dimensional pyramids made from hand-made sand bricks to be completed in a weekend, class productions that need each mother to hand-smock a Victorian gown, themed days where you will be requested to cook peacock pies according to authentic recipes that can only be sourced from archives buried in locked vaults in Liverpool. That sort of thing.'

I thought she might be having a breakdown, but wouldn't mention it to her because I knew how annoying that can be. 'So what's the plan of action for the day?' I injected a note of fun and adventure into my voice. Maybe Tally and I could bond through this. She was right. I knew nothing about her life, probably because I'd never been interested enough to ask about it. Or because I thought I knew what it must be like. 'Maybe we could go to the zoo?' I suggested. 'Or Chessington World of Adventures?' Even the memory of the day there with Ed could not spoil this place for me. I must be very shallow.

Tally pressed her lips together to suppress a laugh. 'This isn't the school holidays. We're taking the kids to the dentist, then we've got to do a big shop, back here for lunch, then the older ones will have to be tested on their spellings and tables, then we've got to put the house back together faster than the little angels are destroying it.'

It didn't sound too bad to me. Perhaps we could squeeze in a few hours at the zoo as well. I'd mention that later.

I was still drinking my coffee when Tally opened her mouth and a deafening sound came out of it. 'Jocasta! Ellery! Martha! Five-minute warning! Toilet and teeth *now*!'

I don't know about them, but I was practically up those stairs and into the bathroom in a second. After a minute, during which we heard no sounds of activity, we went and collected the kids from in front of the television where they'd been avidly watching *Nine and a Half Weeks*.

'Upstairs now!' Tally snapped.

They continued to ignore their mother while Mickey Rourke was feeding a blindfolded Kim Basinger with strawberries. I knew what was coming next and took it upon myself to switch off the TV. For Christmas, I fully intended to buy these children a lot of *Tweenies* videos.

They all glared at me demonically before stamping up the stairs to the bathroom. I wondered if I should go with them and sing a cheery toothbrushing song for encouragement. But Tally was doing fine just bellowing at them. Minutes later, they came down. The children looked just about presentable but Tally had been transformed into, well, herself.

I looked at my watch. In less than five minutes, while simultaneously coercing three feral creatures into Gap co-ordinates, she had straightened her hair, applied a subtle veneer of make-up and squeezed into jeans that were at least a size smaller than my own.

I couldn't help it. My resentment began seeping back. It took five hours and a team of professionals to make me presentable for Lisa's magazine but I knew I still didn't look sexy. Tally achieved this in five minutes. I suppose I simply don't possess the raw material. I'm different. This was quite liberating to acknowledge. Perhaps Tally envied my ability to look like Worzel Gummidge without any effort whatsoever.

We manhandled the children roughly into their car seats with promises of bags of sugar and some dangerous toys later. Then came the nightmare of being forced to sing *The Wheels on the Bus* all the way there, and it was a twenty-minute journey. Tally drew the line at Ellery's 'The Axe-Murderer on the Bus goes chop, chop, chop' which reduced the girls to tears.

We were almost barred from the dentist. Martha screamed from the moment she entered the waiting room until we left. This made every other child scream and even one of the adults lost his nerve and left without keeping his appointment. Ellery bit the hygienist and Jocasta threw a jack-in-the-box at the receptionist.

'That wasn't too bad,' Tally declared, as we left. And, compared to the hideous hour we spent at the supermarket, she was right. If I'm ever stopped by those women with clipboards asking me my opinion, even if it's about frozen peas, I'm going to insist that they write down my top tip for retailers: manacles for trolleys. Shopping would be so easy if you only shackled children into their seats. And it should be compulsory, so kids would not be allowed to run up and down the aisles, pulling cereal boxes from the bottom of piles, sticking their fingers into loaves of bread, pushing their mothers' trolleys into the back of my legs.

Tally seemed oblivious to the chaos they were wreaking on the other shoppers. I wanted either to hit them or give them tooth-rotting sweets to shut them up. Somehow we made it to the checkout with three unharmed children, although that was only because I forced myself to keep an arm's length away.

Repeating the *Wheels on the Bus* trauma on the way back, I longed for Tally to speed up, drive through red lights or off a bridge, anything.

I happened to notice the clock in the front of the car. 'Tally, do you realize it's one o'clock. Where has the morning gone?'

She didn't turn her head. 'Are you surprised we haven't had time to fit in a facial? Or a Pilates class?'

My expression gave away that she had read my mind perfectly. 'But actually,' I added, 'it's quite nice when the day goes quickly, don't you think? I hate it when hours drag by.'

211

Tally gasped in disbelief. 'It's not just this morning that has shot by, Jenny. It's the last ten years! Every morning like this, every afternoon the same. I became pregnant when I was twenty-eight then blinked and I was thirty-eight.'

'That's the same for all mothers,' I countered. 'You make sacrifices for children, I'm prepared to do the same.' Although after today, I was coming to the conclusion that I would be sticking to one child and fixing unbreakable locks on our video cabinet.

Tally didn't argue and I felt a little smug that I'd made a valid point.

The afternoon sped by even more quickly. The tables tests went well. I thought it would be fun if Ellery typed the answers on the computer. When I went to check the answers, I found he'd typed *I'm bored* over and over again. Jocasta answered 'twenty-three' to every question.

I listened to them read. They'd both worked out by now that I was a fool and were having a lovely time taking me for a ride.

'B . . . A . . . N . . . D,' I sounded out, when Jocasta was struggling with the word. 'What does that spell?

'Penis,' she replied.

While I was doing this, Martha was emptying all the jigsaws onto the playroom floor. I assumed that Tally was making the most of my presence and was watching daytime television with a glass of wine. When I finally went downstairs, I found her crying.

'God, Tally, it'll all be OK, I know it will. Phil is staying at our flat, a couple of nights of my cooking and Mark's feet and he'll come running back to you.'

Tally looked up at me as if I was a stranger. 'Do you think I'm crying because Phil left me? He effectively left me years ago. Since Ellery was born, he's been leaving the house at seven in the morning and not coming home until eight or nine. Then he's exhausted and just wants to have dinner and collapse in front of the television. By that time, *I'm* exhausted and go to bed. Almost the only time we talk is when we have people round to dinner.'

'But is it his fault that he has to work such long hours? You have an expensive lifestyle.' I felt the need to defend him now that he was living with me.

Tally stared at me. 'What is it with you and this need to blame people for things that don't work out the way you dreamed? There isn't any fault. If there is any, it's mine for thinking that just because I imagined my life would turn out one way, it inevitably would. So, yes, it was stupid of me not to realize that if I wanted a big house and expensive things, then I wouldn't be able to see my husband as well. It was stupid of me to think that I could have children and still have time to read books. And it was unbelievably stupid of me to think that, when I got all the things I'd wanted, I would automatically be happy.'

Now I wanted to cry. 'I had no idea you were so unhappy.'

'Do you think I'm unusual?' Tally asked, curiously. 'You're wrong if you do. Half the mums I know cry regularly and not because their husbands work crazy hours. They cry because they can't remember what they did, who they were before they had kids, and they haven't a clue about what they'll do and who they'll be once the children have gone. It's bloody terrifying!'

'I wish I'd been a better friend and could have helped you in some way,' I said, miserably.

Tally blew her nose unglamorously. 'In a way, you did. You'll be really insulted by this but, what the hell! I used to observe your life that was essentially the same life you'd led since university. Watching films with Mark, eating hamburgers with Mark, going on the same walking holidays, wearing the same clothes, living in the same flat, doing the same low-key jobs, mixing with the same friends, even keeping the same hairstyle. And I thought, well my life may not have turned out the way I'd hoped but at least I grew up and moved on.'

I gasped. 'That's a horrible thing to say! Why does everyone condemn me and Mark for wanting to hold on to something that works? Maybe he's right, and couples do only have kids when they're bored with each other or dissatisfied with their current life and looking for the next diversion.'

'If you believe that, then why have you put yourselves and the rest of us through this horrendous ordeal?'

I don't know. Why have I?

We were both subdued by our first-ever frank conversation. I was bruised and fragile from Tally's revelation that she'd always regarded my life as barren and stationary. All of a sudden, she'd reinvented herself as Boadicea, bravely ploughing on through storms and famines, conquering new territories, while Mark and I

213

huddled in a cave for years, hiding from intruders trying to tell us about the invention of the wheel.

I couldn't concentrate on anything for the rest of the afternoon and sat in the living room with the children watching *The Terminator*. 'We're hungry!' they announced as the final credits rolled. I realized I'd fallen asleep and felt guilty to find that Tally had cleared up the downstairs of the house and had tea ready on the kitchen table.

'I'd better be off,' I mumbled.

Tally was picking breadcrumbs off Martha's fish fingers and brown bits from Jocasta's chips. 'Why don't you stay for the rest of the day? You're going to miss the good bit. Two hours of getting the children to sleep, running up and down stairs to sort out fights, faked sore throats and lost teddies. Then, after we've shredded Mediterranean vegetables for dinner, we can sit and think about all the things we want to tell Phil about our day. About *The Wheels on the Bus*, the dentist, crying because our lives are so empty, that sort of thing.'

I put my coat on, aware that her voice was rising worryingly. She followed me to the door.

Impulsively, I hugged her, feeling her body become rigid as I touched her. 'I'm sorry, Tally, about all the trouble I've caused. I'm going to do everything possible to get Phil back here.'

She smiled sadly. 'Then everything will be fine, will it? Or will it just be the same as it used to be?'

To me, they were both the same thing.

I caught a cab and directed it to Alfie's house first. A neighbour saw me knocking on the door and peering though the window. 'Are you a relative?' she called.

'Sort of,' I answered.

'He was taken to hospital last night. I saw the ambulance arrive.'

Oh no. 'Do you know where they took him?'

The woman thought about it. 'Probably St George's.'

I got the cabbie to drive me to St George's where it took me thirty minutes and a repeated lie that I was his daughter to track Alfie down. He was on a cardiac ward looking old and tired. I kissed him on the forehead.

'Alfie! Why didn't you get someone to call me?'

He sat up painfully, and pulled his shabby pyjama top around him. 'What a lovely surprise! Has your husband thrown you out?'

I frowned at him teasingly. 'Don't change the subject. I left you all my contact numbers on Saturday and told you to call if you felt any worse.'

'I'm fine. They're just making a lot of fuss about nothing.'

I picked up his chart from the end of the bed, having learned how to interpret the figures while Harry was in hospital. 'This doesn't look like nothing, Alfie.'

'That is supposed to be confidential, young lady,' he scolded.

'Hah! This coming from the taxi driver whose job description includes the eliciting of confidential information from one passenger in order to pass it on to the next. I bet all your passengers know about my life.'

Alfie shook his head. 'As soon as I get to the finger-stroking part, they always become confused. "Surely nobody would get in a state about something so trivial?" they say. "Not when she has her health and a husband who loves her and friends who put dots on the guests at her origami parties?" That's what they say.'

We both knew that this was Alfie talking. His passengers were more likely to say: 'Isn't it quicker over Lambeth Bridge?' and 'Will a twenty-pound note be a problem?' They might even occasionally ask if he's ever had Kylie Minogue in his cab, but they wouldn't care about my life or Alfie's heart.

'So what have the doctors said?'

'They said I should retire now. But I'd always planned to chuck it in at Christmas anyway before going to Australia. You never know, I could like it so much, I might stay there permanently.'

'That would be lovely,' I said, hoping his dreadful son-in-law wouldn't spoil his plans. 'And the climate would be good for you.' It was suddenly desperately important that this man found happiness. As if Alfie knew what I was thinking, he took my hand.

'Don't you go worrying about me. Not unless it's going to stop you worrying about everything else.'

'No,' I confessed, 'it just adds to the list.'

'So what have you been up to? But bear in mind I have a dodgy ticker.'

'I've been somebody else for a day.' I told him about my depressing experience at Tally's.

'And you're worried you'll end up like that?' Alfie asked shrewdly.

'Or alone. Or with Mark, the way we used to be, but regretting that I wasn't braver.'

'You know your problem, Jenny?'

I knew many of them and wasn't keen on hearing that I had another. 'Tell me,' I said, reluctantly.

'You and your generation think you have a right to be happy. I don't know where you get that impression. It doesn't even say in the Bible that you have a right to be happy.'

'I'm sure it does,' I said doubtfully. 'Or was it just my parents who said so?'

'Parents do that,' Alfie agreed. 'But they're not doing their kids any favours. And now I'll give you my secret of happiness.' He waited until I was properly listening. 'Don't expect it.'

I wanted Mark. I wanted to tell him about the day with Tally and her deep unhappiness. I wanted him to assure me that we were different, that we had a life worth envying. I walked back to Battersea from the hospital in Tooting. It took an hour but, by the time I got home, my head was clearer. I knew I wasn't going to be able talk to Mark, not with Phil and Kieran staying there. But I hoped I could find an excuse to drag him out onto the patio to spend a few minutes alone with him. I really needed that.

I was surprised that there wasn't much noise coming from the flat. Perhaps the three of them were still suffering from their overindulgence of last night. When I opened the door, my surprise was even greater. The three had become four. Mark, Kieran, Phil – and Ed.

I considered turning around and running away. But judging by recent events, when I did run away, I tended to be followed. So I simply closed the door behind me and stood in front of them all. The lesson I'd learned from last night was to keep my mouth shut until I knew exactly what was going on and what I was accused of doing. It went without saying that I would be guilty of whatever it was, but there was no point in bringing up additional offences if I could get away with them.

Mark went first. 'Ed popped in to see you.' I couldn't hear anything accusing in his voice but that didn't mean anything.

216

Incongruously, Ed was drinking beer with the other men. 'I probably should have phoned. I didn't realize you had a full house.' He saw that I was looking at his beer. 'I wasn't going to stay but he insisted on giving me a beer.' He was pointing at Kieran, who was hunched up, trying to become invisible.

I still wasn't speaking. Neither was anybody else. Ed was drinking as quickly as he could. 'Right then, I'll be off.' He stood up. I glanced at Mark who nodded imperceptibly at me. He knew I had to speak to the man.

I let Ed out and pulled the door behind me.

'I'm really sorry,' he said. 'I thought you'd be living alone again. I know you said you'd split up with your husband for a second time.'

I was finding it difficult to look him in the face. 'You must have got quite a shock to find I was now living with three men.'

Ed smiled. 'Actually, it was a relief. When Mark answered the door, I felt sick. I was sure you'd taken him back. But when I met the others, I realized it was all a temporary set-up.'

'I'll have to remember that rule next time I'm planning an evening of secret debauchery,' I observed lightly. 'One man – suspicious, three men – above suspicion.' Now was my cue to tell him that I was, in fact, back with Mark, that it was just our living arrangements that were a little Byzantine. But I didn't. Tally was right about me. I always want to attribute blame for actions and consequences. Right now I was blaming my day with Tally for my reticence.

I did know her better now and I wasn't judging her so harshly any more. I know that Alfie said that there is no such thing as a right to happiness but surely there is a basic minimum we can expect? And if you don't find it, if it is actually kept from you in the life you've chosen, is it so wrong to snatch a little from someone else's life? Just a tiny bit, so small that the other person wouldn't even notice?

After all, Phil had been able to live with Tally's infidelities for years before I blundered in and spoiled things. Was she supposed to accept an inferior life? To settle?

I didn't know the answers any more but I was not going to be so quick to condemn and discount alternative choices.

'Hello?' Ed was knocking on my head affectionately. 'Is there anyone in there?'

I pulled myself together. 'Sorry! I've got a lot on my mind. Why did you come round?'

'Simple. I've missed you,' he shrugged. 'And once I'd calmed down, I started to think about what you'd done. I can understand why you took Mark back. When my wife left me, those first weeks were unbearable. I didn't know what to do without her and I missed her at every moment, when I was eating, waking up, even pushing a trolley around a supermarket. It was all I could do to stop myself from snatching her off the street and forcing her back with me. So with all the upset of your father-in-law's illness, it makes sense that you'd slip back into old ways.'

He was being so reasonable I could kiss him. 'It was still wrong of me. I should have told you.'

'But, as you said, it only lasted a few days, so why would you?'

At last, someone who understands me. 'I'm sorry anyway.'

'So how are all the aches and pains?'

'All recovered. As if I'd never been riding,' I said.

'Anyway, the reason I came round was to ask if we could, you know, try again. But more slowly this time. I know that everything is difficult for you. But when I asked Mark how his father was, he said that he and your aunt are moving abroad at Christmas. So I presume that you'll be able to make a clean break then. In every way. So what do you think?'

Oh, this was very dangerous. I heard Mark, Kieran and Phil laugh out loud at something on the television. Terrific. I wanted to spend the evening asking Mark if he'd ever cried in despair and, instead, I was going to be refereeing bottle top-flicking contests.

Ed was looking at me. He was nothing to do with the rest of my life, all the messy bits. He wasn't friends with my friends. He didn't know me when I was eighteen. He had no opinion on the way I'd lived my life up until now. To him, I was a talented artist and a desirable woman. Not a finished product but a beginning. A possibility. And that was what I wanted to be.

I needed to think about this carefully but I didn't have the time. Mark suddenly pulled the door open and peered out suspiciously. 'Oh, you're still here. Is everything all right?'

'Yes!' I answered, too brightly.

Mark went back in reluctantly.

I turned to Ed. No, I couldn't do this, I couldn't sustain this

218

level of deception. It just wasn't me. But I knew he'd argue with me if I told him now. And he didn't deserve a quick brush-off.

'Are you free for lunch tomorrow?' I asked impulsively.

Mark watched me carefully when I came back in. I glanced in the mirror to see if there was a brand across my face or whether my guilt was entirely internal. Maybe I should cut out the middle man, shave my own head, don the hair shirt and take my punishment before I actually do anything.

'Everything OK?' Mark asked.

'Fine. Bit of a misunderstanding, that's all. He won't be coming round again.' I was relieved that I could say this with sincerity. Perhaps this really was the beginning of a new, honest era between us.

Kieran walked out of the kitchen carrying some more beers. 'We thought we'd play bridge,' he said. 'Since there are four of us.'

Bridge? We hadn't played since those first two terms at university when we played almost every Friday and Saturday night. Me, Mark, Phil and Kieran. Lisa hadn't been interested in learning and Tally wasn't on the scene. Not legitimately, anyway.

Phil had taught us all how to play and Mark and I had an instant advantage that we knew each other so well. Since bridge requires a partnership where communication is perfectly tuned, we couldn't lose. We found that we were even thinking the same way. It annoyed Kieran, who had to partner Phil. They were both good players but each had his own style and neither was prepared to compromise to meet the other.

Once we'd learned the basics, we were regularly beating them. Mark and I were disappointed when the games broke up but Lisa became fed up of sitting on the arm of Kieran's chair, stroking his hair, adoring him. We switched to Scrabble, always good for a drunken brawl in a university bar where students would fight over non-existent words.

By the time Tally joined our crowd, the games had been banished to Mark's tiny bedsitting room where the two of us played by ourselves late into the night. We became part of three couples, all planning to move to London, all of us smug and confident, with dreams we shared and a few, I now know, that we didn't.

219

As Phil dealt the cards, Kieran looked at Mark. 'Do you realize that we agreed to go into business that very first term?'

'I do remember. We were going to open a gym, nothing fancy, no frills, for men who wanted to get fit but didn't want all the posing and the lycra.'

Phil carried on dealing. 'I don't remember you talking about that.'

Mark explained. 'That's because we worked out that we'd never make much money with a gym. Those were the days where small companies were starting up everywhere making fortunes for young men in their twenties.'

Kieran raised his fist in a mock salute. 'That was going to be us.'

We all picked up our cards and I felt all my tension melt away. I'd forgotten how much I loved this game. It was full of rules, points to count, strategies and techniques to call upon and, above all, a strictly-governed communication system. You were only allowed to use certain words to describe the cards in your hand to your partner. A lot of our success in Bristol came from the sheer amount of time we devoted to memorizing the bidding system.

Our friends probably wouldn't be at all surprised to learn that we spent our time away from them practising for our bridge games. It was like a magic trick to us, like reading each other's minds. But maybe it damaged our other communication skills. Maybe we got into the habit of paring all our thoughts down to carefully regulated abbreviations, always assuming that the other would be able to read the subtext.

Worked with cards, maybe not so effective when planning a life together. Instead of saying 'I love you' a million times, maybe just once I should have said, 'I assume I love you but I can't be 100 per cent sure since I don't have experience of any other men so I don't know what it's like to *not* love a man I'm with.' He wouldn't have understood what I was going on about but he would have at least known that I was going to be more trouble than I'd led him to expect.

But tonight, when anything I said could reveal me as the liar and cheat I'd become, I was grateful that we'd reverted to the old rules. 'One Club', I bid, remembering the old system.

And the years melted away.

After the first hand, I noticed Phil yawning. 'You know that you're prime heart-attack material, don't you?'

He waved a hand dismissively. 'Is that what Tally told you? I bet she had a gleam in her eye when she did. The greatest contribution I've made to my marriage and my family in the past ten years is in taking out a substantial life insurance policy.'

I flinched. 'You don't mean that. You're a great husband and father.'

Phil laughed. 'I don't think Tally would agree with you.'

'Have you ever asked her?'

He reacted as if I'd asked him to stick a finger up my nose. 'Of course I haven't.'

'Have you asked her anything at all about what she thinks of the past ten years?'

Phil concentrated on his cards. 'I don't need to. We've been together forever. I've seen her in childbirth, I know everything about her. There's nothing new she could tell me.'

'Did you know she's cried every afternoon since the day Ellery was born?'

They all looked at me in horror. We'd never formally agreed on the subjects that we wouldn't discuss in each other's company, but private misery was obviously one of them.

'I'll get some tortilla chips,' Mark said, jumping up quickly.

'Is there anything I can get?' Kieran asked desperately.

Phil was just watching me, waiting for a punchline or a comforting cliché. And I was close to breaking my resolve, making him feel better, when the doorbell rang. It was Lisa and she'd been drinking.

'So sorry to intrude on your lovely evening,' she said bitterly. 'But I know you'll all be really pleased to know that I've been fired.'

Chapter Fifteen

She burst into tears. Kieran rushed to comfort her but she pushed him away. Mark immediately rushed over, gently put his arms around her and guided her over to an armchair. Then he knelt on the floor and held her hands firmly.

'What happened, Lisa?' he asked.

'I told them I was pregnant and they fired me,' she cried.

'Are you sure?' Phil asked. 'They can't do that.'

Lisa glared at him viciously. 'Well they did!' She calmed down quickly in Mark's soothing presence. I really did, do love him. 'OK, they didn't fire me because I was pregnant. They didn't actually fire me at all. But they made it impossible for me to stay there so it's the same thing.'

'What did they do?' Phil was in full lawyer mode and I was prepared to hit him if he continued to be reasonable. Knowing Lisa as we all did, this was a guaranteed way of sending her over the top.

'It was awful,' she cried. 'I told everyone in the office that I was pregnant and handed out my maternity leave plans to everyone. I arranged to speak to them all individually, to outline firmly my expectations of them.' I grimaced, imagining how well that would have gone down.

Kieran defended her vigorously. 'That's just a sign of your commitment to the magazine. How could anyone object to that?'

Lisa ignored him completely. 'Then I noticed everyone sneaking out of the office at lunchtime, a couple at a time. I finally grabbed a secretary and persuaded her to tell me where they were all going.' Probably with thumbscrews. 'They were meeting for a drink at the pub so I decided to join them. I don't normally, which I thought was the reason why they didn't invite me.'

I knew where this was going.

'So I got there and they were drinking champagne. Must be someone's birthday, I assumed, but as I came up behind them I heard Petra, my deputy editor, make a toast: "To Lisa Bradford's husband, for making her pregnant and saving us the job of having her assassinated." Then someone said: "You've got to feel sorry for the poor brat" and my secretary, *my* secretary, replied, "Yeah, but not that sorry," then they all laughed and cheered.'

'Lisa, that's terrible!' I exclaimed.

But she didn't hear me. 'They all hate me! All this time I thought I had lots of friends there, that I was popular, and the fact is that nobody likes me. Nobody!'

We were all horrified by her distress but it got worse. She slowly looked around at each of our faces and we watched the truth dawn on her like an unstoppable chemical reaction. 'You knew,' she whispered. 'You knew that they hated me. All of you.' Finally she turned to me. 'Why didn't you tell me, Jenny? At some point in all the years you've been my friend, could you not have told me that I was universally despised? You were perfectly happy to tell me that my husband slept with one of my friends years ago, something that could never cause anything but damage, but you didn't tell me about a bad situation that I could actually change.'

Now everyone's attention was on me. Was I wrong or were they all relieved that they were temporarily off the hook? I wanted to go and get the tortilla chips.

'What did you want me to say?' I asked her helplessly. 'And would you have believed me anyway?'

Lisa suddenly became very pale. 'I don't feel very well.' She looked down. 'I'm bleeding,' she announced flatly.

The ambulance took her to St George's Hospital. Kieran was allowed to go with her but Mark and I had to take a taxi. Phil decided to stay behind. 'Do you think I should let Tally know?' he asked, doubtfully.

Mark and I looked at each other. 'Definitely,' we agreed and left him phoning her.

We sat in A & E, waiting for news. I'd popped up to look in on Alfie but he was asleep. I'd sat next to his bed for a few minutes, hoping he might wake up, tell me to stop chasing happiness before

I went and did so. But his loud snoring persuaded me to give up and go back downstairs.

Mark was pacing the relatives' room anxiously. I gently encouraged him to sit down.

'This is awful!' he said. 'What if this is our fault for causing her all the extra stress on top of her finding out about the company's money problems? Firstly I give my dad a heart attack, then I make Lisa have a miscarriage!'

I took his hand firmly. 'Lisa has never needed anyone else to give her stress, she has a surplus of neuroses of her own that she can draw on. And besides, she may be absolutely fine. She's probably reorganizing the nurses' rota right now.'

But he wasn't listening to me. 'I am actually praying inside, praying that she doesn't lose her baby.'

I looked at him curiously. 'I thought you weren't interested in her pregnancy?'

He started to chew his nails. 'I wasn't. It wasn't actually real or meaningful to me until tonight. But when I saw the way Kieran looked at Lisa as they got into the ambulance . . .' He drifted away into his thoughts and I decided not to intrude. Within minutes he was asleep.

I sat next to him, trying not to disturb him. His body instinctively responded to mine and moved closer, his head dropping onto my shoulder. I envied him the ability to switch off with such ease. It was twenty past midnight when Kieran came in. I jumped up, waking Mark with a start.

'How is she? What have the doctors said?'

Kieran smiled. 'The baby's OK. They're going to keep her in overnight to make sure the bleeding stops but she should be all right.'

Mark and I hugged each other in relief. Then I kissed Kieran warmly. 'That's great news. What are you going to do now?'

'They won't let me stay here with her so I'm going back home to clean up before they let her out tomorrow.'

'And she's happy about you moving back home?' Mark asked expectantly.

'Happy might be something of an overstatement, but she's agreed. This has put everything else into perspective. All that matters now is us and the baby.'

'You're so right!' Mark agreed fervently.

Once more, I looked at him with curiosity. But this was not a good time to talk. That would have to wait.

I took a chance and asked Kieran if I could pop in and speak to Lisa.

He hesitated. 'I can't promise that she'll talk to you or even listen. But you can try. I'll wait down here for you.'

I walked into the ward and saw her sitting up in a bed, scrutinizing the sheets for grime. I smiled to myself. She was on the mend and didn't look completely displeased to see me.

'If you're looking for something to throw at me,' I said, 'don't go for the bedpan on your left – it's still got something in it.'

She didn't laugh, probably because it wasn't that funny. 'Where's Kieran?'

'Downstairs with Mark. He said you might not mind if I came up for a moment.'

'That's because he doesn't know what you and I fought about.'

I raised my eyebrows. 'You didn't tell him you found out about all the phone calls? So what did you argue about?'

'The baby. He hadn't got to that thrilled stage that I'd been expecting. At least that's what I told him. He just thinks my hormones were going crazy making me a little more irrational than usual.'

'So why did you decide not to say anything?' I asked.

'I kept waiting for him to say something to me, to prove that you'd warned him again.'

'I nearly did,' I confessed. 'But I knew you'd feel betrayed again.'

'Can I ask you a favour?'

I sat down next to her. 'Anything. Anything at all.'

'Finish your friendship with him. I know, I know. Nothing happened, but I don't like it.' She shrugged. 'I can't help it. You're my friend. It changes things if you're his friend too. Does that make sense?'

I nodded. It made complete sense. Because, of course, it was more than friendship. There had been undercurrents, real enough, but undefined. And at our breakfast at the Ritz, they came swirling to the surface. That was the thing about undercurrents, just because they were unseen didn't make them any less destructive.

I didn't know whether I dared ask my next question but I had to

– there was enough suspense in my life without this. 'Will you tell Mark?'

Lisa placed her hands on her stomach with unbearable tenderness. 'No. What would be the point?'

'You could do it just to hurt me. I've caused you enough hurt recently.'

'Then what? Mark gets hurt again. It would never stop.'

I felt ill with relief. 'I don't deserve this.'

'That doesn't mean I've forgiven either of you. I intend to punish you in ways you can't imagine. I'm going to take you shopping when you get all that money from your Auntie Lynn and make you buy clothes that I pick out for you.'

I groaned dramatically. 'Please! Ruin my life! Steal my husband! Anything but clothes shopping.' Then I put my arms around her. 'I'm sorry for everything. And starting from today, I'm going to make it up to you.'

'Are you going to turn me into a likeable person as well?'

I froze. 'Lisa . . .'

She shook my arm. 'Only joking! Well, I'm not really but this isn't the time.'

'What are you going to do about work?'

'I'm taking a week off sick then I'll go back until my maternity leave begins. Nobody saw me at the pub so I'm going to bluff it out, act as if nothing's changed.'

I was overwhelmed by her nerve. 'That takes guts.'

'You never know, I might make them like me before I leave. Listen, I'm exhausted. Can you send Kieran back here so I can torment him a bit more before he goes home?'

She kissed me fondly before I left in a great mood. I felt twenty pounds lighter. There were no more secrets between us and we were going to be all right. I was sure of it.

Mark and I got home to find a post-it note from Phil stuck on the TV. *Thanks for everything. Gone home to Tally. Phil.* We were both fairly choked at this.

'So is that it?' Mark asked me. 'We've repaired their marriages, as we planned, just like that?'

I thought about his question. 'I'm not sure we can take the credit for any of it, but it certainly looks as if they're all back together again.'

'And Maria? You didn't get round to telling me just what our marriage break-up had to do with her but is she over her strop, whatever it was?'

'She's fine. You know Maria.' I'd called her the day before and, after ascertaining that she was now happily ensconced with Gary (not Tony), I broke the news that I was back with Mark. Surprisingly, she'd been pleased for me.

'I would have thought she'd have thrown a party when she heard we were getting a divorce,' he said. 'She's never liked me.'

'That's not true,' I lied.

'You're a terrible liar,' Mark laughed, 'I'm pleased to say.'

I began to feel uncomfortable. Something occurred to me. 'Has it really only been a month?'

Mark pulled me onto the sofa. 'And it's been the worst month of my life. But I have this great feeling that now, finally, everything's getting back to normal.'

I tensed initially but, inevitably, we dissolved into each other once more. He was right. Everything was getting back to normal, with one exception: I was going to be meeting my ex-lover for lunch tomorrow.

That didn't happen when I was eighteen.

My new life started on a Wednesday. Mark had moved back into the master bedroom on our return from the hospital. We made love and talked about honesty and feelings. He slept well. I didn't.

'I've been thinking about the business,' he began over breakfast. In keeping with our commitment that we would be returning to normal, we were eating on trays on laps in the living room.

'All our troubles, *all* of them, were caused by money, did you realize that? If I hadn't lost all that money to Clive, then I wouldn't have overreacted when you started pushing about kids and –'

'Mark, we've been through all this –'

'I know, I know. Well anyway, this past month has shaken me up. Yesterday, before we came home, Kieran and I came to a decision.'

Oh no, not more decisions. 'And?'

'We're going to dismantle the company, sell on all our contracts and open a gym, just as we'd always planned back in Bristol.'

So this was how it was going to be. We weren't just going back to a month ago, we were going back to the beginning in every way. Not many people get the opportunity to do that, to turn back the clocks, take different paths, make different choices. Maybe there's a good reason why it's not possible. We were about to find out what that reason was.

'I think that's a great idea.'

Mark beamed. 'We worked it out. We're going to use the ware-house where we were going to store all our equipment. And we're going to work like crazy so that the gym will be open for Christmas. I want Dad to see it before he moves. Of course, it will take every penny we have but that won't matter because we've got Dad and Lynn's money coming at Christmas. That will cover all our operating costs for a couple of years while the gym takes off. We can use that time to make real plans.'

'Like what?'

'Well, nothing definite. And I'm not promising anything. But, well, I've been thinking since that night at the hospital with Lisa and, well, I'm still not 100 per cent sure but I'm not totally against it and . . . maybe we could consider starting a family?'

Family. He said the word.

So he was offering me everything I wanted. I had dragged every-body around me through all nine circles of Hell and achieved my goal. Oh yes, and not only was I keeping my husband and having a baby, I was building a lucrative, creative and fulfilling career. Oh yes, and on top of that, we were being handed £250,000. Now might be a good day for me to buy a lottery ticket.

And they say that 'want' doesn't mean 'get'.

This redoubled my determination to tell Ed that I could never see him again. After all, there was nothing he could offer me that I didn't already have.

'Are you sure you're OK about being here?' Ed asked. 'You seem very distracted.'

I looked around me. I'd never been to a restaurant like this. It was spread over seven floors and landings, each area decorated differently like an eccentric relation's dining room. Our zone was an illumination-fest: Tiffany lamps, bizarre statues with light bulbs in their orifices, little stars carved out of the walls with candles behind. Sitting under a revolving yellow sun, Ed looked seriously jaundiced.

'Sorry. I've got two friends in hospital.' I told him about Lisa and Alfie, feeling bad about using them to excuse my distraction but they weren't lies as such. Not really.

The food was ethnic; I think that's the correct word. We started with some thin slices of reindeer on slices of cardboard, followed by zebra and mush. I don't know what it really was because, by the time it arrived, I'd forgotten what I'd ordered. That was Ed's fault.

'Come away with me for the weekend,' he said suddenly.

'Sorry?'

'You're not going to be comfortable about staying out all night while Mark is staying in the flat and I understand that. I respect it too. You've been together all your life and you want this divorce to be as easy as possible on him.'

This was when I should have told him that I wasn't going to divorce Mark and I wasn't going to embark upon an affair. At this point, the food arrived and my mind became completely blank.

Ed went on as the waitress served us. 'So I suppose that means we'll be snatching afternoons and evenings when we can until Christmas, when he moves out. And I'm willing to accept that. If we can just start things properly.' From nowhere, he pulled an air ticket wallet and slapped them on the table.

At this point, I lost my appetite.

'New York,' I whispered.

'It's fantastic at this time of year, cold and crispy. You'd love it. And Americans will love you!'

'Because I'm weird?' I suggested.

'No!' he protested. 'Well, you are a bit . . . unusual.'

I bit into whatever it was that I'd ordered. It was definitely meat and a lot of garlic had been used in the preparation. I would have to eat mints all afternoon before I went home, and clean my teeth when I got in. And floss. And gargle with mouthwash.

I took a deep breath, ready to let him down gently. I stopped, suddenly aware that I'd never done this before. I'd never had the formative experience of dumping a boyfriend that most girls would have added to their repertoire before leaving school. I quickly trawled though my store of famous dumping scenes from films I'd seen but I'd lost my faith that movies could provide me with appropriate scripts. Also, I was no longer as certain that I wanted to finish this. This made me a terrible person, I knew that,

230

but I remembered all the new possibilities he represented, the excitement, that afternoon in his flat.

What was I thinking? I was here to draw a line under this insanity. I'd won, got everything I'd wanted from Mark. It was time to settle back down. And yet, I don't know, sitting here, looking at him, I felt . . . I don't know what I felt, so I stalled for time.

'Ed, that's such a lovely idea, but I can't just take off for New York. I'm worried about Lisa and Alfie. And my father-in-law's not fully fit yet. I'd feel terrible if something happened to any of them and I was on the other side of the world.'

His face dropped. 'You're turning me down.'

'No! If you ask me again after Christmas, then I promise I'll say yes. I promise.' What was I saying, making long-range promises like this? I didn't even know what I would be doing that evening. I was supposed to be letting him down gently then returning to the perfect life I'd wanted with Mark, the life I'd fought for with no thought for the casualties that might suffer under friendly fire.

Yes, this was definitely a breakdown, the sort of hormonal implosion that led premenstrual or menopausal women to murder traffic wardens and steal polyester blouses. I was all over the place, wanting Mark, wanting Ed, even wanting Kieran at one stage.

Ed thought about the problem, unaware of the volcano simmering below my expressionless exterior. 'I've got a compromise. Let's go away in England. Just down to Sussex. That way, if you're needed, you can be back in an hour or so.' I didn't raise any immediate objections and he was encouraged to sell harder. 'I know a little place in Selsey, near Chichester. It's empty at this time of the year. We can walk for miles and not see a soul. Saggy bed, log fire, pushy landlady, Cumberland sausages for breakfast, and –' he made sure I was listening '– the restaurant does the biggest and best toad-in-the-hole you will ever taste.'

I suddenly knew that I wanted to go. I really did. And I really didn't. This was all wrong. I found myself concentrating on the logistics, mainly to distract myself from having to consider the moral implications. The only time I'd ever gone away without Mark was when I'd been to health farms with Lisa. How could I find an excuse to get away for a whole weekend? If I said it was an origami contract, he'd insist on coming with me. I always went with him on his business trips.

'OK,' I said impetuously, not having any idea how or even if I was going to do this. I could work the rest out when I was alone.

Ed stared at me. 'Really? Oh, Jenny, you won't regret it.'

I regretted it already.

'Then why did you agree to it?' Maria asked.

I'd met her at a reception for a fashion show where she was selecting swimwear for the following summer. It was not my idea of a fun afternoon but it was the only time she could fit me in.

'I don't know. Well I do. There's a possibility I might love him. I might not but I might.' I shrugged, hoping she could make sense of this. I certainly couldn't.

'But you love Mark; you always have.'

'But what if I don't? What if that's just familiarity? I mean, you've had loads of men –'

'Thank you –'

'So you know all the degrees of feeling you can have. And I vividly recall you saying that you thought you loved your first boyfriend.'

'Everybody loves their first boyfriend.'

'Exactly!' I lunged forward, spilling champagne down both of us. 'So what happens to someone who only has one boyfriend?'

Maria was dabbing at the champagne stain. 'I know this is going to sound callous but I think you're deluding yourself about Ed. I'm sorry to disillusion you but all the feelings of "love" you've described since you met him, well, they sound like plain infatuation to me.'

This irritated me. 'I know the difference between love and infatuation. I'm not a child.'

'In this area, you *are* a child,' Maria pointed out, with uncharacteristic gentleness. 'And if you'd had any experience of men in the past, you'd be able to recognize this.'

I saw an opening here. 'So finally I have the opportunity to gain some experience. How can you deny me the chance?'

Maria applauded my gambit and reluctantly gave up that argument. 'So what do you think you'll gain by going away with Ed?'

'I'll know. We'll be away from everything so there'll be nothing to remind me of my other life. It'll just be me and Ed. Just as I've had a thousand weekends of me and Mark. It will either

232

feel right or wrong. That's all I need, just this one weekend. Then I can make my decision.'

'And what if you can't? What if you decide you love Ed then, as soon as you get back to Mark, you remember that it's him you love?'

'Because I've made up my mind,' I said, hoping I could convince her of my resolve. That would at least give me hope that I might be able to convince myself. 'This is going to be it. My last deception. Absolutely. So what do you think?'

Maria looked at me seriously. 'I think it's a mistake and I think you're crazy. You could end up losing it all. But if you've made up your mind, I know I can't dissuade you. So why did you have to see me in such a hurry?'

'Because I need you to supply my alibi.'

A procession of underweight girls in bikinis walking past gave Maria time to consider my request.

'This isn't fair.'

'Why not? You don't even like Mark.'

'I dislike lying even less. This isn't like you, Jen. I think everything that's happened has unbalanced you and you're not thinking straight.'

'One weekend, that's all I'm asking for. Then I will either choose Mark or Ed. You've always said it was a mistake for anyone to settle down with someone when they hadn't lived properly. That was why you didn't approve of Mark for me. Well, I'm not planning to have lots of affairs or even one long one. Just one weekend. Please, Maria!'

She agreed.

'Why are we here?' I whispered.

'Because you are heavily obligated to me and I am calling in the favours while you still remember them,' Lisa replied cheerfully. 'Now shut up, it's about to start.'

I'd had to postpone a business meeting and a shopping trip with Ed to accompany her to this Whole Woman seminar.

As she'd only given me a day's notice, I'd had no time to find out what we were in for. 'What exactly is this about?' I shouted as loud, electronic music throbbed around us.

Lisa folded a pashmina over her stomach to protect her foetus from the noise. 'Not totally sure. They wrote to me ages ago and offered me free tickets. I didn't need them at the time but I didn't throw them away.'

'You could always have given them to one of your team,' I suggested.

Lisa looked at me sharply. 'Is that a criticism?'

'You told me to be honest with you. Well, one of the reasons your staff don't like you is that you keep all the freebies for yourself even when you don't want them.'

'That's not true. I handed out some sachets of Slim Fast last week.'

'Yes, but you kept the Chanel lip gloss for yourself and it wasn't even your colour of Slaughterhouse Scarlet.'

She corrected me wearily. 'Sarajevo Scarlet. OK I take your point. Anyway, we were doing this series on motivational speakers and we received all of these invitations. I sent writers to all the famous and controversial ones but there were still some that I couldn't include.'

'But they must have sent you some information. What are their aims? I can't help thinking that we already are whole women. We're trying to be nicer ones.' And I wasn't just speaking for Lisa, either.

'I think they said something about shaking our perceptions of womanhood. What are you complaining about? It's not costing anything.'

A woman wearing a golden helmet marched out on stage and the audience erupted. This told me that these were people who watched too much Oprah on satellite. I clapped politely in case they singled out non-participants for special humiliation. I was taking no chances.

Lisa's eyes were shining. She had thrown herself into the quest for self-improvement as every other project in her life. It was a new list and I was sure that, if I asked to see the list tomorrow, there at the bottom would be: *Give free anti-wrinkle cream to typists*. But I was trying to support her because I felt guilty for, well, everything.

The woman in the helmet picked up a microphone. Her image appeared on massive screens above the stage, showing that it was not a helmet but hair. Her entire face appeared to be part of the same helmet, with a plastic sheen that was unreal. Even her clothes were unnatural. It looked as if she was wearing a stiff

234

woollen suit, but they didn't move when she moved. The effect was bizarre. Lisa was impressed. This was a woman with serious control over her appearance. 'Is there anyone here who wants to be made whole?' she screamed.

We all screamed back. I didn't scream, but I waved politely.

'OK, OK, OK! Now I have one thing to say to you! What is stopping you from being a whole woman?'

That was a valid question. I was going to put up my hand and say: 'I've only had one real boyfriend and now I'm not sure if I ought to have another one, just to see how I feel,' but this wasn't A-Level Geography and nobody was putting up their hands.

The women around us were screaming wildly about their thwarted goals and crumpet thighs.

Helmet Woman was touching her right ear as if she was listening to every one of these mad harpies. Then she asked for silence, screamed for silence.

'You're right, all of you are right, but, do you know, there was one word I didn't hear. The one word that is holding you back from attaining true, valid womanhood and do you know what that word is?' She waited for total silence.

'*Domination.*' At that, she grabbed the front of her suit and ripped the whole outfit off in one fluid gesture to reveal that she was wearing a leather basque and a thong studded with vicious nails. From offstage, she was thrown a whip and a leather stick of some kind. As if a button had been pressed, all around us, women reached into their bags and pulled out entire ranges of bondage weaponry.

Lisa and I were glued to our seats as we tried to assess whether we would be allowed to get out of this place without demonstrating some kind of violent tendency. When they started to play the theme from *Buffy the Vampire Slayer*, we made a run for it.

When we got outside, I marched Lisa straight to the nearest restaurant and ordered champagne.

'I'm pregnant,' she protested, 'I can't drink.'

'It just so happens that I have the answer to that.' I pulled out the sheaves of articles Maria had prepared for me, weeks earlier, on the value of Modest Champagne Drinking in Pregnancy. They'd been in my handbag ever since and were finally proving their worth which is evidence that hoarding has some merit.

'Just a small glass,' she conceded.

235

'There is a reason I've brought you here,' I said. 'We are not going to any more seminars or buying tapes that make us visualize ourselves as blossoming lilies. Instead we're going to go out once a week, drink champagne and laugh, I'm going to tell you to lighten up, you're going to tell me to smarten up and we're both going to do what the other suggests.'

Lisa was doubtful. 'If there is any way you can represent that in a list format, you have a deal.'

We shook on it and I congratulated myself on rescuing my most valued friendship from almost fatal injury and restoring it to a healthier condition than it had originally enjoyed. Of course, it still wasn't an honest friendship because I hadn't told her that I was still seeing Ed. I couldn't. I knew she'd be terrified that I was once more about to destroy the fragile web interconnecting us. But we were close again and I'd made that happen.

That smugness was to last, ooh, a day until it came crashing down from where I least expected it like an avalanche in August.

I must have believed I had some sort of magic power that was inflicting happy dust on everyone around me. Lisa was so mellow that she left a tip of more than 5 per cent in the restaurant for the first time ever. Maria was so infatuated with the new man that *I had found for her*, that she was almost happy about providing an alibi for me. In two days, I would be going to Selsey with Ed, so he was blissfully happy. Mark and I were getting on well and I was keeping the lies to a minimum so he was not being hurt. Besides, after this weekend, I would be able to chose between them and the lies would end.

Everything I touched turned to happiness. And if I'd stopped there, maybe I'd have got away with it. But I wanted the full house. I had managed to persuade Phil to go back to Tally; now I needed to rebuild my friendship with her and make it even better than before as I did with Lisa. So I invited her for lunch.

She didn't sound that pleased to hear from me. 'Lunch isn't very easy. You must remember what my days are like.'

'But that was when you had the kids at home. Surely you have more free time when they're at school?' After all, you found the time to shimmy over to my husband's office as soon as you found out he was available, I thought. But I'd forgiven her for that. Almost. Practically.

'I suppose I can meet you tomorrow as long as I'm away by 2 o'clock to pick Martha up from nursery.' It wasn't the most enthusiastic reception to an offer of magical happy dust.

I felt guilty for not fully forgiving her so I chose an expensive restaurant in Pimlico, near Ellery and Jocasta's school. I was determined to woo her, to make her like me more than she did a few weeks ago when I ruined her dinner party and her marriage.

She'd dressed casually for me in jeans and shirt similar to the ones I favoured, but better fitting. Still, I was touched by the gesture.

'I've ordered champagne,' I told her after a very clumsy greeting kiss.

'But I'm driving. Did you forget about the school run?'

Yes I did. 'Oh well, you can have one small glass.'

'As long as it's very small.' She then made a major event of draping her hand dramatically over her glass whenever a waiter approached.

'So how are things going at home?' I asked.

'Phil's back so the children are pleased.'

Her tone dismayed me. 'But aren't you? I thought you wanted him back.'

Tally ran her finger around her untouched glass of champagne. 'I did but I thought everything would go back to the way it was. Phil is driving me mad. Yesterday he came home in the early afternoon with flowers and insisted on sitting down with me and talking. And he brings me tea in bed every morning. He's trying so hard.'

'But that's exactly what you wanted!' I was thrilled that my interference had paid off.

Tally was doubtful. 'It was only when we started talking that I finally realized why we'd stopped talking in the first place. We have nothing in common any more, apart from the children.'

I felt uneasy. 'But surely that's because of the children. I've read about things like this. You become so wrapped up in being parents that you forget how to be partners to each other. You need to go back to how you were before you had children.'

Tally looked at me coldly. 'That's what we *have* done. And it's reminded me that the reason we had children was most likely because we'd reached that inevitable point where we didn't know what else to do with our lives.'

Suddenly the answer to this, to all of our crowd's problems, was very clear. 'Then you haven't gone back far enough.'

'I don't understand.'

'It's no good you and Phil going back to a stage in your life when you weren't happy – you need to go back to the time when you were.'

Tally fingered her hair absently. 'University?'

'And those first years in London when it was just the two of you,' I reminded her. 'You were so wrapped up in each other then.'

She became wistful. 'I can't remember how we filled our days back then.'

I was encouraged by the softening of her mood. 'You need to go back there, work out when it started to go wrong and stop it from happening. That's what Mark and Kieran are doing with their business.' And it's what I'm doing with my own life, but that's my secret.

Tally was tensing up again. 'I still don't see how you can avoid that moment when the fairy tale ends and you stop caring.'

I didn't want to hear this. I drank too fast because I was uncomfortable and the food was modern; in other words, there wasn't enough of it. 'Mark and I never reached that moment.'

Tally laughed unpleasantly. 'You just did! That's why you've put him and the rest of us through all this. But I have to admit that you and he took a lot longer to get there than anyone else.'

The waiter filled my empty glass with the dregs of the champagne. In forty-five minutes, I'd finished the bottle. 'That's not true,' I said shakily. 'I wanted children because of some, I don't know, biological imperative.' That isn't easy to say when you're a little drunk. 'Mark and I were as happy as ever. Everything was perfect.'

'Really?' Tally said. 'But you thought everything was perfect in those shiny golden days at university and that proved to be an illusion.'

I flushed. 'I know he made a mistake back then. I've forgiven him. We're all entitled to make one mistake.' I was doing a swift philosophical calculation in my head to decide if Ed counted as one mistake or if every lie was an individual lapse.

'What about two mistakes? Is everyone entitled to make two mistakes?'

238

I shivered. Well, the champagne was very chilled. 'What do you mean? What was his second mistake?'

'I'm sure it was as meaningless as his "mistake" with me but, on his very first day in Bristol after the Freshers dance, he slept with Lisa.'

Chapter Sixteen

Like the loyal friend Maria had always been, she took the day off when she heard the desperation in my voice.

'Shopping?' she'd repeated. 'With me? Are you sure you don't mean playing Connect 4 and showing me your origami sumo wrestler with moveable abdominal muscles?'

'I want a whole new wardrobe. And who else would I ask when I have a leading fashion buyer for a friend?'

'Aren't you still working off your debts to the Rottweiler?'

'Those are cancelled,' I said, tightly. 'Besides, she's not up to shopping. Morning sickness.' I hoped this would close the subject of Lisa. I wasn't ready to face it, not yet.

Maria was waiting for me to elaborate but I refused to acknowledge her unspoken question. 'So what did you have in mind?'

This was an easier question. 'I want you to think back to when you first met me when I was a twenty-year-old student. Do you remember you said you'd love to get your hands on me and put me in some decent clothes? I tried to put you off by saying that I'd let you do it when I left university and got my first proper job.'

Maria pretended to search her memory. 'I think I may have said the same thing once or a million times since then as well.'

'So now I'm taking you up on the offer. I want you to imagine that I'm a normal graduate, trying to put her student image behind her and move on, grow up. It may have taken me a little longer than everyone else, but now I'm ready.'

'Are you sure you don't just want sexy new clothes to impress Ed on your weekend?' she teased.

'I *am* sure actually.' I was surprised by my own certainty.

'OK. But I have one condition.'

'Which is?'

'I won't make you buy something you hate but you have to try on everything I give you.'

'Fair enough.'

We started at Selfridges where, as usual, none of the women in the perfumery hall sprayed me with their noxious scents or offered me a mini makeover. Maria, on the other hand, had to fend them off by swishing her hair aggressively.

'Why does nobody ever ask me if I would like to try this season's blusher or J-Lo's anti-ageing cream?' I grumbled.

'Because you dress as if you either don't care about your appearance or can't afford to do anything about it. We're going to change all that.'

We came off the escalator on the first floor and marched past dozens of racks laden with clothes that smelled expensive and were all totally unsuitable. 'Nope. Nothing here,' I said. 'Let's go somewhere else.'

Maria exhaled impatiently. 'Where? The camping shop? Just follow me.'

We stopped in front of a section that dazzled me with its range of colour. 'I think this must be the clown section,' I whispered, hoping the vicious-faced saleswoman nearby wouldn't hear me and identify me as the style philistine I knew myself to be.

Maria was ignoring me and pulling out some wide-legged aubergine trousers and a rust fitted blouse with multi-coloured buttons. 'Go and try these on,' she commanded.

I slumped off to the fitting room like a sulky teenager forced to try on a pretty dress by her desperate mother. When the clothes were on, I stared at myself in the mirror, searching for clues. What difference did they make? My waist appeared smaller and my legs longer but did I still look like a woman who had committed herself to an identity at eighteen and got stuck? Surely anyone with eyes could see that I was just a child wearing somebody else's clothes.

I reluctantly pulled the curtain back to show the result to Maria. 'Perfect,' she pronounced with satisfaction before handing me a mid-calf-length, gently flared brown skirt with panels of garish florals and psychedelic swirls. To go with it, I was expected to try on a long-sleeved, tie-dyed cotton top with satin cuffs and a lacey collar.

242

'These look dreadful,' I declared as I walked up and down under sufferance.

Maria followed my eyeline. 'You're just saying that because you don't like people looking at you.'

'That's not true,' I protested. Was it? I studied my reflection again. I was disturbed by the thrill I experienced at finding myself looking so different. This was a step even beyond my transformation at the hands of Lisa's magicians. They had merely used paints and potions to apply a mask over the real me. Even the dress they had chosen was unthreatening, probably because they were trying to turn me into someone marketable.

Now I was wearing the sorts of colours and shapes that would always turn heads whichever face and body was poking out of them.

'Yes, it is true,' Maria insisted. 'You don't want anyone looking at you and do you know why?'

'Yes I do.' Because, all at once I did. I liked being safe. I was a safe person. It had taken me thirty-eight years to find out precisely who I was and now I knew. Safe. Stick to the first boyfriend who wants to stay with you in case the next one wants to leave you. Stick with the first friends who accept you in case you make new ones who change you. Stick to small jobs that you're good at rather than attempt a brave career that you fail at. Even when I break out and embark on an ill-advised affair, I stick to Mark in case Ed doesn't work out.

'Try these.' Maria was standing in front of me, a pile of clothes over her arm, amused by my distraction.

I obediently put them all on. Tight skirts, baggy trousers, clingy dresses, funky jackets. With each item, I broke a link of the chains to my past. As I held in my stomach and zipped up the skirt, I squeezed out my fear of change. In the trousers, I let go of my ever-present terror of regrets. In the dress, I uncrossed my arms from across my chest and allowed myself to become visible. And in the jacket, I simply felt attractive and entitled to feel it.

'Are you buying all of it?' Maria asked, astonished by my compliance.

'I can afford it,' I replied. 'Even without Auntie Lynn's money, I'm doing well. I'll even treat you to lunch.'

But Maria wasn't listening. 'Isn't that your friend with the slutty wife?'

243

I turned around and saw Phil, wandering miserably around the lingerie section. After paying for all my purchases, we went over to say hello.

'Oh, Jenny, thank God you're here!'

'It's not Tally's birthday, is it?' I asked.

Phil's mouth tightened. 'Why do you assume I'm buying something for Tally? Why can't I be having an affair like everyone else seems to have been doing? Perhaps I have mistresses all over London.'

I kissed him on the cheek. 'Because you're not like that.'

He stiffened at my sisterly affection. 'I didn't think you were like that. So it proves that none of us can really know anyone else.'

This was getting thorny. 'So what are you looking for?'

'I've been trying my best with Tally but she's still so unhappy. When I ask her how she feels, she just clams up. We're back to talking about the kids and my job and the house. It's an improvement on not talking, but only a little. I don't know what else to do. So I thought I'd buy her a nice nightie.'

'What is wrong with the lot of you?' Maria wailed. 'Did you all jump into some kind of time tunnel at Bristol that airlifted straight into middle age?'

Phil cringed before continuing. 'She said you had lunch the other day, Jen. Did she give you any idea what was on her mind?'

Oh yes. She took great pleasure in communicating to me what was on her mind. 'I can only tell you what we talked about, which was going back.'

Phil screwed up his forehead. 'Going back where?'

'She mentioned that you appear to have gone back to just before you had children – buying flowers, breakfast in bed, making an effort?'

'How can making an effort possibly be a bad thing?'

'I could be wrong but I think she wishes you could go back to the time when you didn't *need* to make an effort, when everything came naturally.'

'I always needed to make an effort with Tally,' Phil said mournfully. 'She was out of my league from the beginning.'

'But it didn't seem like that to her, not for years. Anyone could tell that you made her happy.'

Phil wasn't convinced. 'I don't remember that I was doing anything different.'

244

'Then I recommend that you spend some time trying to remember.'

'And a rule to bear in mind, Phil,' Maria interjected, 'is that broderie anglaise nightdresses are not acceptable wear for any woman under the age of ninety.'

Mental note to self: unpack broderie anglaise nightdress that I was planning to take to Selsey.

Mark became subdued as I took all of my new outfits out of the bags and transferred them to hangers. 'What's this all in aid of?'

'I couldn't keep going to all my business meetings in that one purple dress. My work's really taking off and I need the clothes to go with it. And, look, I've got some things for you.'

After a drunken lunch with Maria, I'd asked her to help me choose some things for Mark.

'Have you ever bought him clothes before?' she asked.

'Loads of times. It's always been easy because we can both wear the same size jeans and we're roughly the same height. But I want to get something different for him.'

'To turn him into Ed or to alleviate your guilt about Ed?'

'Just because I let you choose my new wardrobe doesn't mean you now have fresh insights into my psyche.'

'They're not fresh insights, they're old, stale ones. Your new appearance may have fooled the lady from the Estée Lauder counter but I know that, deep down, you haven't changed.'

'That's where you're wrong. Look at me taking risks! I'm wearing a low-cut top without a scarf.'

'But you do keep touching your throat nervously like Julie Andrews in *The Sound of Music* when the Baroness said that Christopher Plummer fancied her.'

I let my hand drop self-consciously. 'So are you going to help me or not? I don't know anything about men's clothes.'

'All right,' Maria sighed.

She was more conservative when selecting things for Mark and stopped me from going for the same bold colours she had picked out for me.

'What's wrong with a man in yellow?' I asked.

'With his bald head, he'll look like a sunflower. Look, Jen, are you sure this is a good idea? Just because you've decided to break out of your safety zone, can you assume that Mark is ready to do the same?'

With all the zeal of a new convert, I'd announced over lunch that I had been visited by a revelation, that I now recognized myself as someone hard-wired to make safe choices. Furthermore, I'd identified Mark as suffering from the same affliction and I was going to lead him into the light swathed in rainbow fabrics.

Maria raised an objection. 'Once you've reinvented him as a Disney cartoon character, what happens when, if, you leave him?'

'*If* I leave him, *if*, then I will have helped him prepare for his new life by taking the first few steps with him.'

Maria lifted the tablecloth. 'Are we being filmed? Why are you talking like the narrator on a bad reality TV show?'

I didn't rise to the insult. 'I mean it. I feel great in these new clothes. But I feel even better about making the decision to change. And it doesn't matter what happens this weekend and what I decide. I want Mark to move on too.'

'Sounds like a serious case of encroaching to me.' But she helped me, curbing some of my more extreme temptations.

Mark gingerly lifted the clothes from their bags as if they were alive. 'It's pink. You've bought me a pink shirt.' He just kept staring at it. But I'd anticipated this reaction.

'And I've bought an orange shirt for me. We're making a new beginning, aren't we? But we've been wearing the same things forever. You'll feel different in bright colours. I was amazed by the effect.'

'But I don't want to feel different. I'm quite happy feeling the same.'

I recoiled as if he'd slapped me. These were precisely the same words he'd used when I first asked him for a baby. Now I knew how Tally felt about stepping back in time to the wrong time.

'I want us to change,' I said, softly, 'just a tiny, tiny bit. Not in the things we do but in the ways we are.'

'Is there something you're not telling me?' Mark asked shrewdly. 'Because you're behaving very strangely, completely out of character.'

Good, I thought, it was my character I was trying to escape. 'I'll take them back if you really want me to. I suppose it was a bit mad to think I could ever prise you from your Fruit of the Loom T-shirts.'

'This weekend with Maria will be good for you,' he said kindly, grateful that I had backed down. 'You can get whatever it is out of your system with her, drink too much, listen to her calling me a hobbit. Hopefully, after a weekend with fashion buyers talking about skirt lengths for forty-eight hours, you'll be glad to get back to normal. I'll be glad too.'

He kissed me and held me a little more tightly than before.

Alfie was surprised to see me. 'They were going to send me home in an ambulance,' he explained. 'You didn't need to bother coming.'

'Don't be ridiculous,' I said. 'After all the times you've rescued me when I needed a lift, the least I could do was pick you up today.'

'Ah, but I was making you pay for your lifts. They were business.'

'What makes you think I'm not going to charge you?' I teased.

He'd refused to lean on me, determined to show that he was back to full strength, but I could see he'd lost weight. The hospital door opened automatically and revealed his lift.

'A taxi?' he gasped. 'Somebody else's taxi?'

'Now's your chance to see how Londoners have suffered for decades,' I whispered.

He sniffed the air inside the cab. 'This hasn't been cleaned for some time,' he muttered.

When the cab pulled out, throwing us back against the seats, he swore impressively. 'Is he trying to kill us? Doesn't he know I've just come out of hospital?'

'He is focussed on his destination,' I intoned. 'Nothing else matters.'

I think all taxi drivers should be forced to travel anonymously in another cab at least once a month. They'd soon learn that a Simpsons air freshener is no substitute for a complete set of intact vertebrae.

I helped him into his house and unpacked the shopping I'd bought.

'You can make me a cup of tea while you're out there, love, and then come and tell me how things are going back home.'

While I waited for the kettle to boil, I thought about my friendship with Alfie because I considered this a proper friendship, different to what I shared with Lisa and Maria, or had once shared with Kieran, but just as real. What differentiated this from the others was that this was perhaps the only relationship I had ever known where I'd been completely honest. I don't know why, maybe because whenever I was with him, I found myself remembering that stupid fortune cookie. I'd never lied to Alfie even though I'd done my fair share of things worth lying about.

So it was when I made the conscious decision to lie about my weekend with Ed that I knew my deception was no longer harmless.

When I got home, there was a man on the doorstep. This was an improvement on finding men *in* my flat. He looked vaguely familiar so I surmised he must have come to my origami party. If he'd worn a red or blue dot, it would have helped. Bearing in mind Maria and Lisa's warnings of serial killers, I maintained a guarded distance.

'Hello?'

'Jenny. Hi!'

His pleasure at seeing me was scary. 'I'm really sorry, but I don't remember your name.'

'Gary,' he said. 'From Kittenz?'

Of course! Gary/Tony. 'I would have recognized you if you'd been leaning on a bar with your friend, holding an overpriced beer and trying to hide from me.'

He laughed. 'We found you amusing. It was like one of those films where an innocent is snatched from his world and plonked down in an alien environment. Like *Crocodile Dundee . . .*'

'*George of the Jungle . . .*'

'*Starman . . .*'

I reappraised him in the light of this exchange. 'You like bad films?'

'I do, but I'm capable of bluffing on the subject of good films as well.'

'That's essential if you want to be regarded as postmodern rather than thick,' I agreed.

We stood on the pavement just enjoying the bond.

'Now you've ascertained that I'm not going to hit you with a cosh and rip the fillings from your teeth, is there any possibility that you might invite me in?'

'I'm so sorry! Come in.'

I experienced a momentary panic that Mark might be home and wonder why I was bringing yet another man into our home. But in a rare case of serendipity, this was the first occasion in recent weeks where I'd walked into the flat and not been greeted by an unwelcome surprise.

While I threw some clothes into the bedroom, Gary did the usual visitor's thing of reading our book titles and feigning interest in our paintings. 'Anybody else would have asked me what I was doing here or how I got their address.'

I went into the kitchen to see if I had milk or biscuits before I offered anything. 'If Maria has ever talked about me, then you'll know I'm not very good on my people skills.'

'She talks about you a lot. I've heard all about your origami party.'

Thank you, Maria. So this had been my major contribution to our friendship, to be a figure of fun, a subject to fill one of those frequent tricky silences at the beginning of her relationships. 'And after my unsubtle approach to you at Kittenz, you must now be convinced that I am certifiable. I'm astonished that you're not worried about being alone with me.'

Gary was now crouched in front of the video cabinet. 'What a fantastic collection! You've got *The Postman*! That's the worst film ever.' He spoke in hushed awe.

'Tea? Coffee?'

'Tea please. Wow, you've got some serious games here.'

'You like games as well?' A pang of anxiety stabbed me. Could I be accused of encroaching when he came to me rather than the other way round?

'Who doesn't? I was president of the Games Society at university. And there's a bar in Hammersmith where we all meet to play. We go there for the old games like Mouse Trap and Hats Off, but there are some of the Dungeons and Dragons weirdos too.'

Bad, very bad. 'Tell me, Gary, have you spoken to Maria about this side of your life?'

'Not yet. You know what it's like in the early days.' No I don't. Ask me after the weekend. 'You've probably found, yourself, that some people are put off when you mention that you like to play games. They think you're either childish or odd.'

249

'Speaking for myself, I'd have to say I'm both of those things,' I confessed.

'But that's not all you are,' Gary countered. 'You're a gifted paper artist, I've heard.'

OK. It was time to draw this encroachment, whoever was doing the encroaching, to a halt. Since I didn't know if I would ever want to face Lisa again, I couldn't afford to strike Maria from my dwindling list of friends as well. 'So, Gary, to go back to your earlier question, what are you doing here and how did you get my address?'

'I got the address from the book next to Maria's phone. Why I am here is more delicate. You're going to be very shocked when I tell you. I expect you trust your partner completely.'

No, he wasn't being ironic. Maria can't have told him that story. She must be saving that for a long winter evening when there's nothing good on the telly. 'I doubt very much if anything you say will shock me,' I said with confidence.

'I heard her planning this weekend away with you but when I tried to talk to her about it, she became secretive. Then I phoned the hotel. I was going to surprise her with flowers and champagne when she arrived. And they didn't have a reservation in her name, although they did in yours.'

His forlorn expression informed me that Maria had every right to be optimistic about this man. He wasn't just mad about her, he cared about her. Bless her for maintaining the fiction with him for my benefit. But I couldn't let her jeopardize this relationship for my sake.

I explained why she was lying. His disappointment at my role in this made me feel ashamed. 'She was going to tell you after the weekend and she hated going along with it.'

'I realize that I've just met you but this sounds insane. Maria tells me that you have an incredible marriage. She really envies you for it.'

'Envies me? She calls my husband a hobbit!'

'How long have you known her? For me, it's been just over a week and I already know that she wants a stable marriage and possibly the chance of kids more than anything in the world. You have got everything she longs for.'

Before I could comment on this, the phone rang. Gary signalled that he needed the bathroom and I pointed down the hall as I answered.

250

'Hi, Jen, it's Maria.'

'Maria!'

'Why are you whispering? Have I called at a bad time?'

'No. I've just got home from picking up Alfie from the hospital. I thought Mark might be having a nap but it looks like he's not here.' My hands were clammy from the lies.

'I was ringing to check if you're definitely going ahead with the weekend. Because you'll need to keep your mobile on at all times, just in case I have to contact you in a hurry. And I'll do the same. I'm still not happy about this, Jen. You can still pull out now, you do know that, don't you?'

'Every hour I change my mind,' I admitted. 'When I speak to Ed, I want to be with him, then when I'm here with Mark, I can't imagine why I would ever betray him. What's wrong with me?'

'You're just a typical teenager struggling to choose between two boys,' she said, not unkindly. 'A teenager who just happens to be a thirty-eight-year-old married woman. And if –'

'Have you got a plaster?' Gary came out of the bathroom holding his hand up. He'd cut his thumb on the broken shelf where Ed had smashed the bottle of nit shampoo. Mark hadn't got round to fixing it.

Maria's voice began to climb. 'That's Gary in the background. Gary is at your flat. My boyfriend. What the hell are you playing at, Jen? Have you got some sort of disease that turns you into a predator, working your way through every man you encounter?'

'Maria, he just came round to –'

She slammed the phone down before I could finish.

'What did she say?' Gary asked nervously.

It was what she didn't say that worried me.

I spent the rest of the afternoon trying to track her down. Her mobile wasn't switched on and I couldn't encapsulate my explanation in the twenty seconds available on her particular message service. Her secretary told me that she'd taken the rest of the day off and her tone suggested that this was my fault. I had to speak to Maria, to clear this up before I went away with Ed tomorrow. If I went. When I went. If I went. Whatever.

When you've been friends with someone for twenty years, when you've spent hundreds of evenings together, spoken for thousands of hours, you would feel entitled to say that you know them. So how was it that I wasn't sure where to begin to find her on an average Thursday afternoon in October?

Think! I told myself. Where did she like to go when her life was hemming her in and she had to get away from her flat, her office? She'd never mentioned it happening but it must have. It happened to everyone. And all the boyfriends she'd had. Where did she go with them? She talked about pubs and clubs and bars and restaurants but I couldn't recall a single name. Her world was a generality to me, lacking in details.

Would she be able to find me if I was running away from a situation? Easily. She'd go to the café in Battersea Park or the steps outside the Tate Gallery, or Streatham Odeon or Auntie Lynn's. I sank into my sofa in despair. I'd been a terrible friend to her and that was before I started my unintentional encroaching pattern.

I walked to her flat and rang all the neighbours' doorbells until one of them let me in. After watching her carefully secure her safety chain, I asked the elderly lady downstairs if she knew where Maria liked to go. I must have appeared agitated because she made to shut the door in my face. I stopped her before she broke my nose.

'I'm going to call the police! If you were her friend you'd know where she liked to go. She left here in a dreadful state half an hour ago. I know who you are – you're one of those crazy stalker ladies who kill their love rivals. I hear about it all the time on *Crimewatch*. Well I'm not going to tell you anything, even if you hold a knife to my throat!'

She managed to slam the door then. As I left, I saw her at the window, speaking excitedly into the phone. Terrific, there'll be a photofit of me all over London within an hour. I'll be arrested for asking intrusive questions about my best friend. At least if I was in a cell, I would be saved the dilemma of having to decide if I was going through with my weekend away. And they serve big meals in prison – they have to, something to do with human rights. Solitude, locked doors, lots of food. My kind of place.

I wasn't going to give up. I'd walked all the way here and hadn't bumped into Maria, so the only option left open to me was to keep walking and see if I could catch up with her. Mad, I know, but when I faced her I wanted to be able to declare that I had tried everything to find her.

I started out toward Clapham Common, going into every pub,

252

bar, café, Starbucks, every shop selling hand-painted pine chests, imported Mongolian incense and organic baby clothes. I walked around the common, taking in every bench, even sticking my head in the public loos and the Circus ticket office.

I didn't find her, of course I didn't, but the walk calmed me down. Gary would find her. He'd know how to contact her and he'd explain why he'd come round. He'd make it absolutely clear that I didn't encroach.

I'd been walking for almost three hours by the time I got home. I was exhausted and aching and very hungry. So I was looking forward to ordering a takeaway, collapsing in front of a video and not having to talk to Mark. He'd understand I was tired and would just stroke my finger, make me hot chocolate and pack me off to bed early.

But when I saw him, he was wearing that look again, the quizzical, accusatory look, that meant I was not going to be eating for ages.

'Gary rang,' he said.

Here we go again. 'Mark, I –'

He stopped me from interrupting. 'It's OK, I know he's Maria's boyfriend. He just said to tell you that Maria's at his flat and she's fine. Something about you being worried that she'd left the office unwell or something.'

Thank you, Gary. 'That's good.'

'Are you OK?' he asked strangely.

'Why?

Mark looked down at the bloodstains on the living room carpet. 'I was just wondering who's been bleeding in our flat?'

Couldn't do it. Couldn't explain it. My exhaustion had spread from my body into my mind and my mouth. My brain couldn't form any more lies and my lips couldn't form any more words. If there was a point where I was willing to concede that I might be having a breakdown, this would be it.

'I don't feel very well,' I said hoarsely and went to bed.

Chapter Seventeen

I woke up with a bad cold.

'Jen, you look terrible! You do know that flu is going around? I hear that Phil's got it and Tally and the kids.'

'It's just a cold,' I moaned, dragging myself out of bed. 'I'll be fine.'

'Don't be so silly. You need to stay in bed. You haven't got any meetings today, have you?'

'No but –'

'You can't possibly be thinking of going on this weekend with Maria, not in your condition.'

'Let me see what we've got in the medicine cabinet. I might just need some Day Nurse.'

Mark was exasperated by my stubbornness but he let me pass. When I got to the bathroom, I noticed that he had fixed the bathroom shelf and cleared up all of Gary's bloodstains. Something else I'd have to explain away. Another time. I opened the cabinet and was relieved to find that my usual foresight had prepared me for the next five years of illnesses.

There was Day Nurse, Night Nurse, nasal sprays, Benylin in Dry, Chesty and Congestion formulas. We had Vicks Vapour Rub, an electric vaporiser with essential oils, sticky pads that you place on your forehead to cool it down, eardrops, throat pastilles, even some utterly useless homeopathic tablets that I enjoyed swallowing by the handful just to annoy Lisa, who swore by them. And there was much more behind all of that stuff. But this would do for starters.

I piled up all the appropriate remedies and carried them into the living room. Arranging them by symptoms and ingredients, I drew up a drug schedule that I estimated would keep me going for the next forty-eight hours.

It went without saying that I'd gone over the top by now. By anyone's definition, I must be unhinged. But finally there was a time limit on my madness. In two days this could all end, would definitely all end, just like the final scene in *Butch Cassidy and the Sundance Kid*. Without anyone actually dying, I hoped.

I was going away with Ed. If I didn't, I'd have to postpone it and then I'd be forced to go through all this again. There was no question of just not doing it, of calling him up and explaining that I was happily back with my husband and couldn't endanger that on the off chance that my perception of love might be favourably altered. No. Too safe. Not me. Couldn't face the prospect of living with the regrets.

Mark watched me reading labels, calculating paracetamol levels. He didn't bother pressing me to reconsider, largely because I think he knew that I had already distanced myself from him.

It was a satisfying hour and by the time I'd organized all the medicines and tablets, the first dose had kicked in.

'So you're definitely going?' Mark asked one last time.

'I don't want to let Maria down,' I replied. 'and I think it will be good for me, for us, to have this weekend apart.'

'Personally, I've had enough time apart from you. But if you need to do this, then you must.'

I was prevented from crying by the combination of tablets that had dried up every secretion in my head. Mark left for work shortly after this, kissing me on my head to avoid catching my cold. He didn't say anything momentous and neither did I, just the usual garbled 'byes' and 'love yous'.

Then I was alone. I'd arranged that I would go to Ed's flat and we'd drive down to Sussex from there. He'd rescheduled his workload so that he would have the day off because he wanted to miss all the Friday commuter traffic.

I caught a taxi on the street after checking that Alfie was OK and had plenty of food left for the weekend.

Ed kissed me warmly but he was concerned about the heat blazing from my face. 'Jenny, you don't look very well.'

'It's just a cold,' I said. 'I've got plenty of drugs with me so I'll be fine!'

'If you're really unwell, then we can postpone, do it another weekend.'

'I want to go today,' I urged. 'The sea air will clear my head. Please, Ed, let's not put this off.'

He reluctantly agreed and, by lunchtime, we'd arrived in Selsey. We pulled into the hotel's car park and I woke up with a start.

'Is my company that dull?' Ed teased. 'You slept all the way.'

'Sorry, but I feel loads better.'

'I'm pleased. Come on. I'm dying to show you the room.'

A large woman in a scary suit was standing behind the desk but her fearsome features dissolved into a crinkly smile when she saw Ed.

'Mr McLaren!'

'Hello, Mrs Turner. You're looking gorgeous!'

Mrs Turner blushed attractively. I liked her. 'We haven't seen you for ages. Welcome back. And this must be . . .?'

'This is my friend, Jenny Stafford. I've told her all about this place and she's as excited to be here as I am.'

'Will you be riding while you're here?'

Ed glanced at me mischievously. 'I don't think so.'

The landlady looked surprised. 'That's not like you.'

'Jenny's not feeling too well. She has a nasty cold, so we're just going to take it easy, have some gentle walks, eat a lot, sleep a lot, let this place work its magic.'

My drugs were wearing off. The only magic that I needed was of the pharmaceutical kind. Ed picked up the key and carried our bags upstairs. When he opened the door, I revised my opinion. This room could well cure me of all my ills. It wrapped itself around me like a quilt, the sheerest gauze curtains allowing the dazzling light to dart about, illuminating the pale floral wallpaper and the carefully-chosen prints of local seascapes. The bed was old and saggy, as Ed had warned, but its age was a comfort, a symbol of endurance. And it called to me with a plaintive cry: 'Come and lie down, Jenny,' it intoned, 'the pillows are fat and soft, the sheets are crisp and cool, the duvet light and enveloping.'

'Would you like a nap?' Ed asked tenderly, intercepting the telepathy between me and the bed.

'I would love one but –'

He kissed me. 'It's OK, I wasn't planning to join you. I can see

257

you need to rest. I'll leave you in peace for a couple of hours. I might even go and have a ride. I'll come back later and we can have afternoon tea together.'

'That sounds wonderful,' I said, overflowing with gratitude. After taking the next two tablets on my schedule, I fell onto the bed without even taking my shoes off and slept the sleep of the innocent.

I woke up an hour and a half later, feeling miraculously better. I accepted that this was just the effects of the medicine but I enjoyed the remission and got out of bed. I must have sweated a lot because I felt sticky and uncomfortable and in need of a bath, and what a bath! It was the biggest cast-iron tub I had ever seen and, when I turned on the taps, the water filled the room with steam. After pouring in the new bath oils that I had bought from my new best friend, the perfume counter lady in Selfridges, I climbed into the bath and sank into paradise.

I don't know how long I lay there, enjoying the silence, letting all my conflicting plans battle it out for supremacy in my mind. But I wasn't complaining when the bathroom door opened and Ed joined me. Not just in the room but in the bath.

'What on earth have you put in this water?' he asked, wafting away the strong scent all around him.

'It is a very expensive bath preparation,' I scolded, 'that is only sold to women in nice clothes who are deemed worthy of such luxury by discerning consultants in white coats on substantial commission.'

'At least it will take away the smell of the horses,' Ed sniffed.

'I can't smell a thing,' I pointed out. 'My nose is so thoroughly blocked up that you could have been mud-wrestling in manure with pigs and I wouldn't have noticed.'

'Then why did you bother with the bath oil?'

'Stop asking me complicated questions. I'm too ill to think straight. I'm also hungry and I need scones and cream and at least fifteen cups of tea.'

Ed's hand reached out and he interlaced his fingers with mine. 'Is there any chance you might like to work up an appetite first?'

'In the short time you've known me, have I ever needed to work up an appetite? On the other hand . . .'

It was four-thirty by the time we'd got dressed and ambled downstairs to the garden room where a single table was set for us. Mrs

258

Turner was carrying through a tray laden with scones and fruit cake, in quantities which suggested that she knew why we would be particularly hungry. My face turned bright red but this could have been because my temperature was soaring once more.

'You really are sick,' Ed observed worriedly. 'Now I feel like a monster, making love to you when you're in such a dreadful state.'

'Do you recall me fighting you off?'

'Perhaps you were too polite to say no.'

'Perhaps I wanted to say yes.' We hadn't stopped holding hands since we'd left the room. I sensed that this must be what a honeymoon felt like. Although Ed and I had spent that fantastic, albeit awkward, afternoon in his flat after Chessington, this was different, special, real.

When Mark and I had gone on our walking honeymoon, it was just another holiday. We didn't even make love on our wedding night because I had blisters all over my feet from the new shoes that Lisa had made me wear. I know it sounds ridiculous now but it was a perfectly valid reason to me and to Mark. We respected each other's comfort. Besides, after so many years, it was just another night. I didn't think I minded at the time but I must have because I couldn't stop thinking about it now. I minded that Mark didn't mind.

Mark. The betrayal overwhelmed me instantly like an impenetrable fog. He was at home, Mark, my husband, worrying about my health, missing me, probably tidying the flat up ready for my return. And here I was, comparing our honeymoon dismissively to a couple of hours with a man I barely knew.

I hoped that my sudden inability to breathe was down to the illness raging through me rather than a suffocating guilt. The arrival of a second pot of tea pricked this particular thought balloon.

Ed watched me pouring two more cups with undisguised joy. 'I'm already imprinting this moment on my memory as one of the happiest of my life.'

I almost dropped the pot in relief. 'Oh Ed, me too! I was dreading us being uncomfortable with each other, that you wouldn't have felt what I felt, that I –'

He leaned over and placed a finger over my lips. 'You're babbling, sweetheart. I think you need to go upstairs, take some more of your potions, snuggle up in the armchair in front of the window with a blanket around you and watch the sunset. And I'm going to sit with you.'

It was exactly as I'd dreamed it would be, when I was sixteen, when I was twenty-six, when I was thirty-six. If a quartet of gypsy violinists were to appear right now playing 'O Sole Mio', I might even cry. And not with laughter,

We sat there in silence of the most perfect kind, folded together like paper under a blanket, watching the light change from bright to dim to red to hazy. It was changing for us; we both felt it.

Oh, this was easy. I had done the right thing and it hadn't been the safe thing. I had been brave, taken a massive chance and it had paid off. I knew without any doubt that my future lay with Ed. Nothing could compete with this. Mark couldn't compete with this. Maybe it was the fever talking because even I could tell how awful this made me appear. For maybe a second, a warning voice inside told me not to trust my feelings. But I was becoming vaguely deaf, probably because the infection was now causing my ears to buzz and throb ominously.

'You're burning up again, Jen.'

I wanted to put one of those cold gel pads on my face to cool me down but I felt that this was a bit much on our first night together. It would be like letting him see me with one of those strips across my nose that sucks out blackheads. Far too soon for that.

I stroked his face, enjoying the sense of entitlement. 'I'll take something. I'm saving the strong stuff until we go to bed otherwise I'll disturb you all night coughing and sniffing.'

'Maybe I'd like you to disturb me.' I slapped his hand lightly, jumping in alarm as my mobile phone rang. The display revealed that it was Mark. If I'd been thinking more clearly, I would have cut him off, blaming it on a bad reception later. But my brain was addled and I answered it without thinking.

'Hello? Jen? Are you there?'

'Hi.' I held the phone tightly to my ear, hoping that Ed wouldn't hear my caller's voice.

'I just called to make sure you got there safely and to see how you were feeling.'

His kindness was impossible to bear. 'I'm fine. Just a little groggy, that's all.'

'You sound as if you need to be in bed. Listen, I won't keep you, just to let you know I'm thinking about you. Make sure you get plenty of sleep and don't let Maria drag you out. I won't call again – I don't want to wake you up if you're having a nap. Hello? Are you still there?'

'Yes, sorry.'

'Go to bed *now*. That's an order. Love you.'

'Bye,' I mumbled, hating myself for not being able to tell him I loved him too. Hated myself for not even knowing if I did. Actually, I hated myself full stop.

'Who was that?' Ed asked casually.

'Just Maria,' I replied, lying with ease, wishing it hadn't been so easy.

After dosing myself up again, I changed my clothes for dinner and paid unusual attention to my make-up to disguise a nose that was becoming swollen and cheeks that were chalk-white and beginning to flake. Ed hugged me, stroking my hair affectionately and I forgot about Mark once more.

Still holding hands (Would I ever tire of this? Not possible), we strolled downstairs, talking in our new private language that was in the early stages of development. I tried to ignore the ache that was winding around my bones and was proving immune to the chemical barrage I'd thrown at it.

Stopping at the foot of the stairs to look at the menu, Ed abruptly dropped my hand.

I grabbed it once more only for him to shake it off again. 'Are you OK? What is it? Are you feeling unwell?' I'd been a bit off myself the night before when a sudden sense of illness over-whelmed me. He could well have caught the cold that I was finally accepting was more likely to be flu.

'Ed, please. What is it?'

He wasn't listening to me. He was staring at the reception desk where a woman was checking in with two children.

'It's Rachel. My ex-wife.'

Let's run away! I wanted to shout. We'll go and hide in our room, make love for forty-eight hours, have food sent up by room service then creep out on Sunday night, drive home and nothing will be spoiled. But it was too late. She'd seen us, or rather the kids had.

'Eddie,' they cried and came running over to him. He opened

261

his arms and caught them both, lifting them off the ground as if they weighed nothing.

'Sacha! Lulu!'

'Mummy, it's Eddie!'

'Mummy' was coming over to join us. Shimmying over. It was as if she'd filled in a list of attributes that would enable her to be everything I'm not. Unless Ed had chosen me because I was so different to her. She was a good four or five inches taller than me with endless legs that she showed off in skintight jeans. Typical that I should give up wearing jeans just when I learn how it's done properly. Her hair was a pale shade of blonde and chopped into a spiky short crop that only a very pretty face such as her own could carry off. She looked about twenty-four although I knew that she was the same age as me. I tried not to peer at her to see if she had the same lines that Ed had called attractive but which I had grown to despise in recent weeks.

She kissed Ed on both cheeks with enviable cool. If I'd been her, I would have thrown him on the floor and begged him to come back to me. 'Hello, Edward. This is a surprise.'

Edward? He was visibly flustered by this encounter and looked over to Mrs Turner on the desk, who was holding her hands up helplessly. Rachel spotted the exchange. 'Don't blame Peggy. I booked in under my new married name, so she had no idea I was coming. If this is going to be awkward, the kids and I could go somewhere else.'

'But Mum, you promised! You said we could help muck out the stables and go riding before breakfast.'

'Please, Mum! We don't want to go anywhere else. We want to stay here and see Eddie!'

'It won't be a problem,' Ed insisted. I cleared my throat which turned into an unattractive phlegmy cough from which both Ed and Rachel shrank back in distaste.

Ed took the hint. 'Oh, sorry, Jen. Rachel, this is Jenny Stafford, Jenny, this is Rachel.'

I smiled my most sophisticated smile, the one that got all the perfume ladies in Selfridges fighting to spray me and sell me the perfect crow's feet reducing cream. 'Nice to meet you, Rachel. I've heard a lot about you.' There. Now who's the cool one? Not a smidgeon of jealousy or angst.

'Hello, Jenny.'

Some bustle in the background reminded us that we were blocking both the staircase and the entrance hall. Ed moved me to one side with an odd arm movement that avoided any actual physical contact with me.

'You'll be wanting to get the kids to bed?' he asked, watching them with great fondness as they jumped off the stairs suicidally.

'They're starving so I was going to bring them down to get something to eat first.'

'You must join us –' he turned to me '– mustn't they?'

No they mustn't. 'Of course they must.'

Ed beamed at me, which made the sacrifice worthwhile. 'I insist, I mean, we insist.'

'OK then. We'll be down in five minutes. Come on, kids! We're having dinner with Eddie.'

They both punched the air with excitement. 'Yes!'

Ed watched them until they got to the top of the stairs and turned right. Towards the bedroom next to ours. This just got better and better. I should have brought a compendium of games with me.

He must have seen that I was looking unhappy. 'Jen, this can't be ideal for you. Maybe we could move on tomorrow. I don't want to spoil the weekend for you, I mean, us.'

'It'll be fine,' I said, bravely. But I'll be packed and ready to move on at 7.30 in the morning.

We went into the dining room where we had to drag two tables together to accommodate our cosy, but modern, extended family group. The aching had moved to my head and the tablets I'd taken earlier didn't seem to be having any effect. When Rachel returned minutes later, my misery was complete. In deference to my feeble attempts to dress for dinner, she'd done the same and was wearing an utterly plain shift dress in chocolate brown linen, accessorized only with a chunky gold necklace. I immediately felt overdressed.

I was glad I hadn't read more of Lisa's articles because I had a horrible suspicion that they might have confirmed that this woman chose this ensemble using powers of cunning that I could never comprehend or match.

'So what are we all having to drink?' Ed asked, establishing that he was the host for the night. 'Rachel, some Sancerre?'

'Of course,' she replied. 'They've got the best in England in their cellar.'

'And Coke for the kids,' he said to the waitress without needing to ask. 'And I'll have some Sancerre too, so why don't we have a bottle?'

And I'll have some hemlock and a sword to fall on.

'Oh, Jenny, what about you? Will it be all right to drink with all the tablets you're on?'

I don't care. Death would be a glorious release. 'I'll share the Sancerre, if that's OK?'

When it came to the food, I was in my element. Ed liked women to eat well – he told me so. Admittedly, I wasn't remotely hungry. I now knew that I was very ill and couldn't face so much as a peanut but I wasn't going to let this woman defeat me in every event.

'I'll have the toad-in-the-hole,' I told the waitress triumphantly. Ed had mentioned that this was the speciality. 'With fried pota-toes, carrots and peas.'

Rachel's mouth twitched slightly. In jealousy? 'Just a green salad for me, please.'

Ed looked up from his menu. 'I noticed you'd lost weight. You're looking incredible! In fact, I think I'll join you with a green salad. We had an enormous tea a few hours ago.'

Oh, that is fabulous. Now I'm going to be the greedy pig along-side the eminently self-disciplined ex-wife.

Ed touched the children's faces fondly. 'So what have you kids been up to since I saw you last?' They both spoke at once, eagerly sharing tales of school trips and birthday parties and homework difficulties.

'And Uncle Richard left as well,' Lulu added as an after-thought.

Ed's head shot up at this. 'You didn't tell me, Rachel. When did this happen?'

'It was a few months ago. I was hoping it wouldn't be perma-nent so I didn't say anything, but he's moving all his things out this weekend, which is why I brought the kids here. I wanted to spare them a messy separation.'

'I'm sorry it didn't work out,' Ed said sympathetically.

'I thought you'd be pleased and say that I deserved it. You told me I was making a big mistake and you've been proved right.'

'That doesn't mean I like seeing you unhappy.'

'I'm not that unhappy. Everything you said about Rich was

264

true. He was selfish and vain and he started looking around the minute he became bored of me.'

I considered setting the children's hair on fire with the candle to break up this moving exchange. I would have set myself on fire but I fully expected them to ignore the flames unless they happened to get close to the best Sancerre in England.

'We're glad he's gone,' Sacha piped up. 'He was mean. We like you best.'

Ed ruffled the boy's hair. 'I like you too. So are you looking forward to going riding in the morning?'

'I can't wait! Are you coming with us too? Oh please say yes!'

'Yes please, Eddie! You have to come, doesn't he, Mummy?'

Ed looked across at me uncertainly. 'I *was* planning on going for a ride. But it's up to Jenny, really.'

'Hooray!' the children screamed.

There was not a chance in Hell that I was going to sit in the room while Ed went riding with Gwyneth Paltrow and her perfect children. 'Why don't I come as well? It'll give me an opportunity to get to know Sacha and Lulu.'

They clearly didn't relish the prospect of getting to know me. 'Are you sure you'll be up to it?' Ed asked. 'It wasn't a great success last time and that was when you were in full health.'

'I'll be fine,' I insisted. 'I wouldn't miss it for anything.'

Rachel and Ed were both looking at me with strange expressions. Ed leaned over to me, conspiratorially. 'You have a drip hanging from your nose,' he whispered.

Best evening of my life. No question.

I was prepared to make love that night even though I felt dreadful. I needed to recoup the losses I'd sustained over dinner. But Ed wouldn't hear of it. I couldn't help but ask myself if it was because Rachel was next door. The walls were very thin, a fact I deduced when I heard Lulu announce with absolute clarity: 'I don't want *her* to come with us. She's ugly.'

Ed acted as if he hadn't heard. 'You need to get some sleep if you're determined to go ahead with the riding. Listen, Jen, I know why you're so keen on coming, but it isn't necessary. Rachel and I split up a long time ago. I'm with you now.'

'No, really,' I stressed, 'I want to come for your sake. You love this place for the riding first and foremost and, if I want to spend as much time with you as possible, then I'm going to have to ride with you. It'll be much easier this time. You'll see.'

It might have been a touch easier if my temperature hadn't settled merrily at 101 degrees and refused to come down, even when I risked ridicule and stuck the cooling patches all over my face for half an hour before getting dressed.

I sweated so badly in the night that Ed had ended up sleeping on the armchair cushions on the floor. I took a deep bath in the morning to wash away the stale smell of illness from my body, leaving the door ajar in case Ed decided to join me again. He didn't.

I hadn't brought suitable clothes for riding, for obvious reasons, so I had to wear the baggy aubergine trousers Maria had chosen for me. I knew they looked ridiculous with the jacket and riding boots that I had to borrow, but I consoled myself that at least they co-ordinated with my nose, which was now deep purple as well as dripping profusely.

Rachel appeared in full gear, looking fresh faced and beautiful. I noticed that she and Ed wore matching jackets. How lovely. 'You don't look at all well,' she mentioned sweetly. 'Have you taken anything for it?'

'If there is anything I *haven't* yet taken for it, I would be interested to try it.' I wanted her to shut up so that I could focus on conquering my fear. The horse I was being given, Daisy, was smaller than Toffee had been but friskier. Good thing? Bad thing? It didn't matter, I would have mounted a rabid lion if Rachel had done so first.

I got on without too many difficulties. Maybe all the drugs had dulled my phobic impulses. And when we started out from the stable, I fully expected to be able to get away with this. Ed had gone in front, followed by the two children with Rachel right behind. A boy from the stable was leading my horse, having ascertained that I was clueless and possibly a danger to the animal.

With every step Daisy took, a cannon reverberated through my body, causing untold pain. But my riding was more relaxed, mainly because I was using all my powers of concentration to focus on not passing out rather than not falling off. If I were ever to go riding again, I would pass on this tip to the instructor.

I was also trying to hear the conversation in front. I was sure it would be innocent, with me tagging along, but if there were any seeds that Rachel might be sowing, I wanted to know so that I could rip them up.

'Eddie, can we go for a gallop?'

'Oh yes, please Eddie!' The kids were pleading and I longed for him to refuse them. If this made me callous and hard-hearted, putting myself before the needs of two children, then that's what love must do for you. Although I didn't recall ever becoming a bitch when I was with Mark, even in the early idyllic years which I assume must have existed. Was this some sort of acid test? Was love supposed to make you nice?

I wished I'd read some of the complimentary copies of *Modern Woman* that Lisa kept on sending me. I could have done one of those quizzes, How Do You Know If It's Real? '*If you answer mainly A, then you love Mark and should go back to being a nice person; if you answer mainly B, then you love Ed and should resign yourself to being portrayed by Joan Collins when they film your life story; if you answer mainly C, then you are a social and cultural misfit and you have no place buying this magazine. Go and sort your own life out, loser.*'

I'd been thinking of Mark on and off through the night, in between sweating fits and pill-popping. And about Ed. And love. I had to know exactly how I felt before I made my big decision. I remembered everything that Maria had said about my inexperience making me deluded, that my feelings were no more than infatuation. But I didn't believe this. Surely this was too real to be a delusion? Even if it was being fuelled by all the drugs I was swilling down indiscriminately, surely I'd recognize it as such?

I tried really hard to recall the early days with Mark. I could picture the things we did, the first time we kissed and held hands. I could even remember when I knew I loved him, but the feelings? Nope. Couldn't get them back. And this struck me as a far worse betrayal of Mark than the lies and the infidelity.

I was roused from my reverie by Ed, who had trotted back and was staring at me with concern. 'You're not well,' he said firmly. 'Lee, could you take Jenny back? Jen, I'll see you at breakfast. We won't be long.'

And they were off, the four of them galloping off into the distance, a perfect nuclear group, satisfyingly symmetrical. I let myself be led back, humiliated, distraught and sick. But not

267

defeated. I'd started this weekend with a lover, new clothes and a brave new attitude to life. I intended to end it the same way.

I had another bath, having sweated off a further few pounds during the brief trek. The aubergine trousers were covered in mud and I had to put on the clothes I'd worn the day before. I hadn't brought that many clothes with me because Ed had led me to believe we would be spending most of the weekend in our room. I wished I'd brought my best broderie anglaise nightie and could pull it on, crawl under the duvet and ask Mark to make me up a hot water bottle. He'd stroke my head and put Lucozade next to the bed and look in on me every hour or so. Did I say Mark? I meant Ed.

I sat in the armchair in front of the window so that I would be able to see them return. I didn't dare lie down even though the bed had begun calling me again. I'd only end up sweating more and I couldn't spare the clothes.

I was still throbbing from the effects of the ride on my already aching limbs. It was as if my body had come out in sympathy with my mind, which was in torment. How could it have all gone so wrong? I had just discovered that I loved Ed and wanted to spend the rest of my life with him. He had claimed to feel the same way. Then she appears, without even an orchestra warning me by playing some sinister minor chords. Now it was all hanging before me either to be grasped or snatched away. And there was nothing I could do about it.

I couldn't make myself more desirable than Rachel or present a couple of wholesome children who need a daddy. I couldn't lie naked on a rug and let him ravage me because the cold floor against my boiling skin would send me plummeting into hypothermia. I couldn't even get on a horse and gallop after him.

How ironic, I thought. I'd come away thinking that all I had to do was decide who I loved and then make my choice. Not for one moment had I considered the possibility that the decision might be taken out of my hands. Maria, for all her much-vaunted experience of men and relationships, hadn't warned me of this.

Of course I fell asleep in the chair but was woken by screams of laughter approaching from outside the window. Ed was carrying Lulu on his shoulders, even though she was far too big for him, and chasing after Sacha. He was stumbling under her weight and threatening to drop her. Rachel was smiling indulgently at all the nonsense.

They looked so right together, the four of them. Don't let him leave me. Don't let him leave me. Don't let him leave me.

Ed came upstairs a good twenty minutes after they'd returned to the hotel.

'What were you doing?' I asked, hoping I didn't sound too shrewish. 'I saw you get back ages ago.'

'The kids wanted a quick game of table tennis. We always did that before breakfast.' He saw my face drop and rushed over to me, kneeling in front of my chair and placing his hand gently on my damp hair. 'I'm only doing all this because they're upset about their mother's marriage breaking up. All these changes are bad for them. I wanted them to enjoy a bit of stability and routine, just for an hour or so. Anyway, are you coming down for breakfast?'

I wanted to so badly. I couldn't leave him alone with Rachel for a second more than necessary but my body had given up on me. I burst into tears. 'I don't feel well,' I wept.

He held me tightly, kissed me on the head and helped me over to the bed. I switched off my mobile phone without thinking and, within seconds, I was asleep. Just before I dropped off, I wondered why he hadn't repeated the offer to change hotels.

When I woke up, the room was dark. Looking at the clock, I saw it was half past five. I sat upright, too quickly, and had to lie down again. The bed was soaking and I was shivering in my damp trousers and top that I'd been too exhausted to take off. I grabbed a couple of tablets. I didn't know what they were and I didn't care.

Pulling myself up, I looked in the mirror and scared myself. I had turned into Jacob Marley's Ghost, a spectre of deathly pallor and gloom. I decided to take a quick shower before going to look for the others. In desperation, I had to put on some of Ed's clothes and enjoyed a momentary pleasure that I was still allowed an intimacy that was out of bounds to Rachel in her status of 'ex'.

I trowelled on enough make-up to give me a disturbingly orange complexion that I hoped was more attractive than the red-and-white combo underneath.

Feeling almost human, I went downstairs, already rehearsing the witty lines with which I would entertain Ed and devastate

Rachel. But the script would forever lie unread and unspoken. At the small table where Ed and I had held hands over scones yesterday, where I'd experienced my first encounter with real love, he was telling Rachel that he still loved her.

I knew this because I could read his lips.

Chapter Eighteen

I wondered which one he'd choose: the classic 'I didn't mean for this to happen', the succinct 'it just happened', or the morally unassailable 'it's for the sake of the kids'?

As I curled up on my side of the bed, the door sprang open and he rushed over to me. 'Jenny, I'm so sorry. I didn't mean for you to find out like this.' I hadn't thought of this one, but that's good too. I waited for the next one on his list but it was apparently my turn to speak. I wouldn't know, never having played this scene before. That's right. Thirty-eight and never been dumped. Never had a broken heart. I couldn't even say that my heart was broken during the split with Mark because my overriding emotion had been rage that he wasn't going to give me what I wanted and terror of the uncertainty before me.

So this was what it felt like. I'd wanted to sample the intense emotions that I felt I'd missed in my sheltered life with Mark. My wish had come true. It required effort to isolate the pain of a lost dream from the overwhelming discomfort of flu but I had a fairly accurate idea which was which.

'The thing is, Jenny, it was never just Rachel, it was the whole package. We were a family. It worked for them and it worked for me. How can I not have another go at it?'

How indeed? How could anyone compare a package, a family, years of shared experiences and common memories, to an unbalanced paper-folder with whom one happened to have shared a few unfortunate dates and a small number of hours in bed? And a bath.

He was now stroking my shoulder. 'Talk to me, Jenny. Please!'

'I'm not well, Ed. Go away. Pack your bag and take Rachel and her children and go away so I don't have to see any of you again.'

I closed my eyes tightly, like a child desperate to avoid seeing the doctor approach with an injection. Go away, I prayed; go away. He sat there on the bed for what felt like hours before finally complying with my request.

Then he was gone and I was alone. For the first time in my life I was entirely alone. I was in a hotel in Sussex without a car and too ill to get to a bus stop or station. I didn't even have much cash on me. I switched my mobile phone back on, fully expecting to find that there was no reception. This would have been in keeping with the general theme of the weekend.

Inexplicably I had a full signal and could contact anyone I chose. But I had nobody I could call, nobody I could see, nobody I could ask for help or advice. Maria was the only person who knew I was here and why, but I couldn't ask her to rescue me, not when she was unhappy about being involved in this deception in the first place, and especially since it had led Gary to my door. No, that would be an encroachment too far. Auntie Lynn, Lisa, Kieran, even Tally or Phil? I couldn't tell any of them what had happened. They'd all, quite rightly, judge me and I couldn't face that, not while I would be judging myself for the rest of my life.

I was also just about in possession of enough self-control to realize that this would have to remain a secret if I didn't want it to ruin every other part of my life on top of my own personal happiness.

There was only one person I could call. Alfie. He'd tell me what to do.

'Hello?'

I recognized that voice. 'Lisa? What are you doing at Alfie's house?'

'Oh Jen, he's had a heart attack! A paramedic's with him now and we're waiting for an ambulance. He tried to call you but you had your mobile switched off. So he found my business card in his wallet. Isn't it awful? He didn't have anyone else to phone apart from us.'

I closed my eyes. 'How is he?'

'The paramedic says he's stable but he's very weak. Where are you? Mark's been phoning you constantly. So has Maria. Is something going on that I don't know about?'

You could say that. 'Lisa, I'm in Selsey, down in Sussex. Don't ask why. I've got flu and no money and I don't know what to do.'

My voice broke at the end and I bit my hand to prevent myself from weeping too openly. I didn't deserve pity and couldn't bear for Lisa to be kind to me.

This was her kind of situation. 'OK. Let me think. My company uses a car service and I believe they have branches all over the country. I'll call them and arrange for them to pick you up and bring you back. They can transport you straight to the hospital, if you like.'

'I would love to come straight there but I don't think I should. I'm really sick and probably contagious, so I ought to keep away from hospitals. The last thing I'd want is to give Alfie flu. Or you, in your condition.'

'Good point. Right, then just go home and I'll keep you posted. Maybe you could send Mark to the hospital.'

'I'll never be able to thank you enough for this, Lisa.'

'Yes you will. I'm dragging you to another seminar as soon as you're better. "Organized Pregnancy – How to Survive a Baby without Disrupting your Life" – they even supply you with pre-printed lists.'

I loved Lisa. She was my sole source of continuity, a steadying hand, at a time when I felt I'd been ploughing aimlessly into walls with my eyes shut. After I'd given her the hotel details, I packed and trudged downstairs, forgetting that this woman I loved was the same woman who'd slept with my husband on their first day at Bristol years ago. Forgetting that I was supposed to hate her.

The journey back was awful. I had to make the driver stop a number of times so that I could be sick. I think I'd taken too many medicines or mixed them or something. Unlike Alfie, this driver had no interest in my problems and didn't want to know how I'd ended up in such a state. He was more concerned about his uphol-stery and would have refused to take me if Lisa hadn't offered him twice the fare.

We reached Battersea at half past ten. Mark opened the car door to help me out. He must have been watching by the window, waiting for me to arrive.

'Thanks!' he called to the driver, who sped away before I could cough one more germ onto his paintwork. 'Come on, Sweetie Pie,' he said tenderly, as he helped me into the flat. I hadn't been aware I was crying until he gave me a tissue and guided me straight to bed. My nightie was folded on the pillow ready for him to help me into, and there was a hot water bottle on my side of the sheets.

I couldn't speak but, at the same time, I knew I didn't have to, that Mark wouldn't expect it. I lay down slowly until my head found its familiar impression in the pillow. I fell asleep, lulled by Mark stroking my head, saying over and over again, 'It's going to be all right.'

I stayed in bed for six days without a fight. Mark called a doctor, who diagnosed pneumonia and said I was lucky to avoid being sent to hospital. He prescribed a lot of antibiotics which Mark collected and doled out to me carefully. Days and nights blurred into a haze of self-recrimination and fever. Every so often, in my more lucid moments, Mark would update me on Alfie, who was rallying and expected to make a full recovery. But he never asked me what had happened. Not then, at least.

The following Saturday morning, I woke up at 7 o'clock and felt for the first time that I was going to live. I was so weak I could hardly walk and I was still coughing like a forty-a-day smoker, but a window of clarity was demisting in my head.

I made myself some tea using a mug of water boiled in the microwave because I couldn't lift a full kettle. Carrying it through to the living room, I noticed that Mark had moved all his stuff back in. He'd returned all the furniture and paintings to their original positions. Even the books were back the way they used to be, stuffed in haphazardly between knick-knacks and tacky souvenirs and all our favourite framed photos. I wondered when he'd done this. Not while I was ill because I would have heard him. It must have been when I was in Selsey with Ed.

So he was reassembling our life while I was blithely dismantling it. At the very moment when I knew with absolute certainty that I would be leaving Mark, he was possibly standing in front of the kitchen cupboard, merging my coffee cups with his toast rack, believing each item replaced would restore a brick in our broken relationship.

I sat down, still dizzy when I moved too quickly. I sipped the tea, my tongue unconsciously searching for the crack from when Mark had dropped the mug a year or so earlier. It was a cheap mug that he'd bought me on our honeymoon from the Beatrix Potter museum. I was devastated when it was damaged and he'd ordered

274

some expensive ceramic repair glue from America to fix it. It had become my most treasured possession. At the same museum, I'd bought him a Peter Rabbit tie that he said he'd wear every year on our wedding anniversary.

Our wedding anniversary. It was next month, on 15 November. I'd forgotten all about it – hardly surprising when we'd been going through an on-again-off-again divorce. The first anniversary is paper. I'd often been approached by people asking me to create special presents for their spouses from paper. Sometimes, it would be a flower from the wedding bouquet or a symbol of a country visited on honeymoon. What would I make Mark? I knew a nifty fold that produced a heart with a realistic jagged centre section – the perfect broken heart. What was I thinking? That would be the perfect present for me, not him.

'What are you doing in here?' Mark had got up without me hearing him and was crouching in front of the sofa. 'You should have called me. I'd have made you a cup of tea.'

He extended his hand and I reached for it, letting it rest gently in mine. 'I wanted to get up. I'm feeling a bit better. I might try and have a bath in a while.' A bath. When would I be able to have a bath again without thinking of Ed joining me?

'Will you be OK if I go over to the gym?'

'The gym?'

'Don't you remember me talking about it? You must have been more out of it than I thought. We've started work on the conversion and are on schedule to open on Christmas Eve. It's going to be tight but we're getting there. Thank goodness we've got Dad and Lynn's money coming. Once we open this place, we will be completely and absolutely broke!'

'I vaguely recall you talking about that.' But in truth I hadn't been able to listen to anything he said, apart from the updates on Alfie. All I could think of was Ed. I was like a teenager with a crush on a pop star and I didn't know what to do about it. I needed a mother to tell me to pull myself together. Then I could go into a sulk, refuse to eat or wash my hair for a week, tell her that she was too old to understand, then immediately transfer my allegiance to Justin Timberlake.

'There's soup in the cupboard and lots of bread. Just don't try and do too much on your first day up.'

I could tell he was pondering whether he dared kiss me or not.

275

We were saved from his dilemma by the doorbell. It could only be the postman at this time. Mark opened the door and Lisa walked slowly in, her face bare and her eyes red.

'Oh Jen, I'm really sorry. Alfie died.'

They delayed the funeral for over a week so that his daughter could arrange to come back from Australia. It also gave me some extra time to regain some strength.

Mark had been worried that the news of Alfie's death would be a setback for me, that I'd blame myself. Of course I blamed myself. Not for his heart attack, but for not being there when he needed me and not being with him when he died. When I weighed up the amount of time we'd spent in each other's company, it was obvious that he had given a lot more than he'd received. And relationships shouldn't be like that. I believed this now, having been on the receiving end of so much kindness over the past week, from Mark and my friends.

I kept thinking of our last conversation when he told me not to expect happiness, how that was his secret of happiness. I understood it now. I'd gone chasing something that was not rightfully mine and abandoned something that was, because I believed that I was entitled to happiness. In doing so, not only had I landed myself with some ugly scars but I'd hurt everyone around me too. Especially Mark. No more. No more.

It was odd going to the funeral of someone I'd known for such a short time. But, although it had only been six weeks since Alfie had joined me on my stalking escapade, it had seemed longer because the whole period was so intense. Lisa, Kieran, Mark and I sat near the back of the packed church, trying to guess who all the mourners were.

We recognized Katie, his daughter, from the photos. Her feckless husband wasn't with her, a fact that I knew would have pleased her dad. The service was bland, hampered by the vicar not knowing Alfie. He invited people to come to the front and share something about the deceased.

A man shuffled to the front and turned to face the congregation. 'Alfie could get to Staples Corner from anywhere in London quicker than anybody else, even if the North Circular was closed. Thank you.'

276

Mark and I exchanged amused glances. The next man to come forth was equally specific in his eulogy. 'Alfie could get any drunk out of his car in less than ten seconds, without threats of physical violence.'

We heard murmurs of approval buzz around the church. 'They're all taxi drivers,' Mark whispered to me.

'We should pay attention,' Kieran whispered. 'We might pick up some tips about short-cuts around the Hanger Lane Gyratory System.'

Lisa and I began to giggle and a few stern faces turned to frown at us. I remembered where I was and became sad once more. I decided to say something myself. Alfie would have liked that.

'Erm, I didn't know Alfie for very long but I will always have one very special memory of him. He bought me breakfast at his favourite café one day when I was in a bad way. The waiter brought over a fortune cookie and, when I opened it, the fortune read: BE TELL TRUTHING TO HIMSELF.' There were a few laughs. 'Yes, I sneered as well. But it came at a time when I was not being honest with myself and, as a tribute to Alfie, I'm going to try and be "tell truthing" in the future.' Mark's expression told me that he approved of the gesture. It was a good moment for us.

Before I could step down, a cockney voice shouted from the back, 'That wouldn't happen to have been Billy Tong's caff down the Brixton Road, would it, love?' I nodded in surprise. 'Only we weren't laughing at the words, we were laughing at Alfie's cheek. Billy's been flogging those fortune cookies for fifteen years and there's only ever been the one fortune in them, and they all say exactly the same thing!'

Everyone collapsed laughing in collective appreciation of cabbie humour at the expense of the hapless passenger. I left sheepishly, glad that I could now add to my list of achievements over the last two months: butt of joke at taxi driver's funeral. I bet no fortune cookie in the world could ever foretell that one.

Lisa and Kieran had to dash off for their first baby scan at the hospital.

'We must meet up,' she said to me as she kissed me goodbye. 'Now that you're getting back on your feet, we should go out and have dinner. I'm hoping the scan will show that I'm having triplets because I'm eating for four already.'

277

'I'll call you,' I said vaguely. I was still undecided about whether to confront her about Mark. Somehow it had become less important but I wanted to regain the moral high ground in our friendship. It was the only area in my life where the moral high ground seemed reachable without jet propulsion.

Mark felt bad about all the teasing back at the church and wanted to comfort me. 'Sorry about the laughter. That was unfair of them.'

I shrugged. 'They were right. It was a good joke but that doesn't take away the gift from Alfie. He wanted me to remember that it was important to be honest and I'm going to do my best.'

Mark and I had been summoned by Harry and Auntie Lynn to tea. We made quite sure that Harry hadn't been given any bad news from doctors before we went. Both Mark and I had become surprise-phobic. There was probably a Latin word for this but we didn't know what it was. Our vocabulary was severely restricted by our reliance on words acceptable and achievable in Scrabble.

Lynn had laid the table for a full English tea with crustless sandwiches and tiny cakes. When she bought a plate of warm scones through, it hit me again. My memories had been permanently tainted by the weekend with Ed. Despite years of sharing cream teas with Mark all over Britain, this experience would now always evoke a sordid deception that ended in my humiliation and heartbreak.

Even when the pain ended, which I had to believe it must, the memories would live on, contaminating all the precious ones that I'd accumulated before and since. And I'd been so sure that the experience would bring nothing but clarity and certainty, that anything would be better than the regret of not giving in to temptation just once.

Well, I'd been wrong. I was permanently scarred by having and then losing Ed. And it didn't matter whether it had been 'real love', for the sense of loss was as real whatever the underpinning emotion. I could not regret anything more deeply than my decision to go away with him that weekend.

'I did extra scones,' Lynn announced. 'They're Jenny's favourites and she needs building up.'

This would be my punishment. I'd escaped the ducking stool and the branding with a scarlet letter but I would be force-fed food

278

that reminded me of Ed forever more. With stoic acceptance, I picked the two smallest and placed them on my plate.

'So what's all this about?' Mark asked. 'I'm not being rude, but I have to be at the gym every minute of the day right now. The builders slack off if Kieran or I are not there to motivate them with Digestive biscuits.'

Harry coughed. 'We hope that you're not going to be too upset about this.'

'I knew it!' Mark slammed his cup down. 'I knew something was wrong. It's your heart, isn't it?'

'There's nothing wrong with me. I'm in perfect health.'

Mark sat down again, embarrassed by his outburst. The funeral had made us both a little sensitive.

'Sorry,' he mumbled.

'Anyway, Lynn and I were talking about what we'd do in Spain. We've been watching the two of you working to ... you know, with your marriage.' He was finding it excruciating to talk about this sort of subject with his son. Lynn rushed to help him. She sat beside him, her hand on his shoulder.

'What he's trying to say is that we've been impressed by the way you've sorted out your problems and got back to normal.' If only they knew. 'And that's because you have solid foundations. Like us.'

'Are you renewing your wedding vows?' I asked, curious to know where this was going.

'No,' Auntie Lynn replied. 'That isn't necessary. Not for us,' she added pointedly. 'We've always worked together, Harry and I. It's what we talk about, how we spend our time, how we spend our money, what we love to do.'

'The way you two love to watch films,' Harry added.

Lynn continued. 'So we've decided that we want to continue to do so. Nothing too taxing, just a little plant nursery in Spain. Moving abroad is a big change and we think that too much change in other areas might be difficult to cope with.'

'It can shake the foundations.' Harry was enjoying his little contributions.

'Anyway, the reason we're telling you,' Lynn said, 'is that now we're going to need all the money that we'd promised you, so I'm afraid that you'll have to wait until we pop our clogs before you can give up buying your lottery tickets!'

So we were not going to be given £250,000 after all. That left us in something of a pickle.

We sat on the bus, a careful inch of space separating us. 'Déja vu,' I said.

'What is?' Mark asked, gloomily.

'All this. Losing a load of money from the business that you'd been banking on. An uncertain financial future. Big risks ahead. But there's a difference this time.'

Mark looked at me hopefully. 'Which is?'

'This time, there are no secrets and we're going to get through it together.'

He relaxed an inch, enough for his body to make contact with mine. It wasn't *Last Tango in Paris*, not on a 319 to Battersea, but it was an improvement.

'Good grief, I don't believe it!'

I leaned over Mark to see what he was looking at. Alongside the bus was a stretched, open-top Cadillac. In the back was Phil, his sparse hair gelled up and his face made up in the David Bowie style he'd worn to that 1980s disco in Bristol when he first met Tally. Next to him, Tally was resplendent in her Abba blue sequinned cat-suit, the one she'd bought in the charity shop to wear to the grad-uation party. She, Phil, Mark and I had performed *The Winner Takes It All* and won £50 which we blew on beer and crisps.

I couldn't believe she was still able to get into it. She looked twenty-one and I hated her all over again for reminding me of Rachel. And for sleeping with Mark. And for telling me about Lisa. Phil looked fifty-one and bore a passing resemblance to Doctor Who, but he was enjoying himself. He had taken my advice about going back literally. It hadn't been what I intended but who was I to say if it was a good idea or not? Every idea I've had for myself has proved a total disaster. Maybe I'll ask him for advice in future.

The Cadillac turned off at the lights and then I knew exactly where they were going on a Tuesday evening – eighties night at Kittenz. I hoped they had a better night there than I did.

When we got home there was a message from Maria on the answering machine. 'Hope you're feeling better. If you're up for a drink, so am I. Give us a call.'

280

I looked at Mark and he ran a finger over my face, which had become angular with all the weight I'd lost. I was probably as slim as Rachel now. There I go again! Stop it!

'Go and see her,' he told me. 'Sort things out. Then when you get home, you can sort things out with me.'

I think I'd rather have faced a night accosting strangers at Kittenz.

'You've got cheekbones,' Maria cried, with envy. 'Now you truly are the woman with everything.'

I rolled my hand back and forth to indicate this wasn't absolutely true.

Maria considered this. 'You are the woman about to inherit two hundred and fifty thousand pounds without having to undergo actual bereavement?'

'Er, no.' I explained about Lynn and Harry's change of plans.

'Well, you are the woman with the fabulous lover who whisks her away on romantic weekends?'

'Er, no.' I explained about Ed, trying to make it sound funny so that I wouldn't be reminded how tragic it all was. She laughed like a seal at the description of me trying to be seductive while riddled with pneumonia.

'OK, well, you are the woman who alienated all her friends but then, in one heroic creative spurt, won them all back?'

'Er, no.' I told her about my lunch with Tally and what she'd told me about Lisa and Mark. This sobered her up pretty quickly.

'What are you going to do about it?' she asked.

'I think I made up my mind at Alfie's funeral that I was going to let it go.'

Maria widened her eyes. 'But it will sit there festering. Every time you look at Lisa and Mark, you'll imagine –'

'Thank you, Maria!' I exclaimed, stopping her before she became graphic. 'Look at what's happened and where we are now. She's pregnant and happy with Kieran. She's going to be dragging me to seminars where I'm going to learn to love my breasts as individuals and apply eyeliner in a perfectly straight line. If I confront her, then what? She feels guilty, lashes back out at me, I discover that Mark slept with the entire netball squad, all at the same time, and then the cycle starts over again.'

'You've become well adjusted!' she accused me. 'And you haven't gone through the menopause yet. That's unheard of in a woman.'

I smiled slightly. 'So as you can see, I am no longer the woman with everything. I'm the woman who's got exactly what she started out with but will have to live with the knowledge of what she might have had.'

'Is that good or bad?' Maria asked. 'Before I prepare the correct facial response.'

My answer was immediate. 'Bad.'

We sat in silence, playing with our glasses. Maria spoke carefully. 'You do know that none of it was real, don't you?'

I didn't know this but I was too tired to argue with her so I nodded. 'It doesn't make me feel any better.'

'Look at how crazy it all was: leaving Mark, the origami party, meeting Ed, indulging in that what-if game with Kieran, the weekend away, even Alfie. You've crammed a whole lifetime of experiences and mistakes into one short month. And now you've caught up with the rest of us, you can go back to your comfortable life with Mark in the knowledge that you haven't missed out on anything.'

'Maybe I wish I *had* missed out on it all,' I murmured.

Maria didn't press this when she heard the choke in my voice. 'Well, anyway, I dumped Gary.'

I looked at her sadly. 'Oh no, Maria. But didn't he explain about –'

'Yes, yes, that was all your fault, I know. Sorry I jumped to the wrong conclusion. No, it was the old story about finding out that we had nothing in common. It was quite a coincidence that he was into all your weird anti-social interests. I was actually dating Mark with hair!'

I laughed, feeling my equilibrium return. 'I had a funny thought when he was with me,' I began. 'He really liked you a lot even though he knew you didn't enjoy games or bad films. So I was wondering why it was necessary for your boyfriends to like all the things you like and vice versa?'

Maria stared at me blankly. 'That's an idiotic question. Of course you have to have things in common.'

'Yes, but you don't have to do all the same things. Paul Newman and Joanne Woodward don't like each other's hobbies but they've been happily married for years.'

'But I don't spend hours drinking with them,' Maria argued. 'I do know you, however, and you've got the strongest relationship

I've ever seen, which appears to be based on you doing everything together.'

I groaned. 'Don't tell me that Mark and I represent the pinnacle of human relationships to you, that you are aspiring to our dizzy heights?'

Maria stuck her bottom lip out. 'It sounds a bit foolish when you put it like that. But you're not far wrong.'

'God, no wonder you haven't been able to find a man. There aren't many lustrous-haired men who wear the same size skirt as you and enjoy flirting, shopping and having their facial hair bleached.'

Maria flicked a crisp at me. 'I don't know why I stay friends with you.'

'Because I'm honest?' I tried.

She raised an eyebrow. 'Since you brought the word up, what are you going to tell Mark about that weekend? It sounds as if he needs some answers and he's waited long enough, quite frankly.'

'I made a promise to myself today in Alfie's memory that I would be truthful. And since I made another promise to myself a couple of weeks ago to be brave, I've decided I have to tell him the truth.'

'Don't do it,' Maria said bluntly.

I sat back in surprise. 'What?'

'Don't do it. He's put up with enough from you already. If you tell him the truth, you'll be doing it for yourself, not for him. And certainly not for Alfie, who only wanted you to be happy. Why not, just this once, put Mark first? Invent a plausible story, one you can maintain – maybe a plot from a film he fell asleep in.'

This was all wrong. 'But then I have to live with the lie.'

'It's either that or forcing him to live with the truth. You decide.'

Mark had two mugs of Ovaltine in the microwave ready to heat up when I got in. I loved him for it. I loved him for all the small gestures and vowed to try and claw back the passion that I simply couldn't recall from our early years together.

'So how was Maria?' he asked, handing me the Beatrix Potter mug.

'Same as ever,' I replied, knowing that he didn't really care, that he was tentatively opening doors, hoping I might finally jump out from behind one of them.

283

'You never did tell me why she didn't drive you back from that weekend.' He was sipping his drink with exaggerated nonchalance and studiously avoiding eye contact.

So here it was. My opportunity to lay the foundations for our future, foundations of truth or deceit. I remembered Maria's warning and knew instantly that she was right, that Mark's feelings were more important than mine right now. I would have to live with the guilt. It was the price I had to pay.

'There was a dinner being given by one of her most important clients on the Saturday night. She had to be there for that.'

Mark nodded. 'So why did Lisa have to arrange the car home? Surely at a business function, they must have had arrangements with local cab firms?'

You'd think so, wouldn't you? I thought wearily. 'It was Lisa's idea. When I called Alfie to see how he was, she answered the phone and, when she heard how bad I sounded, she insisted on organizing one of her company's cars for me. I was too ill to argue with her.'

Mark carried on nodding, taking all this in, really wanting to believe it. I hated lying to him like this after resolving at Alfie's funeral to be honest. I made a decision then. If Mark asked me one more question, then I would answer it truthfully, whatever the consequences.

Twice he lowered the cup from his lips, about to say something. Twice he changed his mind. Finally he put the cup down. 'You probably shouldn't have gone in the first place.'

'I realize that now,' I agreed. That was not a lie.

'Still, you're OK now, aren't you?'

But what he meant was 'we're OK, aren't we?' I knew that and he knew that I knew. We'd always been like that.

'I'm OK now,' I replied, relieved that I could answer honestly, relieved that he'd said 'OK' and not 'fantastic' or 'back to normal'.

And we both knew what I was saying. We were OK.

Chapter Nineteen

My legs became weak and I thought they might give way.

'Are you all right, love?' the newsagent asked.

I nodded imperceptibly and picked up the magazine, throwing the money on the counter and running out of the shop before anyone got a look at my face. How could I have forgotten about the article? Well, it was obvious how. I'd been preoccupied with getting myself back to full health, taking on as much work as I could do without exhausting myself, and helping Mark and Kieran with all the promotional material for the new gym.

I was also now officially Lisa's birthing partner after Kieran was the first expectant father ever to be sick while watching the video of an uncomplicated delivery. 'He can't do it,' Lisa told me, matter-of-factly. 'Never been any good with blood. You'll be much better. Kieran can wait outside and you can relay information. Now I have a list of duties for the birthing partner . . .'

I wasn't sure that it was strictly necessary for me to be there while she was measured up for a maternity bra. However, it was a new experience for us both and we relished any opportunity to move away from the past.

But since reinventing herself as the first woman of thirty-eight ever to get pregnant, she'd ceased to be a magazine editor to me. So I'd put the whole episode of the 'Who Will Buy This Desperate Woman?' feature behind me. And now the magazine was out. Just when Mark and I were back on an almost even keel.

I sat on a doorstep round the corner and opened the magazine with quivering hands, wondering which photos they used, hoping they wouldn't be too provocative. But I didn't need to worry. They didn't use the provocative photos. They didn't use any at all. The article was about Maria.

Maria was flushed with excitement. 'She invited me out to dinner a week or so after your origami party. We went to this terrible restaurant in the Fulham Road, where they gave me three mangetouts and one baby sweetcorn and called it a vegetable medley.'

Of course! That had been when Ed was bringing me back from riding. Not a good day.

'Since when did you and Lisa become such good friends?' I tried not to sound jealous, knowing that this was a childish reaction.

Maria didn't notice my churlishness. 'Sharing the adventures of your origami party and that first date with Ed was a real bonding experience. We were like kidnap victims, having undergone unimaginable trauma together.'

I sighed. 'So you formed your own private survivors group?'

Maria smiled. 'We just realized that we didn't hate each other, that's all. And while everything was so crazy, it was good to have someone to discuss it all with, someone who knew all the people involved.'

'Someone who wasn't me,' I observed.

'It was mainly you that we were discussing,' Maria admitted. I couldn't argue with her. I decided to be grown up and feel pleased that my two closest friends were now getting on so well, especially when the outcome had been to save me from tabloid humiliation.

Maria went on. 'Anyway, she called me because she had a problem with the feature and she didn't want to tell you while you had so much else going on. She was really embarrassed about it but she had been overridden by her directors. They felt you were not representative of the typical *Modern Woman* reader. What made it worse was that the editor of *Upscale Man* refused point blank for his magazine to be involved when the subject – you – was so . . . unconventional.'

'That's outrageous! There must be thousands, millions of women who don't fit into the rigid little moulds these magazines create and then perpetuate!'

'Yes, but they don't buy *Modern Woman* – they fold paper or go fly-fishing.' She gazed at me from below her eyelashes, recreating

286

the main photo they'd used. 'I, on the other hand, am a marketing dream; interested in fashion, going out, drinking, socializing, all the things that cost money. The advertisers will love me. And the responses are already pouring in. Do you know why?'

'Because you've said that you love sex and never wear a bra?'

She sat back, her arms open in an expression of sincerity. 'Because I'm uncomplicated.'

'Hardly!' I scoffed.

But she just shook her head and laughed. 'Compared to you, Jenny, compared to you.'

OK. Fair point.

On our first wedding anniversary, Mark had brought me breakfast in bed. He was carrying a tray on which everything was made of paper. The toast was perched on an incredible origami rack. I recognized the knife, fork and spoon set as being made by a folder in Manchester that I'd met at a conference a month earlier. Mark had come with me and even joined in some of the sessions.

But the star piece was the cup. It was beautifully folded. I'd made a similar one myself in the past, but this one was filled with tea. 'How did you manage this?' I picked it up and turned it round in my hands, breathless with admiration.

Mark looked pleased. 'I found someone to make the cup, then I contacted a paper company and got them to supply a sheet that had been coated in silicon. The timing was a bit tight so I had to go and collect it from Reading last week to deliver to the folder.'

I loved him for this, for the effort, the time, the imagination, the thought. Then, as I picked up the cup, there was an envelope underneath. I opened it. It was a letter from the court, acknowledging Mark's request to stop the divorce proceedings. 'I'd forgotten about this,' I murmured.

'I'd hoped for some kind of imposing certificate,' Mark explained, 'but we have to settle for a pre-printed letter from a clerk. It hasn't even got a real signature, just a computer-generated one.'

I ran my fingers over the formal note, not needing embossing or ink for this to be significant to me. 'Thank you,' I whispered.

Then I reached over to my side of the bed and pulled a package out from the drawer.

'I always knew this would be your favourite anniversary,' he said as he untied the elaborate ribbon from the box. 'So what does one of Britain's newest, brightest origami artists create for her husband on this special day?' He looked confused as he removed the flat piece of paper from the box. 'Flat origami?'

'Read it out loud,' I told him.

Dear Mark,
Thank you for the past year and the previous nineteen. Thank you for the cups of tea you made and the shoes you polished. Thank you for catching all those mice and not minding when I made you catch a bus to Putney Common to set them free. Thank you for giving me the coffee Revels even though you like them too. Thank you for saying that you'll think about starting a family. My present to you is that I've decided to wait. Maybe forever. We'll see. I've come home for good.
Love
Me
XXX

He gazed into my eyes emotionally and held both my hands before whispering tenderly, 'I'd been hoping for a Sony Home Cinema System.'

I hit him with the tray and pulled him under the covers, laughing.

We got a few cards when the post arrived, all very low key under the circumstances, and only one present, well two if you counted the cheque for £100 from Auntie Lynn and Harry.

Mark shook the final padded envelope vigorously. 'I didn't expect Tally to send us anything. You don't think she's been manufacturing anthrax in her blender, do you?'

I snatched the packet and opened it.

'That's an odd present for a wedding anniversary, isn't it?' Mark said.

I looked at the CD entitled *The Greatest Love Songs From The 1980s* and smiled. 'I think it's more of a thank-you-and-sorry gift, and it's perfect.'

Later that evening, as I was cueing up *The Towering Inferno*, he came in with a tray of cake, champagne and a small box. A ring box.

288

'I can't believe it! How conventional is that?' I laughed. 'You've bought me an eternity ring for our anniversary. That's what normal couples do. The next thing, you know, we'll be having wine and cheese parties and collecting china figurines.'

Mark pushed the box towards me, smiling mysteriously. 'Aren't you going to open it?' he asked.

I picked up the box and untied the ribbon around it. Lifting the lid off, I stared at the gift inside. How could I ever have thought he would be conventional? Of course he didn't give me an eternity ring.

It was a jelly baby.

'It's the best news we've had in a long while,' Mark said as we all passed the magazine round. 'The sooner we get Maria married, the better. If I can put my vote in for the Alaskan salmon farmer –'

I snatched the magazine away and slapped him with it. I'd never told him that Maria had been holding our relationship up for all these years as a paradigm of emotional perfection. He would have been convinced that she was making fun of him and been offended as he usually was by everything she said.

'She's having a ball,' I told everyone. 'Her suppliers are all offering her free clothes to wear on the dates and she's got enough men lined up to last her until she's forty. Then she's going to choose the best one and make him marry her.'

'You can't make someone marry you,' Phil interrupted, bringing champagne round. The room fell silent at this observation. Nobody dared look at Mark or myself.

I swiftly moved things on. 'Speaking of which, I forgot to thank you for the anniversary present, Tally.'

She was sitting cross-legged on the floor in front of the Christmas tree, dressed in jeans and a tight, sequinned, black crop top, an outfit that was as casual as Tally could manage. 'I wanted to send something suitable,' she teased.

'I know you think that women have the monopoly on good ideas,' Phil insisted, 'but this one was mine.'

'He's right,' Tally confessed. 'He bought a copy for me after our mad 1980s night.'

'How *was* that?' Lisa asked, who had refused to believe me when I described the clothes Phil and Tally had been wearing that night.

'It was the most ridiculous night of my life. We were the only ones dressed in costume. The place was full of these sad women all trying to attract the attention of equally sad men. Anyway, Phil ordered me to sit on a barstool and then pretend I didn't know him when he came over.'

'Because that's what happened when we met at Bristol,' Phil explained.

'But by the time he'd got two drinks and was bringing them to my table, I was being chatted up by a short hairdresser called Gus who told me I could have some free highlights if I'd walk over his bare chest in my stilettos.'

'So I asked him outside for a fight, only meaning it as a joke –'

'Phil always did use satire inappropriately at university, so this was a true recreation of those days,' Kieran interrupted.

'And the hairdresser started to cry. Then the bouncers came over and Phil had to give them twenty pounds each to let us stay . . .'

By now they had forgotten that we were there and were reliving the evening for themselves. It was a new memory and an old memory all in one. Maybe that was the key, the big secret. If you like a place, go back there. Stay there if you want. If not, revisit often.

This Christmas we were breaking a few traditions. After a few drinks at Phil and Tally's house, we were all going to the gym to have an opening ceremony. It wouldn't be open to the public – that would be in the New Year, providing I got paid for some work I'd just done which we could then use to pay the gym staff. It was tight but we were managing.

The taxis arrived at half past seven thanks to Lisa's foresight in making friends at Alfie's funeral. On her way out of the church, she'd introduced herself to the least intimidating group of cabbies as the woman who'd called the ambulance for Alfie when he had his heart attack and held his hand when he died (which was true). Once she'd made them feel thoroughly uncomfortable, she stroked her stomach dramatically and announced that she needed to get to the hospital. Kieran had cringed at her shameless, but effective, freeloading but was nonetheless impressed when she obtained the private phone numbers of five separate drivers with guaranteed discount rates.

When we arrived at the warehouse, Lynn and Harry were already waiting, huddled together against the cold.

'You should have gone in, Dad!' Mark cried. 'It's freezing out here.'

Harry shook his head firmly. 'This is a big day for you and I respect you for wanting to do things properly. You've worked hard, you and Kieran and Jenny, to get this far and I'm proud of you.'

Lisa rescued the moment from descending into sentiment. 'Yes, I'm proud too, but I'm pregnant and bursting for the loo so can you say your bit then open the doors very quickly?'

Kieran and Mark both knew that tone and were rightly stirred into action. Mark delivered the speech. 'Thank you to everyone who helped us get here: to Phil for reminding us that we'd wanted this all along; to Jenny for saving us a fortune by doing the work of twenty even when she was ill; to Dad and Lynn for bringing cakes and soup over when we were working late; to Tally for posing for some sexy promotional posters; and, of course, to Lisa for getting pregnant which has prevented her from terrorizing us with her organizational skills.'

'Yes, yes,' Lisa said, 'very funny and, as soon as I've been to the loo, I'll remember to laugh. Now please *open these doors.*'

'I declare the MarkieFit Men's Gym well and truly open,' Kieran hastily declared.

'Praise the Lord!' Lisa exclaimed and pushed past us all to be the first one in. I followed her to the bathrooms since this was the first opportunity I'd had to be alone with her for weeks. We were constantly attending classes and courses and seminars but we were never alone and I wanted to make sure we were OK.

I heard her moaning in ecstasy. 'That is the most wonderful feeling in the world, I could sit here all day.'

'I hope you won't mind if I don't join in this particular pregnancy experience with you,' I called from the other side of the door. 'There are limits to every friendship.'

'I think we went to the limits of ours this year,' Lisa replied dryly, as she emerged from the cubicle.

I was tempted to tell her that I knew just how far over the boundaries she'd transgressed all those years ago. I could even have justified it under the umbrella of my new policy of honesty and openness. But I didn't.

That weekend with Ed marked both the end and the beginning of my life with Mark and with my friends. As I struggled to close the door on the new emotions that Ed had stirred up, I decided to exclude some old destructive ones at the same time. I'd had greater success in ridding myself of the jealousy than I had in forgetting that afternoon in the hotel room in Selsey. But I was working on it.

Lisa stood in front of the mirror, rearranging her dress.

'Why *are* you wearing that tent?' I asked, wondering if this fell within our limits or not. She was wearing a preposterous gingham smock, which was unnecessary because her stomach was still almost entirely flat.

'I have waited a long time to be pregnant, I may only be pregnant once, and I intend to enjoy every second of it. Since my reputation at *Modern Woman* has rendered me almost unemployable in the business, I am going to make motherhood my new career. And do you know why?'

'Surprise me.'

'Because mothers are supposed to be despised. Even if they try to make their kids like them, they'll fail. I was born for this.'

I hugged her, glad to hear her making fun of herself even though I knew she was still smarting from the animosity she'd encountered at her office. 'You'll be a good mum – scary, but good.'

'So will you,' she countered. 'Will you?' she added, tentatively.

I turned towards the mirror to examine my eye for a non-existent speck. 'I might.'

Lisa turned me back by the shoulders. Her eyes were shining with excitement.

'You mean, you and Mark have finally agreed to try for a baby? That's fantastic! Our kids can grow up together and be best friends. We'll share school runs and go on holiday together . . .'

I held up a restraining hand. 'Lisa, don't get carried away. Before you add me to all your new lists, we can't assume that I'll get pregnant as easily as you did. If at all.'

Lisa patted my hand. 'Of course you will! You're bound to! After all you've been through to get Mark to agree to this, after all you've put the rest of us through, you *have* to.'

I looked at her calmly. 'The funny thing is, if it doesn't happen, it won't be the end of the world, the way I thought it would be. Mark and I will be fine, whatever.'

'But you'd be better than fine if you had kids,' Lisa insisted.

I shrugged. 'Yes I would, but Alfie taught me that happiness is a gift not a right. I nearly threw away my life with Mark, my greatest gift, on a whim that something different might be better, might make me happier. When we fixed what was wrong between us, everything else became simple. He became less entrenched in his determination not to have children, and I stopped demanding them as my inalienable right.'

Lisa looked dubious. 'I don't see why you couldn't have worked this out at the beginning.'

'Because we didn't know how to, then. Now we do.'

'I'm glad I'm not like you,' Lisa said finally. 'Your life is so complicated.'

'Do you know the real difference between us, Lisa?'

She thought about this. 'I always wear two coats of lipstick and blot in between. And you always wear two pairs of socks to keep your feet warm.'

'You expect to be happy and I expect to be loved.'

'Aren't they the same thing?'

'They can be but they are not always. Mark loves me and I love him. That makes us phenomenally privileged. We're going to try for a baby but we're not going to chase this new dream at the expense of everything we have already.'

'Personally, I'm chasing love, happiness, babies, fulfilment, the lot.'

'You've spent too much time reading your own magazines!' I laughed.

'You've spent too much time watching bad films!'

We linked arms to go and join the others. Yes, we were OK.

'So everything is all right, you're quite certain?' Auntie Lynn asked for the fifth time.

'I'm positive! Go to Spain. Be happy. Grow olives and eat paella. We'll be over at Easter if Mark can get away from the gym and if I'm not snowed under with work.'

'Don't overdo it,' Lynn warned. 'You're still not completely fit.'

'I know, I know.'

'And don't let work come between you and Mark, not again.'

'It wasn't work, Auntie Lynn, not really.'

'I know that, love.' And she held my gaze for a few seconds, telling me with her eyes that she really did know.

I blushed to think I was that transparent to her. 'It was nothing,' I explained hastily. 'Just a moment of madness. I might even have *been* mad. I certainly felt . . . different.'

'And are you better now?' she asked.

'Worse actually, but that's what I have to live with,' I replied evenly. 'And I'm working to make things between me and Mark better every day. I won't repeat my mistake, that's for sure.'

'That's good, then,' she said, patting my arm affectionately.

'Yes it is,' I agreed, after thinking about it for a moment. 'Yes, it is.' And the second time I said it, I meant it.

When we got home, Mark went straight into the kitchen to rummage in the cupboards. I bent down at the video cabinet. 'What do you fancy?' I called through. *'The Matrix? Moulin Rouge? Ocean's Eleven?'*

He poked his head round the door. 'The original or the remake?'

I gasped. 'The remake of course.'

'Go for it,' he grinned.

While I fast-forwarded the trailers, Mark brought a tray through with Coke, popcorn, Kit-Kat Kubes, prawn crackers, cold frank-furters, some grapes and my tablets, and sat next to me on the sofa.

'Happy Christmas, Jenny.'

'Happy Christmas, Mark.'

Without looking at each other, our hands zig-zagged back and forth, each reaching for our favourite snack in our favourite order with pinpoint accuracy. When our hands bashed, one of us would mumble 'sorry' and the other would mumble back, 'I should think so.'

He didn't throw me across the Ikea coffee table and eat the grapes off my naked body, as proof that his love for me was as alive and vibrant as when we were eighteen.

But he did let me hold the remote control. And that was good enough for me.